Against
All Evil

Also by Howard Schneider

Snapshots: Flash Stories from Random Lives
Howard Schneider with Mizeta Moon
(e-Book, 2015: paperback, 2019)

Survival: Collected Short Fiction
Howard Schneider and Mizeta Moon
(e-Book and paperback, 2018)

Word Storms: Original Fiction
Howard Schneider, Mizeta Moon & Silver Gladstar
(e-Book and paperback, 2017)

Monkey Casserole: 33 Selected Short Stories
Howard Schneider, Mizeta Moon & Linda Burk
(e-Book, 2016)

Also by SpearPoint Publications

45 Pieces of Turkish Delight
Patricia Morgan

Danger Wears Pantyhose!
Mizeta Moon

Seeds of Change
Patricia Morgan

Aliens, Fish Tales & Flying Hooves
Mizeta Moon

Embracing Evil
Mizeta Moon

Against All Evil

Old-Time Radio-Style Serial Adventures

By

Howard Schneider

SpearPoint Publication

Cover designed by Keith Buckley at Zap Graphics, Portland, Oregon.

Grateful acknowledgement is made to the International Institute for Social History, Amsterdam, for permission to use the image of a family gathered around a radio, as shown on the front cover.

ISBN 978-1-67815-408-0

Published by SpearPoint Publications
Portland, Oregon
2020

Contents

Dedication

This book is for my maternal grandmother,

Exer Rosa Eugenia Hanson
1877 - 1974

My younger brother, Jerry, and I loved it when our maternal grandmother came to live with us. She was a major part of our lives and left us with lasting memories of her kindness, generosity, sweetness, adventurousness, and sense of humor. In our view, she was a perfect grandmother.

But as wonderful a woman as she was, the reason this book is dedicated to her is because she is the one who introduced me to radio serial adventure stories. Like so many others in the1940s and 50s, she was devoted to her afternoon soap operas—Stella Dallas, Our Gal Sunday, Ma Perkins, and a host of others. She listened attentively while ironing, mending, fixing dinner, all the things to help keep our lives intact.

But it wasn't her afternoon soaps that turned me into a devoted radio listener—it was the evening programs—the irresistible serial adventure stories. Ones I listened to every weeknight on the radio turned up loud enough for me to hear in bed—and for grandma to hear in the adjacent room.

As I remember, the stories started around six, maybe earlier, and went to around ten, a different adventure every fifteen or thirty minutes. Programs like Boston Blackie, The Green Hornet, Sky King, The Lone Ranger (Grandma's favorite), The Cisco Kid, The Whistler, Batman, Sergeant Preston of the Yukon. These fast-moving episodes of danger, intrigue, and tension not only kept me glued to the airwaves, but vividly stimulated my imagination as I pictured the scenes and characters inside my head—it was active listening, not passive like watching TV.

It is the mood of these stories I wanted to impart in this "Against All Evil" collection. All of these adventures have been posted monthly over the past five years on the SpearPoint Publications website. Hopefully, this book will expand their audience and further introduce new readers to a compelling story-telling style of the past, hopefully one that will not only entertain, but also probe imaginations, and maybe even inspire readers to create their own writing adventures, just as those stories did me.

Acknowledgements

I thank my understanding and supportive wife, Leslie, for her encouragement during the preparation of this book. Also, I express my gratitude to Maurice Posada and Mizeta Moon for valuable editorial contributions, and to Keith Buckley at Zap Graphics for his cover artistry.

Preface

The adventures in this collection, although not in the exact script format of the radio-style "to be continued . . ." cliffhanger stories of the 1930s and '40s, were inspired by prototypical characters featured in those stories who triumphed over a multitude of evil foes. Examples include the Lone Ranger and Sargent Preston, and superheroes like Batman, The Green Hornet, and Captain Marvel, to name only a few.

The superhero concept is illustrated in these "Against All Evil" stories, albeit it in an exaggerated sense, by Max and Lena Manus (*The Intruders, Tale of the Scorpion, Hijinks Underground*). Max is a brilliant scientist, now retired, who had accidently discovered a way to activate superpower energy mechanisms buried deep in our genetic past. His wife, the resourceful and intrepid Lena, is a retired CIA assassin who must use her well-honed skills to help Max protect his superpower secret from evil powers that would steal it to use for their own malevolent purposes. His discovery allows them both to call forth physical and mental powers far greater than those of normal humans. But even as effective as they are in combating evil, the unrelenting parade of villains they must confront may never allow them to attain the peaceful retirement they long for.

In *Undercover Agent,* exceptional strength of character, although not at a superhero level, is revealed by the challenges a physically handicapped, homeless woman, Karla Hammer, faces. In her case, it's intelligence, determination, and moxie that allow her to overcome formidable odds and survive dangerous life-threatening situations. In her own way, she is as heroic as any superhero.

In *Jack and Storm*, set in the far future, the protagonists overcome prejudice and social rejection by discovering their true natures. Capabilities that had been dormant until needed for survival allowed them to find acceptance and respect in a new world—a world of their own kind.

The Intruders

Episode One

Portland, Oregon, 2013

Max Manus was jolted from deep sleep by a vivid image of a man he'd never seen before lying in a pool of the man's own blood. Awake and intensely alert, Max immediately realized that something about him was drastically different, that he had changed, that he was not the same as he was when he'd come to bed only a few hours before. He seemed to be vibrating with some kind of energy, as if a pulsing motor inside his chest cavity had been switched on. Even though his glasses were on the nightstand, he could see clearly in the darkened bedroom. He made out the position of the hands on the dresser clock across the room; it was 2:35.

Rising to a sitting position, he noted his wife, Lena, stir sleepily on her side of the bed.

"What is it, Maxie?"

"Nothing, Liebchen. Just a dream. Go back to sleep."

"Are you getting up?"

"Yes. The bathroom. That's all."

She knew that was nothing out of the ordinary for her 67-year-old husband and rolled onto her other side.

Still on edge from the intensity of the dream, Max remained absolutely still and listened for unusual sounds. But there was only the quiet late-night hum of their modest Southeast Portland bungalow—the purr of the refrigerator, the soft sound of the furnace. He also heard far-off traffic and the gentle rustle of a light breeze caressing the two giant Douglas fir trees in their backyard. As far as he could tell, there was nothing out of the ordinary, no hint of danger.

He lifted back the covers and shifted his right leg over the edge of the bed and down to the floor. After bringing down his other leg, the one with the bad knee—arthritis from some previous trauma—he stepped into his slippers, side-by-side where he'd left them on the floor next to the bed and rose to his feet. Standing still, he listened once more. Again, there were no sounds he didn't recognize.

What was it that woke me? he wondered. *Was it just the dream, or did I hear something?*

Finally deciding all was in order, he started for the bathroom. But suddenly he froze in place when he heard a faint sound he *didn't* recognize. It came from the living room, down the hall. Then he heard it again. It sounded like scratching at the front door. Or was it just an echo from the dream that had awoken him so abruptly? Not sure what was happening, if anything, he remained still and continued to listen. A second later he heard it again, then once more, only louder. Then he heard the front door creak open and someone enter the living room. The muffled footfalls were unmistakable. Then a second person came in. He heard their every step as clearly as if he were in the room with them.

He started to wake Lena, but perhaps foolishly, he decided not to disturb her. *I can deal with this,* he thought to himself, maybe overconfident because of the strange energy he felt.

The door from the living room to the hallway, which led past the bedroom, was partially closed, allowing him to rush unseen from the bedroom into the kitchen before whoever breached their security and entered their house had time to get their bearings. During his dash to the kitchen, he couldn't help but notice the absence of pain in his arthritic knee.

Standing in the kitchen at the open knife drawer, considering his options, Max was suddenly overcome with raging anger that someone had broken into his home. That the intruders must have thought they might do as they please with him and his wife. As he thought about it, his confidence increased, and he became convinced beyond any doubt that he could cope with whatever threat he was about to encounter. That he would be able to protect his sleeping wife, expel the invaders, fight for his life if he had to, even kill if necessary. He felt invincible, a feeling he'd never experienced before. And he liked it.

Coming to his senses, he scanned the blades neatly organized in the drawer by function and size and grabbed his custom-made Messermeister nine-inch boning knife. With his thumb he carefully tested its finely-honed edge and sharp point. This knife had served him well in the past for his culinary pursuits. Now, at this crucial moment, he had no reason to think it wouldn't serve him just as well for self-defense if it came to it.

As he quietly eased the heavy drawer shut, he noticed a stream of flickering light spilling under the closed door leading to the dining room. Then an unmistakable sound, the creak of a loose dining room floorboard, alerted him to someone treading lightly toward the kitchen, someone who would probably come through the swinging door in a few seconds. He quickly moved to the other side of the room, positioned himself behind the door, and pressed his right shoulder firmly against it.

A moment later a footfall sounded close to the threshold. He shoved against the door with all his weight, slamming it with such force and momentum that when it crashed into the unsuspecting intruder, he was propelled backwards, landing him against the edge of the dining table with a dull crack in his lower back. The interloper cried out and dropped to his knees. A mix of surprise and terror spread across his face. Unable to remain upright, he collapsed to the floor, dropping his flashlight as he went down.

When Max sprang over the threshold and sped into the dining room, the disabled man reached out with both arms in a feeble attempt to entangle Max's legs. But Max nimbly stepped aside, then dove forward and plunged the knife into the man's thigh. Max felt a solid thunk when the keen point

3

pierced deep into an oak floorboard underneath. The man screamed as blood gushed from the wound and pooled along both sides of his immobilized leg.

At the very moment Max's knife was slicing through the man's flesh, a grotesquely large head appeared from around the half-open hall door. Max heard raspy, heavy breathing and looked up to see a giant of a man edging into the living room holding a pistol in his huge hand. The man, Gorgon the Giant, halted, looked at Max, glanced at his helpless partner lying half under the table with blood gathering around his impaled leg, then took a step forward, pointing the gun directly at Max's head.

"So, old man. You're the famous Max Manus," Gorgon growled with a thick Russian accent. A malicious sneer formed by his thick lips dominated his ugly, scarred face. "Now you will please to pull knife from friend's leg. Then we get your wife and you come with us. Someone I know wants much to meet you."

The Intruders

Episode Two

Gorgon slowly advanced toward the dining room where Max knelt next to the whimpering man he'd pinned to the floor with a knife through his leg. But before he'd covered half the distance, he suddenly screamed, dropped the gun, then lunged towards the front door. A number-ten metal knitting needle protruded from his back. Max's wife Lena was close on his heels, another needle gripped in her raised fist. But before she could strike a second blow, her foot caught the rug that Gorgon crumpled up in his rush to escape. Unable to halt her fall forward, her head slammed into the doorjamb as Gorgon stumbled out the door. She collapsed onto the floor.

Max ran to where Lena lay unmoving and checked her pulse. She was alive but stunned. As Max reached for the nearby phone to call an ambulance, she opened her eyes and tried to sit up.

"Lena, are you alright? You had an argument with the doorjamb and lost. Don't move until we know how badly you're hurt."

Hearing the screech of tires on concrete, Max glanced through the half-open door and saw a black van speed away from the curb. The man with the knitting needle in his back quickly vanished into the misty Portland night.

"What about the guy with the gun? Did he get away?" Lena asked.

"Yes. There was a van out front, probably intended for me. I'll get an ice pack. At least you're not bleeding."

"I'm okay. I've had worse," Lena said, feeling the top of

her head. "What about that guy over there with the knife in his leg? Looks like you were able to take care of one of them, anyway. Let's see what he has to say. If this is about what I think it is, we're in for trouble."

Knowing Lena's resolve once she'd made up her mind, Max didn't try to stop her. He extended his hand to help her get up. She accepted it and rose slowly to her full six-foot height.

Holding Max's hand, Lena went with him into the dining room. After observing the writhing intruder for a moment, she nudged Max aside and squatted down next to the man who was sobbing hysterically, obviously in great pain. She didn't say anything, just rocked back and forth on her bare feet and stared at him intently, waiting for his crying to stop. She caressed his cheek with the backs of her long, scarred fingers. Finally, when he calmed a little, she leaned in and whispered a few words close to his ear. He looked up at her and shook his head. His panicked expression was a desperate plea, as if he were wordlessly begging her to accept his inability to tell her what she wants to know.

She waited for him to speak. To confirm her strong suspicion. "Tell me!" she finally said, leaning in close to his face.

He uttered a sputtering reply. "I ca-can't tell you anything. They'd kill me if I do. My fa-family, too. You know what these people are like."

Saying nothing, Lena grabbed him by the hair and jabbed the knitting needle she was still holding into his right eye. Viscous fluid and thin blood exploded onto her faded blue nightgown. He screamed and grabbed out at her. She slapped his arm aside, then yanked his head up and slammed it forcefully onto the floor. Grimacing with pain and fear, he whimpered like a lost child.

"Who sent you? Tell me or lose the other one," Lena said.

"It's . . . it's the Killoffs," he blurted out, tightly closing his remaining eye. They want the formula. They sent us to capture Max and take him to Nicki Killoff. Don't you know by now—they'll always find you. You'll never escape them. Their eyes are everywhere."

Satisfied with his answer, Lena let his head fall back onto the floor. She stood up and told Max he could call 9-1-1.

While Max was reporting the break-in to the Portland police, Gorgon the Giant was slouched in the back seat of the van being driven by Nicki Killoff's cousin, Boris. Gorgon was telling the man who sat next to him, Stefan Stravorski, how all hell broke loose after they got into the Manus house.

"He came out of nowhere and stuck Rustoff to the floor with a kitchen knife . . . and his half-wild she-wolf bitch wife almost killed me with this spike." He waved the knitting needle Stravorski had pulled out of his back in front of Stravorski's face. "I barely got out alive. She's an animal!"

It saddened Stravorski, a loyal Killoff gang member, to see this once-powerful man, a brutal enforcer for the Portland Russian mafia, now mortally wounded and slumped next to him blubbering like a baby. Blood from a punctured artery pulsed from a hole in his back. A giant defeated by an old woman.

Realizing that if these two soldiers, who were on loan from the local Russian mob, were to link the Killoffs to this break-in, he'd be in serious trouble, he pulled out his pistol and fired a single shot into the side of Gorgon's head. He also had to make sure that Rustoff, the one Max pinned to the floor, didn't talk when he was in police custody. He called the mob's contact at the East Portland police precinct to arrange Rustoff's unexpected suicide before he had a chance to spill his guts. That accomplished, he returned to his own dark thoughts. To the Killoff gang's quest to capture Max Manus and get their hands on the weapon he possessed, a weapon so formidable it could change the balance between the forces of evil and the powers for good.

The weapon the Killoff syndicate wanted was a potent plague bacterium. If released into the world, it could destroy all humanity in a mere few weeks. This mutated organism was the unintended consequence of Max's research into a completely different subject—mechanisms controlling cellular energy production. Amazingly, during Max's long research career, he had discovered how to manipulate subcellular regulatory mechanisms in a way that channeled unimaginable amounts of energy to all levels of body function, cascades of dynamism that could affect the entirety of physiology—yielding an incredible enhancement of human potential.

But it was not Max's enhanced energy discovery that the Russians were after, that was still a secret known only to Max and Lena, and to them alone. No, the Russians were after a plague agent: a mutant bacterium known only as LX29. Much to Max's regret, during his early research he'd inadvertently discovered that the metabolic amplifying process was also able to further energize an already existing deadly plague organism, increasing its killing power to a level far beyond anything previously known. Its potential as a germ warfare agent demanded that the enhancement process be kept secret from those who would use it for their own sinister ends. But somehow, knowledge of the existence of this organism and its lethal properties had escaped his lab and was now unrelentingly sought by organizations and individuals who *would* use it for evil purposes—like the Killoff Russian mafia gang.

But Max had focused his energy enhancement research on the human body, not bacteria. He'd discovered the potential to increase physical, sensory, and mental functions to a phenomenal degree—to what could even be considered a superpower level. But he had only tested this discovery on himself and Lena, and even then, only under rigorous laboratory conditions. However, these experiments, albeit preliminary and not yet sufficiently investigated, confirmed the possibility of super-human powers beyond his wildest imaginings. Protecting both of these two secrets, LX29 *and* energy enhancement, was a challenge Max and Lena must not fail to meet no matter what was required of them or what the cost. The consequences of dissemination of either one of these discoveries were too horrible to imagine, and their safeguard had become the focus of their lives.

On the other hand, this challenge was increasingly in

conflict with their desire to escape their life of danger and retire to a life of quiet solitude and peaceful pursuit of their own interests. Max to his music, his writing, his research; Lena to her rose hybrids, her charity projects, her gardening and cooking, to her book club and reading, maybe even to the memoir Max was urging her to write. They also yearned to spend more time with their beloved adopted daughters, Rana and Zula. Balancing these opposing demands was becoming especially difficult as they entered the time of life when most normal people retire from the demands of making a living and enter a period of winding down and taking time to smell those so-often-spoken-of roses. The question is, will the world let that happen? Or will reality continue its unrelenting intrusion into their quest for tranquility?

Meanwhile, as Max and Lena patiently waited for the police to arrive, they commiserated over the discovery of their whereabouts by the Russian mobsters.

"Will it always be like this, running every time they find us?" Max asked. "What do you think, my little flower. What should we do?"

"Run and hide. That's what we've done in the past, Maxie. But not this time. This time, we need to fight back. To put an end to it."

"Yes, Liebchen, I agree. You're right! It's what we should have already done. No more running away."

"Good!" Lena said. "And I don't want to move away from Portland. I like it here. So, it's now or never."

An hour later, in response to Max's 911 call, the police arrived to find the bloody man bandaged and tightly bound. Max and Lena told the officers only what they wanted them to know— that they had no idea who the would-be burglar was, that they had surprised him and together had been able to subdue him. The police took over the crime scene as the old couple faded into the background. Ignored by the police for a short while, Max and Lena collected the few things they needed and quietly snuck away unnoticed.

Meanwhile, as the black van made its way along Lombard Street, Stravorski was organizing his thoughts before meeting the younger Killoff, Ivan Killoff's son, Nicki. Ivan was head of the North American branch of the international Russian mafia, *Now that Manus and his barbarian wife know we're close again, they're probably on their way out of town. The Killoffs will be furious at this repeat of Max's escape two years ago when they located him living in Denver. I don't look forward to telling Nicki about what happened tonight.*

Boris and Stravorski soon arrived at a nondescript, all-night laundromat in North Portland that belonged to the local Russian mafia gang. It was serving as the Killoff gang's makeshift local hideout while they were in town to capture Max. Boris parked in the rear lot and accompanied Stravorski through the back door, then down to a dingy basement. Nicki, sat at a small table in a dank back room, anxiously awaiting their arrival. He was acutely aware of the importance of capturing Manus. He had worked long and hard to reach this moment. He also knew he couldn't fail his father again, like he did in Denver.

When Boris and Stravorski came into Nicki's room without Max, Nicki stood up so violently the chair tumbled to the floor behind him.

"Where is he? You failed again, didn't you," Nicki screamed before the two men had a chance to say anything.

Stravorski had been right; Nicki was furious. He barely listened to Stravorski's description of what had happened at the Manus house. The only thing that mattered was that Manus had escaped. But Nicki's anger was also laden with fear of what he would face when he reported to his father. Trying hard to calm himself, Nicki, picked up the chair and sat down at the wobbly table he was using as a desk, shifted his gaze to Boris and nodded. At once Boris stepped behind Stravorski and with his powerful practiced hands broke Stravorski's neck with a single sudden twist. The loud snap echoed throughout the basement like the sound of a cracked whip. When Nicki began to scream at him, Boris let the body drop to the filthy floor.

"Find them!" Nicki shrieked. "We've got to get that formula. Search everywhere from Canada to California. Bring them to me! Soon! Or else . . ."

The Intruders

Episode Three

Nicki Killoff called his father, Ivan, as soon as Boris removed Stravorskie's body from the basement of the North Portland laundromat Nicki was using as his Portland headquarters.

Ivan, waiting in his office in the gang's trucking warehouse on the edge of Oxford, Mississippi, answered on the first ring. "Did you get them?"

"Well, ah . . . not yet. But we'll find them. I pro . . . promise," Nicki stammered.

"What? They got away again? This is their second escape, Nicki. Your promise is meaningless. Obviously, you're not up to this task. Stay close to the phone and don't do anything. I'll call back soon."

"But father, we had a good plan. But they must have known we were coming and were prepared. They fought like wild animals."

"I'm not interested in your flimsy excuses and won't accept any more of them," Ivan replied in a stone-cold voice, then cut the call.

Meanwhile, later that same night, having turned over the captured intruder to the police and left their house, Max and Lena were comfortably settled in a cozy cabin on a remote slope of Mt. Hood. It was a neighbor's weekend retreat where they'd been before. They sat together in front of a low fire, both lost in deep thought.

"The Killoffs will hound us forever if we don't destroy

them once and for all," Lena said, finally breaking the silence. "There's no choice. We have to annihilate then. Every one of them," emphasizing what they had decided after learning the identity of the would-be kidnappers who invaded their home.

"You're right, Lena. We can't let them, or anyone else for that matter, get hold of the LX29 formula. I wish I'd never tested the energy enhancement concept on the plague strain. But it was the only one we had in the lab at the time, and I was anxious to confirm the generality of my discovery, to see if it applied to any form of biological energy production—even a simple bacterium. I should have waited to get a less dangerous one, a mistake I will regret for the rest of my life. LX29 could turn a person into a bloody corpse within forty-eight hours. It would be a horrible way to die—massive internal bleeding, spasms, excruciating pain. And it's highly contagious. I don't know why those bastards want it so badly, but I know damn well it's not for the good of mankind."

"Max, Don't fret," Lena said in her calming manner. "What's done is done. But now, . . . now it's time to conclude this game. So, get on with your planning and I'll get on with mine."

About 5 a.m., with Lena asleep on the sofa, Max saved the document he'd been diligently working on, made a backup copy, then closed and put aside his laptop. He went out onto the cold grass and breathed in the crisp, clean mountain air. After stretches and yoga exercises, he hurried back into the warm cabin. But, in his haste to get on with the task ahead of them, he didn't notice the fresh boot prints in the damp dirt below the living room window. Back inside, he showered and shaved, then ate a hastily prepared breakfast. Finally, he was ready.

"Lena, let's talk," he called out from the little kitchen where he sat at a table set with two steaming cups of green tea.

Lena was already awake, finishing her isometric exercises. She smiled and answered immediately. "I'll be right there." She too was ready. Anticipating possibilities that Max might come up with, she had already made inquiries, called in a few favors, and issued orders. Her people were standing by and could be deployed at a moment's notice.

While Max and Lena were in the mountain cabin formulating their plan, at the gang's hideout in North Portland, Nicki Killoff had just answered a call from his father. Ivan told his son that someone to help find Max was on the way. "And Nicki . . . we have to have the formula no later than ten days from now. Our client moved up the delivery date. They mean business. There's no room for mistakes," Ivan added before hanging up.

Three hours later, Boris ushered the man sent by Ivan into the basement hideout. Nicki was sitting at his rickety table in the dingy room. With a sullen smirk he greeted a well-muscled, hard-looking man of medium height. He appeared to be in his mid-fifties, was bald, and was dressed in black. To break the tension, Boris introduced Nicki, but had no idea what the stranger's name was.

The man stepped forward, leaned over a bit, spread his big, thick-fingered hands on the table and looked directly into Nicki's eyes. In a low, gravelly voice he said, "Tell me what you need, Nicki boy. All I know is that you want a couple of old people grabbed, right? So, who and where are they? And what's the big picture here? If I'm gonna do what I'm being paid to do, I gotta know what's going on. Ivan didn't say much. Just to make sure you got it done. And done soon."

Nicki blinked nervously, but otherwise held his own, trying as best he could to maintain control of the situation. "Who the hell *are* you? What *have* you been told?" he spat out, as if he were the one in charge of the gang rather than his father, who was far away and at the other end of a phone line.

"Relax, junior. I'm The Albanian. I provide special services, so to speak. Your old man hired me to capture the two targets you're looking for. I deliver them *alive*, I get fifty thousand apiece. *Dead*, I get nothing."

"Well . . . all right," Nicki mumbled, reluctantly accepting the fact that he had no choice but to cooperate with the hired enforcer. "I'll tell you what we know."

The Albanian sat down in the chair in front of Nicki's

table.

"The old man is Maximilian Manus," Nicki started. "He's a scientist. He made some kinda killer bacteria thing. Like the plague from a long time ago. Only worse. He's the only one who knows how to make it. There's gotta be a formula or recipe—whatever it is we gotta get it. If it's not written down, or on a disk or something, then we'll have to make him tell us what we need to know. His crazy bitch wife, a tall woman named Lena, is always with him. We want 'em both."

"So, what's the problem?" asked The Albanian. "There's just two of them, right? And they're old, aren't they?"

"Yeah, . . . but there's a few complications."

The Albanian didn't say anything, just waited in silence.

Nicki continued, "Two years ago in Denver, where they were living, they escaped when we tried to capture them, and then they managed to escape again last night. We've got to find them and get that formula. We gotta have it within ten days. There'll be bad consequences if we don't meet our client's demand."

"Don't worry, Nicki. I don't do failure. Tell me, how did these two geriatric relics manage to escape? Twice, right? Do they have some kind of secret army? Is there something special about them? If there is, I need to know what."

Nicki glanced down at the open notebook on his table and said, "The old man, Max, is some kind of science genius in biochemistry and neurobiology, whatever that is."

Nicki looked up for a second from the open notebook, glanced at The Albanian, then continued.

"There's a rumor that he discovered a way to increase his power. Like science fiction, you know, superman kinda stuff. And that he's the only one that knows how to make it work, and his wife helps him keep it secret. But even if that's true, which it couldn't be, anyway, it's not what we're after. We want his formula for a plague organism. It says here he might have created it accidently. Like a test experiment or something."

"Okay, I get the picture. Sounds to me like this old guy's a little nuts. But he's sure as hell no superman. But maybe no dummy, either. That doesn't mean we can't capture him. Whatever he's got, we'll get. What about the old lady? This Lena dame? What's her story?"

Nicki withdrew a printout from a file box under the table, leafed through it, then began reading, word for word:

Lena Hock: born 1948 in Blauberg, Switzerland.

Father: General Gustav Hock, Swiss army; Jewish, highly intelligent, excellent leadership qualities; deceased.

Mother: Irena Cordreseau, Carpathian gypsy; WW II anti-Nazi partisan; tall, cunning, ferocious; descendant of Genghis Khan; deceased.

At a young age, Lena was acknowledged to be intellectually and athletically precocious.

Disappeared in 1968 at the age of 20. Suspected to be a member of Israel's Mossad, although never substantiated.

She remained under the radar until she escaped from Syria's maximum-security prison in 1975; resurfaced in Israel the same year.

Revealed to be a CIA assassin in 1989 when she was outed by a Russian intelligence officer.

No further knowledge of her actions until she met Manus in 1995 during a covert Central Asia high-tech CIA operation; they were married in 1996.

After marriage to Manus, she remained out of sight until a rumor of Manus' plague bacterium was leaked in 2005.

She retired from the CIA in 2006 at the age of 58.
She is considered extremely dangerous and to be avoided
The Albanian stared at the young Killoff for a moment with a

look of disbelief, then said, "What? You're afraid of these fossils? Come on, Nicki. They're old—past their prime. They're antiques. Let's just find them and grab 'em. I'll collect my bounty and get the hell outta here. You'll make your client happy, your daddy will pat you on the head, and you'll all live happily ever after."

"Right, but first we have to find them," Nicki responded. "We've got a dozen of the Portland Russian guys out searching. It shouldn't take long to track 'em down. They couldn't have gotten far."

Then Boris's cell phone rang. He recognized the number and answered at once. When he ended the call, he turned to Nicki and said. "We found them. Let's go!"

The Intruders

Episode Four

It was nine a.m. when Max and Lena left the remote cabin near Mt. Hood and started up the slope to a shortcut through the woods to where they had hidden their car the night before. Halfway up the hill, Max suddenly came to an abrupt halt. Lena stopped next to him.

"Did you hear that?" Max asked. "It sounded like a car door closing. Wait! I hear people running . . . on a dirt road."

"Max? Are you sure? I don't hear anything. How can you hear something that must be so far away?"

"It's like last night in the house. When I heard the intruders fiddling with the front door. When I woke from that dream."

Then a flash of reflected light caught Lena's attention. "There's someone coming along the road. See. There, through the trees?" She pointed off to her right. "There's a bunch of them."

Max looked where Lena was pointing. "Yeah. I see them. Let's get out of here. We're not prepared for visitors. Not yet, anyway."

Max couldn't help but notice how invigorated Lena was as they raced up the hillside.

"This energy's incredible," she said to Max as he ran along side of her, matching her speed and length of stride. "I think I could run like this forever."

Is this what I think it might be?? Max wondered. *That's how I felt during those energy enhancement experiments I conducted on Lena and myself. What the hell's going on?*

Could it kick in automatically? Is there a trigger that responds to danger? My God! What if this is real? I've got to check this out as soon as we take care of this damn Killoff problem.

Two hours later, back in Southeast Portland, Max and Lena separated when they reached the corner of Martin Luther King Boulevard and Hawthorne. She drove on to a boarded-up, abandoned machine shop under the ramp to one of the bridges spanning the Willamette River. Max walked across the Hawthorne Bridge and up to a secret level-4 cell culture laboratory at the Oregon Health Sciences University Medical Center. They both had work to do since they intended to engage the enemy that night. They understood the tactical advantage of surprise and were determined to use it to their advantage.

Lena arrived at her operation center a few minutes later. The upgraded space housed computers and other electronic gear in a central room, a office for Lena, a kitchen with a table and three chairs, and another lab for Max. The computer equipment was the responsibility of her faithful Indian companion, Raj Rajgupta. He greeted her without turning away from the images scrolling on his three wide-screen, high-definition monitors.

Ignoring his greeting, Lena snapped, "Why didn't we know the Killoffs were in town?"

She had contacted Raj immediately after the previous night's attack in their home and instructed him to find out what was going on. He had worked all night and had answers.

"Sorry, Lena. There was no word of their arrival. They're here under the cover of the local Russian mafia. I learned from street-level scuttle-butt and some hastily set up phone intercepts that they arrived two days ago, failed in your kidnapping, missed you on Mt Hood, and are now on their way back to town. Three members of the Killoff gang are here from their headquarters in Mississippi: Ivan's 26-year-old son Nicki; Nicki's lieutenant, Stefan Stravorski; and Ivan's nephew, Boris. My guys saw Nicki and Boris this morning, but there's no sign of Stravorski. And there's one more, another out-of-town guy, an assassin and bounty-hunter called "The Albanian." He arrived today and is with them now. They've also enlisted a bunch of the local Russian mob guys to help find you two. Looks like they really mean business this time."

"The Albanian? Damn!" Lena said, interrupting Raj. "Where are they holed up?"

"In the basement of a laundromat on North Lombard Street. Arnie Axman, one of my guys, set up surveillance from an empty dumpster in the rear parking lot while they were out looking for you and Max. He'll let me know when they return." Raj turned back to his screens.

"Good work, Raj," Lena said, somewhat mollified. She went into her little office and powered up her own computer.

Lena didn't like it that The Albanian had joined the Killoffs. She knew him to be ruthless and cunning, having encountered him many years ago when he was a young KGB hit-man. During that encounter, he thought he had killed her. But he hadn't. Although seriously wounded, she survived a gunshot that barely missed her heart. "This time will be different," she muttered as his face filled her screen. Her back-door access to restricted CIA files served her well once again.

Meanwhile, across the river and up the hill in his biohazard lab, Max was preparing a special treat for their Killoff foes. Alone in the lab, sitting at a HEPA-filtered exhaust hood, he cautiously removed one milliliter of a milky liquid from the freezer vial he'd just thawed and carefully transferred it into a sterile tube. Next, he added ten milliliters of growth medium, screwed the cap on tight, wrapped the tube in impervious, plastic sealing tape, slipped it into a small padded envelope and put it into a padded pocket of his backpack. Then he put the resealed freezer vial back into the liquid nitrogen storage tank, discarded his biohazard-suit into a burn chamber, erased his entry record from the secure lock-pad, and left unseen through a seldom-used utility tunnel. He left no trail of having been there.

Max joined Lena and Raj back in Southeast Portland thirty minutes later in time for lunch at their favorite fast-food spot, a Burgerville near Lena's lair. Seated at a window table looking out onto MLK Boulevard, they reviewed their plan of attack while savoring black bean veggie burgers and organic rhubarb milkshakes. After due consideration, they concluded that the unexpected appearance of The Albanian wouldn't change their plan as it was laid out. If it worked, he'd go down like the others.

Max slurped up the last of his shake, then addressed Raj. "Find out from Axman when and where the Russians will be tonight. Once you know they're together, set everything up for the attack. Now, I need some time in my lab," Max added as he rose from the table, grabbed his pack and headed for the door. Lena and Raj followed.

A little later, not far away in North Portland, two dusty vans pulled into the littered lot behind the laundromat and parked across from an unused, rust-coated dumpster. Nicki, Boris, and The Albanian headed for the building's rear door. The other men divided up and left in separate directions down the alley. Once inside the laundromat, Nicki made another call to his father, fearful at the prospect of reporting yet another failure.

Even Boris and The Albanian, standing just outside the door to Nicki's make-shift office, could hear the Killoff boss's anger (or was it panic?), then a loud threat of severe consequences if the formula was not in hand by the deadline.

"Find them!" Ivan screamed. "If you don't have them by tomorrow night our client will send in his own people. And Nicki, they wouldn't leave witnesses. Like you, for instance."

After hanging up, Nicki waved the other two into the room. "All right, let's get busy, We've got to find him."

Five hours later, at 7:20 p.m., with their plan in place, the three thugs took a break for dinner.

"We'll regroup in half an hour," Nicki said. Looking at Boris, he continued, "Get the local Russians guys back here so we can start the search for Manus tonight. We don't have time to lose."

Back at Lena's hideout in Southeast Portland, at 7:35 p.m. Max came out of his lab and joined Lena in the kitchen.

"My part's ready. How about you?" he asked anxiously after he sat down at the table.

Lena, noting the concern in his voice, replied in her usual confident manner. "Everything is ready, Maxi. The Russians are still at the laundromat. One of them went to the pizza shop down the block. They do have to eat, you know. Axman will call when they're together again. The microphone he attached to the back wall is picking up everything they say. Now we just have be patient. So, how about a little Schnapps, a few pretzels, and we listen to some Brahms until it's time to go. Would The Third Symphony be okay?"

Max smiled as concern drained from his face. He grabbed a handful of pretzels and accepted the little glass of clear liquid Lena offered him. "Okay, Lena, you're right. Prosit!"

It was 8:13 p.m. when Axman called from the dumpster. "They're back. The local guys are here, too. Everything's ready.

"We'll be there in fifteen minutes," Lena said as she punched the OFF button on the CD player.

They were in their Subaru Outback and on the way two minutes later.

The Intruders

Episode Five

Twenty-two minutes after Axman informed Lena that Nicki Killoff and the others were together again, Lena was seated in front of a row of washing machines and dryers in the all-night laundromat that housed the Killoff's hideout in its basement. She was the only person there and was disguised as a disheveled, gritty old woman with a black plastic garbage bag full of wet clothes on the floor in front of her. As she rose from a sticky yellow plastic chair to put the clothes in a dryer, a door on the other side of the room slowly eased open. A balding, powerfully-built man stepped into the room, stood unmoving, and looked around. He focused on the old woman a moment, then closed the door behind him. Apparently satisfied with what he saw, he went out the front entrance, crossed the street, and went into a 7-11 minimarket.

When the man looked at her, Lena instantly recognized him as The Albanian and sat back down. Quickly pulling her thoughts together, she concluded he had come up from where Nicki and the others were meeting in the basement and assumed that he needed cigarettes or something and would return soon.

She was right. A few minutes later he entered through the front door and started towards the stairs to the basement. But as he passed Lena again, he looked a little closer and noticed a tiny earbud barely visible through her scraggly wig. Reacting immediately to his suspicion, he moved with lightning speed to where she sat and jammed a pistol hard against her

23

forehead. When Lena looked up at him from her seated position, surprise flooded his face. He recognized her at once.

"It's you! I thought I killed you thirty years ago," the surprised assassin said. "But I won't fail this time."

Then, as The Albanian was about to pull the trigger, a bumbling old man, smelling of filth and mold, crashed through the front door pushing a wobbly grocery cart full of dirty rags. In the fraction of a second that The Albanian glanced in Max's direction, Lena's hand shot up and grabbed the thick wrist of his gun-hand in a vise-like grip. She twisted his arm backwards and pulled him down towards the floor, at the same time sweeping his feet out from under him with a powerful kick. His legs catapulted upward as she pulled his upper body down onto the concrete floor with so much force that his bald head split like a cleaved melon before he had a chance to comprehend what had happened. With her other hand she easily caught his dropped pistol.

The old bum, Max in disguise, threw off his reeking coat and rushed to help Lena pull the body aside. They had to get the dryer going before the others in the basement wondered why The Albanian hadn't returned. Max assured Lena that Axman had successfully rerouted the dryer vent's exhaust hose into a basement window. Lena put the wet clothes into the dryer, added the milky liquid Max had given her earlier, inserted six quarters into the coin slot, and pushed the START button.

In the basement below, Nicki and Boris were filling in the Russian mob guys on their plan to find Max and Lena. Suddenly they all started sneezing, followed quickly by a burning sensation in their eyes, then difficulty breathing.

"What the . . ." were Nicki's' last words before collapsing. Two of the thugs went down next, then Boris and the rest of them.

Max stopped the dryer five minutes later. Fifteen minutes later, he and Lena went down to the basement—by then the air had cleared. Nicki and the others were out cold and would be for at least eight hours. Max and Lena cuffed everyone, grabbed the box of documents under Nicki's table, then called the FBI with an anonymous tip about a Russian mafia gang incapacitated in a laundromat basement. They also mentioned the dead assassin lying in front of a washing machine. They found Axman where he was hiding out back, loaded his equipment into the Subaru, and left without leaving a trace of having been there.

Back in Lena's abandoned machine shop thirty minutes later, Max and Lena learned from Nicki's files that the Killoff gang's headquarters was in Oxford, Mississippi. The gang had moved there from New Orleans after Hurricane Katrina destroyed their warehouse operation near the waterfront. The Killoff's control of drugs, weapons, and human trafficking had only been temporarily interrupted by the storm and was now back in full swing.

Max and Lena knew that to have any peace in their lives, and to protect Max's secret, they had to go to Mississippi to complete their task. Ivan Killoff, his ruthless younger brother Vladimir, and their gang of ex-KGB goons, had to be eliminated. But, since there was no mention of any "client" in Nicki's files, they were unaware of the real danger that lay ahead.

"What we did tonight was the easy part, wasn't it," Lena said, then took a liverwurst and onion sandwich from the platter Raj had prepared.

"Yes, Liebchen, you may be right. What we did tonight might turn out to have been simple compared to what we could encounter next. We shouldn't underestimate the Killoffs. Maybe you should call the girls."

"That's a good idea," Lena said as she picked up her secure phone.

"They'll meet us at the Hyatt in Oxford, Mississippi in three days," she said, after disconnecting a few minutes later.

"So Maxi, should we drive or fly?" Lena asked as she reached for another sandwich.

Max considered her question, thinking how easy it would be for their enemies to monitor the airports.

"Let's take the Mercedes. It's more comfortable than airplane seats. More secure, too. We'll leave first thing in the morning."

What Max didn't say was how he looked forward to some quiet time to think about the possibility of self-induced superpower. A long drive would provide that opportunity. They also needed time to plan for their confrontation with the Killoffs. Besides, he loved driving his big Mercedes 600 limousine—in his view, the perfect automobile.

When Max and Lena left Lena's hideaway later that night, they noticed a man lying on a blanket on the damp sidewalk half-way down the block. They weren't alarmed though, assuming he was just another Portland homeless guy who'd found a dry spot to pass a wet night in peace. But, if they had looked a little closer, they would have seen an olive-complexioned, bearded man who was pointing a Nikon 35 mm camera equipped with a telephoto lens at them. The time would come when Lena would chide herself for the oversight.

Far away, in the early hours of the following morning, Ivan and Vladimir Killoff huddled in the back office of the Transit Trucking warehouse. They were concerned about why they couldn't reach Nicki or Boris in Portland. Even their calls to the Portland Russian gang went unanswered. Equally worrisome was what to tell their client? A client who they had never met in person, who spoke with an accent they didn't recognize, and who demanded immediate results. Ivan had come to regret his decision to take on the contract to capture Max and obtain the plague formula, especially since his gang had failed to do so two years earlier. It was a task that had turned out to be even more difficult than he remembered from their attempt before. When the phone rang precisely at 2 a.m., he knew who it would be. The call he expected but dreaded.

The Intruders

Episode Six

After Max and Lena came out of Lena's secret sanctum and left in their Subaru Outback, Abdul Farhadi, barely visible in the dark shadows down the street, called the leader of his al-Qaeda sleeper cell. Fifteen minutes later, a tan Toyota sedan arrived, and two bearded men joined him. When they smashed through the door of Lena's hideout and rushed in, they discovered Lena's partner, Raj Rajgupta, sitting in front of a bank of computer screens. After an hour of unspeakable torture, Raj revealed what he knew about Max and Lena's travel plans. Satisfied that he'd told them everything, they decapitated him with Lena's bread knife and left his head in the refrigerator, ghoulishly displayed on Lena's favorite porcelain platter.

While Raj was being tortured in Portland, 2400 miles away in Mississippi, Ivan Killoff answered his phone on the second ring. After listening in silence for a moment, Ivan sputtered, "There was a change in plans, a minor delay. I guarantee we'll have what you want by tomorrow night." The line went dead without further comment.

Five minutes later a windowless van pulled up in front of the Killoff warehouse. Two men got out and jimmied the building's front door. They made their way silently to the office where Ivan and Vladimir were still trying to contact Nicki in Portland. The two Killoffs were taken by surprise when the assailants burst into the room. Before Ivan and Vladimir could do anything to protect themselves, two pistol

27

shots echoed through the dark warehouse. The killers doused the brothers' bodies and much of the office with gasoline and lit it on their way out.

And so it was: with two bullets and a single match, the Killoff cartel's leadership ceased to exist. Its dozen low-level gang members would have to seek similar employment, if their criminal deeds can be called that, with other gangs. But for Max and Lena, a far more dangerous adversary had taken the cartel's place in the quest to find the formula for the Max's plague agent, as if fate were upping the ante in its attempt to punish him for an unforgivable transgression.

Back in Portland, a little before dawn, Max readied his car for the drive to Mississippi. Over the years he had lovingly restored an armored, super-charged 1968 Mercedes-Benz 600 Grand Limousine that he had discovered in a Munich junkyard years before. For Max, this vehicle was the perfect combination of design, engineering, performance, and reliability, and he eagerly looked forward to the trip.

Later that morning, cruising smoothly down I-5 South a few miles south of Salem, Lena told Max she thought they were being followed. "That tan Toyota Camry back there has been on our tail since leaving Portland."

"I noticed it, too, but wasn't sure. What do you think, Liebchen? Should we lose it or find out what's going on?" Max asked. He had a strong suspicion what her answer would be.

Lena put down her binoculars and said, "There are three men. We need to know who they are and why they're following us. A divide-and-conquer tactic should work. We'll disable two of them and capture the other one. Pull into the next rest area." Max nodded in agreement as Lena described her plan.

Twenty minutes later, Max took the rest area exit and parked at the far end of the nearly deserted truck parking area. There were few other visitors: a single semi idled as the driver tested tire pressure with a big hammer; an elderly couple holding steaming paper cups sat at a picnic table; and a lone woman walked a leashed dog.

The Camry arrived a moment later and parked near the bathrooms. The three men remained in their car.

A minute later, Lena got out of the Mercedes and walked towards a nearby stand of trees. Max got out at the same time and ambled toward an information alcove near the bathrooms.

Seeing the woman heading for the trees, the burly man in the back seat eased out of the Camry and followed her. The other two remained in the car and watched Max.

Twenty yards into the woods, Lena glanced over her shoulder and saw that the man trailing behind her held a pistol with a silencer attached. When she went around a sharp bend in the footpath a second later, she stepped off the trail and out of sight behind a large oak tree. Apparently afraid of losing her, the bearded man sped up. When he came to where Lena was hiding, his increased momentum added to the force of her powerful, lightning-like kick that shattered his ribcage and ruptured his lungs. He dropped to the ground as a muffled gurgle of blood erupted from his mouth. She made sure he was dead with a powerful blow to his throat, then rushed back to the edge of the woods. She saw Max standing in the information area studying a wall map.

When Max spotted Lena across the lot, he and headed toward the bathroom. The two men got out of their car and followed him. Lena trotted across the parking lot without the men noticing and approached the information area as the second of the two men entered the bathroom behind Max.

Inside the bathroom, Max was in one of two stalls; its door was closed and latched. The two men were waiting for him to come out. The younger of the two held a pistol and the other one held a loaded syringe. Lena entered the open door behind them as quiet as a cat approaching its prey. With expert precision she downed the one holding the gun with a powerful chop to his neck with the hard edge of her clinched fist. Then, in one continuing dance-like motion, she turned, stepped down on the other man's foot and rammed her hand into his chest.

He catapulted backwards, smashed his head hard against the cinderblock wall, and collapsed unconscious to the floor.

Lena propped the dead gunman on the toilet in one of the stalls while Max injected the other one with the contents of the syringe the man had been holding. After making sure no one was nearby, they put the comatose assailant into the trunk of the Mercedes, then gagged him, tied his wrists behind his back, and shackled his ankles. Then they hurried into the wooded area and pulled the man Lena had dispatched earlier off the path and covered him with brush. Before leaving the rest area, they collected the men's IDs and other possessions. A minute later they they were back on the highway.

When Lena couldn't reach Raj by phone, she sadly realized how the men who followed them must have discovered their travel plans. The passports they took from the assailants' car had been issued in Yemen; the names were Arabic. Max and Lena speculated that the men were al-Qaeda operatives and suspected that the Killoff gang had been hired by the terrorist organization to steal Max's plague formula. Although they had believed they could have defeated the Killoffs, Max and Lena knew well that this jihadist group was a horse of a different color. Al-Qaeda made the Killoffs look like Keystone Cops. But at least, one way or another, they would be able to confirm their suspicions and learn more when they interrogated the man stashed in the trunk after they reached their destination, a CIA safe house on the outskirts of Sacramento that Lena had used in the past.

It was late afternoon when they got there. She punched in some numbers on a keypad next to the security gate. After the gate swung open, they proceeded along a winding, tree-lined gravel driveway to a plain, single-story house hidden by a dense hedge of tall laurel bushes.

"What about the guy in the trunk?" Lena asked after Max parked.

"We'll leave him for now. He should be ready to talk by tomorrow morning. If he isn't, an injection should help. And if that doesn't work, you'll have to persuade him with methods from your old days," Max replied.

Lena nodded in agreement, got out of the car, walked up the sidewalk to a covered entryway, and said a few words into the microphone by the front door.

The next morning, the safe house manager, who knew Lena from past visits, didn't question her request to use one of the sound-proof rooms in the basement. Max and Lena hauled the weakened Arab out of the trunk and half-carried, half-dragged him down a flight of stairs to a brightly-lit chamber where they strapped him to a metal chair bolted to the floor. Max inserted a venous line into his arm. As soon as Lena removed the gag, the prisoner cried out in Arabic for water. His lips were cracked and bleeding. His voice was raspy and dry. The back of his head was matted with blood.

Lena ignored his pleas and said, "Who do you work for?"

"For Allah. You infidel dogs are not worthy to even crawl in our shadows," he croaked, seemingly trying as best he could to project the brazen bravery of a zealot on the threshold of divine martyrdom.

Lena ignored his response. "What did you do to my friend?"

"To the glory of Allah, we cut off his head after he told us what we wanted to know."

Lena dug deep into her reserve of will power to suppress the temptation to repay him then and there for brutally killing her loyal friend. But she knew the importance of the information they needed, and that a fanatic jihadist like this one would talk only after time-wasting torture.

She stepped back and turned to Max, "Is the truth serum ready?"

"Of course," Max replied, then injected a mixture of scopolamine, temazepam, and sodium thiopental into the IV line he'd inserted into the man's vein.

31

The Intruders

Episode Seven

The al-Qaeda soldier that Max and Lena had captured the day before, Ahmed Hussain, spilled his guts after an injection of Max's truth serum. As Max and Lena suspected, Hussain was a member of one of a dozen al-Qaeda sleeper cells spread around the country. The terrorist organization was after Max's plague formula to use as a threat to force foreign powers out of Yemen. Their intent was to take over the country and establish an Islamic Caliphate. The al-Qaeda leaders planned to challenge the UN at the upcoming annual meeting by announcing their possession of a plague organism which they would release in major cities around the globe if their demands were not met. The Killoffs, whom the U.S. al-Qaeda leader had coerced to capture Max by a combination of money and intimidation, had failed, and the two Killoff brothers had been killed and incinerated the night before to eliminate any link to the terrorist organization.

Later that morning, after the serum wore off, the captive screamed his threats at Max and Lena: "You can martyr me. It won't make any difference. Before you ambushed us yesterday, we had already informed our brothers of your travel plan. They will find you. They'll capture you—and they'll learn your secret. It is the will of Allah."

"Even with the help of Zula and Rana, we're no match for these fanatics," Max told Lena after they handed Ahmed over to the safe house agent. "We have to consider other alternatives. There must be a way to out-maneuver these crazies other than direct confrontation. But I need time to

32

think. I need to talk to my colleague and friend, Ben Goodman, at Cal Tech. We should be able to devise a solution," he continued. "Call the girls and tell them to meet us in Pasadena instead of Mississippi."

Lena was disappointed with the delay in confronting their newly discovered foes but understood Max's reluctance to plunge ahead unprepared. She also well-knew his ingenuity when it came to devising ways out of sticky situations.

"The girls will be there in two days," she said after ending the call. Then she arranged for a replacement car. Much to Max's regret, they had to leave the Mercedes at the safe house since it was now known to their enemy.

They left Sacramento mid-morning, both wondering from their own unique perspectives how they would be able to overcome the most determined and vicious opponent they could have imagined in their wildest fantasies. Their destination was Pasadena, where they both hoped to find an answer.

Later that evening, Max relaxed in Goodman's Cal Tech office waiting for his old friend to return from a graduate student's thesis defense. Max was recalling the time when Goodman had been a researcher with him at MIT when they were working on Max's energy enhancement discovery. After leaving MIT for Cal Tech, Goodman had received numerous scientific awards for his brilliant work in virology. His discoveries had landed him the directorship of Cal Tech's Institute for Viral Genomics. If anybody could help Max contrive a way other than physical combat to defeat the al-Qaeda fanatics, it was Ben.

While Max was waiting for Ben to finish the doctoral exam, an Imam, Sheik Rashid al-Saaladi, was telling his five senior followers about the devastating loss of their three men in Oregon and Max and Lena's escape. They were in a back room of a strip-mall mosque in Minneapolis.

"We won't allow this setback to prevent us from driving the godless devils from our land. Allah is only testing our resolve, forcing us to be more cunning and ruthless in carrying out his divine will. We must capture this nonbeliever and obtain the weapon to deliver us from the grip of the Great Satan. But to find him, we have to identify and locate everyone in his past, then post our spies to see where he goes to hide. But have no doubt, Allah will lead the way. He will not be able to escape the eyes of God."

It was not all that difficult for al-Saaladi's young computer whiz, his college student nephew, Faisal, to identify Max's past students and scientific collaborators by means of an exhaustive internet search. With that information in hand, by early that evening instructions had been given to each cell around the country; soon thereafter, surveillance of everyone who'd been identified was in place. It was not surprising, then, that when Max and Goodman left Goodman's office later that evening, they were followed to Goodman's house. Unfortunately, the ever-vigilant Lena hadn't been with them. She, unlike the two scientists engrossed in their planning and less aware of their surroundings than they should have been at that particular time, would certainly have spotted the car, with its two bearded and dark-skinned passengers, that followed them all the way to Ben's neighborhood.

Instead, Lena was with Anna Goodman at the Goodman house in South Pasadena waiting for their husbands to return for the dinner she and Anna had prepared while catching up on family and mutual friends.

Max and Ben arrived home at 8 p.m. A minute later, the bearded driver parked the nondescript Nissan Altima down the street, half a block south of the Goodman house. Its tinted windows prevented anyone seeing inside. The man in the passenger seat called al-Saaladi to report their success.

"Stay there and keep watch," the Imam instructed. "But don't do anything. Just keep a watch on the house. Reinforcements are on the way for an attack early tomorrow morning. Let me know if anything changes."

Later that evening, after dinner and dessert, Anna asked Lena to accompany her while she took their dog, Hannibal, for his evening walk. He was a big, three-year-old, mastiff-wolf hound mix, trained in personal protection. Ben had got him because of a high crime rate in their part of town. The two women headed north on the sidewalk in front of the Goodman house, intending to cut through a small park down the street and then around the block and back home. Hannibal trotted off-leash a little ahead of them.

The two scientists were happy to stay home and continue their planning. They had developed a plot to entice the al-Qaeda gang to steal a lethal dummy sample of the bacterium. After all, they concluded, if the Greeks were able to use the Trojan Horse trick at Troy, they should be able to make it work in Pasadena. They just had to figure out the details of how. Not only would it be a major scientific challenge, but also a dangerous risk with the possibility of worldwide consequences if they failed. Yet circumstances required that they try. And these two were not the types to retreat form a challenge, even one of this magnitude.

Meanwhile, as Anna and Lena were completing their walk and approaching the Goodman house from the south end of the block, they noticed Hannibal's raised hackles and low throaty growl as they neared the brown Nissan parked at the curb.

Invisible inside the Nissan, the big man in the driver's seat, holding a photo of Max and Lena, turned to his equally brawny companion and said, "A woman that looks like the Manus bitch is approaching from behind us. I see her and another woman in the side mirror."

"Yes. Here they come," the man in the passenger seat said as he turned and watched the women approach along the sidewalk.

"If we eliminate her now, it'll be easier in the morning when we attack the house to capture the old man," the driver responded excitedly. "We'll do it as soon as they pass us."

"No!" his companion objected. "The Imam said we should wait for reinforcements. They'll be here in the morning."

"Don't worry. Al-Saaladi will be pleased with our initiative. Follow my lead."

A little past the car, alerted by Hannibal's warning and hearing the quiet creak of the car doors opening behind her, Lena spun around to investigate. At that very same moment, the man from the driver side sprang out of the car and rushed at her. He was moving forward rapidly, lining up a karate kick to her midsection. Seeing him springing toward her with his boot approaching her chest, she side-stepped to the right and turned counter-clockwise. As he flew by her, she grabbed the attacker's calf in the palm of her big hand, her long fingers clutched firmly against the far side of his leg. She yanked his leg toward her and rammed her right hand against the toe of his boot. The sharp crack of the spiral breaks of his leg bones was followed by his ear-shattering scream. Without hesitation Lena tightened her grip on his leg, looped the fingers of her other hand around his ankle and continued her powerful pivot, swinging the man further around in an accelerating arc. Her swing came to an abrupt halt with a loud skull-crushing crunch when his head smashed into the solid trunk of the maple tree that graced the front yard of one of the Goodman's neighbors. She released her grip and let him drop to the ground like a dead weight.

At the same instant that the attacker's head smashed into the tree, wild pistol shots fired by the other man kicked up chips from the sidewalk. Lena felt the sharp pain of a bullet rip into her calf. When she turned to attack the shooter, almost falling onto the sidewalk as she twisted around, she saw Hannibal half-ripping off the assailant's gun arm. The dog then pulled him down onto the street and locked his huge jaws around the man's throat and immobilized him against the curb. Blood gushed from the man's shredded arm.

Realizing that the situation was under control, Lena glanced at Anna, who was standing nearby paralyzed with shock. "Anna! Call Max and Ben! Tell them to get down here! Tell them to bring a couple of tourniquets."

The Intruders

Episode Eight

Max and Ben reached Lena and Anna soon after Anna's summons. Ben called Hannibal off the mauled assailant and then called 9-1-1 for an ambulance. Max applied a tourniquet first to Lena's leg, then to the jihadist's arm that Hannibal had torn open.

"I'll be okay. But the bullet has to come out, it's still in there," Lena said through clenched teeth.

"Hang on, Lena. An ambulance is on the way. But before the medics arrive, I'm going to get this guy away from here," Max said, glancing at the jihadist next to the curb who was staring at the dog's teeth six inches away from his face. We don't want the police or anybody else finding him and sticking their noses in our affairs. This is a problem we have to take care of ourselves. Interference from incompetent bureaucrats and over-zealous FBI agents is the last thing we need."

Max tied the jihadist's hands together, pulled him to his feet, and steered him along the sidewalk to Goodman's back yard and down a flight of steps to the basement. Max gagged him and tied his legs together. After he secured the man to a metal support column, he ran back to where Ben and Anna were watching over Lena. The ambulance had not arrived yet.

The first thing Max noticed at the scene of the attack was the dead al-Qaeda fighter lying lifeless under the tree.

"He tried to kill me. I had no choice," Lena said.

"We have to get rid of him, too," Max said. "Ben, give me a hand."

Max and Ben loaded the dead jihadist into the Nissan, and Max tossed in the pistol they found in the gutter. Ben drove the car to a deserted lot behind an abandoned auto parts store four blocks away. He parked in an out-of-the-way spot next to a dumpster, wiped Max's prints off the gun, and grabbed the men's IDs and cell phones. He rejoined Max and Anna just as the ambulance pulled up.

"Must have been another one of those random drive-by shootings," Max told the medic who was examining Lena's leg.

The doctor who removed the bullet from Lena's leg said she would be okay but recommended an overnight stay as a precaution. It was a little before midnight when Max and Ben left the two women and got back to the Goodman house. Anna had stayed with Lena at the hospital. Max and Ben immediately went to the basement to confront the wounded al-Qaeda soldier.

"So, Mr. al-Saeed, tell us why you and your companion were sitting there in your car, watching and waiting. Why did you attack my wife? Whom do you represent?" Max asked the man tied to the column. Max held the man's driver's license in one hand and his mobile phone in the other. "I see from your phone that you recently called someone in Minneapolis. Who was it?"

"I will die before I tell you anything, you spawn of the Devil. You can torture and kill me, but we will win. With Allah's guidance we will grind you and your corrupt country into the dirt where you belong. We'll feed you to the jackals and laugh as they fight over your bodies."

"Yeah, right. We'll see about that," Max said as he loaded a 20 ml. syringe with truth serum.

It took only 15 ml of the serum to make the wounded man talk since blood loss and trauma had reduced his resistance. He told them about the attack planned for early the next morning. How reinforcements from an Oregon-based al-Qaeda unit would arrive at dawn. Then he told them about the Minneapolis mosque headquarters of Imam Rashid al-Saaladi and about how he planned to use Max's plague to create a terrorist haven in Yemen.

Finished with the interrogation, Max turned to Ben. "We have work to do. First, you have to retrieve the Nissan. I'm sure Mr. al-Saeed will be happy to join his partner after I give him a high dose of barbiturate. You can return the car with the two men in it to wherever you took it before. I'll brew a pot of coffee and start working out the details of what we still have to do tonight. Hurry back. We don't have the luxury of time."

An hour later, Max and Ben were sequestered in Ben's study. They concluded that when the al-Qaeda soldiers arrived the next morning and learned that their two lookouts had disappeared, they would either abandon their plan, or, more likely, break into and search the house as instructed by the Imam. Max and Ben agreed it would be the latter. Anticipating an attack, they would have to set up the Trojan Horse subterfuge that night instead of over the coming days as they had originally planned.

After intense back-and-forth discussion, Max summarized the plan they finally agreed on. "Hopefully, the al-Qaeda reinforcements will assume that we discovered their advance lookouts, the two guys in the Nissan, and that we concluded that there would be an attack soon and left in a hurry. We'll leave the phony bacteria in your freezer as if it had been abandoned in our rush to escape. We'll make it seem like the lookouts broke into the house and made a quick search for the formula, but not finding it, set out to try and locate us again. I'll use al-Saeed's phone to send a text confirming that story."

Max turned on al-Saeed's phone and typed, "Manus and others escaped. We are looking for them. House needs thorough search by team arriving tomorrow morning."

"Let's hope that al-Saaladi will be desperate enough to believe the message is from al-Saeed. Ben, go to your lab and prepare the material we discussed. I'll stay here and get everything ready for our departure," Max said as he powered off al-Saeed's phone.

Ben got to his lab fifteen minutes later. He put on a bio-hazard suit, turned on the robotic safety hood, retrieved the required samples from the freezer and set to work. First, he filled a glass vial with a liquid containing harmless bacteria. Then over the outside surface of the vial he swabbed a highly contagious and pathogenic bacterium—one he had previously created through a unique mutation process he had been investigating because of a similar Russian sample captured by a U.S. Army Biodefence unit. This mutated bacterium could be absorbed through the skin and transmitted through exhaled breath or fluid of an infected person. Fortunately, a critical property of this mutant version was loss of lethality upon subsequent passage, making it unable to cause an epidemic. Instead, it would only kill those it initially infects—anyone who touches the vial, or anyone whom that person transmits it to by sneezing or breathing in their presence.

Ben placed the vial contaminated on its outer surface into a slightly larger glass jar and swabbed the outside surface of that jar and its lid with the same lethal organism. He put that jar into a standard shipping box and sealed it with tape. He was back at his house twenty minutes later. He hid the package under a large frozen salmon at the bottom of the chest freezer in his basement.

While Ben was in his lab preparing the Trojan Horse, Max ransacked the house, creating an appearance of it having been rapidly searched. Max also prepared a false description of the plague production method and downloaded it onto a flash drive, which he hid in a desk drawer in Ben's study.

With their work accomplished, Max turned to another matter which had been on his mind. He called his adopted daughter Zula.

"Sorry to wake you, honey. There's a change of plan. You and Rana will have to meet us in Minneapolis instead of Pasadena."

While Max filled Zula in on the details, Ben called his neighbor across the street and arranged for Max and himself to take refuge in their house. From there, they could keep watch on the Goodman house and monitor the next move by the al-Qaeda agents who should be arriving soon.

The Intruders

Episode Nine

Watching from a curtained window of the darkened living room in a house across the street from his, Ben Goodman whispered, "Max! I think they're here. A van just pulled up down the street. That guy," nodding at a man walking away from the van, "he just got out. He's heading towards my house."

Max peered through night-vision binoculars. "There're three more in the van. This guy must be checking out the house before they do anything."

The man from the van walked past Ben's house to the end of the block, stood in the shadow of a tree for a moment scanning the area, then retraced his steps. "The house seems to be empty," he told his companions in the van. "Our scouts said the target and the others left. But we've still got to check it out. Let's go."

The four men spent the next hour searching the house. They found the packing box hidden in the freezer and the flash drive with the phony instructions.

"With Allah's help we've found the weapon," the leader said. "We'll wait to hear from our men who are following Manus, then capture him and his woman. We'll kill his friends."

"What should we do with this box and the flash drive?" one of his men asked.

"Tomorrow morning I'll send them to Minneapolis. I'll call the Imam now and give him the good news."

Meanwhile, across the street, every word of the jihadists'

conversation was clearly audible—Max had installed microphones in Goodman's house the night before. The two scientists were relieved that their Trojan Horse had been found and that the terrorists had taken the bait. So far, their plan was going as they had hoped.

"When Lena recovers, she and I will go to Minneapolis and confront the Iman, that is if our surprise package doesn't kill him first. One way or the other, I intend to finish this business once and for all," Max said.

A few minutes after the jihadists drove off, Max and Ben returned to the hospital to check on Lena. They found her awake and in a single room, her bandaged leg elevated on a couple of pillows. Ben's wife, Anna, sat next to Lena's bed reading aloud from a book of poems by a local poet. Both women seemed relaxed and to be enjoying their quiet time together. As it turned out, the bullet had missed bone and major blood vessels and was easily removed with a minimum of surgical trauma. Lena said she wasn't in pain and that she could be discharged the next day.

Max was relieved by the lack of serious injury and knew that Lena would soon be back to her normal "fighting condition." He described the night's activities and told her about his intention to take the battle directly to al-Saaladi at his mosque in Minneapolis.

Lena agreed and told him she'd be able to travel in a day or two. She grabbed her secure phone and made the necessary travel arrangements. Then she called Rana and Zula.

"The girls can meet us in Minneapolis the day after tomorrow," Lena said after she ended the call.

"Good." Max replied. "That'll give us time to formulate a plan. We'll stay with Ben and Anna tomorrow night and fly out the next day, but only if you're up to it."

At 4:48 p.m., Flight UA 382 touched down in Minneapolis. Max and Lena checked into the Airport Crown Plaza forty minutes later. Lena changed the bandage on her wound, then slept for an hour with her leg elevated. Max meditated for twenty minutes, then finished reading the book of poems he'd borrowed from Anna. They left the hotel in their rental car at 7:15.

At 7:30, they entered the middle eastern restaurant adjacent to the Muqdir Alevi mosque. "This is as good a place as any to start our surveillance," Lena whispered while they waited to be seated. The bearded waiter looked at them closely before leading them past the front counter. Signs proclaiming, "No Cell Phones" and "No Alcohol" in Arabic, Urdu and English were conspicuously displayed next to an ornate cash box. He led them to a small table near the rear of the crowded restaurant, dropped menus in front of them, then walked away without saying a single word.

Waiting for the dinners they'd ordered from another surly waiter who'd eventually showed up, they glanced around at the other patrons. All were Middle Eastern or South Asian. A few of the women wore head scarves, but most were enshrouded in black burqas. Every male in the room was bearded, and many of them cast scornful glances at Max and Lena. As they dug into the humus appetizer the server had abruptly put down in front of them, Lena's phone vibrated in her jacket pocket. Checking the identity of the sender, she said, "I'll take this outside. It's from my contact here in Minneapolis. I'll be right back."

Out front, with her back to the restaurant's window, Lena stood facing the parking strip in deep conversation. Meanwhile, Max used the pita pieces to scoop up more of the humus while he waited for Lena to return. He was deep in thought about how they could achieve their goal of destroying the al-Qaeda cell and was unaware of three men approaching from behind him.

Lena returned to their table five minutes later, anxious to tell Max what she had learned about Imam al-Saaladi and the layout of the mosque. But Max wasn't there. *He must be in the men's room,* she thought. When Max had not returned a few minutes later, she became concerned and called him on his mobile, ignoring the cell phone ban and angry looks from the leering waiter and some of the other diners. After four rings she connected.

"Max, where are you?"

"Hello, Lena. I've been expecting your call," a man answered in Arabic. Lena knew at once who it was. The Syrian accent and rasping voice told her everything she needed to know. It was a man she would never forget, one who had haunted her nightmares for decades. She started to reply but was distracted by two Arabic men walking toward her. A young muscular guy in a black tee shirt positioned himself behind her. The other one, older, bearded and wearing thick, tinted glasses, sat down across from her in what had been Max's chair. His right hand remained under the table.

Lena said nothing. Instead, she abruptly shut off her phone and returned it to the side pocket of her jacket. She then zipped the pocket closed, her movements deliberate and unrushed. She stared intently across the table at the bespectacled man, who, like Lena, had said nothing. The smirk formed by his grossly thick lips visible through his black beard was all he needed to communicate his intent. She instantly realized the gravity of her situation, how the events fitted together: Max's disappearance, these two here to abduct her, the proximity of the restaurant to the al-Qaeda gang's headquarters in the mosque. That's when she felt a surge of energy building inside her body. The same sensation she had when she had overwhelmed The Albanian in the North Portland laundromat.

Suddenly she bolted upright like an explosion while at the same time ramming the table into the chest of the unsuspecting man sitting across from her. He and his chair catapulted backwards onto the floor. His single pistol shot ricocheted off the underside of the table and hit a burqa-clad elderly woman sitting close by in her left eye. At the same time, Lena jammed her right elbow hard into the solar plexus of the man standing at her back, halting his attempt to grab her from behind. Spinning around to face him, she smashed the palm of her left hand upward under his chin with such force that the snap of his cervical vertebrae echoed around the room. The attacker fell back onto the table behind him. A platter of hot jasmine rice splattered over nearby diners as he collapsed to the floor.

Without interrupting her smooth pirouette, she spun back to the first man as he reached for the gun he had dropped. In a single, liquid move she slipped the knife from the scabbard under her jacket sleeve and hurled it with unerring accuracy to pierce the man's throat with enough force to slice into his spinal cord. He crashed into a close-by table, then to the floor. Steaming lentil soup rained down on his glasses to mask his lifeless eyes.

Lena cautiously edged around the up-turned table to where the man lay. She reached down and withdrew her knife from his throat and wiped the blade clean on his shirt. Then she stood to her full six-foot height, defiantly looked around the room at the stunned patrons, re-sheathed her knife, and left through the front door without bothering to look back.

Sitting in the car they had parked three blocks away, Lena called an unlisted number in Virginia. The encrypted conversation lasted less than a minute. She then called Zula.

"I need you now! Tell Rana. Then call this number." She gave Zula the Virginia contact.

"But, Mama, I have to lead a class tomorrow morning and then prepare for the—" Zula responded, but was cut off in mid-sentence by Lena.

"Zula! Come *now*! They've captured Max! Call that number. Flight arrangements are being made as we speak. You and Rana will be here by early morning."

"Oh, my God! We'll be there, Mother. Don't worry. We'll get Papa back!"

Exhausted, her leg hurting, Lena just wanted to return to the hotel and get some sleep before her daughters arrived. She inserted the key into the ignition, but then paused. She withdrew the key, got out of the car and called a taxi.

The Intruders

Episode Ten

The tall, almond-skinned, former Syrian Secret Service enforcer and assassin, Hamid Hassan, rose from a chair where he'd been resting and told the al-Qaeda soldier standing nearby to help him to attach electrodes to both feet of the man strapped to the narrow wooden table in the middle of the room. After the electrodes were in place, Hassan went over to the table and studied the old but wiry and well-muscled body. All five fingernails of his right hand had been torn out and the raw wounds were still bleeding. Bruises and lacerations covered his arms, legs, and trunk. His face was swollen from repeated blows. Saying nothing, Hassan slapped the prostrate man across the face three times, then once more, finally arousing him from a deep meditative state into which he had escaped.

"Wake up, Max! It's party time again. Only this time you will tell us what we want to know about the package that arrived yesterday. We need to know how to prepare it for release. The false instructions on the flash drive you planted in Pasadena have already wasted too much of our time. Nobody knows where you are. No one is coming to your rescue. You belong to me now. You may as well talk and save yourself from the horrible things we will do to make you cooperate," Hassan said, staring into Max's bloodshot eyes.

"Do what you want. You'll get nothing from me," Max croaked, his voice rasping from a throat raw from thirst.

Hassan took the control box from the man standing next to him and switched it on. Max's scream bounced off the

46

unpainted brick walls of the basement room in the mosque in which Imam Rashid al-Saaladi was preparing for the morning call to prayer.

At the same time Max was undergoing unrelenting torture in Minneapolis, in California the four al-Qaeda operatives who found the genetically modified bacteria in the Goodman freezer the night before woke earlier than usual. They were all suffering severe headaches and having difficulty breathing.

"Are you sure you didn't open the vial inside that jar?" one of the men managed to ask as he gasped for breath.

"No, you fool. I only took the jar out of the box to make sure it wasn't broken. A vial inside the jar must have contained what we're after. I didn't open that jar. I put it back in the box and took it to the Fed Ex office," he said, wiping away thick, yellow discharge oozing from his nose.

Meanwhile, in a Minneapolis hotel four miles from the mosque where Max was being viciously interrogated, Lena, Rana, and Zula were refining their rescue plan. They intended to be ready for the morning prayer service. Lena knew Max was being held by Hamid Hassan, the Syrian Secret Service officer who had relentlessly tortured her in Syria's Sednaya maximum security prison almost forty years before. She knew how bad it must be for Max and was determined to find him as soon as possible.

A short time later, five minutes before the prayer service, a tall, heavily bearded man entered the front door of the Muqdir Alevi mosque. He was clad in traditional Arabic dress, a white, floor-length throbe with a red and white-checkered gutra on his head. He was followed at a respectable distance by two women shrouded in black, full-face, eye-slotted burqas. They divided to go to their separate areas. But instead of entering the central prayer room, the man slipped unnoticed into the narrow hallway along a wall separating the mosque from the restaurant next door. A moment later the two women fell in step behind him.

"There should be a door leading to a basement at the end of this hall. I believe they'll be holding Max down there," Lena, disguised as the bearded Arab, whispered to Rana and Zula, still encased in their bulky garments.

They found a locked steel door at the end of the hallway. Rana immediately stepped forward with her lock pick and opened it in less than a minute. At once they heard muffled moans and the zapping sound of electric discharge, a sound Lena knew all too well. She fought hard to control her rage and the temptation to rush down the narrow stairway. They first had to assess the forces they would encounter when they did go down. She motioned to Zula, who was standing close behind her. Zula, as stealthy as the Zulu warriors of her childhood, eased past Lena and silently crept down the stairs far enough to gain a view of the dimly lit room. After a quick scan, she returned to where Lena and Rana waited.

Close to tears, Zula described what she had seen. "Papa's strapped to a table and they're shocking him with electrodes. There are five of them. An older man is holding a box with wires coming out of it. A younger man is standing near him. The others are across the room watching. Papa isn't saying anything. He's just moaning."

"Okay. Rana, you take out the three watchers. Zula, the young guy near Max is yours. The old bastard questioning Max is mine," Lena whispered. At that instant, she felt her energy level suddenly rise, her confidence increase. She felt for a quick moment that her daughters might be absorbing some of that power, but then turned her full attention back to the basement. "I'll go down first. Come when I call," she mouthed as she started down the stairs.

Lena, still disguised as a bearded Arab man, boldly descended into the room and brazenly confronted the surprised men.

"What's going on down here?" she challenged in perfect Arabic and imitating a man's voice. "The Imam asked me to see why the lights are dimming so frequently. What are you doing? Who's that strapped to the table?"

Max knew at once that it was Lena. The anguish in his face was replaced by relief, even though he understood that she confronted five fierce fanatics, each of whom would want nothing more than to kill her with utmost speed. But then he sensed Lena's power and knew she would prevail. He also felt that Rana and Zula must be somewhere nearby and would join her any moment. He strained to break loose from his straps, but to no avail. He could only watch and hope for the best.

Hassan was momentarily confused by this intrusion, but quickly realized that something was amiss. "Who are you? How did you get down here? The Imam wouldn't have sent you. He knows what we're doing," he yelled, anger creasing his shadowed face.

Perceiving his doubt about her, Lena quickly called for Rana and Zula. They leapt into the room from halfway down the stairs, burqas, fists, and feet flying. Zula landed first, turned to the surprised burly thug next to Hassan and landed a solid, roundhouse kick to his jaw, then followed with a powerful punch to his throat. When he hit the floor, she rammed her boot down on his chest. The cracking of his sternum and ribs told her that he was no longer a threat.

Landing behind Zula, Rana twisted around to confront the three mujahedeen standing next to the wall. Instantly recovering from their surprise, they rushed forward to where Rana stood as if she were waiting to greet them. But her greeting was not what they would have chosen. When they were close to her, she darted to the right, turned and quickly stepped behind them before they knew what had happened. She spun around and landed a powerful kick to the back of the closest one's knee, immediately putting him out of commission with a blown-out joint and experiencing excruciating pain. She followed the kick with three quick karate chops to the neck of the man who had been next to the one whose knee she'd just ruined. He went down to the floor and stayed there. But she wasn't fast enough to prevent the third man from twisting around and landing a heavy fist in her face, then kicking her in her midsection with enough force to send her flying backwards onto the wall. But when he rushed

49

at her to deliver a fatal blow, he was stopped by a jolting kick to the small of his back, propelling him forward into the wall as Rana jumped aside. Stabilized by the wall, he turned to see who had attacked him and was greeted by Zula's high kick to the middle of his face. The force smashed his head back hard against the moldy brick wall. Before he could recover, Rana grabbed his arm and spun him in a half circle to slam him face-first into the hard surface behind her. When he dropped stunned to the floor, she delivered two rapid kicks to his kidney, then one to his throat that ended his life.

While Rana finished off her attacker, Zula ran over to the one with the damaged knee as he was trying to get up, favoring his left leg. She landed a rapid kick to his chest, causing him to collapse back onto the floor gasping for breath while blood from his ruptured lung trickled from his gaping mouth.

At the same time her daughters were using their martial arts skills to dispatch the four so-called jihadist warriors, Lena had attacked Hassan. Her rage at what the vicious sadist had done to Max was no doubt heightened by recalling the treatment she'd received from him years before and by the realization that she was now finally able to settle that old score. With lightning speed, she grabbed Hassan by the hair and smashed his face into the rough brick wall he was standing next to. The rage she felt gave her power far in excess of the ferocity with which Hassan tried unsuccessfully to resist her onslaught. She bashed him against the wall two more times. Broken teeth erupted from his bloody mouth. His nose was crushed beyond recognition. Facial bones were broken, and deep lacerations spurted more blood.

"That's for forty years ago," Lena screamed.

Bouncing back off the wall, Hassan, even though nearly paralyzed with pain, instantly recognized her voice—this falsely bearded creature was the woman prisoner he had repeatedly and unmercifully tortured when he was a security agent at a Syrian prison. In a half-blind rage, he recovered enough to smash his fist into Lena's chest hard enough to knock her back against the stair rail. As he lunged forward to smash his other fist into her face, she deftly ducked his wild swing, threw her shoulder into his midsection and raised him high enough to throw him upside down over the stair rail. The lower half of his body landed hard on the metal stairs. The upper half landed head-first on the concrete floor with a loud cracking sound. The blood spilling from his fractured skull mixed with the widening pool forming from blood streaming from his mangled face.

"And that's for what you did to Max," Lena screamed as she kicked him violently and repeatedly in the ribs for extra measure, alarming her daughters with her near-crazed fury.

"Mother, stop! He's dead! We have to get Papa out of here," Rana said, pulling Lena away from the Syrian splayed over the wet floor and blood-spattered stair steps. They undid Max's restraints, wrapped him in the throbe Lena had been wearing and carefully carried him up the stairs, down the hall, and unseen out of the front entrance of the mosque. Zula hurriedly brought their car around. Twenty minutes later they were back at the hotel.

A physician and two nurses arranged by Lena's former colleague spent most of the day treating Max's extensive wounds. Fortunately, no permanent damage had been inflicted, although the doctor predicted a long recovery period would be required for Max to completely heal from the severe beating he'd received. Max didn't argue with him on that point. The doctor assured Rana that the blows she'd taken hadn't broken any bones or injured any internal organs, although the bruises would linger for a while.

That evening, when Lena and the girls were tending to Max's wounds, Rana, with her slightly musical south India inflexion, said, "Papa, you and Mama need a vacation after this nightmare. Why don't you go to our hacienda in Mexico? I know how much you love it there."

"That's a good idea. Maybe we should. But I need to rest up here for a few days before I can travel. Anyway, I want to see what happens at the mosque. We have to make sure our Trojan Horse did its job," Max said in a scratchy voice, grimacing from the effort to speak.

The next day in his private chamber at the mosque, Imam Rashid al-Saaladi was keenly aware of the headache that had started during the night and had now intensified. He was also having difficulty breathing. The two companions who'd been with him when he opened the package from California had the same symptoms. This condition was far more than just a panicked confusion over Max's escape and the slaughter of his fellow jihadists. The symptoms progressed rapidly throughout the day; by evening all three were nearly comatose, seriously dehydrated from fluid loss and elevated temperatures.

The following morning, the Imam and his two associates were dead. The mosque custodian discovered the bodies around noon. The corpses in the basement were found a little later. By that evening the FBI, alerted by an anonymous tip, had arrested twelve additional members of the group whose names they found in the Imam's files. They closed the mosque and raided the restaurant next door. The discovery of arms and explosives in the restaurant storage room and in the mosque attic space led to indictment of a dozen collaborators. Over the following week, more than thirty al-Qaeda operatives spread around the country had been arrested thanks to records found at the mosque and in the restaurant. The al-Qaeda plot to blackmail the world with Max's plague had been successfully derailed—terminated just like the Minneapolis mullah and his deluded followers. The only unsolved mystery in this momentous series of events was who had massacred the jihadists found in the basement and the identity of the mysterious tipster.

There is one more thing of note. No traces of Max, Lena, or their daughters, were ever found at the mosque, at the hotel, or anywhere in Minneapolis, as if they had never been there.

The End

With this challenge successfully met, Max and Lena had prevailed in yet another battle in their war against those who resort to violence and mayhem to satisfy their evil aspirations. At last, the two weary warriors could retire to the quiet, peaceful existence they craved. A time in which they could pursue their own desires rather than react to events beyond their control.

But alas, as our planet continues to spin on its mighty axis, humanity perseveres in its perilous voyage along the uncharted tides of time. With this irrefutable reality in mind, it should not be surprising that three days later, as Max and Lena were savoring breakfast on a private plane headed to Cabo San Lucas, the notorious Mexican cartel leader, Don Arturo Mendez, was inserting himself into their future.

Mendez and his cousin and legal adviser, the suave Leon Cardosa, were lounging on the shaded deck of Mendez's sprawling hacienda near Ensenada, Mexico. They were gazing at the calm turquoise surface of the Pacific Ocean while savoring one of Mendez's exorbitantly expensive tequilas.

"Do you think that rumor about some American scientist discovering a way to increase physical power could really be true? Like some kind of superman thing?" Mendez asked, as he nursed a 35-year-old añejo.

"I have to admit, it does sound improbable, but my source seemed convinced," Cardosa replied before taking a long pull on his Dos Equis chaser.

"See what you can find out, Leon. A power like that could make a big difference in our fight with the Sinaloa Cartel."

"Sí, Arturo. It would. I'll check it out," Leon said as he reached for his phone.

Tale Of The Scorpion

Episode One

A dusty pickup pulled off a narrow dirt track a mile past the bleak village of Mota Hilarto. The driver eased into a spot relatively free of prickly pear cactus and scrub brush that populated the dry landscape. Three men got out, glanced at their cargo in the long bed, then walked around the area with their eyes focused on the ground. Soon, one of them found what they were looking for and hollered to the others. Two of them took wooden stakes and hammers from the bed and went back into the desert. When they got to the right spot, they drove two stakes into the hardpacked dirt. The stakes were about ten feet apart, one on each side of the entrance to a Mexican Fire Ant colony, equally spaced from the hole where a parade of quarter-inch-long, reddish-brown ants were busily coming and going.

Back at the truck, the third man released the tail gate and grabbed a rope tied around the ankles of two naked men who were tied together face to face. He pulled them out and let them crash to the rocky ground. Their hands and feet were secured with duct tape, and their bodies were bruised, broken, and bloodied. The man kicked them away from the truck, then went to the cab and took out a large jar of thick, yellow-orange honey.

When the driver's fellow cartelistas returned to the truck and told him the stakes were in place, he carefully poured the contents of the jar onto the faces and bodies of the captives struggling at his feet. Ignoring their pleas for mercy, he turned to his men and said, "Okay, amigos, they're ready." His companions grabbed the rope and dragged the captives over rough terrain through clumps of fishhook cactus to the ant bed, then tied them to the stakes so their bodies were stretched across the entrance. The two men stomped the ground, brushed off crazed ants swarming over their boots, and ran back to the truck.

After the driver made a brief phone call, he backed into the dirt track, changed gears, and drove off in a thick cloud of swirling brown dust.

Nearby villagers ignored anguished screams, even though they lasted late into the night. They knew it was best to ignore Narco-Cartel business.

While a half-dozen Black-Headed Mexican buzzards fought over the last remnant of flesh on the bones of the two Sinaloa cartelistas the following morning, 1200 miles to the north, the president of the Society for Experimental Physiology was welcoming an audience of research scientists to their annual meeting in San Francisco. He finished his introduction by announcing, "And now Dr. Benjamin Goodman will present the keynote lecture. His topic is, 'Epigenetic Regulation of Cellular Energy Production.'"

After Goodman's presentation, when the usual probing questions had been dispensed with, an elderly gentleman in the front row spoke up. "Dr. Goodman, weren't you a research colleague of Dr. Max Manus at MIT twenty years ago?"

"Yes, Dr. Smithers, I was. We worked together for several years. I believe you were chairman of the Chemistry Department at the time, is that correct?"

"Yes. I'm retired now. My question is about a rumor circulating then that Manus discovered a way to increase cellular energy production beyond normal levels. Some claimed the process produced a "superman effect," so to speak. And that he had successfully tested it on himself. Is that true?"

"Uh, well, uh, no! Certainly not. No. There's no truth to that rumor. How could anything so improbable be possible? In fact, Dr. Smithers, if I may be so bold, it's unbecoming that a scientist of your status would bring up this matter in public, especially at a forum such as this," Goodman replied, his initial hesitation having quickly turned to irritation.

Smithers, as well as others in the audience, were surprised at Goodman's openly defensive response. That response was especially noted by a certain Stanford professor sitting in the front row.

Meanwhile, back in Mexico, twenty-three miles northwest of Cabo San Lucas and situated on a gently-sloping, cactus-covered hillside above the Bay of Pesado, the tiny village of Agua Verdosa was welcoming a cool ocean breeze softening the sun's unrelenting heat. The village had only two attractions of note: the grimy Three Lizards Cantina and a small marina at the bottom of the slope. Twenty miles further up the coast, behind an eight-foot, razor wire-topped wall at the end of an overgrown dirt track, a seldom-used hacienda sat on a hillside overlooking the Pacific Ocean. It was in this secluded hide-away that Max Manus, a brilliant retired scientist, and his wife Lena, an ex-CIA assassin, enjoyed a justly deserved reprieve after defeating the al-Qaeda cell that had captured Max in Minneapolis three months earlier. The jihadists had intended to steal a bacterial plague organism Max had created in his laboratory years earlier. Before his rescue from the jihadists by Lena and their two adopted daughters, Rana and Zula, Max had been tortured unmercifully. While recovering in quiet isolation in Mexico, he was using the time to further explore his amazing discovery of auto-induced enhancement of energy and mental function. Lena was determined that nothing would interrupt his recovery or his research.

But there's always a catch; a fly makes its way into the sugar bowl no matter how tight the lid. In this case, the fly was an astute and politically-connected Mexican lawyer, León Cardosa. Quite by chance Cardosa had learned from his sister's husband, a professor at Stanford, about a rumor that an American scientist may have discovered a way to increase physical and mental energy, raising the possibility of generating something like superpower. And, to add frosting to this cake, Cardosa was the cousin and senior adviser of one of Mexico's most ambitious and ruthless drug cartel bosses, the infamous Don Arturo Méndez. Méndez, known as *The Scorpion* because of the lethal sting he was capable of inflicting, was the uncontested leader of the small but powerful Baja Narco-Cartel and was feared by all who knew him, and by many who didn't.

Cardosa's casual mention of the rumored superpower during one of their family get-togethers got Méndez's attention. Open to any possible advantage for advancing his goals, no matter how improbable, he instructed Cardosa to investigate further. Lounging on his luxurious, shaded patio overlooking the Pacific Ocean, Méndez raised his glass of vintage tequila to toast the possibility of such a weapon. "Here's to getting the secret of that power, León," Méndez said.

León sipped his tequila as he listened to Méndez's fantasy about taking over his enemy, the larger and infinitely more powerful Sinaloa cartel, and eventually assuming leadership of all Mexican narco-cartels. And then, ultimately, establishing an all-powerful Narco-North America.

Changing the subject, Cardosa said, "I heard we recently captured two Sinaloa gang members spying in our territory."

"They were checking out our sea routes to San Diego. The Sinaloas need more revenue to fight off the Gulf cartel. Taking over our routes would help. But we sent a message. Stay away or be served to the ants and buzzards! Another tequila, León?"

As a senior partner in one of Mexico City's prestigious law firms and an adviser to the Mexican National Cabinet, Cardosa was well positioned to extend quiet feelers to the U.S. legal community, including one of the leading intellectual property firms. A week later, his contact at the patent firm of Sharkey and Wrathe discovered a 1996 patent issued to Max Manus related to cellular energy mechanisms. Even though the patent only obliquely referred to something called "metabolic up-regulation," Cardosa's astute contact realized the patent might be what Cardosa was looking for and immediately sent the link. The next day, after studying the patent, Cardosa urged Méndez to arrange a meeting with Manus. Even though the claims were vague, and the methods only scantily described, Cardosa suspected the inventor knew much more than was revealed in the official document.

Since Lena had carefully concealed their identity, their hasty departure from Minneapolis, and their subsequent travel to Mexico, it took Méndez' agents several weeks to discover that Max owned a hacienda on the Baja peninsula. Another two weeks were required to discover its location.

When Lena spotted a cabin cruiser outfitted with deep-sea fishing rigs slowly motoring past their beach, she thought nothing of it; just another fishing party out of the Agua Verdosa marina. Little did she know that photos of her and Max sitting on their patio watching seagulls flutter in the boat's wake were being transmitted to León Cardosa's iPhone.

Later that week, José Valdez, Max and Lena's loyal property manager and guard, woke to frenzied barking of his two Rottweiler-Giant Chihuahua cross breeds. The fierce dogs roamed the property day and night, providing backup to a sophisticated electronic security system. José immediately called Lena at the main house. She'd heard the commotion as well and checked the monitors but didn't see anything out of the ordinary.

But trusting the dogs, she and José set out to investigate and followed the frenzied barking to the north section of the wall where it connected to an electrified fence stretching across the beach. They didn't find any intruders, but later when they reviewed the recording, they saw a clear view of a man's head and shoulders peering through the razor wire barrier. He'd disappeared when the raging dogs arrived.

"Probably just a curious local," Max said, as he and Lena had their breakfast the next morning, more to assure himself than her.

"You're probably right," Lena said in her soothing yet noncommittal way. However, following her well-honed instinct, the night before she'd sent the security video to contacts in D.C. and Mexico City. Then, as Max was pouring another cup of coffee, Lena's secure phone buzzed. Reading the text, a dark frown spread across her face. Their quiet time had just come to an end.

Tale Of The Scorpion

Episode Two

Lena put down her secure phone and looked at Max. "That call was from my contact in the Mexican Federal Police. The man caught on camera last night is a soldier in a Baja drug cartel run by someone called *The Scorpion*. His name is Arturo Méndez." She refilled her cup from a pot of herbal tea and squeezed in juice from a wedge of lemon. "They kidnap for ransom, among other more lucrative activities, so they must think we're rich Americans. What else would they want? They couldn't know about your superpower work, could they?"

"I don't think so," Max replied. "In fact, they shouldn't know anything about us at all since you've done such a good job of keeping us off the grid down here. José's dogs must have scared that guy off last night. But I know you'll keep a close lookout just in case," Max replied, savoring the last swallow of his favorite Mexican coffee.

A few days later, and a thousand miles away, Méndez was updating his adviser and lawyer, León Cardosa, as they finished lunch on Méndez's patio.

"The drug route to the U.S. is working out okay," Méndez said. "The old freighter we bought from that crazy Chinese shipping company docked in Long Beach with eighty million dollars' worth of cocaine and thirty million in meth. Pot production in California will bring in at least twenty. If this keeps up, within twelve months we'll be able to take on the Sinaloa cartel," Méndez said.

"Congratulations!" León responded. "That's great. But maybe we should think about phasing out marijuana production. It's going to be legal in the U.S. soon. That market will disappear. The future is cocaine, meth, and heroin. America will never legalize those. At least not in our lifetime. It's one of their ways to keep the masses under control."

"Yeah, I know. But before we abandon pot, we've gotta increase our supply and distribution channels for the hard stuff. Then we'll take over the other cartels," Méndez said, reaching for tequila. "Then we won't need what we get from pot."

A moment later, after lighting Cuban cigars, Méndez brought up the other topic on his mind. "What about that superman thing your brother-in-law told you about? You haven't forgotten that, have you?"

"Certainly not, mi amigo. The scientist is an old man named Max Manus. Not much is known about him after 1994 when he left that MIT university. But I did learn that he and his wife arrived in Cabo about three months ago. Yesterday, we found a walled hacienda on the west coast north of Agua Verdosa where an old Gringo couple lives. I have a photo of them. Tomorrow, I'll get a scan of Manus's passport photo for comparison. A friend in Immigration Services is doing that to repay an old favor. I'll let you know if it's Manus," Cardosa answered.

The next day Max's mobile phone rang as he and Lena finished a late breakfast. Other than their daughters, Rana and Zula, his good friend and colleague, Ben Goodman, and Lena's CIA contact, no one else knew the number.

"Yes," Max answered, frowning at the unfamiliar caller ID.

"Good morning, Dr. Manus. My name is Arturo Méndez. I want to talk to you about something beneficial to both of us. It's important."

"Sorry. Wrong number. There's no one here by that name," Max answered, preparing to end the call.

"Wait, Señor. From where you are now, you can see me

on a yacht anchored off your beach. I know who you are, and I don't take no for an answer. If you know what's good for you and your wife, you'll meet me at the Three Lizards Cantina at five o'clock today," Méndez said, then hung up.

"That was Arturo Méndez. He knows who I am and wants to meet today. Important things to discuss, he says."

"He's a dangerous cartel leader. We shouldn't get involved with him," Lena said forcefully, watching the big yacht speed to the south.

"You're right. But now that he knows about us, we have to do something. We can't just ignore him and hope he leaves us alone. We'll meet in Agua Verdosa and make it clear that we want nothing to do with him."

Lena shook her head in disagreement but knew that once Max made up his mind there was no changing it.

At five p.m., Max and Lena entered the Three Lizards Cantina through louvered, swinging half-doors. A stench of sweat, stale beer, and rancid cooking oil hung in the air. Méndez and two burly bodyguards were the only ones there. Méndez sat alone at a single table with two empty chairs in the middle of the room. One of his men stood at the bar. The other one ambled over to the swinging doors, leaned against the doorjamb, and folded his arms across his broad chest.

"Buenas tardes, Señor, Señora. Please, sit down. Thank you for coming," Méndez said, beckoning the two to join him. "Would you like something to eat or drink?"

"What do you want that's so important?" Max asked after he and Lena sat down, ignoring the offer of hospitality.

"It's a pleasure to meet you at last, Dr. Manus. You are such a famous man, but it's been hard to find you. Not much is known about what you've been up to since leaving that university."

"What do you want?" Max repeated, disregarding Méndez's banter. "We know who you are."

Lena said nothing, just watched and listened, maintaining her usual alertness, ready for whatever might happen.

"All right. I'll get to the point," Méndez said, noting Max's blunt reply. "It's rumored you can turn into superman. Is that true?"

"That's ridiculous," Max barked. "If that's why you invited us here, we'll be leaving now," he said, glancing at Lena and sliding his chair away from the table.

"Not so fast, Dr. Manus! I think that instead of leaving, you will come with me to my hacienda for a more serious discussion." Mendez beckoned toward one of his men. "Arnaldo, you and Felix escort my new friends to the helicopter." Max glanced at Lena, then erupted from his chair. With three long strides he reached the front door as the bodyguard started to draw his holstered pistol. Before the gun was halfway out, Max kicked him in the midsection with such force that the man was lifted a foot off the ground and propelled backwards through the swinging doors. His head smashed into the post supporting the porch roof. The loud crunch and splatter of tissue told Max the man was of no further concern.

In the same split second that Max jumped up, Lena leapt to her feet and rushed to the cartel soldier standing at the bar. When he went for his gun, she grabbed the wrist of his right arm and twisted it clockwise, then yanked it upwards. Her move was so forceful his shoulder was dislocated, and his arm dropped useless at his side. Without pausing, she grabbed his left arm and swept his legs out from under him with her right foot while pulling him down to the floor. His face smashed into the brass rail below the bar. Teeth and blood exploded onto the filth below. For extra measure, she rammed her booted foot into the back of his right knee, crushing everything in its path, grinding splintered bones into the floorboards. Only then, as he lay writhing in a spreading pool of blood, did he realize what had happened.

Max and Lena were surprised by the speed and ferocity of what they'd just done. They glanced across the room questioningly at each other, then went to where Méndez sat at the table. He appeared paralyzed by what he'd witnessed.

"Don't contact us again. Next time, it'll be your turn," Max said furiously.

He and Lena looked around the cantina, then left through the swinging doors. They stepped around the lifeless body sprawled on the porch, got into the pickup they'd borrowed from José, and headed north towards their hacienda.

After Max and Lena left the cantina, Méndez quickly took out his phone. "León, the old man and his woman took out my two best men in five seconds. Whatever his power is, it's real. We've got to have it. Meet me at my hacienda this weekend. Get Sánchez out of prison and bring him. We'll need all the help we can get."

On the way back to their hacienda, Lena and Max were having a hard time understanding the change that came over them at the cantina. Lena was the first to speak. "Max. What I felt was greater and came on faster than anything I've known before. What happened back there?"

"It was the same for me," Max said, thoughtfully. "It's possible that new energy regulation networks in our brains have emerged, or perhaps been rediscovered, and that they're reinforced when they're activated. It could be they're not only permanent components of our defense mechanisms now but are more pronounced—and quicker to take over. If what I suspect is true, they'll be switched on automatically whenever we sense danger. If that's the case, the ability to generate incredible power when it's needed most would be truly awesome. And, if I'm right, the power will become stronger with every time we use it."

Absorbing the significance of Max's explanation, Lena said, "If you *are* right, we're changed into something altogether different. We've progressed beyond the increased energy I've been experiencing lately. We might be at a point at which this superpower turns on spontaneously."

After a long moment of silence, Max answered. "Yes, you may be right. I suspect we *have* been transformed. We may not be able to fly, Lena, but we may be capable of just about anything short of that," Max said, grinning in a way Lena had never seen before.

After a short pause, Lena asked the obvious question.

"Will we be able to turn it on at will?"

"We'll see," Max answered. "I need more time in the lab. Then I'll know for sure."

Tale of the Scorpion

Episode Three

Back at their hacienda after their confrontation at the Three Lizards Cantina, Lena turned her full attention to how to deal with their newly discovered opponent, Don Arturo Mendez. She found Max in their library room. "After what we did to his men at the Three Lizards Cantina today, Mendez will be more determined than ever to add your superpower to his arsenal."

Max was in his favorite chair engrossed in a Brahms symphony. "What did you say?"

"Mendez! He's going to come after us. There's no doubt about it. We have to anticipate the worst. I've already taken steps to prepare for his next move. José is installing alarms and cameras to extend a mile beyond our wall, a safehouse in La Paz is ready if we need it, and Rana will be joining us tomorrow. I also received copies of classified DEA files on Mendez, his consiglieri Leon Cardosa, and on the operations of his Baja Cartel. We'd never be able to defeat them by ourselves with the number of men he has and the weapons at their disposal, no matter what kind of powers you can conjure up."

"You may be right," Max replied after he turned off the stereo. "No matter how much superpower we can activate, we couldn't match their strength. We'll have to defeat them some other way. I have an idea, but I need time to work it out." After a pause, he continued, "Why did you send for Rana?"

"We have to know their every move. Rana's job in a army intelligence has made her an expert in surveillance and eavesdropping. She's bringing the latest hi-tech listening and transmitting devices."

"How can we make use of that stuff? The cartels are more security-conscious than any law enforcement agency," Max said with obvious skepticism.

"Max, please. Concentrate on your science. Listen to your beloved Brahms, or even Mozart if you have to. But don't worry, Rana and I will take care of everything.".

"Yes Liebchen, of course. I was just curious, that's all," Max replied, as he headed to his lab.

The next day at the Los Cabos airport, José Valdez, Max and Lena's faithful hacienda caretaker and resourceful guard, recognized Rana immediately from a photo Lena had showed him. "Señorita Rana. My name is José. Your mother sent me. I'll take you to the hacienda. My truck is outside."

Before complying, Rana called Lena to make sure the man was who he claimed to be. "Yes, Mother, he matches your description." Turning back to José, she noticed how handsome he was. "Okay, José, let's go," she said with a smile.

After two hours of idle chat and a few side-glances at each other, José and Rana arrived at the hacienda.

Rana was pleased to see how well Max had recovered from the torture he'd endured in Minneapolis at the hands of the al-Qaeda operatives before Lena and the girls rescued him. After coffee, and catching up on family matters, then extensive discussion of the situation with Mendez and his cartel, Max brought up the subject of his renewed research on the superpower discovery he'd made years earlier.

"Oh, yeah. That's really interesting, Dad," Rana said as she rose from of her chair and went to retrieve the backpack she'd left by the front door. "Maybe we can talk about it later."

Undeterred by Rana's apparent skepticism, Max continued, "I'm working on a protocol for its application to others, too. Including you. Hopefully, I'll have an answer to that soon."

Digging through her pack, Rana didn't seem to be listening to Max. She'd been hearing about his scientific breakthroughs since her adoption at the age of seven and had become a little jaded to what to her seemed like outrageous fantasies.

"Dad, I really would like to hear more, honest, I would. But right now I need to show Mom this new voice recording system and figure out the best way to take advantage of it."

Lena, noticing Rana's lack of enthusiasm about Max's energy research, with an encouraging smile said, "We'll get back to that later, Maxie. Rana and I have our work to do, too. Like winning a war with the Baja Cartel."

After Lena gently sent Max back to his lab, Rana removed a small package from her backpack and spread out its contents on the dining table. "Since we can't overcome their greater numbers and military weapons, we need to know their plans so we can anticipate and counteract their every move." Picking up one of the items, she continued, "These will allow us to do that." Then, pointing to another gadget, she said, "That one's an ultra-sensitive, miniature microphone and transmitter that links to satellites through cell phone towers with a wavelength we can monitor with these little receivers. It also serves as a location beacon."

"How on earth do you plan to deploy all this stuff?" Lena asked. "You can't just walk into their offices, or houses or cars, and hide them."

"Why not?" Rana asked. "I'll visit Cardosa at his office in Mexico City. As for Mendez, we'll send him a present he won't refuse," Rana replied. "It's something I discovered in the file you got from the agency."

Two days later, at 10 a.m. in Mexico City, Leon Cardosa's secretary, Juanita, announced that the woman from Ares Munitions had arrived for her appointment.

"Show her in, and bring two coffees," Leon instructed, curious what this visit was about.

Leon was momentarily taken aback by the striking beauty of the elegant, raven-haired woman entering his office. She sat down in the chair in front of his desk, politely turning down the coffee he offered.

"Thank you for seeing me, Mr. Cardosa. My name is Maria Delblanco. I represent a private Israeli company that supplies sophisticated weapons to military and law enforcement organizations. We don't advertise and we maintain a low profile, so you may not be familiar with us. Because of your unique connections to the Mexican government, as well as to a wide range of other organizations, we would be interested in retaining your services to introduce us to appropriate people who might benefit from our new products. Naturally, discretion is of the utmost importance. Is that something you might be interested in?"

"Of course, Ms. Delblanco. Our firm frequently does work of that type. But I do need to know more about your company. Are you sure you wouldn't like a cup of coffee?"

Seeing that Cardosa was hooked, she slowly crossed her shapely legs and allowed her short skirt to slip up another few inches. "Well, yes, perhaps I will. With milk, please. No sugar," she replied, smiling appealingly.

When he got no answer from his secretary, he stood up. "Juanita must be away from her desk. I'll get the coffees myself, I'll just be a moment," he said, walking toward the door.

As soon as he left the room, Rana quickly took a nano-mic transmitter from her pocket and attached it to the underside of his desktop. She was sitting as if she were an unmoving marble statue smiling her enticing smile when he returned a minute later with fresh coffees.

An hour and forty minutes later, having finished her visit with Cardosa, she was back on the sidewalk in front of his office building hailing a cab. She instructed the driver to take her to the Mexico City airport. She only had two hours to make her flight to Cabo.

The next day, after a lunch of steak and potatoes, Galtero Sanchez was reclining in his green, simulated leather Lazy Boy lounge chair watching a raunchy Hong Kong porno movie he'd already seen at least six times. As he poured his third Margarita, the prison warden appeared at his open cell door. "Sanchez, you're escaping tonight. El Scorpio needs you. Be at the soccer field at nine. His helicopter will let down a rope ladder."

Sanchez slowly lifted his massively muscled body out of the recliner and stood to his full six foot-seven-inch height. A multicolored wrap-around tattoo of the deadly Sonoran Bark Scorpion covered every square inch of his body from his giant feet to the top of his shaved head. "It's about time, Warden. I'm bored with this filthy dump. I need some action. Something to do. Somebody to kill."

Two days after Leon Cardosa's meeting with Maria Delblanco, he and Sanchez were meeting with Mendez at Mendez's hacienda. They were planning how to capture Max and force him to reveal his superpower secret. Their conversation came to a sudden halt when Mendez's housekeeper came out to the patio holding a pair of handsome black Chihuahuas. "Señor, these two dogs just arrived by Fed Ex. This note was with them."

Mendez, whose love of Chihuahuas was well-known, happily took the dogs onto his lap and told Cardosa to read the note.

"'Don Arturo, please accept this gift in appreciation for your generous contributions to our community.' It's signed, 'A friend'," Cardosa added.

These are magnificent specimens. Thank you, friend, whoever you are," Mendez said as he admired his new companions.

Ignoring the dogs and the note, Sanchez addressed the challenge head on, "It'll be no problem to destroy the hacienda wall and capture Manus and his woman. We can torture her until he talks. That always works, especially if we make it bad enough. And we know how to do that real good, right Amigos?"

"All right, make the arrangements," Mendez told Sanchez. "Do it next week."

After Sanchez left, Mendez and Cardosa turned to other matters.

"Have you heard from that Israeli company about those military weapons?" Mendez asked.

"Not yet. She said they'd send a proposal in a few days. I'll let you know." After a moment, Cardosa said, "One more thing, Arturo. The Sinaloa Cartel is making more advances on our sea routes to California. The Russian mafia is supporting them. We need outside help as well. Now that the Russians and Iranians are taking most of the Afghanistan poppy crop, the Asians are getting less than they would like. Our poppy fields in *Guatemala* could supply their needs. We can sell them meth and cocaine too. Since the Russians have Europe tied up, maybe we should move into Asia with the help of the Chinese. If you want, I can make inquires."

"Yes, do that. I've been thinking the same thing. Globalization is the solution to our problem," Mendez replied, as he scratched one of the Chihuahuas behind its ears, in no way suspecting the nano-mic chip embedded in its leg muscle—the device that was sending a steady stream of their conversation to Rana's receiver at the hacienda.

In the middle of the following week, it was a little after midnight when the new alarm woke José in his casita and Max, Lena, and Rana in the big house. The cameras showed four SUVs slowly approaching the hacienda from a mile away.

Forewarned of the attack, Max quickly secured the false basement wall to conceal his lab. Lena and Rana gathered up the supplies, equipment, and armaments they would need. José met the three of them at the entrance to the tunnel to the boat house. His guard dogs ran ahead, leading the way. When they arrived at their destination, they sealed the hidden entrance behind them.

By the time Sanchez blew the front gate apart with a massive charge of C4, José had already launched the high-speed motorboat and they were well out into the bay.

"There's nobody here! They were here yesterday, we have a photo of them on the patio," Sanchez screamed angrily at his men. Looking out to the water, he glimpsed the disappearing wake of a sleek boat, then noticed the boathouse at the edge of the beach below the hacienda with its door standing open. He quickly took out his phone.

"Don Arturo, they escaped. They're in a speedboat headed south. Probably to *Cabo San Lucas. Can you arrange a reception for them?" Sanchez yelled excitedly into the phone.*

"Damn! All right, no problem. We'll be there to greet them. If they go someplace else, my contact in the Mexican navy will let me know," Mendez answered angrily and also with what would turn out to be highly unwarranted confidence.

Tale of the Scorpion

Episode Four

"Full speed due south," Max instructed José, as he unfolded a Baja coast navigation chart. "Méndez probably expects us to head to the Cabo San Lucas boat basin. I bet he has informers in the local Mexican navy patrols, All the cartel do. They'll surely locate us soon. So, we'll do the unexpected. Instead of heading to San Lucas where Méndez will be waiting, we'll dock at the boat ramp at Agua Verdosa. Then we'll drive to the safe house Lena set up in La Paz."

Max took the wheel while José called his brother. "Raúl, meet us at the ramp with your SUV and boat trailer. You have to take us to La Paz. Hurry! We'll be there soon."

While José was talking with his brother, an enraged Méndez, in a helicopter on the way to intercept Max at the San Lucas boat basin, was talking to Sánchez. "Meet me at the basin with six of your men. Send the other three to Agua Verdosa in case he goes there. Get it right this time."

The conversation between Méndez and Sánchez was not picked up by Rana's devices since the Chihuahuas with the chips were at Méndez's hacienda in Ensenada.

When the three cartel soldiers reached Agua Verdosa, they checked the Three Lizards cantina. Finding it empty, they proceeded to the boat ramp. As they approached it, they spotted a Chevy SUV with a trailer in tow, which was half-way into the water and positioned to load a boat. A single man stood nearby scanning the bay with binoculars. They quietly pulled behind a ridge and cut the engine without being detected. The one in the back seat called Méndez to report the situation.

"Stay put. If Manus docks, capture him and the woman and kill anyone else," Méndez ordered.

As José guided the boat toward the trailer, he waved to his brother, then commanded his two dogs, Jupiter and Zeus, to jump into the water, swim to shore, and check out the beach area. The dogs eased over the side and into the water without a sound.

A few minutes later, as the boat approached the dock, the dogs signaled three sharp barks. Lena understood their meaning. "Rana, let's see what the dogs have discovered," she whispered. She and Rana, clad in black tee shirts and jeans, put on their water shoes, slipped over the stern and silently swam to the beach. They reached the shore a little beyond where the barks originated.

Hearing the boat bump against the trailer, the three cartel thugs, with Uzi's in hand, crawled to the edge of the yucca-covered ridge for a look-see. Spying only three men, two on the boat and one next to the trailer, they didn't hesitate to carry out Méndez's orders. They stood upright and one of them yelled, "Hombres, hands in the air! Get out of the boat. Ándale!" They cautiously picked their way down the ridge toward the boat ramp with their weapons pointed directly at Max and his two companions. Carefully maneuvering over the rocks and around the yucca, they didn't notice two silent shadows closing in on them from behind.

Lena, faster than Rana had ever seen her move before, did a flying leap over the man a few steps behind the other two. As she sailed past him, she slammed her fist into the side of his head then grabbed and threw aside the Uzi he flung into the air as he catapulted down the slope. He didn't notice cactus needles piercing his body as he rolled over them since he was already dead. Rana caught up as Lena landed behind one of the other men with her left arm across his throat, reaching around with her other hand to grab his gun as she crushed his windpipe. At the same instant, Rana landed a powerful kick under the chin of the other as he was turning back to see what was happening, fatally snapping his neck with a loud crack. Lena pulled her two bodies behind a patch of yucca while Rana maneuvered the other body under a creosote bush. They collected the guns, took all the extra clips from the men's pockets, then rejoined Max and the others.

The two black Giant Chihuahua cross breeds, standing atop the ridge, each barked once, then bounded down the slope to José, wagging their stubby tails in perfect harmony.

Together at the ramp, Rana stared at Lena in wonder. "Mom, I've never seen you move like that. Like a guided missile or something. I've always knew you were good in martial arts, but that was way beyond anything I've seen you do before. Is this what Dad's superpower thing does?"

Lena glanced at Max, then said to Rana, "Ask your father, honey. Maybe he can explain."

Max said, "Well, it may be hard to believe, and even harder to understand, but Lena and I seem to be undergoing a change of some sort. As I mentioned when you arrived yesterday, it's based on that energy enhancement discovery I made a long time ago."

Rana, immediately realizing the implications of such power, said, "When you referred to it then, I thought you were exaggerating. I pretty much forgot about it, but obviously I was wrong. Could I learn how to use it?"

"We can work on that. We should include Zula, too," Max replied. "But right now, we have to get to the safe house in La Paz before Méndez figures out what's going on. Don't worry, Honey, we'll continue this conversation."

Not far away, still in the helicopter heading to Cabo San Lucas, Méndez called for an update from the men Sánchez sent to Agua Verdosa. Getting no answer, he suspected the worst—that Max had gone to that boat ramp and discovered and outwitted his men. He called Sánchez, who was on his way to Cabo San Lucas. "Go to Agua Verdosa. I'll meet you there."

Twenty-five minutes later, Méndez joined Sanchez and

his compadres at the Three Lizards cantina to plan their next move. At the boat ramp, they discovered fresh tire tracks and realized their quarry had escaped again. They found the cartel SUV behind the ridge, then after a quick search, the three hidden bodies. Méndez was confronted once more with Max and Lena's cunning and power, doubling his commitment to have it for his own use.

Infuriated, Méndez angrily instructed his men, "Question everyone in this stinking village. See if anyone saw a boat pulled by a truck or SUV leave the area within the last two hours."

They found an old man leading a burro loaded with firewood. He reported such a vehicle heading south on the dirt road, and that there were at least four or five people in it. Following this lead, forty-five minutes later they discovered the same vehicle had stopped at the gas station in El Pescadero on Route 19, then headed north toward La Paz. Méndez called his man in the Mexican Air Force and demanded helicopter surveillance of Routes 19 and 1. He provided a description of the target. Twenty minutes later, Méndez learned that a Chevy SUV pulling a speedboat on a trailer was approaching the junction of Route 19 with Route 1, about 15 miles south of La Paz.

"Stay with them," Méndez ordered the pilot. "I want to know where they go. Don't fail me. If you do, your wife, your four children, your girlfriend, your mother, and your dog will all die. Suffering more and longer than you could ever imagine."

The black helicopter dropped back far enough not to be noticed by anybody in the SUV he was following. Half an hour later, the anxious pilot gave Max's location in La Paz to Méndez, then returned to his official flight path.

Racing toward La Paz with Sánchez and the others, Méndez excitedly gave new orders. "Sánchez, get more men. Prepare to attack early tomorrow morning. This time they won't escape."

Meanwhile, in his office in Mexico City, León Cardosa was

formulating a plan to expand the Baja Cartel drug business to Asia. He was convinced it was a market ripe for exploitation. He was finishing an e-mail to a friend of his father's, General Dong of the Chinese People's Liberation Army. Dong oversaw community relations in the Guangdong province, and as such, was the Army's primary contact with the Dragon Fire Triad, the gang which controlled distribution of illicit drugs throughout southern China. The e-mail was an invitation to meet in Hawaii the following week to discuss a mutually rewarding opportunity. As an afterthought, Cardosa added, "We also have access to an amazing scientific discovery that enhances physical and mental power, something in which you or the PLA might have an interest."

A few seconds after hitting "*Send,*" Cardosa called Méndez to find out how his effort to capture Max was going.

The Tale of the Scorpion

Episode Five

Max and his entourage—Lena, Rana, José, and José's resourceful brother, Raúl—reached the La Paz city limits close to midnight. Alert in the passenger seat of Raúl's SUV, Lena noticed a helicopter following them, although it had dropped back to barely be in sight. When she told Max about the helicopter, he said, "I noticed it, too. Méndez must have conscripted it from the Mexican Air Force. He's probably following close behind. We'd better lead them to a false location instead of the safe house you arranged." Then he said to Raúl, "José said your uncle has a vacant house in La Paz. Can we lead them there? After the helicopter retreats, we could go to the safe house Lena found."

"Good idea. Uncle's Rubin's car is there, too," José said.

"Mom, you and Dad were the only ones that heard that helicopter. Does the superpower thing make you hear better?" Rana asked.

"It must," Lena responded. "I've noticed an improvement lately. How about you, Max?"

"Maybe . . . I'll check into it after we finish with Méndez."

A little later, the helicopter pilot observed the boat-towing SUV enter a walled hacienda compound on the outskirts of La Paz. He reported its location to Méndez, then turned back to Los Cabos.

"The chopper's gone. We'll leave the SUV and boat here in plain sight, then take Rubin's car to the safe house," Lena commanded, quickly assuming control. "Méndez should be arriving soon. We wouldn't want to be caught unprepared."

Twenty minutes later, in the safe house a few miles from the uncle's hacienda, Lena called everybody together and laid out her plan. "Méndez should reach Rubin's hacienda soon. He probably called for reinforcements from Ensenada after discovering the dead guys at the boat ramp. It'll take time for them to get here, maybe until early tomorrow morning. That gives us enough time to get ready. Raúl, your job tonight is to find street vendor's disguises for me and Rana, a fully stocked tamale cart, and a little wagon full of bottled water and sodas. Max, finish that special treat we're going to use to spice up the tamales and drinks."

"No problem, my little Edelweiss. As they say, better living through chemistry," Max replied, a sly grin revealing his anticipation of another fun-filled night of what for him was chemistry lab 101.

Meanwhile, as Lena detailed her plan to her little army, Don Arturo Méndez, in the back seat of a cartel van speeding toward La Paz, was barely able to contain his rage as he screamed into his phone at one of his cartel captains. "I want twenty men and big weapons here by six tomorrow morning. No later, or your next meal will be tortillas soaked in battery acid."

The La Paz morning finally dawned. A radiant sun climbed over Rubin's hacienda wall like a fiery torch piercing the dark blanket of night. Méndez's four men were spread around the locked metal gate blocking the entrance to the property where they waited for reinforcements from Ensenada to supplement their ranks before an attack. At 5:45, two pickup trucks and three SUVs arrived. Machine guns were mounted in the truck beds, and the SUVs were packed with heavily armed cartelistas.

As the new arrivals joined the others gathered at the gate to receive orders from Méndez, they heard distant cries of, "Tamales, hot tamales." Then, a younger sounding voice called out, "Refresco, agua. refresco, agua fría." As the shouts grew louder, two ragged vendors appeared around the north end of the hacienda wall, an old lady pushing a tamale cart and a younger one pulling a wagon filled with cold drinks.

"We better eat something while we have a chance," Sánchez yelled. "Señora! Señorita! Over here!"

Lena, disguised as the tamale peddler, and Rana, masquerading as her companion hawking the drinks, quickly distributed food and sodas to the hungry, thirsty men. After collecting pesos from Sánchez, Lena and Rana continued down the empty street, their smiles hidden by the shade of the cart's umbrella.

Twenty minutes later, a disheveled Méndez emerged from the van where he'd been trying to sleep. As the men finished the tamales and gulped the last of their drinks, Méndez took stock of his forces gathered around the gate waiting for his instructions. There were twenty-six men in all and included all the leaders of the cartel—Méndez's captains and lieutenants.

Sánchez, noting the wild look in Méndez's eyes and obvious agitation in his demeanor, drew him aside, out of hearing of the others. "Don Arturo, are you okay? You seem different this morning."

"Of course I'm okay, you fool. We're close to having fantastic power. Just do your job and capture Manus. If you don't, I'll personally peel you like an onion. I'll make a speech to inspire the men and then you can knock down this damn gate and attack."

It was then, as Méndez began to speak, that his world was turned upside down. Because at that very moment, vivid visions materialized from the dark depths of his men's clouded psyches to seize control of their minds. Detachment from their present reality severed all connections to whom and to where they were. They experienced visitations and conversations with long-dead friends and relatives, innocent victims, and unrecognizable beasts of every imaginable shape and size. They relived horrors of their pasts, had fleeting glimpses of the future, saw colors and heard sounds never seen or heard before. They were launched through barriers of time and space to what must have seemed like different worlds. Existence evaporated, then returned, then disappeared again. Nothing mattered other than the technicolor apparitions playing on the screens of their garbled minds.

At first, Mendez's loud, haranguing voice droning on the edges of their mental aberrations was barely audible. But as it continued to increase in volume and intensity, it became unbearable to the unhinged men sprawled in the dirt around the gate. Suddenly, one of the men yelled, "Shut up, you loud fool!"

Attacking whoever was on the other side of the gate was the last thing the incapacitated men wanted to do at that moment. And unwilling to tolerate Méndez's yelling at them any longer, Sánchez cleared his head enough to stand up and rally his men: "Who's this madman screaming at us?"

"The devil," someone yelled.

"Amigos! We have to destroy him!" Sánchez cried as he grabbed a machete from the nearest truck, then led the crazed men forward in a frenzied rush.

What little was left of Don Arturo was soon indistinguishable from the fetid debris floating in the gutter winding its way to the crystal-blue waters of the Gulf of California.

As soon as the stoned cartel men had ended their rampage, the Mexican Federal Police, summoned by Lena, arrived in force and took control. The still disoriented cartel soldiers offered no resistance and were easily stripped of their weapons and herded into police vans. The slaughter of Méndez and arrest of his drug-addled men resulted in the sudden and inglorious end of the formerly fierce Baja Cartel. Lena, shed of her disguise, directed the police action with confident forcefulness that not only intimidated the Mexican captain in charge, but compelled his unquestioning respect. Whatever her power was, it was effective, not only destroying the Cartel, but also enabling Max and Lena to return to their beloved hacienda where Max could get back to his scientific experiments and Lena to her pursuits.

Meanwhile, General Fu Chung, a high-ranking and thoroughly corrupt member of the army's controlling inner circle, was holding a private, unscheduled meeting in a dimly lit, sound-proof room deep in the bowels of the Peoples Liberation Army headquarters in Beijing. "So, General Dong," Chung said as the conference was ending, "if your claim, and the information our own research has uncovered, is true, we would be remiss not to accept Cardosa's offer to include us in acquiring Manus's superpowers. But, if for some reason the barbaric Baja Cartel fails to meet this objective, then naturally we will have to assume control."

"Of course, General. We will be prepared for such a possibility," General Dong replied. "I will meet Cardosa in Hawaii in a few days and arrange the next phase of this operation."

Tale of the Scorpion

Episode Six

Midmorning of the day on which Max and Lena had destroyed the Baja Cartel in La Paz, Captain Hernando López of the Federal Police burst into León Cardosa's Mexico City law firm office. "Don León, Don Arturo is dead. He was killed by his own men in La Paz early this morning. They went crazy and attacked him with machetes. But they say they don't remember doing it. They don't even remember their own names, or why they were there. Must have been some kind of mass hysteria. They've been arrested. What should we do?"

At first Cardosa was overwhelmed by this news. But after a few moments of reflection, he focused on what needed to be done. "Our biggest worry," he said, "is that the men will recover and tell the Federales about you and me."

"That won't be a problem. My cousin runs the La Paz jail and will make sure they don't talk. But what about our drug operations?" López asked, pacing frantically around the office.

After a moment, Cardosa said, "You and I have to take over. Our distribution networks will be okay; they're secure, but we'll have to concentrate on our supply. We need to keep the coke and heroin coming in from Guatemala, the crystal meth from our labs here in Mexico, and marijuana from California."

"But that's what the men arrested in La Paz were doing. Who's gonna do that now?" López asked, doubt reflected in his eyes. After a moment, he continued. "I hate to say this, but maybe we should join forces with the Sinaloa cartel. They'd be happy to get our distribution networks, and they could even supplement our supply needs."

"You may be right," Cardosa said thoughtfully. "But before we decide anything about that, I have another problem to take care of. I've offered to supply drugs to the Chinese. It's a big opportunity."

After López left, Cardosa reluctantly called Dong.

"General Dong? This is León Cardosa. I have bad news. We have to delay our meeting about the topic we discussed earlier. There's been—"

Interrupting Cardosa, Dong said, "Mr. Cardosa, we'll talk about product distribution another time. In view of your sudden organizational change, which our contacts have already told us about, that topic can wait until you work out a new business structure. However, we will proceed with the Manus superpower matter."

"But General Dong, it was Arturo Mendez who was going to steal Manus's superpower secret. I wasn't involved in that," Cardosa responded, a hint of panic in his voice.

Ignoring Cardosa's response, Dong continued, "You will arrange a meeting between Manus and me next week in Los Cabos. By the way, give my regards to your beautiful wife, Martha, and your two charming daughters, Maria and Lucia. It would be a shame if something were to happen to them," General Dong said menacingly, then abruptly ended the call.

After his conversation with Dong, Cardosa sat at his desk desperately trying to figure out what to do. "Oh my god, what have I gotten myself into?" he mumbled. "How can I arrange a meeting with Manus? I wouldn't even know how to approach him."

Meanwhile, back at Max and Lena's hacienda, Rana played the recordings of Cardosa's conversation with Captain López and his phone call to General Dong, both picked up by the microphone she'd planted in Cardosa's office. Even his mumbling was recorded.

"Well Papa, it seems that now the Chinese army wants your secret power," Rana said, unable to disguise the concern in her voice.

"We sure as hell can't take on the Chinese army. Not even with Lena's remarkable talents, and yours, as well," Max said. "We wouldn't stand a chance."

At this point, Lena laid her knitting aside and said, "Max, hold on a second. Let's consider our options. First, this General Dong, whoever he is, can't represent the entire Chinese army. That's not the way it works. He's probably just a crooked, loony-tune renegade. I know, I've dealt with these types before. I'll have him checked out by one of my CIA buddies. And this León Cardosa character. He's just the remnant of the Baja Cartel leadership. Obviously, he's in over his head and he'll be pushed aside quickly by this Chinese general—probably assassinated. So, it's easy. We deal with Dong. It's either that or go into deep hiding, something I refuse to do anymore."

"What are you suggesting, Mom?" Rana asked as she adjusted the settings on the recording equipment.

Lena responded at once. "Here's my suggestion. When Cardosa calls, play along with whatever he says. Let him set up a meeting in Cabo with the general. But we'll have our own version of a meeting with him and put a quick end to his fantasy of becoming a Chinese superman. Rana, can you stay a little longer to help out?"

"I'll stay as long as you want. Anyway, Papa promised to teach me about his power transformation, didn't you Papa?" Rana said, then continued without waiting for Max to answer. "Shouldn't we get Zula down here, too? She wouldn't want to miss a chance to become a superwoman. She can help with the Chinese, too. I doubt the general will show up alone."

Max got up and went to the record cabinet. "You're right, Lena. No matter how much we hate this constant struggle, we can't run away. They'd eventually find us. And Rana, I'll keep my promise. We'll work on your training. Come on, let's go down to the lab. We may as well begin now. And call Zula,"

Max said, as he carefully put a vintage Brahms LP onto the turntable to help Lena formulate her plan.

Cardosa called the next morning. "Hello," Max answered.

"Is this Max Manus?"

"Maybe. Who are you? I see from caller ID you're calling from Mexico City."

"My name is León Cardosa and I'm an attorney-at-law. I'm calling on behalf of a wealthy client interested in establishing a tropical medicine research institute here in Mexico. Your work on drugs to treat exotic diseases is of interest to him. He's anxious to meet you to discuss his plans. Would you be willing to talk with him?"

"Perhaps. This is an area in which I still have a strong interest," Max lied. "Who is this mystery man?"

"For security reasons he doesn't want his identity revealed at this point. He'll disclose everything about himself when you meet him."

When Max agreed, they arranged for Max and the unidentified Chinese philanthropist to meet the following week at the plush and very private Tropicana Deluxe Hotel, a resort on the coast north of Cabo San Lucas.

After talking with Max, Cardosa called General Dong to report his success in arranging the meeting.

"Well done, Mr. Cardosa," Dong said. "I'll organize a little surprise for Dr. Manus. I'm sure he'll enjoy a visit to our facilities here in Beijing."

Dong then called his superior, General Fu Chung. "General, I need a Black Dragon team in Mexico next week where I'll meet Manus. We'll capture him at the resort where I'm staying and bring him to Beijing." After Dong paused, listening to what Fu Chung was saying, he added, "Yes . . . of course this operation is top secret."

After ending the call, Dong called in an officer who'd been waiting in the anteroom.

"Our plan is moving forward, Colonel Fang. You'll lead a Black Dragon team and abduct Manus in Mexico six days from now. Work out the details. I want to see your plan tomorrow morning."

The big man was unable to hold back a barely detectable smile. "Sir. I will not fail." He saluted and waited to be dismissed.

"Of course you won't fail, Colonel. That's not an option," Dong replied, returning Fang's crisp salute.

Tale of the Scorpion

Episode Seven

Several days before the trip to Mexico, General Dong became concerned about the Black Dragon team's ability to capture Max. Chinese army spies, charged with learning about Manus, reported that Manus, aided by his wife, always managed to outwit and defeat those who'd attempted to capture him in the past. Worried about this possibility, he called Colonel Fang to his office. "Use a North Korean Army Stealth Team as backup for the Manus abduction. They're responsible for kidnappings in South Korea. Have them and our Black Dragons there before I arrive."

"Sir, we can do this without them. Manus is an old man," Fang protested, unable to hide his wounded pride.

"That may be true," Dong replied, "but intelligence reports suggest that he may be surprisingly resourceful. I can't risk failure. Nor, for that matter, can you."

"I understand, Sir. I'll arrange everything with Colonel Kim."

Meanwhile, in their remote hacienda on the other side of the Pacific Ocean, Max was conducting a training session with Rana and Zula. They absorbed the technique quickly, both being not only skilled in martial arts, but also because Max had honed the instructional process to its most basic elements. It was effective and highly efficient.

When finished, Max told the two of them with fatherly pride, "You've done well. We're ready to confront the Chinese general and his special forces. This morning Lena learned that he's bringing Black Dragon commandos. She doesn't know how many, so we'll have to prepare for the worst."

"We're ready, Papa," Zula said, determined to do whatever was required to protect her adoptive parents.

"And to use this superpower you've discovered," Rana added.

The Cabo San Lucas Tropicana Deluxe Hotel is not a typical tourist destination. It's not listed with travel agents and doesn't have a website. The isolated property is unseen from the highway, surrounded by an eight-foot-high wall, and is heavily guarded. It is frequented by guests who can afford total privacy and absolute security in a setting of extravagant luxury; the rich and famous, high-level business types, crooks and politicians. Sixty lavish villas are scattered throughout lush, magnificently landscaped parkland. This is where General Dong found himself a little before noon on Monday, a day before the day he would have dinner with Max and Lena. Dong had just been delivered to the resort by a silent driver who met him at the airport, and he was now being escorted to his quarters by a strikingly beautiful hostess.

"I need to contact Colonel Fang at once," Dong told the young woman.

"He is in a large villa with dormitory sleeping quarters. Dial 013 for a direct connection. He and the soccer team are in a single facility; they arrived two days ago."

Dong called Fang as soon as the woman showed him around the villa then left, promising to return later.

"Fang, come to my place in two hours. I want an update."

Fang reported exactly two hours later. "Six Black Dragons and six North Korean Stealth Team soldiers are here, more than enough to handle a single old man and a woman. What's your plan for the meeting tomorrow evening, Sir?"

Dong, displaying an officious attitude of higher rank, said nothing until he finished stirring the martini he'd started before Fang arrived. After placing two glasses into the under-counter refrigerator, he said, "We'll have dinner at the seaside restaurant at eight. Afterwards, I'll invite him and the woman, if he brings her, to my villa to finish our discussion. Your team will grab him on our way here. If the woman is with him, kill her and dispose of the body. Keep him in your villa overnight. The next morning, sedate and secure him in the coffin you brought. We'll leave at 8 a.m. for my Air Force jet parked at the Los Cabos airport. Then, back to Beijing."

"Yes, Sir," Fang responded, anxious to return to his men now that a plan was in place.

General Dong then said, "There can be no problems, Fang. Make sure your men know that. Dismissed."

As soon as Colonel Fang left, Dong poured the martini into chilled glasses and returned to the plush bedroom where the amiable hostess awaited his return.

The next morning at the Manus hacienda, after a breakfast created by Rana—sweet lassi, chapatis, and spicy Kerala-style deviled eggs drenched in squid and okra sauce, Lena addressed the family gathered on the deck overlooking the calm cove below. José, their loyal friend and trusted hacienda manager, was also present, accompanied by his two Rottweiler-Giant Chihuahua crossbreeds, Jupiter and Zeus.

Lena detailed the plan for that evening. "While Max and I are with Dong at the restaurant, the rest of you will station yourselves around the property. According to what we've learned from the microphones Rana planted in Cardosa's office, Dong intends to kill me, capture Max, and take him to China where Dong will extract information about superpower transformation. He's smuggled in a team of commandos to do the dirty work, at least six Black Dragons. They're equivalent to our Navy Seals and are commanded by a Colonel Fang, a giant of a man known for his combat skills and blind obedience to orders."

Lena continued. "I've prepared our own plan to counteract Dong's. Since it's unlikely they'll attack in the restaurant, it will probably be after we finish the meal and leave the building. I suspect Dong will invite us to his private villa for further talk. I'll keep each of you informed through your ear buds." She held up an exquisite turquoise pendant for them to see. "This has one of Rana's audio transmitters in it. It'll pick up every word of our dinner conversation. Rana and Zula, and I, should be able to take out the six commandos: two each. José, now that Max has trained Jupiter and Zeus for superpower transformation at your command, be ready to use them if they're needed. Stay close to Max. Max, you'll have to disable Dong and Fang. Can you do that?"

Max looked around the table, then returned his focus to Lena. "Yes, Lena. I think I can do that. I say that confidently because I have something important to tell you. As amazing as it sounds, it appears that the power we're able to generate actually increases with each activation. It's the same for sensory perception and speed of movement. Not in huge increments, but noticeably. I have no doubt that this incremental increase in power will occur with each of you as well. It appears to work like a straight-forward neural network reinforcement process."

The stunned group was speechless, as if having difficulty understanding what Max was telling them.

After a few moments, in a low voice, Zula said, "Papa, are you saying that we'll become even stronger each time the transformation is triggered?"

"Yes, Zula, that seems to be the case. At some point, we'll probably reach maximum empowerment, although that doesn't seem to have occurred for me, at least not yet. This discovery is truly an unprecedented advance in human biology. Its potential for good is unlimited. But, so too is its potential for evil. For this reason, we must do everything in our power to keep the process secret. It's up to our family to protect this discovery with our lives if necessary. That includes you, too, José. But, just as important, it's also our responsibility to use this gift for good. It's an awesome responsibility."

Zula was the first to respond, sure she would be speaking for the others as well. "We understand, Papa. I think I speak for all of us when I say we accept this responsibility." She glanced around to make sure she hadn't misspoken. There were no objections—the others nodded in agreement.

Suddenly, Rana interjected, "But Papa, you have one more to train. José and I are getting married. Our family army will expand by one. Or three, if you count the dogs," she added, a radiant smile accentuating her radiant South Indian beauty.

Rana's announcement caught Max and Lena by surprise, and they were ecstatic at the news. They had great affection and respect for José, and they knew Rana would only choose a man of sterling qualities as a mate.

Zula, on the other hand, with the observational skills of her ancient African tribal heritage, was not surprised, and was thrilled for her beloved adoptive sister. "I knew something was going on with you two," she said, nodding her regal, closely-cropped head.

After congratulations and a champagne toast, Lena returned to her plan to confront Dong and the Chinese army commandos that evening. She took them through every detail one more time, as if it were just another of her many CIA operations.

Meanwhile, at the Tropicana Deluxe Hotel, Colonel Fang led his Black Dragon team around the hotel grounds for the third time that morning, checking ambush sites between the restaurant and Dong's villa. Later that afternoon, when he reported to General Dong, Fang confidently claimed the abduction would proceed as planned. He reassured Dong that when Manus and the old woman arrived that evening, he and his men would be ready. They would accomplish the objective and return to Beijing triumphant.

After Fang left, Dong poured his third martini and gleefully fantasized how he would use Max's magical power.

Tale of the Scorpion

Episode Eight

Max and Lena arrived at the heavily guarded security gate of the Tropicana Deluxe Hotel in their old Toyota sedan at 7:55 p.m. The hotel security team consulted a list and directed them to the Green Dolphin restaurant where General Dong awaited their arrival. On the drive along the resort's path to the restaurant, Lena spoke into a tiny microphone built into the turquoise pendant hanging around her neck: "Rana, where are you?"

While Lena was talking with Rana, the security guard assigned to monitor the twenty-four resort surveillance cameras noticed one of the screens was blank. After he fiddled with the controls and reset the program with no results, he yelled to his supervisor, "Camera four's out."

"Did you reset the program?" the supervisor asked.

"Yeah, but it didn't come back on."

"I'll let maintenance know."

As the security supervisor prepared a work order, Rana responded to Lena. "We're at the north wall, out of sight of the front gate. I deactivated the hotel security camera for this area before we slipped across the perimeter. I'll reactivate it after we get onto the hotel grounds and find a hiding spot." Then Rana turned to the others. "All right, we have to be quick and hope the surveillance guy doesn't notice the camera blackout right away. Zula, you're first."

Zula took a position six feet from the wall and stood with her eyes closed and a look of intense concentration on her face. Then she bent her knees and sprang gracefully upward, clearing the eight-foot-high, cinder block wall in one seemingly effortless motion. She landed softly on the hotel's lush grass near a clump of azalea bushes that was right where the satellite image showed it should be. She quickly crawled underneath their intertwining branches and pinged Rana.

"I'm in the bushes and well-hidden. The coast is clear."

Next, at José's command, his two dogs, both given modified versions of Max's training, cleared the wall and joined Zula. But when José tried, he failed, unable to make it any higher than six feet.

Rana went to his side. "Try again. Concentrate. Give it all you've got."

Again, José jumped with all the strength he could muster, but fell short of the top by a couple inches.

"We're running out of time," Rana said anxiously. We'll do it together." Rana grabbed him around the waist; "Concentrate, like Max taught you. One, two, three!" Linked together in a clean jump, they cleared the wall by half an inch and joined Zula and the dogs.

Rana reactivated the security camera, then sent a single blip to Lena informing her of their success.

Back at the security post, the guard monitoring the security cameras yelled, "Camera four's back on. Seems okay now."

"Must have been a fluke. Those things can be temperamental. Let me know if it happens again," the supervisor said, then tossed the work order into the trash bin.

Meanwhile, after an attendant parked their car, Max and Lena entered the resort's elegant restaurant precisely at eight o'clock. The hostess greeted them warmly and led them towards Dong's table.

Although there were several Asian guests scattered around the room, it wasn't hard to pick out General Dong. He was sitting alone at a table by a huge floor-to-ceiling window overlooking the grounds and a well-lit beach with the dark Pacific beyond. He fitted the role of a wealthy philanthropist perfectly. A handsome 50-year old, his attire screamed money: dark gray Brioni silk suit, crisp, white Egyptian cotton shirt,

Charvet tie, Barker-Black, ostrich, cap-toe English shoes. Putting down his martini, he stood as they approached. "Dr. Manus, I presume. And Mrs. Manus. A pleasure to meet you both. I am Chow Lee. Thank you for meeting with me. I hope you'll find my humble proposition appealing."

So began Dong's monolog designed to convince Max and Lena the Chinese billionaire he pretended to be harbored a deep concern for the impoverished, malaria-stricken natives of lower Mexico and Central America. That he wanted to establish a state-of-the-art medical research institute headed by none other than Max Manus himself. Max and Lena listened with appropriately feigned interest, all the while thoroughly enjoying fresh-caught rock fish, grilled vegetables seasoned to perfection, and an exceptionally crisp Chenin Blanc. They capped the meal with a delicate prickly pear sorbet. It was then that Lena, who'd been quiet during most of the conversation, letting Dong do the talking and Max the responding, informed the two men she was going to freshen up.

In the privacy of the garishly-opulent powder room, Lena buzzed Rana: "We'll be finished soon. What have you found out?"

"So far, we've spotted five suspicious men stationed at various points along the path to Dong's chalet. There are two more outside the restaurant entrance. What do you want us to do?" Rana replied.

"Nothing yet," Lena answered. "Wait till we know what his next move is. Be prepared for anything."

When Lena returned to the table, Dong stood and excused himself, also, as he put it, to freshen up. But instead, he hastened to the front door and motioned to Colonel Fang, who was waiting near the door with one of his men. "We're done. But there are too many guests milling around the grounds to risk an attack now. I'll take Manus and the woman to my chalet for a while. When the coast is clear, text me and I'll send them on their way. Make your move when they leave my villa."

"Yes, Sir. It will be done."

Dong then asked, "Where are the North Koreans? I don't think we'll need them but keep them informed in case we do."

"They're in a grounds keeper's shed near your villa. I can summon them at once if we require backup," Fang responded.

Returning to the table, Dong found Max and Lena preparing to leave. "Dr. Manus, we still have details to discuss. Won't you and Mrs. Manus join me in my chalet for a nightcap?"

"Well, it's late, but I suppose we should decide how to get this project started," Max replied, glancing at Lena.

Meanwhile, Rana, Zula, and José were positioned along the walkways between the restaurant and Dong's chalet. They kept out of sight of the Asian men hiding in the shadows but who their enhanced vision allowed them to see. The two dogs stayed close to José, although they paid an unusual amount of attention to a gardener's shed near Dong's chalet. José, never one to question the intelligence of his dogs, wondered what was so interesting about that particular shed.

"Zeus, check it out," José commanded. Jupiter remained heeled at José's side as Zeus quietly trotted to the closed shed door where he stood for a moment, then returned to José. He took his usual position at José's right side, then made a single low growl, pointed his nose toward the shed and moved his head up and down twice. José understood at once. "Rana," he whispered into the miniature microphone pinned to his shirt, "there's something suspicious about that garden shed over there. I'll take a look."

But as José started toward the shed, their ear-buds delivered a message from Lena. "We're going to General Dong's for more talk. An attack will probably be later due to resort guests still walking around the grounds. Stay alert."

Looking back toward the restaurant, José saw the three figures heading toward Dong's chalet and realized that they would have a clear view of his approach to the shed. With the two dogs, he slipped behind a bush in time to avoid being seen. At that same moment, he heard Rana's voice in his ear.

"José, leave the shed for later, you'd easily be seen if you approach it again. You and Zula take your positions and be ready for an attack on Max and Lena after they leave Dong's chalet later."

Once inside Dong's chalet, their discussion continued, with Dong promising this and that, and Max pretending to be receptive to the general's proposal. But while this charade was progressing inside, outside Fang was doing his utmost to ensure the mission's success. As he followed General Dong and his guests back to the chalet, he noticed a dog approach the gardener's shed, then quickly retreat. Being of a suspicious nature, he immediately called Lieutenant Kim, the leader of the North Korean Shadow Team sequestered inside the shed. "Leave the shed through the rear door and post your men near the chalet. It's possible you've been discovered. Prepare them for action but keep them out of sight. Manus and the woman don't know about you. Keep it that way."

"Don't worry, Fang. We know what to do and how to do it. You do your job and we'll do ours," Kim whispered into his phone.

After almost an hour of Dong and Max's pretenses, Dong glanced at his phone then suddenly called the meeting to an end. He promised he'd let them know his decision about funding the next day. He expressed deep-felt gratitude for their interest in his proposition and bid Max and Lena good night as he ushered them out of his front door. Their exit was closely observed by Zula, Rana, José and the two dogs, by Dong's loyal Colonel Fang, all six of his Chinese army commandos, and by the six North Koreans.

As she stepped across Dong's threshold and into the warm Mexican night, Lena made a quick scan of the surroundings, taking in every detail. She saw that Max also made a visual sweep of the area. She met his knowing glance with the barest hint of a smile as they started along the meandering walkway back to the restaurant and their car, not bothering to look back at Dong tightly gripping a fresh martini in his fist as he swung the heavy front door of his villa shut.

Tale of the Scorpion

Episode Nine

Max and Lena felt their bodies change and mental acuity increase as soon as they left Dong's chalet and started along the winding walkway to confront their enemy, retrieve their car, and return to their hacienda. They understood the changes were occurring automatically in response to danger they knew lurked in the deep shadows. They were calm and confident, but also anxious to get this over.

"Max," Lena whispered after they rounded a bend in the path, "did you see two men creep behind those fan palms twenty yards ahead?"

"Yes. I also heard the two behind us. How do you want to handle this?"

Before Lena could answer, they glimpsed two sets of gleaming, white fangs flashing against the dark sky, soundlessly hurtling toward the palms. A muffled impact followed. Startled cries were stifled immediately, followed by sound of flesh being ripped apart. Low growls and the soft crackle of shattering bones were clear signs that whoever they were, they were no longer a threat. While Max and Lena were momentarily distracted by the dogs, two men behind them suddenly rushed forward to attack. Running at full speed, the big one in the lead viciously swung a thick steel bludgeon toward Lena's neck. The man a step behind him thrust a hypodermic syringe toward Max's back. Lena's enhanced reflexes allowed her to turn aside as the bludgeon swept downward, grazing her shoulder enough to cause her to grunt in pain. As the bludgeon-wielding man's momentum carried him past her, she spun around and struck her iron-hard fist into the other man's forearm, knocking the syringe free. Without breaking stride, she delivered a lethal blow to the man's throat with her other hand, then for good measure kicked him in the face as he dropped to the ground. The man wielding the bludgeon was still off balance from missing Lena when Max grabbed him by his right arm and flung him over a bed of Canna lilies bordering the walk. The air-borne commando landed face-down on a huge agave plant. Needle-like tips of the thick stems impaled his masked face while others punctured his chest, abdomen and thighs, trapping him in their deadly clutch as his desperate flailing drove the tips deeper and deeper into his writhing body. His sort-lived screams should have served as a warning to his comrades, as if to shout: "Beware! These are fierce opponents."

From his hiding place further along the path, Fang witnessed the slaughter of the two Black Dragons. He'd also heard the short-lived cries of his two men behind the palm trees. He finally grasped the immense power and skill he and his men were up against. In a state of near panic, he called Colonel Kim, the leader of the North Korean Dark Shadow team.

"Colonel, we've had four casualties. You need to take action. But be careful. This old couple is more capable than we realized. They have dogs, as well."

"Don't worry, Fang. We'll rescue your mission for you. Perhaps now you realize you should have let us lead this operation. We're good at this. We North Koreans do have an advantage over you Chinese since we are a genetically superior race," the smirking North Korean answered into his cell phone as he waved the five black-clad, masked commandos closer to him. After ending the call and giving his men a few brief instructions, they deployed: three teams of two determined killers each silently blending into the dark shadows.

Rana watched Fang from where she was concealed but wasn't able to hear what he said on his phone. Then she saw several men emerge from bushes close to Dong's villa. "Zula," she whispered into her mic. "It looks like there's a team we didn't know about. Fang has called more men into play. There're at least six of them. They're dressed in black and are spreading out from where I am, near Dong's place. They're heading toward Mom and Dad. Keep the dogs with you and stay on the look-out. Right now, José and I are going to take out Fang and the soldier with him. They're coming this way. We'll catch up with you as soon as we can."

While Rana watched this new development unfold, she called Lena to warn her about the additional forces. "Mom, six new commandos are on their way toward you and Dad. Zula and the dogs should be somewhere nearby and will help hold them off until José and I get there. First, we'll take care of Fang and his buddy."

As Max and Lena continued toward the restaurant where the Toyota was parked, Lena said, "I'm ready to end this ridiculous game. Let's finish off the rest of these jerks, go back to Dong's chalet, and do whatever we need to do to protect your secret, then go home. I miss Portland."

"Me too. Especially the rain," Max said, scanning the surrounding lush landscape.

As they walked quietly along the walkway, Lena and Max were alert for signs of the additional men Rana warned them about but noticed nothing suspicious.

Meanwhile, nor too far behind Max and Lena, Rana and José were determined to quickly eliminate Fang and his companion so they could join Zula in time to help her defend against the newly deployed forces. "I'll take Fang, you take the other one," Rana said, as they quietly made their way through deep shadows in search of their targets. "There they are," she whispered, pointing ahead at the two men following in the wake of the North Koreans. Before Fang and the soldier had advanced only a few more paces, Rana and José attacked. They used no weapons, just surprise, speed, absolute silence, and deadly force. Rana hit Fang first, a powerful flying kick into the middle of his back. The power of her blow was like a wrecking ball smashing through a crumbling brick wall. His spine cracked into three pieces. As she flew over his contorted body, she finished him off by jamming her right foot into the back of his neck. Close behind, José, having learned from his failed jump at the resort wall to marshal his power more effectively, leaped over Fang's crumpled body and landed in front of the other man. He spun around and rammed his fist into the man's sternum with such force that he was momentarily blinded by blood erupting from the man's gaping mouth. Quickly wiping away the splatter and shifting to finish the job, José saw the man collapse onto Fang's body. He was already dead.

"Good work, José. Now we've gotta find Zula. Let's go," Rana said, as she and José raced off in the direction the North Koreans had taken.

"Do you hear soft footfalls on grass off to the southeast, slightly behind us?" Lena asked in a hushed whisper as she and Max continued toward the restaurant.

"Yes," Max replied. "Sounds like there may be several of them. They're coming this way."

Rana's voice came in over Lena's microphone again: "Mom, José and I took out Fang and the other man. We're on our way. We'll catch up with these new guys in less than a minute. Be prepared for an attack. Zula and the dogs should be near you someplace."

Because of the attention gunshots would attract, the Chinese Black Dragons and the North Korean Dark Shadow commandos were armed only with knives, clubs, and other martial arts weapons, all intended for silent killing. Colonel Kim was the first to spot Max and Lena about fifty yards ahead of them. He hand-signaled his men to spread out. They would attack from three directions, left, right, and behind. The six men merged into the dark night quickly and quietly, but not quietly enough to evade Max and Lena's enhanced hearing.

"They've changed position," Max said. "I think I also hear the dogs panting." After a brief pause, he continued, "Isn't that Zula behind that bush over there?"

Lena nodded in agreement, then whispered, "You're right on both counts. Let's hope Rana and José get here before this new group decides to pounce. I have a feeling it will be coming very—"

Before Lena finished her thought, they heard two men racing toward them from their left. Their slow-motion sense enabled them to anticipate the attackers' tactics and they turned to face the assailants' rush toward them head-on. But the two North Koreans suddenly changed their pace in mid-run, slowing enough to hurl chain-linked steel balls at Max and Lena's' legs in order to entangle them. But it didn't work. Max and Lena jumped up as the chains flew under their feet. Only ten feet away, the two Koreans resumed their high-speed advance. The one slightly ahead dove forward to tackle Max around the waist and drive him to the ground. But as he came close, Max thrust his knee upwards and caught the attacker under his chin. The attacker's head snapped back with a loud crack and he was catapulted into a bed of red tulips.

Lena turned toward the one rushing at her and shifted to the left. The attacker, unable to stop, swept by close enough for her to spin around and slam her elbow into his back, hurling him forward out of control. He stumbled and fell face-down onto the gravel path. Before he could get up, she kicked him between his sprawled legs, then stomped her foot on the back of his neck, breaking it and killing him instantly.

Ignoring the downed attacker, Lena turned to check on Max and saw Zula standing at his side as they faced two more attackers rushing toward them, one wielding a spiked club, the other swinging a heavy chain attached to a metal rod. When the assailants were almost on them, Max and Zula jumped apart. Unable to halt their momentum, the two nearly airborne men flew past them. Max and Zula were untouched by the swipe of the club or the arc of the chain. Unfortunately for the outmaneuvered attackers, Jupiter and Zeus arrived just then, perfectly positioned to greet the two attackers when they ended up directly in front of the two dogs. Neither dog had to move in order to leap forward and sink their fangs into the throats of the hopelessly doomed men.

Colonel Kim and Sergeant Lee, the two remaining Dark Shadow commandos, witnessed the devastating defeat of their companions from the safety of a clump of bushes twenty yards away. Realizing how futile it would be for them to attack on their own, they turned around and headed toward Dong's chalet. They had to inform him of the night's events and get him away from the resort. Suddenly Kim saw two forms approaching. "Somebody's coming this way. It may be more of the enemy. Here, hide behind this fountain," he whispered.

As they passed by in a rush, Rana and José didn't notice the two men secreted behind the low wall of the gurgling fountain. The noise of the water gushing from a nymph's mouth covered the sound of their breathing. "They can't be too far ahead," Rana whispered, as they continued toward where they thought Max and Lena must be.

A little further on, José grabbed Rana's arm. "There's Zula. She's coming this way."

"Zula," Rana whispered when she spotted her nearby. "What's happening?"

"I was coming to find you. Mom and Dad are okay. They're headed to the car. You should have seen them. They totally destroyed those masked guys. This power thing is amazing. They took out four of them. But according to what you said earlier, there should be six. There's gotta be two more someplace, but the dogs and I couldn't find them. Maybe they went back to Dong's chalet to tell him what's happened."

"That makes sense," Rana said. "Let's check it out." The three of them started towards Dong's chalet.

"Who's there?" Dong asked cautiously when he heard three raps on the front door.

"It's me, Sargent Wu," said the Black Dragon commando who was outside guarding the door. "Two of the North Koreans are here to see you."

Dong opened the door a crack, saw who it was and motioned them in. The Chinese Black Dragon guard remained outside.

Kim spoke immediately, a frantic edge to his voice. "Sir, all the others have been killed by the old man and his comrades. They have unbelievable power. There's no chance of capturing him. We have to get you to safety in case they come back here. What are your orders?"

After three martinis, Dong was slow on the uptake. "Are you saying Colonel Fang, five of his men, and four of yours, are dead?"

"Yes, General. Those two old people are ferocious fighters, like nothing I've seen before. We should leave now! We'll escort you to your car and then to the plane."

Outside on the porch, the Black Dragon guard didn't hear Zula when she came up behind him before she cut his throat, holding one hand tight across his mouth. At the same moment, Dong was inside grabbing documents off the desk when the thick front door shattered, fragments of oak and iron exploding into the room. Rana and José rushed in and quickly dispatched the two surprised North Koreans. Dong reacted faster than expected in view of his blood alcohol level. He deftly snatched a pistol from the desk. But as fast as his movement was, it was far too slow to match the lightning speed of Jupiter and Zeus, who'd entered the chalet with Rana and José. Zeus tore Dong's gun-arm off at the elbow while Jupiter ripped his throat open. Gurgling and gasping, Dong collapsed into a rapidly expanding pool of blood spreading over the tile floor. Jupiter's big front paws were perched on Dong's now-not-so-crisp Egyptian cotton shirt, his eyes fixed on the General's to make sure there was no life left in them.

Rana picked up the desk phone with her gloved hand and rang the house-keeping department. "Could you please send a maid to Chalet fourteen. It's a bit of a mess. You may want to send a carpenter as well. Thank you and have a good evening."

Back at the Manus hacienda the following evening, Max and his jubilant family were gathered around the table on their patio, again overlooking the peaceful Pacific and enjoying a dazzling sunset. They were delighted not only with the outcome of Dong's failed kidnapping attempt, but also with the successful application of their remarkable superpower transformation ability. Zula poured a second round of tequila as they gazed into the fading light.

During a lapse in the conversation, in a soft, yet somber voice, Lena said, "This fight with the Chinese General and other attacks and attempted abductions we've had to deal with over the years may be harbingers of what we have to face for the rest of our lives. Is this the way we want to live? Constant battle? Unending good-versus-evil confrontations?" She looked at each of them, wanting to know how they felt about her question.

Max was the first to respond. "Would you prefer to retire to a life of knitting and pruning your roses?"

Lena took a sip of her tequila, then said, "Maybe. I'm not sure. I realize your superpower discovery is a precious gift. That it must be protected and not allowed to fall into the wrong hands. But I'm tired of fighting and killing. Of intrigue and skullduggery. And, as far as roses go, the hybrids I'm developing do need my attention. I miss working with them. So, yes, maybe I am saying that."

Zula, Rana, and José listened to Lena's musing attentively, but said nothing. All three realized that this was an important moment in their family's life. That the ramifications of Lena's musings would eventually have to be addressed. They each understood, without having to state it, that whatever path Max and Lena chose, each of them would stand alongside them and would do whatever was required to carry out their commands. They were family. And family stood together.

Finally, Max responded to Lena's anxieties. "I understand your concerns, Liebchen. I too have doubts about the kind of future we face. But I don't have an answer for you. Maybe we can devise an alternative that would allow us to lead normal lives and still protect the secret. But for now, how about some Mozart to lighten the mood a little? Zula, pass the tequila. I'd like another."

The End

Meanwhile, as Max and his family enjoyed the mild Mexican

climate and generous gift of the agave plant, 3000 miles away, in a drab office on the 16th floor of a nondescript building a mile from the White House, a young summer intern at a under-the-radar CIA contract firm, Smith and Blacker Security, timidly knocked on Basilos Blacker's closed office door.

"Come in," Blacker said, irritated at being disturbed, but assuming it must be important since it was known that when his door was closed it meant Do Not Disturb. "What is it?"

"Sir, Mr. Coffin asked me to give this to you right away. It's a decoded message picked up by Mexican security. It's from a Chinese colonel to someone in the North Korean army describing plans for smuggling a team of commandos into Mexico. It's a few weeks old, but we just got it today. Mr. Coffin said that since it mentions someone named Max Manus you would want to know about it."

Blacker's head jerked up when she said the name. "Let me see it. Ah . . . what's your name?"

"Alice Jameson, Sir. I'm a summer intern," she answered, placing a folded printout on the edge of his desk.

Blacker looked at her for a moment, picked up the message and glanced at it, then said, "Mention this to no one. Understand? Close the door when you leave."

"Yes, Sir," she responded, retreating quickly.

As soon as the door clicked shut, Blacker unlocked the bottom desk drawer and took out a cell phone. His call was answered on the first ring.

"Sir, you'll never guess whose name just came across my desk," he said, his thin lips forming a sinister smile. "Yes, Sir, that's the one."

Blacker listened for a moment, then said, "Only Coffin and an intern. Don't worry. Coffin's okay. I'll have the intern taken care of."

Blacker put the phone back in the drawer, then buzzed the woman sitting at a desk outside his office door. "Get hold of Bentz. Tell him I want to see him. Now."

Hijinks Under Ground

Episode One

Washington, D.C.; Wednesday, 9:45 a.m.

"It's about time," Basilos Blacker mumbled when his trusted gate-keeper, Margo Katz, buzzed him forty minutes after he'd phoned Bentz.

"There's a man to see you. He won't tell me his name," she said over the intercom.

"Is he a big guy? Bald?"

"Yes, sir," she said, glancing at a wall-mounted monitor.

"Let him in."

Responding to a tap on his office door a few seconds later, Blacker pressed the unlock button and yelled, "Enter!" No one got into Blacker's office without his permission. That was a standing rule, and Blacker's rules were never broken.

"Sit down. I've got a job for you," Blacker said, ignoring formalities of social intercourse.

"I figured that much," Bentz replied.

"You ever hear the name Max Manus?"

"Not that I recall. Who is he?"

"How about *Lena* Manus? Or Lena *Hock*? That was the name she used before marrying Manus."

"No. Doesn't ring a bell. . . . Is this Twenty Questions, or are you gonna tell me what you want?"

"We need to bring in Manus. Our friend up top wants him."

"Who *is* this Manus guy? *Where* is he?"

"Some kind of scientist. Must have done something the government doesn't want known. Or maybe he knows secrets he shouldn't. I don't know what the deal is, and I don't care. But his name's flagged, and I got a call. We—you—gotta find and grab him. He's old, so it shouldn't be a problem. Simple abduction. Get rid of the wife if you need to. There's a guy at CIA trying to find out where they are. I'll be in touch as soon as I find out."

When Bentz rose to leave, Blacker said, "Leave by the tunnel to the garage."

"Yeah, I know. That's the way I came in. Don't worry, nobody saw me."

"Good. Keep it that way."

Hacienda Manus, Baja, Mexico; Wednesday, 8:15 a.m.

Lena was startled when her secure phone rang. She dreaded calls on that line since it usually meant trouble. "Yes?"

Lena recognized the voice. "Thought you should know, someone's looking for your and Max's files and anything connected to your names. Can't tell who it is, but they know their way around the system. Looks like they're trying to find where you are. I'll keep you posted."

Lena put the phone back in its drawer, relocked it, and went out to the patio where Max sat writing in a notebook. "Max. It may be nothing, but a CIA friend just gave me a heads-up. Somebody's searching a secure database trying to find out where we live."

"Damn. Won't the bastards ever leave us alone?"

Lena took the chair next to his. "I was hoping we could go back to Portland next week and to our regular life. Now I'm not so sure."

Max closed his notebook and placed it on the table next to his chair. "Nobody knows about this hacienda, but the Portland house will be easy to find if whoever it is digs deep enough." He stood abruptly and began pacing around the patio. "I don't like this. I just want to be left alone to work on the superpower transformation problem. It's a major discovery, and I need time in my Portland lab to learn more about how it works. How to control it better. I'm fed up with this cloak and dagger stuff getting in the way—someone always trying to steal my secrets. "Lena. Can't you do something?"

After a moment of silence, Lena stood and stepped over to where Max was gazing out at the calm Pacific. "Let's stay in Baja a little longer. I'll see what I can find out. We'll go back to Portland as soon as it's safe." When Max turned to face her, Lena smiled and said, "I'll handle it, Maxie. Now get back to your formulas and equations."

"I know, Liebchen. You always do," Max said, returning her smile.

She started back inside, then stopped and turned back to Max. "There *is* one person who knows about this place. That lawyer in Mexico City, Arturo Mendez's cousin, Leon Cardosa. The bug Rana planted in his office should be still working. I'll turn on the recording system in case whoever's looking for us contacts him."

Lena went inside and retrieved her secure phone to contact her colleague, Arnie Axman, leader of Lena's unconventional 'under the radar' band of loyal foot soldiers based in Portland. With a click instead of a ring, she connected with an 888-number at a phony message center in Panama. "Call," she said, then punched off. While she waited for Arnie to call, she poured another cup of coffee, opened her laptop and entered her password.

Washington, D.C.; Wednesday, 6:25 p.m.

Still in his office, Blacker called Bentz. "I got word on where they live. Get over here."

Hacienda Manus, Baja, Mexico; Wednesday, 6:50 p.m.

Axman called Lena, following their SOP for off-the-grid phone contact.

Lena didn't waste words. "Set up surveillance on our Portland house. Cover the machine shop, as well, in case whomever it is locates our hideaway. I want video and photos of anyone checking out either of them—hanging around, knocking at the door, looking in windows or breaking in; anything! Do it tonight."

"What's going on? Why the rush?"

"Someone's snooping around. I wanna know who."

"Okay. If anybody shows up at either place, we'll have pictures to work with. Then I can hack the NSA and FBI photo ID data bases and find out who it is. If they're in there, that is," Axman said.

"I'm trying to get a line on where the hack of the CIA files originated. Between these two approaches we might get a hit. Stay in touch," Lena added, then hung up, keeping the call as short as possible.

Portland; Thursday, 8:20 a.m.

An unmarked private jet landed at a small airport outside Portland and taxied through the open entrance of an inconspicuous hanger at the far end of the runway. Two men carrying tote bags climbed down from the passenger door and went directly to an unoccupied, white SUV parked close by. The pilot remained in his cockpit. There was no one else in sight.

The man who got into the passenger seat of the SUV took out his phone and typed a short message. "We're here," he sent. To the other man, who was behind the wheel, he said, "Directions to the house are on the GPS. Let's go."

West Virginia; Thursday, 8:58 a.m.

Dr. Gerhart Schlossman sat tapping his fingers impatiently on a polished black walnut conference table, frequently glancing at a clock on the wall.

The conference room was in an underground labyrinth of ultra-high-tech laboratories and well-appointed living spaces a hundred feet below the surface of a bleak, deforested landscape. It was a secret research complex carved out of an abandoned, sealed-over coal mine. The idea for this dazzling facility was conceived by a shadowy three-star army general in charge of a little-known, futuristic high-tech weapons program. Its creation and support were surreptitiously financed through an off-the-books slush fund controlled by the general. The project it supported was even more audacious than the facility itself.

The undisclosed research complex employed seventeen people who, for promised financial enrichment, committed two-year stints to what they'd been told was a highly classified, top-secret research project applying artificial intelligence to human physiology. The group consisted of Schlossman (the project's director), four senior scientists (biologists and computer engineers), two junior scientists (robotics engineers), eight lab assistants, and two support personnel (maintenance specialist and chef). The research was supposed to be cutting-edge, and the amenities were far more than adequate, except in one way—living in this underground facility was like being in prison. The staff couldn't leave for any reason short of death and could have no contact with the outside world.

Precisely at nine, a melodious gong sounded throughout the labyrinth. Two minutes later, six individuals in white lab coats were sitting around a table, anxious to learn why Schlossman called an unscheduled meeting.

"Good morning everybody. I realize that time away from your research is a nuisance, but this morning I received a communication from the chief that is extremely relevant to our program."

"Who is this person you refer to as *the chief*?" Dr. Elizabeth Mortensen interrupted.

"That's irrelevant, Dr. Mortensen. It's the subject of the communication that matters. If you can control your curiosity long enough to hear me out, I'll continue." He held eye contact with her until she looked away, then went on. "Soon we'll be joined by a scientist who is reported to have discovered a way to activate immense physiological energy, such that a person can become phenomenally empowered, achieving what might be called "superpower." According to what's been rumored or, should I say, confirmed, it's supposed to be both physical and mental.

"That sounds more like a comic book version of a fantasy character than a scientific reality. Like Superman? Or Captain Marvel? Are you sure about this?" Mortensen interjected.

"I only know what I've been told— and instructed to do, which is to integrate him into our project. Be patient, Dr. Mortensen. Let's see what this new addition to our community has to offer before drawing conclusions. Now! Back to work," he commanded.

As the group filed out of the room and headed to their respective labs, Schlossman said, "Dr. Mortensen. A moment."

"Yes?" she said, halting at the entrance of the conference room and turning to face him.

"I want you to take responsibility for the newcomer. His name is Max Manus. I'm not sure when he'll be here, maybe in a day or so."

"What exactly am I supposed to do with him?" she asked testily. "I'm not here to be a babysitter."

"We'll see what he has to say when he arrives. Then we'll formulate a plan," Schlossman said, ignoring her sarcasm.

"What if he's just a self-deluded fruitcake?"

"From what I've been told, that doesn't seem to be the case. But if it is, that would be unfortunate, wouldn't it."

"For us, or him?" Mortensen mumbled as she left the room.

Hijinks Under Ground

Episode Two

Portland; Thursday, 9:40 a.m.

A large, middle-aged man pressed the doorbell next to the solid Douglas fir front door of a modest bungalow on a quiet, tree-lined street in Southeast Portland. With no response after a couple of minutes, he pressed it again. He knew it worked because he heard the chime inside. After no answer again, he stepped to the edge of the porch and peered into a large window but couldn't see past a closed blind. He looked up and down the street. Seeing no one, he walked up the driveway to the rear of the house where a gate in a tall board fence, which connected the house to a single-car garage, blocked the way in. The gate was padlocked. He took a lock pick from his jacket pocket and quickly opened it.

A deck was attached to the rear of the house and an oak door with small, square glass panels led inside. It only took a minute to pick the lock, but when he turned the handle the door wouldn't budge. "Damn! Must be bolted or barred," he mumbled. He was tempted to break the glass but decided not to since the neighboring houses were so close. Then, on closer inspection, he noticed how thick the glass was, and that it was webbed with fine wire mesh. Realizing there was no easy way to break in, he left through the gate, relocking it on the way out.

Back on the street, Bentz returned to his SUV. It was parked half a block away and was where Bentz's companion, an uncommunicative guy named Tony, had waited while Bentz checked out the Manus house. "Nobody home," Bentz said. "The place is super secure, probably alarmed, as well. They must be protecting or hiding something. We'll keep an eye on the house for a while in case somebody shows up."

Washington D.C.; Thursday, 1:05 p.m.

"Yeah?" Blacker said after he picked up his cell phone on the first ring.

"He wasn't there," Bentz said. "The house is locked tighter than a drum. Serious security. But it's well-maintained, grass and flowers taken care of. They might just be away for a while. We're gonna stake it out. See if anybody turns up."

"Leave Tony there," Blacker said. "You're going to Mexico City. I got a lead this morning from the record of a conversation several months ago between a Chinese general and a Mexican cartel lawyer named León Cardosa. Cardosa might know where Manus is. I'll text the details. The pilot's got the flight plan."

Hacienda Manus, Mexico; Thursday, 1:25 p.m.

Lena answered at once when her secure phone pinged. It was Axman. "Yes?"

"Someone checked out your house this morning. I'm sending an encrypted photo file as we speak. He was a big guy, bald, well-dressed. He didn't try to break in. There was no vehicle visible at the curb."

"Cruise the neighborhood. See if he's watching the house," Lena said as she sat down at her computer. "I'll take it from here."

Ten minutes later, Lena sent Axman's encrypted surveillance file to friends at CIA, NSA and FBI. She should know more later that day.

Mexico City; Thursday, 5:20 p.m.

"There's an American man here to see you."

"What's his name?" Cardosa snapped at his secretary over the intercom.

"He won't tell me. But he says it's important."

"Tell him to make an appointment."

"I did. He says it can't wait. He's *very* insistent."

"All right. Send him in."

Bentz gave the receptionist a cursory glance as he marched past her and entered Cardosa's office. He glanced around the room, then sat down in the chair in front of Cardosa's desk. "We need some information," he said, not bothering to introduce himself.

"Who's *We*? And who are *you*?" Cardosa said, nervously eyeing the huge man across from him.

"*We* are the US government. Who *I* am doesn't matter. It's what we want to know that does."

"That's ridiculous! You can't just walk into my office and tell me what to do. I don't care who you are. This is Mexico! You don't have authority here."

Bentz pulled a silenced Beretta from inside his jacket pocket and laid it on the desk. "Is this authority enough, Mr. Cardosa? The same Mr. Cardosa who conspired with General Dong of the Chinese army to abduct Max Manus?"

Cardosa was momentarily shocked into silence, then said, "I don't know what you're talking about." As he started to move his hand toward an intercom button, Bentz reached across the desk and grabbed Cardosa's wrist with a powerful grasp that caused the lawyer to cry out in pain.

"You damn-well know what I'm talking about, so cut the crap. I need to know where Max Manus is." Bentz squeezed harder before releasing his grip, to Cardosa's relief.

Cardosa glanced at the Beretta while rubbing his wrist and said, "All I know is that he and his wife have a place on the Baja Peninsula."

"Are they there now?'

"No idea. I don't have anything to do with them."

"Where is this place?" Bentz asked, picking up the pistol and pointing it at Cardosa.

"No need for that. I'll give you what I have," Cardosa said with a quivering voice. He opened a drawer and shuffled through some files until he found what he was looking for. His hands shook when he slid a slip of paper across his desk. "Those are the GPS coordinates."

"You sure?" Bentz demanded when he glanced at the numbers, then put the paper in his shirt pocket.

"Yes. But if you want to capture or kill them, you'll need reinforcements. They defeated a Chinese army detail and a North Korean squad that tried to kidnap them. From what I hear, it was no contest. Before that, they wiped out the leaders of the Baja Drug Cartel. There's something about them that's not natural. Some kind of superpower . . . or something."

"Bullshit! Two old people couldn't do that. I think I can handle them. Me and this little guy," Bentz said. Then he pointed the pistol at Cardosa's face and pulled the trigger.

"Thanks, Mr. Cardosa. Your cooperation is greatly appreciated," Bentz said with a quiet chuckle, then rose to leave. After he walked out the office door, he fired two rounds into the chest of Cardosa's secretary who was just starting to dial a phone. Then he eased the pistol back into its holster and left with no trace of having been there.

Hacienda Manus, Mexico; Thursday, 7:15 p.m.

Max sat in his basement lab completing calculations for a metabolic energy experiment when Lena rushed in. "Max! We've got a problem. CIA has a file on the guy that Axman caught snooping out our Portland house. His name is Raymond Bentz, and he's bad news. He lists himself as a security consultant and provides muscle for whoever hires him. He's been implicated in four assassinations but has avoided charges. He obviously has friends in high places."

"What's he got to do with us?" Max asked, glancing back and forth between Lena and his open notebook.

"Everything! Before Bentz killed him, Cardosa gave him our location. I heard it all through the microphone Rana hid in Cardosa's office. I have a feeling we're going to have a visitor soon."

"It would be nice if José's dogs were here." Max said.

"Sure it would, but they're not. José's in L.A. visiting his sister. He took the dogs with him. But our security system is working, so we'll know if Bentz decides to drop by tonight. And if he does, we'd better be ready. But it's not like we haven't faced this kind of thing before. Anyway, it's not Bentz who concerns me—it's who he's working for that does," Lena said, as she hurried out of the lab and headed upstairs.

35,000 feet above Central Mexico; Thursday, 8:25 p.m.

Bentz was taking his first bite of a medium-rare rib-eye steak when his phone rang. "Yeah?"

Blacker got right to the point. "How'd it go?"

"I got the location of their house in Baja. I'm on my way now. I'll pay a visit tonight. The pilot's gonna land this thing in Cabo. Arrange a car for me and some backup. If they're there, I'll deliver Manus tomorrow morning."

"Do you think they'll be there?"

"It's a good guess. Tony said nobody showed up at the Portland house today. Cardosa said they were involved in some cartel business down here a few months ago. It's worth checking out."

"All right. Keep me posted. And text those GPS coordinates, I wanna know where this place is."

Forty-five minutes later, as Bentz savored the last of an apple strudel smothered in thick cream, wheels touched tarmac and the plane taxied toward a dusty Chevy Suburban, next to which stood two big, unsmiling Mexican guys in dark clothing. Bulges under their jackets told him they were armed.

Hacienda Manus, Mexico; Thursday, 11:45 p.m.

A loud alarm jolted Lena out of a meditative reverie and brought Max's yoga exercises to a sudden halt. Together they hurried to the security system display screens and scrolled through the channels. It showed up on camera seven. An SUV half a mile away was crawling along the dirt track leading from a little-used secondary road to the hacienda.

"Looks like there's three of them," Lena said as she sharpened the infrared camera focus on the vehicle. "No way to know if they intend to kill or capture us. But whatever their intent, it can't be friendly. Not after what Bentz did to Cardosa."

"I'm feeling a surge of energy," Max said thoughtfully as he focused on the screen. "It must be anticipation of danger that activates it. I've got to test this in the lab."

"Max! This isn't the time for scientific analysis. Pay attention!"

"All right, all right. The guy driving is Mexican. I can't make out who's in the back seat, but the man in the passenger seat is a white guy. He's big, maybe in his forties, bald as a cue ball. Is that the man in Axman's tape?"

Peering at the image on the screen, Lena said, "Looks like him. He *is* a big guy. I think we'd better prepare to greet our guests."

"Mr. Hospitality. That's me," Max said as he slipped on a Kevlar vest.

"Max . . . I'm feeling a surge, too. This is really amazing," Lena said as she pulled a black watch cap over her close-cropped silver hair.

A little later, Lena used a remote to open the heavy steel gate separating their courtyard from the dirt track. After they walked through the opening, she closed it behind them. "I'll take this side," she said, stepping into the shadows behind a huge agave plant growing a few yards away.

Max crouched in deep shadows under low limbs of an ancient flowering mimosa tree on the opposite side of the narrow lane.

"There's a gate up there," the driver of the Suburban said, as he eased the vehicle to a full stop. "What now?"

Bentz turned to the man in the rear seat. "Check it out. See if we can ram through it and see what's on the other side. Go!"

The man approached the gate and gave it a couple of hard shoves, then tried to pull it toward him. No matter how hard he tried, it wouldn't budge. He looked through the vertical bars into the courtyard, then along the high wall that extended from the gate in both directions as far as the light allowed him to see. Then he returned to the SUV.

"What's the story?" Bentz snapped.

"It's like a prison, man. The gate is really strong, and the wall is at least eight feet high. Doesn't look like we can get in."

"The hell we can't. We're not going back without Manus. Gun it! Smash through that damn thing!"

The Suburban hit the gate at forty miles an hour. The noise of the crash was immediately drowned out by an explosion under the rear axle, which lifted the stopped vehicle two feet off the ground. The bomb embedded in the driveway was wired to go off if someone tried to breach the gate. When the SUV bounced back down, Bentz scrambled out of his side and crouched alongside the open door. Blood ran down his face from where his head hit the windshield. The other two men, dazed by the impact, stumbled out on the other side and crouched next to the open driver-side door. All three had their guns out and pointed into the darkness but were unable to see anything in the dense vegetation.

From behind the agave, Lena saw Bentz and yelled, "Throw out your gun and lie face-down on the ground."

Bentz, focusing on the voice, fired his Beretta in the direction of Lena's command, blasting six holes in the thick agave stems near where she'd been hiding, but missing her since she'd already moved to the side.

At the same time, the two Mexicans on the other side of the SUV fired their pistols randomly into the darkness until their chambers were empty.

"Are you done?" Max yelled from the shadows when the firing stopped. Getting no answer, he fired a single shot that kicked up dirt between the two men squatting by the open door. His aim was perfect, even in the dim light.

"Don't shoot!" one of the men shouted.

"Toss your guns and phones into the road. Your boots, too," Max yelled.

After they did as he instructed, Max shouted, "Start walking, and forget where this place is. We know who you are, and how to find you. Next time I won't be so nice."

The two men jumped up and started off at a fast pace along the ten-mile dirt track, swearing every time they stepped on a sharp rock or a patch of ground-hugging sticker plants.

While Max was dealing with the two borrowed Sinaloa cartelistas, Bentz managed to scramble under the SUV. He watched as the two Mexicans fired the last of their rounds, then, in response to a man's shouts, toss out their pistols and phones. He saw them take off their boots and walk away. Then he saw two legs emerge from the roadside shadows and approach the vehicle. *That must be Manus,* he thought. He scooted to the edge of the undercarriage, aimed and fired a round, striking Max in the left thigh. Max cried out and collapsed to the ground.

But while Bentz had been scrambling under the Suburban, Lena had crawled through the underbrush toward the SUV. Seeing no one, she sprinted to where Bentz was positioned when he'd shot at her. When she heard the shot Bentz fired, and Max's scream, she ran around the front of the vehicle in time to see Bentz emerging from underneath it, pointing a pistol at Max lying in the dirt at the side of the road. Max's pistol lay a few feet behind him where he dropped it when he was hit.

"Don't move!" Lena shouted.

Bentz spun around to discover a tall woman dressed in black with a pistol pointed at him. Without thinking, he swung his gun toward her and fired, but not fast enough. Lena shifted to the side as a bullet flew past her head and fired at the same time. Bentz's brain splattered over the still open car door.

Lena ran to Max and assessed his wound. Five minutes later, she had him back in the house, a tourniquet applied, and a doctor on the way.

After a few minutes, and assured that Max would be okay, Lena said, "Max, I'm not sure I felt any superpower effects tonight. What's going on?"

Max thought for a moment, then said, "I think you did, but maybe in a more subtle manner than mere physical strength. You dodged bullets aimed at you, and your quick shot in dim light to the exact middle of that guy's forehead was remarkable. No, Lena. It didn't fail you. It was just expressed in a different way."

Washington D.C.; Friday, 5:40 a.m.

The general noted the caller ID and answered. "Do you have him?"

"We have a problem," Blacker said, his voice strained.

"A problem?"

"Bentz was supposed to grab Manus last night, but I haven't heard from him. Haven't heard from the two Sinaloa guys we hired, either. I'll let you know as soon he calls." The general didn't respond. "Who is this Manus guy, anyway?" Blacker added after a moment of silence.

Ignoring Blacker's question, the general said, "This never happened, Blacker. Don't ever call me again." After the line went dead, the general punched in a new number. "Captain, I've got a special job for your squad. Meet me at the usual place in thirty minutes.

Hijinks Under Ground

Episode Three

Hacienda Manus, Mexico; Friday, 7:46 a.m.

"Max! Wake up! There's a helicopter approaching!" Lena yelled, while peering through the bedroom window with a pair of binoculars.

Max sat up and shook sleep away. "What? A helicopter?" He cocked his head to one side, was silent for a moment, then said, "It's approaching from the sea."

"A Black Hawk," Lena said. "That means a special ops team. Must have something to do with that guy who tried to break in last night. It's headed for the beach. We've got three or four minutes at most. If it's a fully armed Delta Force squad, we wouldn't stand a chance. Superpower or not. This is serious."

Max hobbled to the window, grimacing with pain from the gunshot wound in his leg. "It's me they're after. That's obvious from that guy's visit to Cardosa. You have to hide in the tunnel. There's a good chance they'll kill you if you don't. They don't leave witnesses to their dirty deeds. Without you, who would rescue me?"

"You can hide in there with me," Lena said.

"No. Whoever it is wouldn't be sending these guys if they weren't sure I was here. Probably had satellite surveillance on us. They'd tear this place apart to find me, and they'd find you, too. And my lab."

"How will I find you?" Lena cried, revealing a feeling of near-panic, a response she had been trained to avoid, but was now threatening to overtake her.

"Lena! You'll figure it out. Call Rana and Zula as soon as the soldiers are gone. You'll do what you have to do. So will I. We'll survive."

Shaking her head in disbelief, she ran from the room, telling Max over her shoulder that she had to get her laptop and phone. "I'll meet you downstairs," she shouted from the hallway.

"This is really pissing me off," Max said, as he pulled on his chinos, favoring his throbbing leg.

A minute later, Lena ran up to Max in the basement where he was opening a concealed panel that hid the entrance to his laboratory and a steel door to a secret tunnel between the hacienda and boat house. She had a satchel in one hand and a small capsule in the other. "Swallow this. It's one of those GPS trackers Rana gave me. At least we'll know where they take you. Hurry. The copter's already on the beach."

"I'll be waiting for you," Max said as he edged Lena into the space. He embraced her for a lingering moment, then slid the panel shut. A moment later, he heard the crash of the front door being smashed open and sounds of men rushing into the house. He put the capsule in his mouth and limped toward the stairs to greet his visitors.

Hacienda Manus, Mexico; Friday, 8:23 a.m.

"Rana," Lena said excitedly over her secure phone, "Max was hijacked by army commandos a little while ago. We've got to get him back."

"Mom. Calm down. What are you talking about? What happened?"

Lena told her about the man who showed up the night before, the gunfight, how she disposed of the body, even about the two cartel thugs Max sent packing. "Just before they got here, Max swallowed one of those trackers you gave us. He made me hide in the tunnel," she added.

123

"Are you sure they were military? It's pretty scary if they were," Rana said, after Lena finished describing what happened and what was captured on the hacienda security cameras.

'I'll send a file of the monitor recordings. See what you think. Call Zula."

"I'm detailed for a tour in South Korea We're deploying tomorrow," Rana said.

"I'll make a call," Lena said. "This is critical, a lot more important than staring down North Korean troops across a stupid dividing line. Where *is* Zula?"

"She's in Böblingen, Germany. Giving a special forces training course."

"I'll get *her* back here, too. The marines will just have to figure out how to sneak up on terrorists on their own."

After Lena called a Pentagon contact to get Rana and Zula out of their regular duties, she made another call. When the man at the other end of the line heard what Lena wanted, he said, "There's no way I can break into that data bank. It's top secret and has a special access code. I'd be toast if they caught me trying to get past that firewall."

"I understand. But this requires extraordinary effort. Someone has Max."

"Max? Oh my God. But what can I do? I'm not cleared at that level. I'd have to break every rule there is."

"I don't like having to remind you, but you owe me for that time in Bulgaria. Don't bullshit me about how hard it will be. You didn't care how hard it was for me then, did you? Just do it. Now! I need to know who's got Max."

After those calls, she sent the monitor files to Rana, 'For Her Eyes Only.'

Aberdeen Proving Ground, Maryland; Friday, 11:25 a.m.

"Lieutenant Vaidyar, a video file just arrived that's tagged for you. It's encrypted," the soldier standing at the open door to Rana's office said.

"Route it here, sergeant. And close that door!"

After going through the security camera recording for the third time, Rana called Lena. "They're army all right, special ops. Eight of them. Can't tell what unit, or where they're stationed. The markings on the helicopter are blacked out. But, there's one thing for sure. An operation like this had to ordered by someone high up."

"Find out who did," Lena said. "I'm pressing my CIA contact to dig deeper into who was looking for information about Max and me. There must be a tie-in. Your tracker shows Max on a course toward San Diego. I'll let you know where they take him."

Undisclosed location, Northern Virginia; Friday, 12:05 p.m.

The general punched a code into his phone. After a short delay, then some crackling, he asked, "Do you have him?"

"Yes, Sir. On board and undamaged. We'll be in San Diego in thirty-five minutes," the Delta Force captain said over the noise of the Black Hawk.

"Any problems?" the general asked.

"No, Sir. No resistance."

"What about the woman?"

"The old man was the only one there. We searched the place. Lots of security equipment, but no one else."

"What did he say when you asked about her?"

"He wouldn't tell us anything. Not even his name."

"You're lucky he didn't. Everything about this operation is top secret, including his name. Any sign of the bald man I told you about? Or an SUV?"

"No evidence of the man, Sir. But there was a wrecked SUV outside a gate to their property. There was blood in the dirt near the vehicle. But no body."

"All right. Forget what you saw. Or that you were even there. There's a plane waiting in San Diego—CF48U. Hand him over to the officer on board, then you and your squad stand down. Remember, this operation is off the books. It never happened! Is that understood, Captain?"

"Yes, Sir." The captain glanced at Max, sitting between two men in commando garb, his head hooded, and his hands shackled. "Definitely, Sir." When the line went dead, he handed the radio back to the copilot. Looking at the silent and unmoving captive, he wondered who this old man was and why he was so important.

Bluefield, West Virginia; Friday, 8:50 p.m.

"I'm Dr. Smith. How do you feel?" a white-coated man asked, as he pulled the hood from Max's head.

"Thirsty. The gorillas who kidnapped me and the goon that delivered me here were not especially attentive to basic body needs, like thirst. Who *are* you, Dr. *Smith*? Why am I here?" Max asked, as he glanced around. He was shackled to a metal chair bolted to the floor in what seemed like a make-shift medical facility in a storage locker, or maybe a semi-trailer truck.

"Ignoring Max's questions, the white-coated man said, "I'm going to see how healthy you are and give you a few inoculations."

"What the hell's going on?" Max said angrily, straining against the steel wrist and ankle restraints.

"I have to make sure you don't carry contagious disease organisms to your new home. So, settle down, mister whoever you are, and let's get this over with."

Two hours later, the doctor calling himself Smith dialed a number he'd been given by the soldier who delivered Max. "He's healthy. In remarkable condition, I might add. But there are two problems. He's got a gunshot wound in his leg. It's gonna take a while to heal."

"Did you get it under control?"

"Stitched up and bandaged. Gave him antibiotics."

"What's the other problem?" the general asked.

"He had a miniature GPS device in his stomach. I picked it up in an x-ray. When he vomited after I gave him a double dose of ipecac and I found it and smashed it."

"Damn! What time did you get it out of him?"

"About thirty minutes after he got here. Close to nine-thirty,"

"All right. Someone will take him off your hands soon," the general said, a new edge to his voice.

"Good," the doctor replied. "I need to get back to the hospital."

A few minutes later, three men arrived. The one who seemed to be in charge looked at Max for a moment, then pulled out a pistol and fired two shots into the doctor's forehead, He replaced the hood over Max's head and unshackled his legs. Without a word, the other two grabbed Max's arms and guided him out of the exam trailer to a waiting van with its engine purring patiently.

Hacienda Manus, Mexico; Friday, 6:35 p.m.

Lena's call caught Rana in her apartment. "Looks like he's in West Virginia. At an airport in a town called Bluefield. The tracker didn't move for thirty-seven minutes, then went dead. They either found it and got it out or took him somewhere that blocks transmission."

"What do we do now?" Rana asked.

"Don't know yet, but I'll let you know when I do."

Hijinks Under Ground

Episode Four

Bluefield, West Virginia; Friday, 11:10 p.m.

The elevator came to a gentle stop and the door slid open.

"Welcome, Dr. Manus," Schlossman said as two uniformed soldiers man-handled Max out of the elevator. "Take off his hood, there's no need for secrecy down here," Schlossman told the sergeant. "But not the handcuffs."

Max squinted in the light, looked around, but said nothing.

One of the soldiers gave the cuff key to Schlossman, then said, "He's got a leg wound. The doctor who checked him out put on a fresh bandage. He said you should keep an eye on it." Then he joined his companion in the elevator, punched in a passcode and returned to the surface.

"You must have questions, Max. Let's go to the conference room and I'll tell you what I can." Schlossman laid his hand lightly on Max's arm and guided him to a conference room where he offered him a chair at a large oval table. "Would you like something to eat or drink?" he asked when Max was seated.

"Water," Max said.

Schlossman took a bottle from a sideboard and set it on the table in front of Max. "Naturally, you're wondering why you're here. You must be upset about how it was done. I apologize for that, but, believe me, it was necessary." He

128

paused and glanced at Max's hands shackled in front of him. "I can remove those after I explain what we're doing and what your role will be. But only if you pledge to cooperate and promise to not try to escape, which would be a fruitless endeavor. There is no way out other than the elevator, which, by the way, has infallible security."

"Who are you? Where are we?" Max asked, not attempting to hide his anger.

"You can call me Gerhardt. We are a hundred feet underground. Only a handful of people know where, or even that this facility exists. It will be your home for the foreseeable future, where you can perfect the superpower transformation process you discovered."

Max clumsily unscrewed the water bottle lid and took a long drink. "I don't know what you're talking about. But I wouldn't tell you about it if I *had* discovered something like that."

"I understand your reluctance, Max. But you may change your mind after I explain our purpose here. And to be perfectly blunt, if you don't cooperate, the people in charge of this project will do whatever it takes to convince you. I imagine Lena means a great deal to you. I believe you also have two daughters, don't you? It would be a shame to put them at risk simply because you're unwilling to serve your country."

"You son-of-a bitch. I'll kill you if you harm my family," Max said as he smashed the handcuffs onto the tabletop.

"Yes. Of course, Max. But you're no position to know what happens up there. You see, we're sealed off from the outside world. No way to communicate other than by my link to a person who's name I don't even know, and to whom I report each week."

"What the hell's going on down here?" Max asked, his hands straining against the restraints.

Ignoring Max's question, Schlossman continued, "You'll work with Elizabeth, a brilliant neurophysiologist. She'll join us in a minute and we'll get into the details of what we expect from you."

129

At that moment there was a rap on the door, then, without waiting for permission, Dr. Mortenson entered and sat down next to Schlossman. "Dr. Manus. It's an honor to meet you and have an opportunity to work with you. We've been aware of your amazing discovery for some time. If it can be combined with our process, we will change human potential beyond anything anyone ever envisioned."

Max was stunned by what she said and was even more astonished by what she and Schlossman described to him during the following two hours.

Havre de Grace, Maryland; Saturday, 6:35 a.m.

"Zula's plane lands in an hour. I'll leave in a few minutes. Do you want to come with me or stay here?" Rana asked when Lena entered the kitchen of Rana's apartment.

"You go ahead. I need to call my CIA contact. He left a message while I was on the flight from LA." Lena poured a cup of coffee, then got her phone.

Her contact answered at once. "I traced the searches to a computer in D.C.. A private company that does under-the-radar work for government agencies. I'd say mostly military from the files that were searched. The firm's done work recently for a future weapons group, but no names are listed. There's a bunch of files that I couldn't get into; somebody's definitely hiding something."

"Who's the contractor?" Lena asked.

"The principal of the company is ex-CIA, Basilos Blacker. He left the agency under questionable circumstances. He makes big money doing dirty deeds. No references to who's hired him in the past, but people he's employed are listed."

"Anyone match the description of the man we neutralized in Mexico?"

"Might have been a guy named Raymond Bentz. He was wanted for murder and other assorted crimes in half a dozen European countries. Blacker keeps company with some rough characters. Be careful if you tangle with him."

"Where's Blacker located?" Lena asked.

"He's got an office in D.C.. I'll text the address."

"Thanks. Keep digging. I need to know who Blacker's working for."

"I'm already pushing my luck. I gotta back off for a while."

"Keep at it. This is important," Lena said in no uncertain terms before she clicked off.

Undisclosed location, Northern Virginia; Saturday, 7:45 a.m.

"Give me an update," the general demanded, a glass of whisky in one hand, his mobile in the other.

"He's still sleeping," Schlossman said, glancing at a monitor showing Max's room. "Except for a leg wound he's in fine shape. But so far, he refuses to say anything about power enhancement. I questioned him for hours last night. Now he knows what we want from him, and some of what we're doing, but we don't know anything about his superpower process, or how it could be incorporated into our implants. He's a stubborn bastard. Secretive, too."

"Keep trying. You've got to break him. Meanwhile, I'll see what I can do up here,' the general said, ending the call.

Washington, D.C.; Saturday, 9:10 a.m.

"I didn't think I'd hear from you again," Blacker said, wondering what the general wanted. He'd assumed the general had written him off after the fiasco at the Manus hacienda in Mexico.

"Don't give me that shit, Blacker. Listen up."

"How can I be of service, Sir?" Blacker replied, struggling to temper his intense dislike of the man at the other end of the line.

"We have Manus, no thanks to you. I resorted to more reliable means. But he's refusing to buy into the program. We need leverage."

"What does that have to do with me?" Blacker asked.

"His wife and daughters. Find them. We'll use them to convince him what's best for all concerned."

"I have no idea where they are. Everything about this guy and his family's top secret," Blacker said.

"You found their houses, didn't you?—the one in Portland and their place in Mexico. I don't care how you did, and I don't care how you find them. Just do it."

"Maybe you've underestimated this guy, General. Bentz is dead, and he was no amateur. There's no sign of his wife, and there's nothing in CIA files about any daughters."

"Losing Bentz was your fault. You should've been better prepared. I keep you on retainer for a reason. Jobs like this, for example, and I expect success. I don't think you'd like the alternative. Call me tomorrow night with results."

After the general abruptly ended the conversation, he called one of his independent contractors, a Kazak ex-military intelligence operative named Nadya Kaliyev. She and her partner, an ex-KGB assassin known only as Klara, would be perfect for capturing Lena and her daughters. But first, he had to find out where these damn Manus women were. Blacker called his highly paid mole at the CIA and told him what he needed.

Havre de Grace, Maryland, Saturday, 9:35 a.m.

Lena ran to meet them as Rana and Zula came through the front door of Rana's apartment. Lena loved her adopted daughters as if they were her own and glowed with unrestrained joy at seeing Zula. It had been months since they'd been together in Cabo San Lucas when the Manus clan wiped out Chinese and North Korean commandos intending to abduct Max.

"Mother," Zula cried as she rushed toward Lena. At six feet two inches tall and with skin color the dark black of her

Zulu ancestors, her regal beauty defied description. Zula enfolded Lena in her long, muscular arms. "Rana told me about Papa. Don't worry. We'll find him. Whatever it takes–we'll find our Papa."

After a tearful reunion interspersed with more hugs, the three women settled in with cups of hot chai and turned to the problem of rescuing Max.

"Tell me everything," Zula said.

Lena opened a notepad and scanned her notes. "This is what's happened," she began.

"Wednesday morning, I learned that someone was searching restricted CIA files to find our location.

"Thursday morning, while Max and I were in Mexico, a lone man checked out our house in Portland. Axman caught him on a surveillance camera.

"Thursday afternoon, a man paid a visit to León Cardosa in Mexico City and discovered the location of our hacienda. He shot Cardosa after he got the information.

"Thursday night, three men tried to break into the hacienda. We killed one, who was the man caught on Axman's camera, and ran off the other two.

"Friday morning, a military team abducted Max from the hacienda. Max made me hide in the tunnel. Rana's tracking device showed that Max ended up in a town in West Virginia.

"I got here early this morning."

"What about José?" Zula asked.

"He'll arrive this afternoon," Rana said. "He's coming from LA where he was visiting his sister. He's bringing the dogs."

"Mom. Who could be behind this?" Zula asked, interrupting Rana.

"What we know so far points to a black ops contractor named Basilos Blacker. He may be working for someone in the military. No idea who, though."

"That's our only lead?" Zula asked.

"It's a place to start. We'll check out Blacker this morning."

"All right, then, let's get going," Rana said. "There's no time to waste. Papa's resourceful, but whoever has him must have powerful resources as well. But so do we, and it looks like we're going to need them."

Hijinks Under Ground

Episode Five

Bluefield, West Virginia; Saturday, 10:00 a.m.

"**Yes, Sir. He's still fine.** Like I told you before, the leg wound's not that bad. In fact, it seems to be healing faster than expected. He slept through the night but he's awake now." Schlossman said into his phone.

"What have you told him?" the general asked, his words slightly slurred.

"Elizabeth and I spent two hours with him after he got here. We described in general terms what we want from him and what we're doing."

"And . . .?"

"Manus denied his superpower transformation discovery and refused to work with us. He said we're insane and demanded to be set free."

"Hmm . . . has he shown any signs of this so-called superpower? Has he tried anything?"

"No. But he's still in handcuffs and leg shackles, locked in his room. He knows there's no way out of here. I don't think he'll try to escape, if that's what you're getting at," Schlossman said.

"Anything else?" the general asked.

Schlossman summarized the week's progress, focusing on compatibility of the AI chip implant. "Only seventeen-percent rejection with the new version. And the monkeys are easier to handle. Looks like composition of the bioadhesive is the key."

"Good. But you've got to reach zero rejection. No room for screw-ups. And keep working on Manus. Just in case, I'm arranging leverage to convince him if he refuses to cooperate. I'll keep you posted."

En route from Havre de Grace to Washington, D.C.; Saturday, 10:20 a.m.

"Do you think Papa will use his superpower to get away from whoever has him?" Zula asked, from the back seat of Rana's SUV.

Rana, who was driving, glanced at Lena in the passenger's seat. Lena was silent for a while, staring out the window. Finally, she said, "Depends on what they've done to him. He was shot in the leg. No bone or nerve damage, but a nasty exit that tore up a lot of muscle. If they shot him up with drugs to sedate or knock him out, it'll take a while to recover. If he's shackled or imprisoned, there's not much he can do. In short, I don't know. But there is one thing I do know. When Max is back to his usual self, and if unshackled, they'll have their hands full."

"What about us?" Zula asked. "Will what Papa taught us in Mexico still work? I can't believe the incredible power I had when those Korean guys attacked. You felt it, didn't you, Mother?"

"That wasn't the first time. It's real, all right. It's as if a new control center in our brains has emerged that kicks in when we're threatened. For me, there's a shift in energy that makes me feel like a superpowered dynamo. I react faster, comprehend what's going on around me quicker, and can exert more force. It's truly amazing . . . but also . . . . scary."

"Scary?" Rana chimed in.

"In the wrong hands, yes. As you know from the discussion we had at the hacienda, your father and I are dedicating our lives to preventing the wrong kind of people from acquiring this knowledge," Lena said, harking back to the family meeting they'd had when Max was recuperating from their confrontation in Minneapolis with the jihadists. "Your father is a brilliant scientist, no doubt a genius. But, in all honesty, he needs my help to fend off the criminals who want to take advantage of his discoveries. With help from you two, and José and his dogs, we have a reasonable chance of doing that."

"Mom. you know we'll do whatever it takes," Zula said emphatically."

"That's right," Rana said. "But, right now we have to decide what we're gonna do about this guy we're visiting today."

"We'll either capture him or monitor him. We've got to find out where they're holding Max," Lena said.

"We better choose one of those options soon. We'll be there in ten minutes," Rana said, glancing at the GPS screen.

"You brought your bag of tricks, didn't you?" Lena asked.

"You know me. Always prepared."

Camden, New Jersey; Saturday, 10:53 a.m.

"Yeah?" Nadya said, when she answered her cell phone. She motioned to Klara to lower the volume on their flat screen TV. Klara glared at Nadya for a moment, then stood and stomped out of the room without turning the sound down.

"I've got a job for you," Blacker said.

"I'm on vacation. We just finished a tough job and we're gonna take some time off. We need it."

"I heard. Brazil, right?"

Silence for a moment, then, "Okay, so you got ears to the ground. What's up?"

"A quick and easy one . . . a fast fifty K."

"It won't be easy if you're calling me."

"Trust me. It'll be easy. I'm just in a hurry, that's all."

"Who and where?"

"An old woman. Couple of daughters too. Local. I'll know more later. Still got a few things to iron out."

"Any problems?"

"Shouldn't be. What's wrong? You afraid of old women?"

"Don't mess with me, Blacker. What's this about?"

"Hey. No big deal. Military stuff. You know how those guys are sometimes. Afraid of their own shadows. Especially if it's political."

"Yeah, I know the type. All right. But it'll be seventy-five if there's three of them. Text me details when you've worked them out. If it's as easy as you say, I'll try to convince Klara. We'll want half the money up front."

Bluefield, West Virginia; Saturday, 11:00 a.m.

"Good morning, Max," Schlossman said when he unlocked the door to Max's room. "Are you ready for breakfast?"

Max got out of the chair where he'd been meditating and advanced toward Schlossman, who took a step back toward the open door. A short chain attached to ankle shackles brought Max to an abrupt halt. He glanced at his raw wrists where steel cuffs abraded skin, and said, "Get these things off me."

"Have you thought more about our conversation last night?" Schlossman asked.

Max stared at him a moment, then said, "I need to know about your progress up to now. The kinds of technical problems you've encountered. I want to see your experimental protocols and talk to the other scientists. Then I'll know if I can help. As far as this superhero bullshit you keep harping on, there's no such thing. Yes, I want breakfast. And don't worry. I don't intend to attack you this morning, . . . Gerhardt." *There's too much I need to learn before I do anything like that,* he thought as he watched Schlossman nervously fumble through his pockets for the key.

Washington, D.C., Saturday; 11:10 a.m.

When Blacker saw the caller ID, he answered, "Got anything?"

"An unscheduled plane with no flight plan landed at a private field west of Annapolis early this morning. A fuel delivery guy one of my people knows saw a tall, elderly woman get out of the plane She got into a green, late-model Ford Explorer, Maryland plate. The driver was a dark-skinned woman, maybe in her thirties. He said she looked South Asian, like India, or somewhere around there. Might be worth looking into."

Blacker ended the conversation and immediately called another number. Twenty minutes later, he learned there were 324 late-model green Explorers listed with the Maryland DMV. Thirty-seven title holders had Spanish, Middle Eastern or Southeast Asian names; six of those were Indian or Pakistani. A longshot, but at least it was something. He made another call and issued instructions. "Check the Indian ones first," he said before ringing off.

Washington, D.C., parking garage; Saturday, 11:25 a.m.

"Blacker's company's in there," Rana said, pointing at a ten-story office building on the other side of a busy street. Her SUV was parked on the third level of a parking structure with a clear view of the building.

"What now?" Zula asked. "Doesn't do much good sitting here staring at a building."

"We need to know who ordered him to send Bentz after Max. Then identify the army team that got him the next morning. Even better, where they're holding Max," Lena said.

"How do we do that?" Zula asked.

"What if you just confront him and ask him?" Lena said. "I don't expect you'd learn anything. He'd deny knowing what you're talking about. Probably get belligerent. But you wouldn't be there to get information, you'd be there to plant a listening device, like Rana did in the cartel lawyer's office in Mexico City."

"Why me? This kind of thing is what Rana does. Not me."

139

Lena turned around in her seat and looked at Zula. "Because, let's face it, you're a bit more intimidating than your demure sister, even though under that calm exterior she is every bit the killer you are. Play your military officer card. Make up something about your old buddy Bentz gone missing, and that he mentioned a job he was doing for Blacker when you saw him last week. You just want to know if Blacker has any idea where Bentz might have gone. He'll be suspicious and won't tell you anything, but hopefully, you'll have a chance to stick the miniature microphone someplace, then get out. You got any better ideas?"

"What do you think, Rana?" Zula asked. "Would it work?"

"Demure? Mom, what do you mean by that?"

"Rana! Answer Zula. Would this plan work?"

"Yes. As long as the pickup is in the same room he's in. It's very sensitive. Just stick it somewhere inconspicuous. Yeah, it should work all right. We'll be able to hear everything he says on this tablet," she said, reaching behind her and grabbing a tote bag off the rear seat. "If Zula riles him up, maybe he'll call his boss to see if he knows what's going on."

"All right. Let's do it." Lena said.

Washington, D.C., office building; Saturday, 11:35 a.m.

"What?' Blacker answered gruffly, when his intercom buzzed.

"There's an Army lieutenant here to see you. She says her name is Sara Nambeeka."

"Never heard of her. I'm not expecting anybody. Ask her what she wants."

The receptionist looked at the security monitor and said, "What does your visit concern, Lieutenant?"

"A friend. Raymond Bentz."

When Blacker heard what Zula said over the speaker, he felt a ripple of panic, but quickly recovered. "Let her in," he said, then switched off the intercom and slid a side drawer open far enough to reveal a Sig Sauer pistol. He reached in and clicked off the safety. "What the hell's going on?" he mumbled under his breath.

"Come in," he said at the rap on his door. He was taken aback when a tall, imposing black woman strode into the room and positioned herself in front of his desk. Her short buzz-cut emphasized the striking beauty of her African facial features. Her unobstructed blazing dark eyes revealed an intimidating gaze. She stood silent for a moment, then leaned forward and placed her big hands, palms down, on the polished surface of his uncluttered desk.

"Where's Raymond Bentz?" Zula asked, as if she were interrogating an inferior officer. It was easy from her height to notice the grip of a familiar pistol in the half-open drawer next to where Blacker sat looking up at her. "If you reach for that gun I'll kill you, which is not what I came here to do," she added.

Blacker, a practiced field agent, recognized the fierceness of this woman at once, and that she was undoubtedly able and willing to carry out her threat. He slowly pushed the drawer closed, with her eyes following his movements. Then he asked, "Who are you? Who's Bentz?"

Zula, realizing she had the upper hand, pulled up a chair and sat down. Without taking her eyes off Blacker, and considering how to reply to his query, she let her arm drop to her side and stuck the sticky surface of the microphone chip to the underside of the chair. "He and I did a couple projects together a few years back. Been friends ever since."

"What kind of projects?"

"Nothing you need to know about. We were gonna go fishing this week, but I can't get hold of him. A few days ago, he mentioned he was gonna do a job for you. I figured you'd know where he is, and if he's okay."

"How did you find me? I'm not listed anywhere."

"I've got friends in military intelligence. You weren't that hard to locate. So, what can you tell me?"

"I have no idea who you're talking about. Don't know anybody named Bentz. Must have gotten your wires crossed. I'd like you to leave, Lieutenant."

Zula was tempted to take the conversation further, but realizing Blacker wasn't going to admit knowing Bentz, she rose from the chair. Still watching Blacker closely, she said, "Yeah. Must be crossed wires. Have a nice day."

He kept his eyes glued to her as she walked over to the office door, yanked it open and left without another word.

As soon as he heard the door to the main hall close, he called the general.

"This better be important," the general said angrily.

"A giant black woman just barged into my office asking about Bentz. Said she was an army lieutenant. Said her name was Sara Nambeeka. You know anything about what's going on?"

"What did you tell her?"

"Nothing. Said I'd never heard of him. There's something wrong about this woman."

"Hang on," the general said, then entered the name into a data base. "No such person, in any branch," he said a minute later.

"Damn. Who the hell is she?" How'd she find me? What does she want?"

"I've got a feeling this is related to Manus. If she, or whoever she's working for, found you, they might find the lab."

"Impossible. That mine has been off the records for years."

"We can't take any chances. She was captured by your security cameras, wasn't she?"

"Should have been. I'll check."

"Send me her image. My people can probably ID her. Do it now."

When the call ended, Blacker buzzed the receptionist. "Bring me the security camera disc for the last hour."

142

Hijinks Under Ground

Episode Six

Bluefield, West Virginia; Saturday, 11:35 a.m.

Heads turned in their direction when Schlossman and Max entered the common dining room and took an empty table. Handcuffs missing from Max's raw wrists could only mean one thing—Manus was going to cooperate. The chef approached with two cups of coffee.

"The works, Don," Schlossman said, then looked around the room as the chef headed to the kitchen. Schlossman beckoned to a man and woman sitting together, who rose and made their way to the table. They sat down across from Max and Schlossman.

"So, Gerhardt, this must be Dr. Manus," the woman said, looking at Max. "I'm Melissa Covington, and this," nodding at her companion, "is Keith Danforth. We're responsible for fine-tuning the behavior-control algorithm and the primate trials."

"Melissa, I haven't had a chance to fill Max in on the details of our project yet," Schlossman said with irritation in his voice. "Perhaps you could wait until I do before you discuss details about your work."

Max set the coffee aside, stood, and said, "No problem, Gerhardt. This is as good a time as any to dig into the research. I'll start with Melissa and Keith." Then, turning to Melissa, he said, "Let's go to your lab." As he started toward the door, he looked over his shoulder and said, "You told me I

143

had to understand the program if I'm going to contribute anything, right? That's what I'm going to do. Tell Don to send my breakfast along and a fresh pot of coffee."

Schlossman was momentarily speechless as Melissa and Keith rose and fell in behind Max without asking permission or even looking at him. When the three of them left the dining room, Schlossman yelled, "Don! Take his breakfast and a pot of coffee to Melissa's lab," then stormed back to his office.

Washington, D.C.; Saturday, 2:40 p.m.

When Blacker's phone buzzed he saw it was his guy who was checking out the DMV hits with South Asian names. "What's up?" Blacker asked.

"I've got people watching all six of the residences. Three of the vehicles are in sight. We'll keep eyes out for the others. So far, we've only seen three women, all in the same vehicle. They're in a condo in Havre de Grace that belongs to a woman who looks like she's Indian or Pakistani. The name on the DMV registration is Ranaveetha Vaidyar."

"All right. Stick with it and stay in touch."

Fifteen minutes later, Blacker got a call from the general.

"We have ID on the woman who came to your office a while ago," the general said. "Lieutenant Zula Mabanga, Army Special Forces, stationed at Fort Meade. She must be someone special because she was recently transferred to a black ops unit as an instructor. There's no mention of Manus in her file."

"Why the hell was she interested in Bentz?" Blacker asked. "At least that's what she said."

"No idea. Any news on the old woman who came in on that private jet this morning?"

"I'm working on it. I'll let you know if something turns up. What about Manus?" Is he cooperating? Anything new at the mine?"

"I haven't talked to Schlossman since this morning, so I don't know. But I still want Manus' wife and kids as insurance. The mine won't stay secret forever. We have to speed this project up if we're going to keep it under wraps."

144

Noting urgency in the general's voice, Blacker asked, "Is there a deadline I don't know about?"

The general hesitated a moment, then said, "I intend to surprise the Russians when we show up at the 2020 joint U.S.-NATO Military exercises. We need a game changer, and this would be it."

"That doesn't give us much time."

"That's why you need to get your ass in gear, Blacker. Bring me that Manus woman, and the daughters."

"Like I said, I'm working on it, Sir. We might have something tonight. At least the woman. I still don't know who or where the daughters are. Are you sure they exist?"

"It's rumored there's two of them, but I haven't seen anything specific. My intel guys are still searching. I'll let you know if we find something," the general said before ending the call.

Havre de Grace, Maryland; Saturday, 2:50 p.m.

"Mom! Zula," Rana said with a sense of urgency. "Listen to these recordings of calls Blacker just had. One was about surveillance on my car. Someone must be watching now. The other sounded like it was with someone in the military. They've identified Zula."

After the three of them listened to Blacker's conversations, they realized danger was closing in. Lena spoke first. "We have to get out of here without being seen. We'll have to evade whoever's watching Rana's SUV, then find the mine they referred to. It must be somewhere around Bluefield. That's where Max's tracker went dead. Sounds like they intend to use Max's superpower as a weapon and use us as coercion to make Max cooperate. But from what Blacker said, they don't know the two of you are our daughters."

"That may be true," Rana said, "but they're still out to find me. Someone must have spotted me and my SUV this morning when I met you at that airfield."

Zula said, "That makes sense. But right now, we have to get out of here without them knowing. I'll sneak out the back, find the stakeout, and neutralize him. Then we can head to West Virginia and find Papa."

"We'll have to get another vehicle in case they've issued an alert for mine," Rana said.

"We'll take mine. It's parked down the street.," Zula countered.

"No. They know who you are, so they'll probably put out an alert for your car as well," Rana said.

"Hold on," Lena said. "Zula, go out the back, over the parking lot wall, and get out of this neighborhood. Then call Uber for a ride to Fort Meade. Beg, borrow, or steal a vehicle and come back for us. We'll deal with the stakeout then. If you take out the watcher now, they'll know something's wrong and send reinforcements."

Zula glanced at Rana, acknowledged her nod of approval, then said, "Good plan, Mom. I'll leave now."

Washington, D.C.; Saturday, 3:05 p.m.

"What?" Blacker said when he answered the phone call.

"Didn't you say something about a tall black woman coming to your office this morning?" the man Blacker had charged with surveillance asked.

"Yeah, so what?"

"The guy I posted behind of one of the target's condo saw a person like that come out the back door, cut across the parking lot, and climb over a six-foot wall. That got my attention."

"Is it the place with the three women?"

"Yeah. And one of them is old."

"Bingo! Give me the address. I'll take it from here."

After Blacker ended the call, he hit a stored number, desperate for it to be answered. It was.

"What?" the woman who answered asked.

"A location. A condo in Havre de Grace. As far as I can tell, there are three women: an old white one, a South Asian, and a Black. The black one's military, but she took off a few minutes ago. Unless she returns, you only have to deal with two."

Blacker gave Nadya the address and told her he'd transfer half her payment right away. He had his assistant handle the money transfer while he called the general. "We're in play. I'll keep you posted," he said, then ended the call.

Camden, New Jersey; Saturday, 3:10 p.m.

"Klara. Get our stuff. We gotta roll," Nadya said.

"What's doing?" Klara asked, concentrating on a cage-fighting match taking place in gory splendor on a sixty-inch flat-screen TV.

"It's the job I told you about. Remember? The easy seventy-five thousand. We gotta snatch a couple women. It's sixty miles from here. Let's go."

Bluefield, West Virginia; Saturday, 4:10 p.m.

"I can see what you're trying to do, and where there might be a few glitches," Max told Melissa Covington as he got up from the table where he'd been going through their experimental results. "But before we adjust your approach, I need to talk to the other members of the group. Can you introduce me to them now?" Keith Danforth, her assistant, was working at a lab bench across the room.

Melissa closed the notebook and said, "No problem. Jerry Riverton's lab's next door. He's creating the AI biochip implants and working on the biocompatibility problem. He's looking forward to meeting you." She rose and led Max into the hall.

After Max and Melissa left the room, Danforth called Schlossman on the facility's internal network. "Melissa told him everything we're doing. Now she's taking him to Riverton."

"Let me know where he goes after that. I want to know where he is every minute."

Washington, D.C.; Saturday, 3:55 p.m.

Blacker answered the call he was expecting. "Yeah."

"We'll be at the woman's condo in five minutes. Any change in the situation?" Nadya asked.

"No sign of the black woman, and the other two haven't left. Looks like it's all clear. Go for it."

"Where should we deliver the package?"

"Take them to the warehouse in Philadelphia. We'll handle it from there."

"What about the black one if she shows up?"

"Kill her and get rid of the body. She's Army. I don't want any military ties to this operation."

"This is getting complicated, Blacker. What's going on?" Nadya asked.

"Don't worry. Just do what you're being paid for."

"Who's the Indian woman?"

"Don't know. Maybe a friend. But I want her in case she's important to Manus."

"What about your stakeout guys? Do they know we're coming?"

"They know but leave them out of it. They're observers, not fighters. You and your psychopath girlfriend are on your own. Call me when you have them."

Bluefield, West Virginia; Saturday, 4:30 p.m.

It only took ten minutes with Riverton for Max to grasp the full extent of why he'd been kidnapped and brought to this secret lab. They thought they could use his superpower in conjunction with Artificial Intelligence systems to be implanted into human brains. The implants would be microchips integrated into brainstem nerve networks. They were hoping that two plus two would yield five.

It was a military operation with the aim to create super-fighters endowed with super-human powers who could be controlled remotely via satellite. The ultimate human war machines. "This is the work of madmen," Max swore under his breath, enraged not only by their intention to steal his discovery and employ it in such a reprehensible way, but also by their intent to turn men into programmed killing machines.

Havre de Grace, Maryland; Saturday, 4:30 p.m.

"The stakeout guy's still out there," Rana said, peering out of her front window. A few minutes later, she said, "A van just parked down the street and two women I don't recognize are getting out. They're coming this way."

"Probably visiting someone who lives around here, but keep an eye on them," Lena said. Then Rana's phone rang, and Lena answered. "Hello."

She recognized Zula's voice. "I got a car and am almost there. Be ready to leave in about fifteen minutes. I'll take care of the stakeout."

"Zula's on her way. We'll get out of here after she neutralizes that guy out there. Pack what we'll need," Lena told Rana. Before Rana left to gather her equipment, she glanced out the window and saw the two women walk past the gate to her small yard and continue along the sidewalk.

Ten minutes later, there was a knock at the rear door. "Must be Zula. She got here faster than she thought she would," Lena said, as Rana was putting the last of her gadgets and weapons into a duffle bag.

When Lena cracked the door to see who was there, it crashed open with enough force to slam her backwards, then head-over-heels when she stumbled over a half-full laundry basket on the floor.

"Mom! What happened?" Rana yelled as she ran into the back hallway. "Oh my god," she cried when she came face-to-face with a big woman in military fatigues pointing a pistol at her midsection. Behind this woman was another one, petite with curly blond hair, kneeling next to Lena and holding a gun to her head.

"Don't do anything foolish, honey, unless you want this old lady's brains decorating this hallway."

"Get down on the floor! Face down! Now! Klara, cuff her, then this one," the blond said, nodding at Lena.

Lena immediately sensed a growing feeling of strength and an urgent desire to strike out at the woman holding the gun to her head but realized the risk of being shot was too high. She willed herself to stifle the urge to strike out and wait for the right opportunity. She caught Rana's eye and shook her head, instructing Rana not to try anything foolish.

In less than a minute, Lena and Rana were sitting with their backs against the wall and their hands bound behind them with plastic restraints. While Klara guarded the two captives, Nadya called Blacker. "Got em. No problem. You can call off your watch dogs now."

"All right. But before you leave, search the place. Find the old woman's phone, and computer if she has one. Look for any info about her daughters. I need them as well."

"There's a tote bag filled with what looks like military communication stuff, some guns, too," Nadya said.

"Bring it. Must belong to the black woman. She's military."

"All right. Then we'll head to the warehouse. We'll be there in about an hour."

Meanwhile, as Nadya was searching the condo, Zula took an exit off the Pulaski Highway and made her way toward Rana's neighborhood. When she turned onto Rana's street, she noticed the stakeout car pull away from the curb and speed off in the opposite direction. Then she saw four women come out of Rana's condo, one of them carrying a black duffle bag. When she got closer, she realized the two in front were Lena and Rana, and saw their hands were behind them, as if restrained. They also walked with a shuffle, as if their legs were shackled. Then she noticed one of the women, the smaller one with curly hair, held a pistol at her side. Still half a block away, Zula pulled behind a windowless van parked at the curb. *How the hell am I gonna handle this situation?* she wondered, as she watched the women approach slowly along the tree-shaded sidewalk.

Hijinks Under Ground

Episode Seven

Havre de Grace, Maryland; Saturday, 4:50 p.m.

Zula scrunched down in the front seat of the SUV she'd borrowed from a friend and watched the four women approach along the sidewalk until her view was blocked by the van parked in front of her. When they didn't walk past the van, and she heard the side-door slide open, she realized the van was their destination—that it belonged to the abductors. She jotted its license plate number on her arm, then slipped further down in the seat to avoid being seen. When she heard an engine come to life and the sound of leaves crunching under tires, she peeked over the steering wheel to see the van pull into the street and head away. After a moment to let it get far enough ahead, she followed, keeping it in sight from a safe distance.

Philadelphia, Pennsylvania; Saturday, 6: 05 p.m.

Blacker looked at the security camera and saw Nadya's van pull up to the loading dock of the derelict building. "They're here," he yelled. Blacker told one of the men to stay near the window at the front of the building, and another one to monitor the security cameras they'd set up when they arrived earlier that evening. He signaled for the other two guys to join him as he headed to a back hallway where a steel door opened to the dock.

"Take them inside and strap them to those chairs in the other room," he told his two henchman when Nadya and Klara forced Lena and Rana out of the van. "Don't let their hoods slip off," he yelled.

"You need us anymore?" Nadya asked, after the big guys took the captives into the building.

"No. I've got enough manpower. Just get the hell outta here. Your payment's on the way."

"Good. You know where to find us if you need anything else," Nadya said, as she climbed into her van. "Until next time, *proshchay*."

"Yeah, same to you—you crazy bitch," Blacker mumbled under his breath.

Seeing that Lena and Rana were securely bound in the chairs and their hoods had been taken off, and after going through the things from Rana's condo that Nadya brought with them, Blacker called the general. "We've got the old woman. She's Manus' wife all right. Her brown-skinned friend is Ranaveetha Vaidyar. Don't know anything else about her, but I don't care either."

"Her brown-skinned friend, as you call her, just happens to be an army lieutenant stationed at Aberdeen Proving Ground. She heads an intel operation and appears to be highly regarded and well-connected. Looks like you've stepped into a hornet's nest."

"Me . . . or us, General?"

"Don't play that game with me, Blacker. You're the one who grabbed her, not me. So cut the crap, don't do anything stupid, and wait for my instructions."

Bluefield, West Virginia; Saturday, 6:08 p.m.

Schlossman answered at once, anticipating a call from The general. "Yes?"

"We have Manus' wife. Is he cooperating yet?'

"I'll find out soon. He's still talking to the research team, but he should be finished soon. I'll check and let you know." Schlossman hung up and went to find Max.

At the same moment that Schlossman left his office, Max stormed out of Riverton's lab and hurried toward Schlossman's lab, his rage barely under control. He intended to confront the director with what he'd confirmed during his questioning of the scientist responsible for coding remote-control algorithms that would monitor and command troops implanted with behavior-regulating microchips and enhanced by Max's superpower. Riverton had referred to these AI-modified soldiers as CEFs: Controlled Enhanced Fighters.

As Max rounded a corner in the hall, he nearly knocked over Elizabeth Mortensen, the scientist he met in Schlossman's office the night he was brought to the lab.

"What's the big rush?" she asked, picking up the notebook she dropped when Max ran into her. "You look like you've had a shock of some kind."

"I know what you people are up to," Max said, "It's not right. It's a despicable corruption of science. I'm going to stop it."

As he started to march off to find Schlossman, Mortensen said, "Wait. Let's talk before you do anything drastic. You'll only make things worse if you attack Gerhardt."

Not sure what she meant, Max turned back to her and said, "What do you mean?"

She looked around, then said, "Come with me. We need to talk."

Before Max could respond, Schlossman appeared from around the corner and stopped next to Mortensen. He gave her a stern look and said, "Is there a problem, Elizabeth?" Seeing fear in her face, he said, "It appears there may be. I'll see you later." Then, turning to Max, "Before I deal with Elizabeth, you and I need to talk. In my office."

Philadelphia, Pennsylvania; 6:10 p.m.

Zula climbed over the chain link fence and ducked behind a pile of half-rotted lumber at the back of the trash-littered gravel lot. The van that brought Lena and Rana to this abandoned auto parts store had just left, right after two over-muscled men in typically black attire took the two hooded women inside. She saw the man she recognized as Blacker when he came out to the dock, then followed the others back into the building. There were only two vehicles parked by the loading dock, so she didn't think there would be many more guards inside, if any besides the two she'd just seen.

As Zula considered her options for rescuing Lena and Rana, her mobile vibrated an incoming call. "Hello."

"Zula, it's me, José. I can't get hold of Rana or Lena. Where are they?"

"José! Thank God, it's you. We've got problems. Where are you?"

"I just landed in Newark. I flew in from L.A. where I was visiting my sister. What's going on?"

"We can't talk on the phone. Can you get to Philadelphia? I'm keeping an eye on a building where Lena and Rana are being held."

"What? Being held by who? What are you talking about?"

"I'll explain when you get here. You and I are going to take care of it. Okay?"

"I'll rent a car and get there as fast as I can. Where should we meet?"

Zula gave him an address for his GPS. It was on North Beach Street, just off I-95, a spot where he could park without being seen. "You should be able to get here in two hours. Call me when you do, and I'll come get you. Did you bring the dogs?"

"Of course. I don't go anywhere without them. I just retrieved them from wherever they put them on the plane."

"I'll be waiting. Hurry."

Bluefield, West Virginia; Saturday, 6:15 pm.

Max followed Schlossman into his office, waited until he closed the door, then as calmly, yet firmly as he could manage under the circumstances, said, "I can't let you carry out this insane plan to use Artificial Intelligence to create super-soldiers. It's not only unethical and dangerous, it's beyond the realm of civilized behavior. It's criminal. You'd have to be a demented psychopath to think it's permissible to turn men into programed killing machines controlled by someone in a back-room thousands of miles away."

"Dr. Manus, with all due respect, your opinion about this project is totally irrelevant. A government group far more important than you and your outdated rectitude has authorized and supports this project. I don't give a whit about your objections. And as far as what I assume is your intent to not cooperate is concerned, I believe you might change your mind after what you are about to hear."

Schlossman then called the number the general had given him earlier.

"We're here," Blacker answered.

"Put her on," Schlossman said.

"Say hello to your husband," Blacker said, as he held the phone in front of Lena.

Lena shook her head and refused to speak.

Blacker glanced at one of his goons, who immediately stabbed a serrated knife into Rana's thigh, quickly ripped it out and held it above her other leg. Rana cried out once, then gritted her teeth and stifled further outburst.

"She's gonna look like Swiss cheese unless you say what I tell you to say," Blacker said. "Tell him you and your Indian friend will be fish food if he doesn't do what he's told. Unless you won't mind your friend's face carved like a Halloween pumpkin by my knife-wielding companion who just happens to love that kind of fun."

"Max. Don't worry about Rana and me. Do what's—"

Blacker yanked the phone away before Lena could say more and raised his other arm to slap her. But charged by Max's superpower, and enraged by what they did to Rana, Lena anticipated his intent and snapped her head to the side.

Just as his hand approached her face, she caught the index finger of his right hand in her mouth and bit down with all the force she could generate. The crunch of bone was obliterated by Blacker's anguished scream. After she spat half of his finger onto the filthy floor, she said, "You shouldn't have hurt her. Now you and your little boys here are really in serious trouble."

"You shouldn't have done *that*, old woman," Blacker yelled," sticking the bloody stub of his finger in her face. He nodded at the man with the knife, who jabbed it into Rana's other leg. Rana screamed louder this time—the blade had struck bone and sent a shockwave down her entire leg.

Sitting in Schlossman's office, with its polished walnut desk and expensive oriental carpets, Max heard Rana's scream as if he were in the room with her. But from Lena's statement, Max knew at once that Zula hadn't been captured. He also knew that Zula would do everything in her power to rescue Lena and Rana, and that when Zula put her mind to something, she succeeded. There was hope, and he clung to it tenaciously.

But Max was still enraged. Schlossman was terrified by the penetrating look Max gave him and the fierce determination in his eyes. But, Schlossman quickly reminded himself that he was in control, not this old man whose wife his employer had in hand. At least that's what he believed at the time.

Philadelphia, Pennsylvania; 6:20 p.m.

Zula heard a door slam and saw Blacker and another man rush down the dock steps and get into one of the parked vehicles. Blacker was holding a rag around his hand and yelling at his companion. The sedan's tires spun in loose gravel as it sped out of the lot. Zula checked the time and figured José would join her around 8:30 p.m. She wondered if the two men would be back by then, and how many remained in the building.

Hijinks Under Ground

Episode Eight

Philadelphia, Pennsylvania; Saturday, 6:25 p.m.

Blacker was in the passenger seat of a sedan speeding south on I-95 holding a piece of cut-off shirttail around what was left of his right index finger. "We'll take an exit in about two miles, then turn left at the first intersection.," he said, then awkwardly auto dialed the general.

"Is he gonna cooperate?" Before Blacker could reply, the general continued, "Where are you? It sounds like you're in a car."

"No progress yet, but we're working on it. They're playing tough, so we'll get tougher. First, I gotta take care of my finger. She bit it off and I'm on the way to a hospital."

"What? What the hell's going on? Did you say the old woman bit your finger off?"

"I'll fill you in later. Right now, send a couple more guys over there. I left three, but we better play it safe. I'll get back as soon as I can. We're at the hospital now. I gotta go," Blacker said with the general sputtering obscenities at the other end. He jumped out of the car as the driver pulled up to the ER entrance.

Undisclosed location, Northern Virginia; Saturday, 6:30 p.m.

The general placed a call as soon as the one with Blacker ended. "We got a problem. Blacker screwed up again. Send a couple of your men to the Philadelphia location as backup. Blacker and another guy had to leave for a while."

He was silent a moment, then answered, "The old woman bit him. He's on his way to a hospital. When can your guys get there?" A second later he said, "All right, if that's the best you can do."

Then he called Blacker. There was no answer, so he left a message. "Backup will be there in two hours. Keep me informed." He ended the call, opened a desk drawer, took out a bottle of single malt and poured two fingers worth. "Son of a bitch . . ." he mumbled as he lifted the glass to his mouth.

Bluefield, West Virginia; Saturday, 6:30 p.m.

It took every bit of will power Max could muster to restrain himself from attacking Schlossman when he heard Rana scream before the phone line went dead. Instead, he concentrated on remaining calm, stared intently at Schlossman, and said nothing. His thoughts were running through possible scenarios that might be playing out where Lena and Rana were captive. The best option was that Zula would rescue them. Then he remembered that José was planning to visit Rana when he left L.A. Both he and Zula were proficient in superpower transformation, and he knew they'd be impossible to stop if they got a chance to save the two women. His thoughts brought him to the only conclusion that made sense—Lena and Rana would be rescued, and his family would come for him. Together, they would take down this evil enterprise and whoever was running it. But he still couldn't get Rana's scream out of his mind, and hoped Zula acted soon.

"You look worried, Dr. Manus. Your wife and her friend, whoever she is, are obviously in a difficult position. Wouldn't it be better for them, and you, if you cooperate with us? Why subject them to more pain when you can prevent it so easily?"

Schlossman said, when he got over initial shock from the intensity of Max's stare after the call.

Max stood and glared down at Schlossman sitting behind his gigantic desk, as if he were protected by its size. "You're the one who should be worried, Schlossman. Not me. You have no idea what you're up against. But you'll find out soon enough." He kicked the chair away, grabbed the cord of the secure telephone Schlossman used for their call with Blacker and Lena, ripped it out of the wall jack, smashed the phone against the desktop, then left the office.

"What are you doing?" Schlossman screamed, as Max disappeared down the hall. "Where are you going?" There was no answer, only silence.

"Dr. Mortensen, gather the staff and meet me in the cafeteria in ten minutes. But not Schlossman," Max said, when he entered Mortensen's lab.

"What's going on?" she asked.

"A return to sanity, that's what's going on."

"Gerhardt would never permit something like this. Why shouldn't he be part of whatever you're doing"?

"Dr. Schlossman's no longer in charge." The calm and strength in his voice was undeniable . . . and compelling.

"What? Who is?" she asked.

"I am."

"What about Gerhardt?"

"The last time I saw him he was behind his desk raving at the injustice of it all. Is that who you want as your leader?"

Mortensen looked at Max for a long moment, then said, "We'll be there in ten minutes."

Philadelphia, Pennsylvania; Saturday, 6:30 p.m.

Blacker couldn't stand it any longer and stormed up to the admissions desk for the third time since he got there. "When can I see a goddamn doctor? Half my finger's gone. I've been here two hours."

"Sir. We've got four attendings, eleven nurses, and forty-seven people waiting to see them, most with conditions far worse than a hurt finger. I'll call you when we can see you."

"Hurt finger? It's been bitten off. I need somebody to do something right now."

"Do you have the missing piece? Do you want it reattached?"

"No! It's gone. It landed on a dirty floor and somebody stepped on it. I just want my finger sewed up, or whatever it is you people do. Just fix me up so I can get outta this third-world hellhole."

Blacker's description of her waiting room did not sit well with the admitting nurse. "Sir. Go back to your seat and wait till your name is called. Or go to another hospital."

Meanwhile, Zula was still crouched by a stack of lumber behind the derelict auto parts store where Lena and Rana were being held captive by Blacker's thugs. When her phone vibrated, she saw it was *José*. "Where are you?"

"Leaving Newark. I should be there in about an hour and a half. Any change in the situation?"

"Yeah. Two guys rushed out the back-door a while ago, jumped into a car and took off in a hurry. No idea how many are still in there. I still don't know what's going on."

"You're not gonna try anything on your own, are you? Wait till I get there."

"Just hurry. You have my location on your GPS, don't you?"

"No problem. Just stay put. I'll see you soon."

Bluefield, West Virginia; Saturday, 6:40 p.m.

Max surveyed the room, saw that every member of the research group was present, then spoke. "Dr. Schlossman is no longer in charge of this project."

A collective gasp expressed their surprise. "What do you mean?" Someone yelled.

"Exactly what I said. What you are trying to do is unacceptable, and the project ends as of this minute."

Before Max could explain the reason for his drastic action, Keith Danforth stood and said, "You can't do this. We won't let you." He looked around the room, as if seeking support, but there was only silence and confusion. Ignoring the others, he approached Max and said, "*I* won't let you. What have you done with Dr. Schlossman? Why isn't he here?"

"I haven't done anything with Schlossman. As far as I know, he's in his office where I left him a few minutes ago. And as far as *you* preventing *me* from doing *anything*, don't even think about it."

As Max turned away from Danforth to continue his address to the gathered scientists, Danforth grabbed Max's arm and tried to pull him toward the doorway. "We're going to Dr. Schlossman's office and straighten this out. Come on!"

Without warning, Max grabbed Danforth's wrist and twisted it outward until his elbow was strained to the point of snapping out of joint. Danforth screamed at the pain and shifted his stance to prevent its dislocation. "Stop! Let go," he pleaded.

Max released his hold and said, "I don't want to hurt you. But I will if you try anything like that again. If you want to see Schlossman, go ahead. You won't be missed here. Everyone knows you're his informer."

"Don't you realize Dr. Schlossman would've called for help by now. You'll be in shackles soon," Danforth said, as he edged toward the door.

"Get out of here," Max said, then watched Danforth go out the door and start down the hall toward Schlossman's office. He then turned to the group, held up his hand to quiet the chatter, told everyone to sit down, and proceeded to describe his plan.

Philadelphia, Pennsylvania; Saturday, 7:50 p.m.

"Are you here?" Zula answered when her phone vibrated.

"If my GPS is right, I'll be to where you told me to meet you in five minutes. Can you get there by then?" José asked.

"I'll be there."

A few minutes later, a silver Toyota Camry pulled into a Burger King parking lot and parked next to where Zula sat at an outdoor picnic table. Zula quickly greeted the dogs and then she and José hugged and exchanged a few words. Then they hurried on foot across a vacant lot toward a row of abandoned buildings backed up to an alley which was parallel to the street the Burger King was on. "It's that one," Zula said, pointing to a chain link fence-enclosed property with a stack of lumber at the back of a parking lot. A Chevy Suburban was parked next to a wide loading dock at the back of a run-down one-story building. "There's a break in the fence over here," she said, leading the way.

A few minutes after Zula and José, and his two dogs, Jupiter and Zeus, got to the lumber pile, a black SUV pulled into the lot and parked next to the Suburban. Two men were in the front seats. One of them appeared to be talking on a mobile phone.

"Come on José, this is our chance," Zula said as she sprang up and ran crouched low to the ground toward the SUV. José and the dogs followed. When the man in the passenger seat got out, he was greeted by a smashing blow to the back of his neck and dropped to the ground. Zula felt for a carotid pulse—nothing.

At the same time, on the other side of the vehicle, José grabbed the driver's left arm when he opened the door, yanked him out and swung him around a-hundred-eighty degrees to smash him into the rear door. Before the man could recover from the impact, José stepped behind him, put him into a chokehold and held tight as the man thrashed violently trying to breath. He was dead sixty seconds later.

"Now what?" José whispered across the roof of the SUV to where Zula stood.

"We convince whoever's inside that we're reinforcements sent to help guard the captives."

"Okay. Let's do it," José said, signaling the dogs to heel at his side.

Zula led the way up crumbling concrete stairs and pounded on the steel door next to a bank of three tall roll-up doors.

Without delay, someone on the other side said, "Who's there?"

"We're here to help you guys out," Zula bluffed in the lowest voice she could manage.

"Who sent you?"

"Who do you think, asshole. Just open the damn door."

When the lock clicked and the door opened a crack, Zula slammed her shoulder into it with enough force to knock the man on the other side backwards and off balance. As Zula and José rushed in, José signaled a command and nodded at the man pulling a pistol out of a holster on his belt. Zeus leapt forward and clamped his jaws around the man's gun arm and Jupiter jumped up and sank his fangs into the man's throat. Within seconds, the dogs knew their job was done and ran after José and Zula, who were headed toward an open doorway leading to another room.

"What's going on back there?" a voice came from the other room.

"No problem," José yelled. We'll be right there."

"Who are you?" a brute of a guy asked as he charged through the doorway to see what the noise was all about.

"I'm your replacement," José said, then smashed his fist into the man's face and kicked his right knee with enough force to twist it sideways at a right angle. The man collapsed in pain and José commanded Jupiter to guard him. While José was dealing with that guy, Zula raced past him into the big room where she saw Lena and Rana strapped to chairs. When she saw Zula, Lena yelled, "By the front window! Watch out!"

Zula dropped to the floor as three bullets zinged above her and hit the wall. At that same moment, José burst through the doorway, not knowing where the shots were coming from. "Aww, he grunted, and was thrown backwards from the force of another round piercing his left shoulder. He landed on the floor next to Zula, who held a Glock pointed at the man walking toward them holding a pistol aimed at Rana. Without hesitating, Zula fired, and the man dropped. It was over—at least that part.

Zula jumped up and ran to the man she shot and checked his pulse. "He's dead. José, are you okay?"

"I'll be all right. What about Rana and Lena?"

Using her knife, Zula cut Rana and Lena's PlastiCuffs, then focused her attention on Rana, who was barely able to remain upright in the chair due to blood loss and fighting off pain from the stabs to her thighs. Lena rose from her chair and said, "We've gotta get out of here. Blacker might return any moment with more men. Rana needs to get to a doctor. So does José."

Zula picked up Rana and headed to the rear door, "We'll take their Suburban."

Lena picked up Blacker's finger from the floor and put it in her pocket. Then she gathered up the men's cell phones, pistols, and a field knife with an eight-inch blade and tossed them into a tote bag that sat near the doorway. Then she grabbed Rana's bag of equipment and weapons and slung both bags over her shoulder.

"José, help me drag this guy out back. We're taking him with us," Lena said, as she approached the man whose knee José had destroyed. He lay where they had left him on the floor writhing in pain, the dogs looking down on him, alert to his every move.

"Where are we going?" José asked, as he grabbed one of the man's arms.

"To the hospital on Rana's base. They'll take care of you, too."

"I'm not military. Why would they do that?" he asked, wincing with pain.

'Don't worry. I'll make a call," Lena said. Jupiter and Zeus followed, one on each side of the man who cried out every time his damaged leg was jostled as Lena and José dragged him out the door and when he bounced down the steps, then to the Suburban where Rana waited on the back seat where Zula had carefully placed her.

Hijinks Under Ground

Episode Nine

Philadelphia, Pennsylvania; Saturday, 9:25 p.m.

When the sedan pulled up to the loading dock behind the derelict auto store, Blacker jumped out, glanced around, then yelled, "Where's the Suburban?" Then, when he saw two bodies sprawled near the SUV, which he assumed belonged to the backup guys he'd asked the general to send, he realized something was seriously wrong. "Check inside," he told the man getting out of the sedan, although he suspected there would be nothing to find other than dead commandos.

Blacker took out his phone. "Sir, there's a slight change in the situation here in Philadelphia."

"Are you back with the Manus woman? Got your finger fixed?" Then, after a slight pause, "What do you mean a slight change? What's going on?" With a shaking hand, the general poured more Scotch and waited for Blacker's answer.

". . . I'll get back to you as soon as I know, Sir." Before the general could answer, Blacker ended the call and rushed into the building. "What?" he said when he almost bumped into the commando standing next to a body on the floor.

"Only two of our guys are here. One's in there, shot between the eyes," the commando said, pointing through the archway. "This one's throat's torn open, and his arm's shredded. Never seen anything like it. The two women are gone. They must have taken Garth with them."

"How'd they do this?" Blacker bellowed. "What the hell kinda animal *is* she?"

Aberdeen Proving Ground, Maryland; Saturday, 10:05 p.m.

After Lena's call, the base hospital was prepared for Rana and José. The on-duty surgeon, Captain Hamilton, met them at the ER admitting desk. "Take Lieutenant Vaidyar to OR three. This man," gesturing to José, "to four," he instructed the orderlies waiting with gurneys.

Back in the Suburban, where Zula sat behind the wheel, Lena said, "I need to ask our friend in the back some questions. Then we'll figure out what to do next."

"Okay. Where to?" Zula asked.

Lena scanned the parking lot, then said, "Park at the far end, under that big tree. It's dark and there're no other cars there."

When Zula opened the hatch door a few moments later, the man scrunched up in the cargo space opened his eyes and tried to say something through the rag stuffed in his mouth. His hands were cuffed behind him and his feet were tied together. Lena ripped the rag away and slapped him across the face. "Are you awake enough to talk?" she asked, then leaned in next to him.

'My knee! I can't stand it. I need a doctor," he blurted out.

Lena smiled, then slammed her fist onto his knee. He screamed and tried to pull away, but there was no place to go. When he frantically looked around, he saw the big heads of the two dogs staring at him over the rear seat. Their black eyes followed every move he made, and low, throaty growls told him they meant business.

"That hurt, didn't it," Lena said, drawing his attention away from the dogs and back to her. "But it's only a taste of how it'll be if you don't answer my questions. Understand?"

"I don't know anything. I was just doing my job," he blubbered, his face contorted with pain.

"Just doing your job when you stabbed my friend in her legs? You enjoyed it, didn't you? I could tell you did. That made me angry. The kind of angry that does away with mercy . . . or compassion. Know what I mean?"

Panic and fear darkened the man's face. "I was just following orders. I had to do what Blacker told me to do. Please . . . believe me . . . I don't know anything."

"Zula. Get the man's knife. It's in that bag on the back seat," Lena yelled at Zula where she stood to the side trying to ignore Lena's interrogation. She knew what her mother was capable of.

Lena held the serrated knife edge a few inches from the man's face. "Who's Blacker working for?"

"How would I know?"

Like a streak of lightning, the knife flashed close to the man's cheek and sheared off his ear. He screamed louder than before and shook his head side to side, flinging blood over everything around him.

"Shut up and listen," Lena yelled, ignoring the spatters on her face. "I want answers, not bullshit. Next, it'll be the other ear, then your nose, then your lips, then eyes. Nod your head if you understand."

The bleeding man nodded vigorously, whimpering and moaning at the same time.

"Let's try again," she said, and held the knife up to his face. "Who's he working for?"

"He talks to him on the phone. He's a general. That's all I know." He spoke so fast his words ran together.

"Where do they have Max?" Lena shifted the knife, ready to slice off his other ear.

The man's gaze followed the bloody blade, and with a trembling voice he said, "I heard Blacker say something about a mine in West Virginia. But I don't know where it is. He never said."

"Why do they want Max?"

"Some kind of top-secret project. I think the general's in charge. Blacker just does what he tells him to do. Hires guys like me to do the dirty work."

"Where can I find the general?"

"Blacker said he's at the Pentagon. But I don't know where he lives. I've never been there. Don't think Blacker has either."

Lena turned to Zula and said, "We're not gonna get anymore from this guy."

"We can't let him go free. He'd warn Blacker about us," Zula said.

"We'll figure that out later." Ignoring his anguished plea to be let go and the bleeding wound on the side of his head, Lena stuffed the rag back in the man's mouth, slammed the hatch door shut, and said, "Let's check out Blacker's office."

Washington, D.C.; Saturday, 11:35 p.m.

Zula pulled the Suburban into the parking garage across from the ten-story office building where Blacker had his office and nosed into a spot with an unobstructed view of the front entrance. The street was quiet. No one was going in or coming out of the building, and most of the windows were dark.

"Let's go. "Lena said.

The glass door opened into a modest lobby with a security desk next to a bank of three elevators. A sleepy, uniformed, older man opened his eyes when the two women entered. "This building's restricted outside of business hours," he said. "Are you on the access list?"

"We're with Blacker Consulting," Zula said, as she and Lena stepped into the elevator car that opened after she had pushed the UP button.

"Wait a minute," he said, "I gotta check."

"We need to pick up some files. We'll be right down," Lena said as Zula pressed the third-floor button.

"Hey. Wait a minute," he yelled as the elevator door closed. "These damn people. Think they don't have to observe the rules," he mumbled.

Standing in front of the door to Blacker's office suite, Lena took his finger out of her pocket, wiped away the dirt from the parts store's floor, and handed it to Zula. "Give it a try."

Zula pressed the finger against the security pad and the door lock buzzed. She pushed the door open, stepped inside, reached up and twisted the ceiling-mounted camera off its base, ripped out the wires, and led Lena to Blacker's office. The door was locked and there was no security code pad, just a keylock.

"I'll try to pick it," Zula said, as she inserted her pick tool. When she couldn't get it to work, she tried another probe, then another, each time without success. "Damn! Must be super secure."

"Get outta the way!" Lena yelled.

Zula looked behind her to see Lena shoving the secretary's desk toward Blacker's office door as if it were a battering ram intended to break down a palace gate. When the door splintered, the two women rushed through and began searching every drawer, cabinet and crevice. Although they found nothing about a mine, a locked desk drawer they forced open yielded a high-security cell phone. There were only two numbers in the phone's memory.

"One of these could be for the general whom Blacker takes his orders from," Lena said. "My friend at the agency should be able to get a fix on who and where he is." Lena took out her phone, punched in a code, waited a moment, read off the numbers, said a few words, then ended the call. "He'll let me know as soon as he has something. Let's get out of here before that security guard gets suspicious."

On their way out of Blacker's offices, Zula took the disc out of the computer that recorded the security camera images. "In case the camera caught us before I disabled it," she said.

Lena's phone buzzed as Zula pulled the Suburban out of the parking garage into a nearly empty street. "Find anything?" Lena asked, after glancing at the caller ID and answering. Lena listened for a few moments, ended the call and said, "One of the numbers is in the Pentagon system, but it'll take a little longer to finds out exactly who. He'll get back to me when he find something. The other is for a Nadya Kaliyev in

Trenton, New Jersey. Maybe she's one of the women who nabbed Rana and me yesterday. As soon as we know who the military guy is, we'll see what he has to say. We'll settle with Nadya later."

Bluefield, West Virginia; Saturday, 11:40 p.m.

After Danforth, whose elbow Max had nearly torn out of its joint, left the room where the staff had gathered at Max's request, Max explained to the disconcerted group why he was acting as he was. "This project has the markings of a top-secret program run by a rogue individual or group. It's intended to convert a special operations soldier into an AI-enhanced automaton designed for programed warfare. The regular Pentagon staff wouldn't sponsor anything like this. Schlossman must be taking his orders from a powerful puppet master who, if whoever it is follows the typical playbook for an operation like this, won't allow any of us to survive after achieving success. There's too much at stake to risk us revealing what we've done, which would be against laws, policies, and international agreements and guidelines, not to mention basic morality."

"How do we know what you say is true?" someone yelled.

"Think about it. The secrecy, isolation, confinement, remoteness, absolute control, restrictions on revealing details to each other about what you're doing. All of this is far beyond usual practice. Being down here is a death sentence, and I'm not ready to die yet."

"If all this *is* true, what can we do? There's no way out. Only Schlossman can call the elevator down, and if he's controlled by someone like you describe, he won't let us get away," Dr. Mortenson said.

"Then we'll just have to—"

Before Max could finish his sentence two things happened simultaneously. The elevator alarm announced its arrival, and Danforth entered the room with a pistol pointed at Max.

"Come with me, Manus," Danforth shouted, waving the gun toward the open door to the hall, seemingly unconcerned about the elevator alarm. At that same moment, two uniformed guards ran into the room, both holding semiautomatic rifles pointed at the frightened onlookers. Danforth, still holding the pistol, turned toward the closest soldier. The soldier saw Danforth's pistol aimed in his direction and fired several rounds. Danforth catapulted backwards onto a conference table then to the floor. Blood gushed from an arc of holes across his chest.

In the resulting pandemonium and confusion, Max exploded with a burst of furious energy. In one smooth leap he kicked the M16 out of the nervous hands of the shooter and rammed the palm of his left hand under the man's chin as he passed by. The guard's head snapped back with a loud crack and he dropped to the floor. In a continuing, fluid motion, Max landed at the side of the second mercenary. He grabbed the gun by its barrel and ripped it out of the man's tight grip. Like a tornado, he twisted around in a half-circle and smashed the heavy weapon into the side of the doomed man's head before he had a chance to realize what was happening. The second commando joined his companion on the floor, by then awash with Danforth's blood. At that point, twelve seconds had elapsed since Danforth's return.

"Somebody grab the elevator before it closes," Max screamed.

Dr. Mortenson ran down the hall to the elevator and stuck her arm between its two doors sliding shut just in time. "Got it! Come on. Now's our chance to get out of here," she yelled.

Schlossman came running toward the staff members crowded in front of the elevator as it filled to capacity. "Let me on," he cried.

Max, who was making sure the elevator door remained open, said, "Schlossman. Go back to your office!"

"You can't tell me what to do," Schlossman screamed, as he tried to push his way through the group.

When he attempted to squeeze past one of the younger women, Harriet Fleming, the analytical chemistry technician, grabbed him by the lapel of his lab coat and flung him to the rear. "Take your turn, Schlossman. You can't tell anyone what to do anymore."

Max caught Schlossman as he reeled back from Fleming's rough toss, gave him a gentle push along the hall, and said, "You'll be the last one out of here. I don't think you'll like what'll be waiting for you up top." Max watched as Schlossman disappeared into his office at the far end of the hall.

Then Max turned to the people crowded in the elevator and said, "We're not taking this up yet, There's no way to know who'd be waiting. We need a plan to deal with whatever it is we might encounter. But don't worry, we're getting out, and soon."

Hijinks Underground

Episode Ten

Philadelphia, Pennsylvania; Saturday, 9:30 p.m.

When Blacker checked the caller ID on his ringing phone he saw it was the general. "Damn! I don't want to talk to him now. Gotta figure out what's going on first," he muttered to his companion, Jake, as he let the call go to voice mail.

"The old lady's friend has knife wounds in her legs. Pretty bad, too. Maybe they went to a hospital," Jake said.

"Yeah maybe. But where? Which one? We need help if we're gonna find them," Blacker said. "I'll call Nadya."

"You again?" Nadya answered. "Now what?"

"The two women you captured escaped. One of them's wounded, probably went to a hospital. I need you to help find them. Fast."

"It'll cost you."

"Don't worry. You'll get paid."

"Where are you? Where were they?" Nadya asked.

"The warehouse in Philly."

"Who'd you have guarding them? Girl scouts?"

"Maybe they had help, "Blacker said. "I don't know. I'll check the hospitals in this area. You canvass the ones around the Indian woman's condo. Do it in person since you'll have to show phony ID to convince them you're official."

"We'll get on it tomorrow."

"I need to find them tonight. Do it now."

"This is *really* gonna cost you."

"Just do it!"

En route from Washington, D.C., to Aberdeen Proving Grounds; Saturday, 11:45 p.m.

Lena answered on the first ring. "Find anything?

"Yeah. Hang on to your hat. The person Blacker's been calling is an army three-star general named Herbert Hooper. It's supposedly a secure cell phone. Fortunately for you, it hasn't been upgraded to protect against the latest hacking programs."

"Do you have an address?"

"He lives near Reston. I'll text you. One more thing. I set up monitoring of his calls. You'll get a ping when he's on the phone. You can listen in. Thought that would help."

"That's great. I owe you for this."

"I'm not keeping score. I owe you for a lot, as well."

After she ended the call, Lena told Zula, "After we check on Rana and José, we're going to pay a friendly visit to a General Hooper."

"Who's he?" Zula asked.

"That's what we're going to find out," Lena said, then looked at the text with Hooper's home address appearing on her phone.

Philadelphia, Pennsylvania; Sunday, 1:10 a.m.

After visiting nine hospitals in the vicinity of the warehouse, Blacker was convinced Lena had not taken Rana for treatment of the stab wounds anywhere in that area. In the parking lot of the last one, he called General Hooper, worried about what he had to tell him. His call was answered immediately.

"Did you find her?"

"Not yet. But we will, Sir. I've checked the hospitals around here. Nadya said they aren't at any of the ones around where she and Klara captured them, either. The guy watching the condo says they haven't gone there, either."

"I don't like this, Blacker." Hooper's voice revealed worry rather than anger. "I think you've underestimated this woman. We don't know if she has backup, or why her friend is with her. She's a lieutenant in an army intelligence unit at Aberdeen. Maybe she's an analyst or something . . . you never know . . . but it's possible she's not a threat to us. Another thing. I can't get through to Schlossman. He's my contact at the mine. Two of the guards went down to investigate and haven't come back up. And *they* don't answer calls either. There're still two guards up top, one at the gate, the other one at the elevator. Something's going on. I want you and your men to go to the mine now. I'll join you in the morning. Bring Nadya and her crazy partner. We need to be prepared for anything. Captain Winters should get there with a four-man special ops team about six hours from now. Around six or seven in the morning."

Relieved that the general didn't explode in anger, Blacker calmed himself and said, "I've only got one man left, Sir. But with those spec ops guys, and Nadya and Klara, we should be able to handle whatever comes up. We'll head there now. But, Sir. I need to know where it is. All I know is that it's in West Virginia."

"It's an abandoned coal mine near Bluefield. The Hankerman mine, at the end of Hankerman Road, seven miles northwest of the Bluefield airfield."

When Blacker and Hooper ended their supposedly secure call, Lena put her phone away and said to Zula, "There're right about one thing. They've underestimated us. Although I do believe we have a challenge ahead of us. If we go directly from the hospital where Rana and José are, we should be able to get to the mine by eight a.m. or so. From what Hooper said, we'll have quite a reception committee to deal with.

Aberdeen Proving Grounds Hospital; Sunday, 12:45 a.m.

"Are you sure you're up to getting out of here?" Lena asked for the second time as Rana changed from the hospital gown into her fatigues.

"Yes, mom. I'm stitched up, loaded with antibiotics and pain killers, and bored as hell. José only had a flesh wound. No serious damage. He's ready, too."

"Then we're going to West Virginia. Thanks to a General Hooper, we're gonna have a mine party."

"What are you talking about, mother?"

"I'll explain on the way. It's at least a seven-hour drive, so we'll have plenty of time to plan our strategy. Zula's waiting out front with an Army van and enough weapons to ensure our party will be a roaring success. Let's find José and get going."

"Did you retrieve my bag of tricks from the SUV we came in?"

"Of course I did. I know how much you like your gadgets—and how useful they can be."

Bluefield, West Virginia; Sunday, 6:40 a.m.

José pulled the van into the tree-shaded parking lot of a boarded-up Dairy Queen near the tiny Bluefield airport and cut the engine. "Wake up. We're here. The coffee's hot and the donuts are fresh."

Lena opened her eyes at once, noted the time, stretched her long, muscular arms, and said, "Good work José. Zula and I needed the sleep. Looks like Rana got some, too." Rana and Zula awoke almost as quickly as Lena did, and both were instantly alert, looking around and assessing where they were.

"I'm gonna take care of the dogs while you ladies devour that Dunkin Donuts gourmet breakfast," José said. He got out of the van and opened the rear door to let Jupiter and Zeus leap down. A few minutes later, they returned from the woods bordering the parking lot to find pans of water and food, which they attacked with impressive zest.

"How'd you come up with all this?" Lena asked, nodding at the pans.

When José turned, he saw Lena standing by the van's side door, watching the dogs scarf down their meal. " All of you were asleep when I stopped at a Walmart on the edge of town. I figured you and Zula wouldn't have had a chance to feed these guys in yesterday's commotion. They need to be in top condition today."

"We all do, don't we? Speaking of which, let's get on with it," Lena answered.

Zula took the wheel and proceeded along Hankerman Road. She slowed a quarter mile before where Rana's GPS indicated the road ended at the sprawling mine site. She pulled into a secluded clearing in the woods bordering the blacktop approach to their destination.

"José," Lena said, studying the layout of the site on Rana's laptop. "Go through those woods to where you can spot the gate and see if you can tell how many guards there are. The entrance to the shaft elevator is a quarter mile beyond the gate. According to this map, there're seven buildings of varying sizes spread around the property. From what we learned from Hooper's call with Blacker, there could be as many as twelve combatants to deal with. They'll probably be dispersed between the gate and the elevator, so we'll have to clear them away one-by-one. Once we get through those, we have to get Max out of the mine. One of Rana's devices should be able to trigger what is probably passcode-protected access to the only way down."

Rana's phone buzzed five minutes later and José whispered, "Three men inside at the gate They're in full battle gear and heavily armed. The gate looks like it's about ten feet high and is reinforced on top with heavy crosspieces. A ten-foot-high, chain-link fence goes off in both directions and concrete bollards are scattered in front of the gate. A small cinder block building next to the gate has a satellite dish and a bunch of antennas. It must be a communication or surveillance post. This place is as tight as a drum."

When José rejoined the women, Lena said, "The gate's out. We'll have to breach the fence. It'd be best to divide into two groups and go in from opposite sides. That'll divide their forces when they detect us. I'm guessing they've installed cameras around the grounds. If there's twelve of them, the odds are three-to-one against us, so we'll have to rely on a surg of Max's superpower when the need arises—and on the dogs. It's worked before, it should again."

"How should we split up?" Rana asked.

"You and José follow the fence line to the right. Take one of the dogs. Keep to the woods until you find a good place to cut through with the bolt cutter. Zula and I will take the other side."

"We'll take Jupiter. It seems that Zeus has developed a strong attachment to Zula," José added, as Zula passed out Kevlar vests she'd included with the weapons she appropriated from the base when she "borrowed" the van.

"We'll keep in communication with the walkie-talkies. Remember what Max always says in situations like this— strike fast and hard, no half-measures. But also keep in mind what I say as a mother—be careful."

"We'll take out the surveillance system if we can. But we'd have to distract the gate guards to destroy the communication post," Rana said.

"We'll see what we can do once we're in position," Lena said. "All right, let's go."

Ten minutes later, Rana spoke into a mike clipped to her vest." We're still outside, but at a good spot. There's a little grove of pines inside the fence, then a line of gigantic dirt-haulers."

"Okay. Stay there. There's a place up ahead where Zula and I can cut through the fence. Give us a few minutes," Lena responded, then followed Zula along the tree line toward a spot opposite the backside of a flat-roofed shed about 20 x 20 feet in size.

A couple of minutes later, hiding behind a dense bush twenty feet from the fence, Lena whispered into her mike. "We're ready. They're probably monitoring this fence, so they'll know when we cut it, or climb over. Be ready for anything—let's do it!"

"Mom. Hold on a second," Rana said. "We can see the front gate from where we are. Let's see if one or two of the guards go to check it out when you cut through. That would give José and me a better chance to get in and take out the surveillance system. We'll wait to go in until we see what happens."

"Good idea," Lena said, nodding at Zula, who was ready with a bolt cutter.

When they heard a buzzer go off, one of the gate guards, the ex-special ops soldier, Jake, who worked for Blacker, ran into the control shack and checked the screens. "There's a fence breach in sector three," he yelled. "Harlan, you and Buzz take a look. Go!"

Zula squeezed through the six-foot cut in the chain link, ran to the back of the shed, jumped high enough to grab the roof edge, pulled herself up, and scrambled onto the flat surface where she lay flat, close enough to the edge to see the fence. At the same time, Lena and Zeus wedged through the cut and hid behind a row of 50-gallon metal drums next to the shed. Just as Lena got there, she heard Rana's voice in her ear bud. "Two guards are running toward a little building on the far side of the property. Must be where you and Zula are. We're going in now We'll try to take out the other gate guard and the control center."

"Okay." Lena said, but said no more since at that moment two armed men ran up to where the fence was cut, stood looking around for a second, then separated, edging off in opposite directions. One walked slowly toward the barrels and the other one went toward the far corner of the shed. Both held automatic rifles at the ready.

Lena saw Zula's head at the edge of the roof, pointed at the man directly under her, and mouthed "now."

When Zula dropped onto the guard below her, Lena sent Zeus running off to the side from behind the barrels. When the guard heading in her direction turned his head to follow the blur of Zeus speeding away, Lena sprang over a barrel and landed beside him and yelled, "Zeus, gun!" At the same time, she deflected the man's gun with one hand and slammed the other fist into his throat. At that point, the dog reached them and dug his jaws into the man's gun arm and shook it so violently the weapon flew out of his hands. When Lena kicked his legs out from under him, the choking and confused guard fell to the ground gasping for air. With practiced speed, Lena cuffed the man's hands and feet and gagged him while Zeus stood over him.

Meanwhile, the surprise of her attack from above allowed Zula to overpower her target with dispatch, and she took him to the ground. He twisted around to shake her off his back, but the force of her tenacious chokehold quickly made him black out. As soon as he was trussed and gagged like his partner, and their weapons were tossed over the fence into the underbrush, Lena called Rana.

"Two down. Where are you?"

"We're still outside. We'll cut the fence now. Can you get into a position to see the gate guard?"

"Give us half a minute. We're going to put these two in this shed—out of sight. Don't want them found too soon. I'll ping you when we're done."

When Rana's phone pinged three minutes later, she and José cut through the fence and crept to the line of dirt-haulers. Jupiter followed close behind them.

When the security alarm went off again, this time from Rana's cutting through the fence, Jake ran into the hut to check the screens. He was shocked to discover another fence breach. He ran out and looked around, then called Blacker, who was in the building where the elevator was housed. General Hooper and the two assassins, Nadya and Klara, were with him. "We've got a problem. The fence was breached in two places. Harlan and Buzz are checking out one spot. I'll check the one that happened just now."

General Hooper nervously watched concern spread over Blacker's face as he listened to the guard. "What's going on?" Hooper asked when Blacker ended the call.

"The fence was breached. But our guys will handle it. Don't worry," Blacker said. "I'll stay in contact with Jake."

General Hooper took a flask out of his jacket pocket and took a long pull.

Meanwhile, Rana and José hid behind one of the dirt-haulers and watched Jake walk past, his eyes fixed on the fence where they'd cut through. "Attack," José commanded. Jupiter charged forward like a silent missile and sank his fangs into the back of Jake's knee, taking him to the ground instantly. Jake screamed and tried to twist away from the vicious dog. Before he could, Jupiter released his jaws from Jake's ripped-open leg and latched on to the arm that held his rifle, biting through flesh to reach bone. Jake's screams were silenced by a blow to the back of his head with the butt of the automatic rifle José held ready to hit him with again if necessary. But it wasn't, Jake was out cold.

From their hiding place on the other side of the lot, Lena and Zula had a clear view of the gate and saw no other guards in sight. Lena was puzzled by the absence of more men. "If my count's right, there should be more soldiers. And Blacker, too. Why aren't some of them at the gate?"

"Your count's right, Mom. Could it be that the backup army team hasn't arrived yet?" Zula asked.

Lena nodded, then called Rana. "Do you see any more guards? We don't."

"No. The place looks deserted. Should we make our way to where the elevator is?" Rana asked, checking a sketch of the layout.

"That's probably where the others are, at least some of them, or else down in the mine. Only one way to find out. But before we go down that path, you and José hide the guy you disabled, then destroy the security system. If our suspicion is right, it's in the gate house. We don't want to be seen on any screens around this place, or in any recordings.

Five minutes later, Rana informed Lena they'd deactivated the gate house computer and control system. then destroyed recordings of the last hour. "We're ready," she said.

"Follow the fence line until you're even with the elevator house, then wait for my call. Zula and I will proceed along this side, past the target, and approach it from behind. Let's go."

Meanwhile, in the elevator building, Blacker and Hooper were growing more concerned about not being able to reach their men. They were also troubled by the fact Captain Winters and his team had been delayed leaving Fort Dix and wouldn't arrive at the mine site for another hour. "We have to know what's going on," Hooper said, pacing around the little windowless room, taking frequent swigs from his flask. "The elevator won't respond and there's no reply from the two guards who went down there to check on Schlossman. I can't get through to him, either. And nothing from the three men who were guarding the gate. Why the hell aren't there security monitors in here? We don't even know who's out there. Or who the enemy is. Blacker . . . you have to find out what's happening."

Blacker was unnerved by Hooper's unhinged yammering. The old man was losing control and sounded nothing like the person he had been interacting with by phone for the past three years. But Hooper was correct about one thing—they needed to know what was happening. Blacker turned to Nadya, who was watching Hooper with obvious alarm as he repeatedly punched in a passcode and pushed the elevator UP button, paced around the room as if seeking a way out, and sporadically screamed at Blacker.

"Nadya, you and Klara get out there and see what you can find out. If it's the two women who got away from the warehouse, take care of them," Blacker commanded.

"Are you crazy? There could be a whole army platoon storming this place. This old guy's off his rocker, nodding at the general, and you have no idea what we're into."

Blacker pulled out a pistol and pointed it at Nadya. "You and superwoman," waving the gun at Klara, "are on the clock. We're not paying you to be afraid. Get out there!"

Provoked by Blacker's accusation of cowardice, and with deference to the pistol he held, Nadya opened the door a crack and peered out. "It looks clear. Come on, Klara, let's take out these bastards, whoever they are."

Hijinks Underground

Episode Eleven

Bluefield, West Virginia; Sunday, 7:50 a.m.

"I hope it's the old lady and her little brown girlfriend. I'd like to rip their heads off," Klara said with a thick accent, the first words she'd spoken since arriving at the mine site. She grabbed their weapons and followed Nadya through the doorway and along the side of the building to a six-foot-high stack of weather-worn wooden crates. Concealed behind the stack, they had a clear view of the broad, empty lot stretching from the elevator building all the way to the gate.

Nadya scanned the area carefully, then said, "If there's anybody out there, they'd probably want to get to the elevator. We'll stay here for a while and see what happens."

A little later, Klara edged closer to Nadya and said, "We've been here fifteen minutes. There's nothing happening out there. If there *is* anyone here, and if they want to get to the elevator, they're not gonna march down the middle of this lot. I'm gonna move over by the fence and see what's going on there."

Nadya watched as Klara darted across the empty space and took a position in front of a one-story, flat-roofed equipment shed, one of several along that edge of the property.

Staying close behind the flat-roofed sheds spaced along the fence line, Lena and Zula crept silently toward a huge pile of gravel a hundred yards ahead of them, Suddenly Zeus turned back to where they had come from and growled. Zula spun around to look behind her and was propelled backwards by two quick shots that hit her in the chest. Lena dove for cover and tried to see where the shooter was. She saw a flash of camouflage uniform dart around the corner of one of the neatest sheds. She crawled to where Zula lay in a pile of leaves and felt for her jugular vein. The pulse was strong. Then Zula opened her eyes and sputtered, "Damn. That hurt."

Lena glanced at the two quarter-sized depressions in the vest and nodded. Yeah, I know what's that like. You okay?"

"I'm good. At least we know we've got company. Did you see anyone?"

"A single shooter. Behind that shed over there," Lena said, pointing.

"Should we send Zeus?"

"Too big a risk. Whoever it is might see him coming and shoot."

Zula looked at the shed for a moment, then said, "I've grown to like flat roofs," she said, then strapped her rifle across her back and dashed to the end of the shed. She pulled herself up in no time and crawled toward the other end.

At that moment, Lena got a call from Rana. "We heard two shots."

"We're okay, thanks to Zula's Kevlar vest. There's a shooter over here. Zula's going after him. I'll stay put and see what happens. Anything where you are?"

"We're behind a little tool shed. The elevator house is straight ahead, about thirty yards. There's a stack of crates and a pickup truck between it and us. We'll get to the truck and wait until we hear from you."

When Nadya heard the two shots she realized they were from Klara's Uzi—she knew that sound from experience. But she was concerned that Klara hadn't returned yet and wondered what she should do. Then she heard the sound of one or more people running fast on hard dirt. She rushed to the far edge of the stack of crates to catch a glimpse of someone ducking behind a red pickup about twenty yards away. "Shit," she mumbled, and pointed her automatic rifle in that direction.

Crouched behind the northern end of the equipment shed, Klara was listening for anyone coming from the direction of the person she shot. "A clean kill", she mumbled. "Now for the other one." A fleeting image of Nadya telling her to not mumble to herself brought a rare smile to her hard, thin lips. Then she got onto her belly and elbowed her way to the corner of the building and looked around. No one was in sight. "I'll go around the other way." She ran to the front corner and peeked around. Again, no one. She then slowly walked along the front of the shed toward the far end, her Uzi pointing ahead of her. Halfway there, she was suddenly crushed to the ground by a heavy weight landing on her shoulders. The gun flew out of her hands. With the reflexes of a trained martial arts expert, she twisted and turned with lightning speed to throw off whoever it was that had dropped on her from nowhere. When Klara threw her off, Zula's weapon slipped from her hand and landed several yards behind her. An instant later, the cold-blooded Kazakhstani killer and the fearless daughter of a legendary Zulu warrior-chief faced each other across a narrow space of three feet with razor-edged knives as their only weapons, each determined to kill the other.

A flurry of movement and noise of a scuffle caught Nadya's attention at the same time it did that of Rana and José. Nadya rushed back to the other end of the stack of crates and aimed her rifle at the two women across the way but was unable to take a shot because they were moving around each other in a tight circle. At the same time, José signaled Jupiter to attack, assuming the woman they saw moving along the row of stacked-up crates with a gun would be distracted by the fight between Zula and her adversary. The gambit paid off—Nadya didn't know what hit her. Before she could comprehend who or what it was, she was face down in the dirt with a growling monster's jaws clutching the back of her neck. She hated dogs with a deep, black passion, ever since a neighbor's rabid mastiff attacked her at the age of seven. "Get it off me," she screamed.

Rana, automatic pistol in hand, called off Jupiter and said, "We meet again. This time on better terms. At least, for me." She cuffed Nadya's hands and feet, grabbed her coat collar and propped her against the crates. "Who's guarding the elevator?" Rana demanded.

"Screw you," Nadya replied.

"Jupiter. Guard." Rana said.

"Get him away from me," Nadya screamed when Jupiter stepped next to her stretched-out legs and bared his fangs in her face.

"The next command will be worse," Rana said calmly.

"All right. Just take him away," Nadya whimpered.

Meanwhile, on the other side of the lot, Zula and Klara circled each other in an age-old standoff between two combatants who knew they were facing a fight to the death, each one seeking an advantage. Then, before either one made a move, they heard a loud command and averted their eyes briefly enough to see José standing nearby. Pointing Klara's Uzi at its previous owner, he yelled, "You! On the ground!"

"Thanks, brother," Zula said. "You saved me a lot of trouble."

Just then Lena ran out from behind the shed. When she saw Klara face down in the dirt, she gestured at the shed door and said, "Cuff her and take her in there."

A few minutes later, Lena and the other three were huddled in the equipment shed. Nadya and Klara were trussed and gagged in a back corner. With information from interrogation of the two assassins, they were planning how to take control of the elevator away from Blacker and Hooper. Suddenly they heard the unmistakable wop-wop-wop of a helicopter in the distance. "Here they come," Zula said. They all knew who she meant— Captain Winters and his army ranger team. "Five minutes at most," Zula added, after listening at the open door of the shed.

Meanwhile, while his family was battling the enemy above ground, Max was trying to control the growing unrest of the laboratory staff a hundred feet underground. He'd propped open the doors so the elevator couldn't respond to repeated signals to bring it back to the surface. He had no way of knowing who was making the requests or who they would face if they rode up with it. But he also realized that the trapped people were growing more desperate to escape by the hour. Especially now that the program was in shambles with Schlossman out of commission and Danforth and two guards dead. On the other hand, what if it were Lena trying to retrieve the elevator? Lack of telephone communications made it impossible to know. He had to do something—they couldn't stay down there forever. With this dilemma in mind, he decided to activate the plan he'd devised.

"Dr. Mortenson, this is what we're going to do,' Max said as he waved her into an office and closed the door. After he explained the plan, he went into the elevator car and pushed the ceiling hatch cover open. Standing on a chair, he climbed into the space above the car and replaced the cover. Then with the help of a colleague, Mortenson brought Schlossman from his office, forced him into the elevator and let the doors slide shut. At this point, Schlossman was a shadow of his former self, trembling with fear and worry over what his bosses would do about his leadership failure.

As soon as the doors closed, the elevator started its ascent in response to the last UP demand still stored in its computer. A single ring announced its arrival in the ground-level elevator building. Blacker and Hooper were shocked at the arrival and stared at the doors as they slid open. "Who are you?" Blacker asked when he saw Schlossman cowering in a corner.

"Schlossman! What's going on down below?" Hooper yelled. Blacker entered the car and coaxed the trembling director out and sat him in the only chair in the room. While Hooper and Blacker hovered around Schlossman, trying to calm him and get answers to their questions, Max silently removed the hatch cover and dropped onto the floor just as the doors began to slide shut. He stuck his hand between them and they reversed direction. When Blacker spun around to see what the noise was, Max sprang forward with a burst of energy.

Before Blacker could pull the pistol from the holster at his waist, Max slammed his fist into his face and grabbed the gun with his other hand. Hooper, already numbed by alcohol, was paralyzed with surprise. Schlossman passed out and fell to the floor. Before Blacker could recover, Max hit him two more times, causing him to collapse into unconsciousness. He stuck Blacker's pistol in his waistband.

In a state of enhanced power, Max heard the approaching helicopter. He quickly pushed Hooper into the chair vacated by Schlossman, ripped off the general's belt, and used it to secure him in place. Then he opened the door a crack and looked out. Seeing the coast was clear, he stepped outside and surveyed the area.

Across the wide lot, Zula stood just inside the partially open equipment shed door. She was watching for the helicopter that was getting louder. Seeing movement next to the elevator building out of the corner of her eye, she glanced in that direction. "Dad!" she screamed. "It's dad," she yelled at the others. "Over here. Hurry," she yelled at Max as he started across the lot to where he saw her standing by an open door. He entered the shed through the door Zula held open just wide enough for him to squeeze in. The helicopter came over the horizon as the door shut behind him.

Rana watched through a crack in the front wall as the aircraft touched down in the middle of the lot, about fifteen yards from the shed. After a minute or so, she said, "There's five of them besides the pilot. They look like Army, and they're armed to the teeth. One of them's headed toward the elevator building. The others are staying by the chopper."

When Captain Winters entered the building, he was startled at the state of the three men he found there. General Hooper was secured to a chair and smelled like liquor; the man he assumed was Blacker sprawled unmoving on the floor bleeding from a split lip and crushed nose; another man was lying on the floor mumbling incoherently. "What the hell's going on?" Winters asked no one in particular.

"He's a monster! Kill him." Hooper slurred. "Manus escaped from the lab, attacked us then took off. No more than ten minutes ago," he managed to add.

"The old guy we captured in Mexico?"

"Yes."

"Where are the guards? I didn't see anyone out there," Winter said.

"Don't know. They didn't respond to our calls. The two mercenaries we sent out a while ago haven't come back, either. Someone must have come to help Manus. Maybe the two women who escaped yesterday. You gotta take care of this mess."

"That's why we're here," Winters replied, then went out the door and ran to where his team waited. "Those guys in there are useless. They have no idea what's going on, or who we're up against. First, we'll walk the perimeter. Joe, you and Terry take that side," he said, nodding to his left. "We'll take this side. Let's start at the gate."

Rana watched the five men go to the gate, divide into two groups, then start down the fence lines. When she described this to the others, Lena said, "What do you suggest, Max?"

"I'll leave that to you, Liebchen. I've been holed up underground and have no idea what the story is up here. But I do believe there's something very fishy about this whole setup. Schlossman, the guy who was in charge down there, is a sleazy bastard. The lab was run like a prison, and most of the science was second-rate at best. If the drunk old guy I found up top by the elevator is part of this program, that explains a lot. He must be the one Schlossman referred to as *The General*."

"That Blacker guy definitely runs an off-the-books operation," Lena added.

"For sure. And this special ops team is definitely off-the-books. Could be they're taking illegal orders from Hooper. The army wouldn't be using war tactics on behalf of a scientific project. Even a phony one. This whole operation stinks, if you ask me," Zula said.

"Be that as it may, there're five highly trained killers out there who wouldn't hesitate a second to blow us away. So, we better make a plan, and do it quickly," Lena said.

"We better do something real fast because there's a good chance those guys will find the three guards we left out there. Then we'd be up against eight, not five," José said.

"We gotta draw them away from the perimeter. That's where we left the guards," Rana said.

"That'll be easy, Zula said. I'll sneak out there, pull the pilot out and blow up the chopper. That should get their attention."

"Then what?" José asked.

"We'll rely on what's worked in the past," Max said. "Our superpower, and an age-old warfare tactics—divide and conquer, then strike fast and hard."

"So, what's the plan?" José asked.

"How about this?" Lena said. "We split them into separate groups of two or three, maybe one guy alone. Then ambush them or take them down one at a time."

"How can we split them up?" Rana asked.

Zula jumped in. "If I blow the chopper, they'll probably all come running to see what happened. When they do, some of us can be positioned in different spots around the lot. Hopefully, when they see us, and we have to make sure they do, they'll divide and come after us. We'll be waiting in ambush as the targets approach where they saw us. The dogs can help, too."

"These guys have Kevlar jackets, so we'll have to take them down with shots in their legs."

"That's better, anyway. We don't want the army after us for murder. Inflicting wounds in self-defense will be easier to justify." After a moment of silence, Lena added, "Any better ideas?" No one said anything. "All right then. That's the plan. Rana, let's see the layout of this place again."

Five minutes later, Max and his family were strategically positioned in three directions from the helicopter. While they waited, Zula crept up on the helicopter from behind, yanked open the pilot's door and pulled him out. With a pistol in his face, she tossed a delayed-action grenade inside, ran with the pilot back to the shed where she cuffed and gagged him, then tied him to a support post with the other captives. The explosion went off as she stepped out of sight around the corner of the shed to wait for the soldiers to return.

When Captain Winters heard the explosion, he looked in the direction of the helicopter and saw a giant fireball erupt with billowing black smoke rising behind. "The chopper," he screamed. "Come on!" he commanded, as he raced forward with his two men running next to him. Lieutenant Joe Arnold and Sergeant Terry Felix, near the fence on the opposite side of the property, heard Winters' command and rushed to join their comrades. When they all got to the open lot, they stopped short of getting closer to the fiery inferno and stood paralyzed with rage.

"The pilot," Felix screamed. No one said anything. They just stood staring at the flames in horror.

Then there was a sudden flurry of movement: a flash at the corner of a long shed near the burning helicopter; a man next to a small building near a pile of wooden crates; and a quick movement near a long line of huge dirt haulers.

"Captain! Did you see that?" Arnold yelled, pointing at the dirt haulers.

"There was someone by that shed over there, too," Felix said.

"By that little building, too," someone else added.

"I saw it. We're gonna take these bastards out," Winters said furiously as he checked his automatic rifle. "Joe, you and Terry take that shed. You two, that little building down there. I'll take the trucks. Let's go. No prisoners, either."

Suffice to say, the Manus clan's plan worked as smoothly as a Swiss clock, exactly the kind of operation Lena was used to carrying out. Assess the situation, make a plan, execute it with absolute precision and competence. As hard as they tried, and as good as they were, Winters and his team never had a chance against such odds—their defeat was inevitable.

Two hours later, Max and Lena were sharing coffee in the plush cabin of an Air Force transport plane with General Phillip Saunders, head of an Army research unit focused on nontraditional weapons. It was the only military group that was aware of Max's superpower discoveries, at least officially. Hooper, Blacker, and Schlossman were in custody, although specific charges had not been formulated yet, and for national security reasons, might never be. Irrespective of troublesome legalities, their futures were not all that rosy. The research staff had been liberated, and after appropriate debriefing and security arrangements, would no doubt be allowed to return to some version of their former lives. The captured and wounded combatants had been recovered and dealt with, and treatment of serious but nonfatal wounds to Zula, José, and Zeus had been given high priority. All in all, Max and Lena were satisfied with the outcome of this rescue action and anxious to put it behind them. As soon as Max made his report to the President, they would be on their way to their home in Southeast Portland and the peaceful life they craved. Lena to her rose garden, her book club and knitting projects, and to a new-found interest in painting. Max to his basement lab, his music, especially the piano lessons he planned to take, and, finally, to qualifying for fourth-degree black belt in Jiu Jitsu. Life was looking up for Max and Lena now that there were no evil villains seeking his secret superpower . . . at least not that they were aware of.

The End

Undercover Agent

Episode One

It was another mistake, like many others she'd made in her troubled life. It seemed nothing ever went right no matter how hard she tried, as if she were fated for an existence of misfortune—the orphanage, half a dozen abusive foster homes, erratic schooling, a two-year stint in prison, and now—at the age of 34—homelessness. But despite the hardships she'd faced, she was not even close to giving up her quest for a better life. An indomitable kernel of optimism miraculously persisted deep within her. Like many others in her predicament, she was a survivor. But she was more than that; she was a determined fighter as well. She knew she would eventually make a life for herself beyond just getting by on a miserly monthly disability check, panhandling for chump change, and collecting bottles and cans when she got down to her last few bucks. She sought that elusive goal every single day. Never for a moment, even in the darkest of times when others like her would have succumbed to despair, did she doubt that she would eventually reach it. Karla Hammer was determined to be an exception to the rule.

This particular screw-up occurred on a warm, midsummer, Northeast Portland morning. Karla woke to sunshine fighting its way through fully-leafed vine maples illuminating the opening of a large, concrete culvert pipe from which Karla had chased away a feral dog the evening before and in which she'd spread out her blankets. Safe in the solitude of a hideaway not yet discovered by other street people, she luxuriated in its quiet peacefulness and fantasized how the day might go. She knew what she was going to wear. She'd bought the perfect outfit at the Salvation Army store the day before— a red skirt and a bright yellow, long-sleeve blouse. Her nails were trimmed and clean and her hair was freshly cut in a short bob by her friend, Mrs. Tang, an enterprising homeless woman who could be found most Sunday mornings at the Hollywood Fred Meyer supermarket recycling station with comb and scissors and a beat-up wooden stool.

It's only 6:35. I've got plenty of time, she thought after glancing at her old Mickey Mouse watch, the only remnant of a barely remembered childhood. The poster she'd found taped to a telephone pole on 42nd Avenue advertised the need for background actors in a movie being filmed around Portland. They needed people to be in restaurant, shopping mall, and street scenes. Check-in time was nine o'clock and she'd memorized the address: 655 NE 7th Avenue. She knew the bus route to get there and planned to arrive early.

An hour later, fortified with free coffee and donated day-old donuts from the Hollywood Senior Center, Karla headed to the movie staging area where she intended to be among the first in line. It wasn't only the $75 a day that would bulk up her savings that lured her, it was the possibility, no matter how slim, there might be an opportunity for more work, a chance to escape her current life. She was a firm believer in that old adage, "Just showing up is the first step to success."

Karla got to Seventh and Holliday at 8:10 to find a three-quarters-full pay-to-park lot, but no other people. No movie-making stuff, like trailers, lights, barriers, or anything. Nothing. Confused as much as angry, she took the poster she'd ripped off the pole out of her tote bag and limped over to the guy directing newly arriving cars into parking slots. "Where's the signup place for this movie?" she asked.

Between cars entering the lot and checking for messages on his phone, the lot guy barely acknowledged the garishly-dressed woman who had a walking stick in one hand, a yellow sheet of paper in the other, and a cloth bag looped over her arm. She was holding the paper out for him to see. He looked at it for a second, then said, "You're in the wrong place, lady. The address is *northwest*, not *northeast*. See?" He pointed at the address. "If you hustle across the river you might make it. But you better hurry," he said, as he turned to collect money from a BMW driver who'd come uncomfortably close to Karla, as if she weren't even there.

"I'll take the Broadway Bridge, it'll put me close to where I need to be," Karla said over her shoulder to the attendant, as she left the lot and headed north on Seventh. Even with a bum leg she was a strong walker and made good time, especially without her shopping cart. She'd left it chained up and covered with a blue tarp at the construction site where her big culvert pipe was waiting to be buried in a few weeks.

Concentrating on getting to the movie location as fast as she could and focusing on the sidewalk with its occasional heaves and cracks, she didn't notice an SUV creeping along the curb behind her, nor did she pay attention to people walking toward or past her. But she came alive when two pistol shots went off close by and a silver-haired man in a red Reebok running suit a few paces in front of her was lifted off the sidewalk and catapulted backwards. The first thing she did was glance at the SUV. Why she did that was still a mystery to her, but, nevertheless, it's what she did. In doing so, she saw a man pointing a gun out the window. She locked onto his eyes as he locked onto hers. He shifted the pistol toward her but was unable to take a shot because the driver took off like a rocket, leaving the shot unfired and Karla alive. But the shooter knew she had seen him, and in his world that was something that would have to be taken care of—loose ends weren't tolerated.

The police arrived a few minutes later, but since Karla had no interest in getting involved and had her own priority at that moment, she didn't hang around. She kept going as if nothing happened, although she was shaken to the core, knowing the shooter would have killed her if he could have. And she'd heard enough stories about hit men to know he might try again.

When she reached Weidler Street, which was one-way heading east, she went left toward the river, due west. That way she could see cars coming toward her. She kept a lookout for the shooter's SUV as she headed toward the Broadway Bridge about a dozen blocks ahead. She wished she had the cart with her belongings so she could change into something less obvious—the red and yellow outfit was like a flag screaming for attention. The killer would be able to spot her from a mile away.

At Martin Luther King Jr Blvd, she waited in the doorway of a shop for the light to change. When she stepped off the curb into the crosswalk, she saw the killer get out of the SUV, which was idling behind a pickup in the line of traffic stopped for the red light. Her heart skipped a beat and a wave of fear shot down her spine, but a surge of adrenaline propelled her forward. She was halfway across the intersection before the killer got to the crosswalk and started after her. She immediately realized that if she kept going, he would follow until he could take his shot without attracting too much attention, then escape in the confusion. So, she did the unexpected. She spun around and ran directly at him as fast as she could. He must have been surprised because he didn't take out his pistol. Instead, he glanced at the vehicles edged up to the crosswalk waiting for the light to change. He and the crazy woman charging at him were in plain view of dozens of people.

As the killer turned back toward the woman, he heard a loud *whack* and felt an intense pain in his left ear. Then, before he could process what had happened, he felt as if his airway had been blocked and he couldn't breathe. He gagged and turned to run to where his partner waited in the line of traffic. But, tripped by the cane the woman thrust between his legs, he fell to the street. As blood gushed from his smashed ear, he struggled to catch his breath—his larynx had been partially crushed when she'd smashed the cane across his throat. He looked up from where he was lying flat on his back and saw the woman raising what looked like a sturdy, wooden walking stick, as if preparing to bring it down on him. Before he was able to get his pistol out she swung the hefty oak staff down onto his forehead with all the force she could muster. His eyes fluttered and he went limp. Karla kicked away the pistol he'd dropped, stepped back, and stood waiting for whatever would happen next.

An hour later, after the ambulance was gone, traffic was rerouted, and crime scene technicians were combing the area for evidence, Karla was sitting in Captain Tom Tabor's unmarked police car explaining what happened for the third time. He'd just received word that the killer's SUV had been spotted, based on descriptions provided by witnesses. The driver had been arrested. Tabor told Karla that the shooting victim, the man in the red running suit, was a mob informer and the shooter was a notorious killer for hire.

"Is there a reward?" Karla asked. "You wouldn't have him if it wasn't for me."

"There might be. I'll check," Tabor replied unenthusiastically.

"Look, Captain, this little sideshow screwed up my chance to be in a movie. So why don't you make use of that phone you're holding onto like a dog with a bone and find out if there *is* a reward ? I can wait."

By then Tabor was used to Karla's directness, so, instead of putting her off, he made a call to a friend in the local FBI office. After another call, this time to a higher-up, who wanted to know more about the woman responsible for the capture, he smiled and gave Karla the news. "There's a twenty-five-thousand-dollar reward. You have an appointment with the Special Agent in Charge of the Portland FBI office tomorrow afternoon. She wants to talk to you about a job.

Karla was stunned by what Tabor said—overwhelmed not only by the amount of money, but also by the possibility of a job. "A job? What kind of job? Cleaning woman, something out of gratitude? "she asked, her voice reeking cynicism.

"Not sure. Although she did say something about undercover. I think she's impressed by what you did. By the way, so am I."

"Undercover? What the hell does that mean?"

"She didn't say. I guess we'll find out tomorrow. Oh yeah—she wants me to come along too. I'll pick you up. Where do you live?"

"I live in a cement pipe at a construction site on Halsey, a little past Seventy-sixth Avenue. You can't miss it. There's a chain link fence with a Keep Out sign. Honk your horn, I'll be waiting."

Undercover Agent

Episode Two

Karla and Captain Tabor checked in at the Portland FBI office lobby desk at two o'clock on the dot and were immediately ushered to the seventh floor. "She'll be right in. Coffee?" asked the agent who led them into the simply furnished, windowless meeting room. The agent was black, goateed, and sported dreadlocks to his broad shoulders.

"Sure," Karla said.

"Help yourself," he said, nodding at the sideboard where a pump pot stood next to a plate of chocolate-chip cookies. He extended his hand toward Karla. "I'm Darrel James. The chief wanted me to meet you." Then he shook hands with Tabor and said, "I heard about your North Portland meth lab bust."

"Yeah, we were lucky," Tabor replied.

Before Tabor could say more, the door opened and a tall, middle-aged woman in a brown pantsuit entered. She was a couple of inches taller than Karla's five-nine and projected an aura of authority. She glanced at Tabor, and in a tone of voice indicating respect for a fellow law enforcement professional, said, "Captain . . ." After shaking Tabor's hand, she turned to Karla and said, "Miss Hammer, it's a pleasure to meet you. Thank you for taking the time for this visit. You've done a great service to the agency, and to the country. The man you attacked was a wanted killer responsible for scores of deaths. You're a real-life heroine. We don't get to meet many of those."

"I didn't have much choice. He was gonna kill me," Karla said, then stepped over to the sidebar and filled a mug with coffee. "Is he still alive?"

The others followed suit and then sat down at the table. Karla and Tabor were on one side, James and the chief across from them. "I'm Hanna Marx, Special Agent in Charge of this office," the chief said. "Captain Tabor filled us in on what you did. That was pretty gutsy. To answer your question, yes, he's still alive, but in a coma. You must have hit him pretty hard."

"Like I said, he was gonna shoot me. It was him or me." After a pause, she continued, "There's a reward, right?"

"Twenty-five thousand," Marx said. "You earned it. It's all yours. How do you want it?"

"Whaddya mean, 'How do I want it?' A check or money order, or cash, whatever you guys do here."

"I mean, do you want it all in one payment or paid in installments over a period of time? There will be some paperwork, as well," Marx replied.

Tabor saw that Karla was becoming anxious with how the conversation was going. He laid his hand on her arm and said, "Karla, the money is yours. Chief Marx will make sure you get it."

"That's right, "Marx said. "You'll get the money. But there's something else I'd like to discuss with you."

"About a job? Captain Tabor said something about that."

"That's right. A job."

"What kinda job?" Karla asked.

"Undercover agent," Marx replied, getting right to the point.

"What? What are you talking about? Is this some kinda trick to cheat me out of the reward?"

"Let's hear what Special Agent Marx has to say," Tabor told Karla, wanting to calm her growing anxiety.

"It has nothing to do with the reward," Marx interrupted. "We'd hire you as a consultant and pay a good fee. We need someone with street smarts to help us learn more about Portland's human trafficking gangs. Someone who wouldn't be suspected of working with law enforcement. Someone like you."

"That's the craziest thing I've ever heard. I don't know anything about that stuff. I'm just a homeless woman trying to survive from one day to the next. I just want my reward money."

Ignoring Karla's outburst, Marx opened the folder lying in front of her and began leafing through the pages. "From what I see here, you should be able to get close to people running those operations. Two years in state prison for assault. No known source of income other than a paltry disability payment. Let's see . . . broken leg and hip from when you were hit by a city bus. That explains the cane. Speaking of which, you used it pretty effectively on Baldoni yesterday. Where'd you pick up that talent? By the way, wouldn't that be classified as a weapon now that you've used it in an assault, or should I say, another assault? Could be a problem for an ex-con. Especially one who's missed meetings with their parole officer," Marx said, looking at one of the pages from Karla's file.

"Listen lady. A single woman doesn't last on the streets as long as I have without knowing how to defend herself, at least if she doesn't have a pimp. Which I don't—never have, never will. That's not my thing. And another thing—it wasn't assault; it was self-defense. So, don't try to frame me for something that's not true. And don't threaten me with missed meetings from years ago that no one gave a shit about."

"Relax, Karla. We wouldn't do anything like that," Marx said, putting the sheet of paper back in the folder and sliding the platter of cookies in Karla's direction. "So how do you get by, living on the streets? If you don't mind me asking," she continued, as if wanting to quickly change the subject.

"What's this, a social studies class? I just want to get my reward money and get the fuck outta here." Karla barked, her impatience escalating.

"Okay, okay. Take it easy. If that's what you want, no problem," Marx replied as she stood, gathered up the folder and other documents she'd brought in, and prepared to leave.

"Just give your bank account and routing numbers to Agent James and we'll get that done tomorrow."

"Wait a minute. I don't have a bank account. Can't you just gimme the cash?" Karla asked as Marx approached the door.

For a moment no one said anything. Then Special Agent in Charge Hanna Marx slowly took her hand off the handle of the door she'd been about to open, turned back to Karla and said, "It's not quite that simple, Miss Hammer."

Three hours later, Tabor and Karla were headed south on 82nd Avenue on their way back to Her culvert pipe in Northeast Portland. Tabor suddenly pulled into the parking lot of a shabby strip mall, parked in an empty spot, and said, "They've got great burritos here," pointing at a storefront with a bright red neon sign proclaiming, 'Open.' "I'm starving. How about you?"

Seated at a Formica table, with burritos, large Cokes, and an assortment of salsas, Tabor said, "Okay. How do you wanna do this? We gotta have a system. A way to communicate, for Agent James or me to know if you need to meet, or if you're in trouble."

"You're asking me? You're the cop," Karla replied, dipping her burrito into a plastic container of salsa verde. "You got me into this mess, so you better damn-well make sure I survive to collect my money in two years."

"Hey. It's up to you, too. Don't lay it all on me. You agreed to the deal. You'll come out of it with a nice bankroll and a clean record. How else would you ever get your prison time deleted from your file?"

"Yeah, sure. But only if I live. Sounds like these guys they're after are major killers. They'll turn me into dogfood if they find out I'm working for the Feds."

"That's why we gotta play it safe," Tabor replied. "A cell phone is out—a homeless woman couldn't afford one. And it would be a risk, anyway. If someone got suspicious and checked it, and discovered contacts with us, you'd be floating down the Columbia with a bullet in your head."

"So, what do you suggest? Smoke signals?"

"A drop site. Someplace we can leave messages and check it every day without arousing suspicion."

Karla was silent for a while, savoring her carne asada burrito, then said, "How about using my mailbox at the Hollywood post office annex? It's where my disability check is sent each month. I'll give you and James the combination."

"That should work. Which brings up another matter. How do you feel about James?"

"Do I have any choice?" Karla asked. "From what that Marx woman said, at least what I thought she said, you two are double-teaming me. Like some kind of joint effort, and I'm the fall guy, so to speak."

"It's not like that. Think of us as your backup. We'll give you whatever support you'd need. At least the FBI and the Portland police are working together for once. James is a straight shooter. I trust him."

"Look, Captain Tabor, I couldn't give a rat's ass for your love affair with the FBI. Or whether James gets the Man of the Year award or sings in a church choir. What I do care about are two things, and two things only. One—I get a bundle of money in two years, then you, and they, are out of my life. Two—if I run into trouble, you and Jimmy-the-Boy Scout come to my rescue. Does that compute?"

A little later, Tabor pulled up to the gate of the construction site where Karla had claimed the culvert pipe and left the shopping cart with all her worldly belongings. The site was still closed and locked up, waiting for city and county permits before actual work started.

"What the . . .?" Karla screamed. "That guy's digging through my stuff!" She opened the car door, jumped out, and ran toward the side of the lot where there was a break in the fence.

Tabor scrambled out and followed her.

"Get away from there, asshole. That's mine!" she yelled, as she ran toward the man, her cane bouncing along the hardpacked dirt.

206

The man, a scruffy young black guy in dirty jeans and a filthy sweatshirt, looked up from digging through the cart's load of clothing and other stuff. "What you gonna do, old lady, make me stop?" He laughed and continued rifling through Karla's belongings as if she weren't coming his way. The next thing he knew he was sprawled on the ground and the woman who yelled at him was standing over him holding a cane with its tip pressed hard against his chest. "Hey, back off. I thought it was abandoned. I didn't take nothing," he croaked.

At that moment, Tabor joined them and asked, "Is there a problem here?"

Karla looked at him as if she didn't know him and said, "Buzz off, Buster. This is none of your business."

Tabor, realizing his mistake of being seen with Karla, said, "Whatever! I was passing by and saw what was going on. I thought you might need some help." He turned and left without another word.

After Tabor was gone, Karla took her cane off the man's chest and said, "You're not from around here. I know everyone in Hollywood. Who are you?"

The guy sat up and rubbed the knee Karla had hit. She stepped back a pace and watched him painfully rise to his feet. Glaring at her, then nodding at the cart, he said, "There's nothing in that mess I'd want, anyway. Can I leave? Or are you gonna hit me with that thing again?"

"Where are you from?" Karla asked, ignoring his question. "You sound like you're from somewhere in Africa." From years of living on the streets and meeting all kinds of people, she'd developed a good ear for accents. "Where you been hanging out?"

"What's it to you?"

"Just curious, that's all," she replied, then remained silent for a moment, as if turning something over in her mind. "I scored a few bucks today. Wanna share a bottle?"

The man hesitated a second, then said, "Why are you so generous all of a sudden? What do you want from me?"

"Nothing, I just wanna make up for attacking you, that's all. Sometimes I get a little excited. Is your leg okay?"

He flexed his knee and grimaced, then said, "You whacked me pretty hard with that damn stick."

"Sorry. I didn't mean to do any permanent damage. I just wanted to stop you from stealing my stuff. How about something to drink while you recover?"

He started to step around her, but then hesitated, licked his dry lips, and said, "All right. Why not?"

Ten minutes later, Karla returned with a jug of cheap red wine and joined the man where he sat in the shade of an ancient maple that would be taken down soon to make room for another boxy apartment building.

"My name's Sue," she lied, after sitting down across from him. She twisted off the screw cap and handed the gallon jug to him.

He took a long pull, then sat the bottle on the bare ground in front of her. "Baku. Yeah, I'm from Africa—Nigeria. Came here with my mother when I was nine."

"Are you living on the streets?"

"When my mom died, I had no place else to go. I bounced up and down the coast for a few years. Now I'm in a homeless camp in North Portland. Been there three years."

"What are you doing in Hollywood?"

"Why the questions?"

Karla heard suspicion in his voice. She took a light swallow from the bottle and passed it back it to him, then said, "Just curious, that's all. No harm meant."

After a long pull on the jug, then another, he said, "Checking out opportunities."

"Opportunities? For what?" she asked.

"What do you care?"

"Relax. Forget I asked. But I know what you mean. Pickings around here are getting scarce—too many of our kind have moved in." She took another swallow of the wine. "In fact, I've decided to leave this area. Maybe I should try North Portland. Whaddya think?" She sat the bottle on the ground in front of him.

"Might be okay. There's space available where I am. It's in a patch of woods on the Willamette River—about a mile south of Kelly Point Park. It's not a bad spot. You'd be safe."

"I've heard the Russian mafia can be a problem in that part of town."

"Not if you stay out of their business. They won't bother you if you don't bother them."

"Are you sure about that? People say they're dangerous. That they control everything—that they want a piece of anything profitable."

"Just stay out of their business, that's all. But there are others you gotta watch out for."

"Yeah, like who?"

"Other gangs, that's all."

"How can you be so sure about that? How do you know what their business is?" she asked, pushing harder to get him to reveal his connection to a gang, if any.

He snatched up the bottle and took another deep drink, then said, "Trust me, I know."

"Okay, I believe you," she replied, the force of his statement suggesting that maybe he did have a connection.

An hour later they started off toward the Hollywood Transit Center MAX Station together. What she kept of her belongings were crammed into two scruffy packs, one on Baku's back, the other on hers. Her stout walking stick made every step a little easier.

Undercover Agent

Episode Three

It was late afternoon when Baku and Karla reached the North Portland homeless camp where Baku lived. The first thing Baku did was introduce Karla, whom he knew only as Sue, to the half-dozen inhabitants gathered around the central fire pit, talking about their day's successes—and failures. His sponsorship of Karla as a new member of the camp, and vouching for her character, would be critical for her acceptance into their community. As it turned out, his standing as a trusted member of the group carried enough weight to win her a place.

A little later, after she'd pitched her tent and stowed her meager belongings, she was back at the fire sharing stories of her life on the streets and learning what she could about her fellow campers. It didn't hurt that she'd brought along the rest of the gallon of wine left over from what she'd bought earlier for Baku. Now she was using it to help fortify her acceptance into this little village of modern gypsies.

When Karla woke the next morning, her first thought was that she had to let Captain Tabor and Agent James know about her new location. Since it would be out of the question for her to travel ten miles to the Hollywood post office annex every day to leave messages, she'd have to set up a new drop site, one that was close by. She told Baku and a few of the others that she was heading out for a day of scrounging and also wanted to check out the area. Baku told her that Rachel, one of the squatters, would hang out all day to keep an eye on everybody's stuff so she didn't have to worry about her belongings being ripped off.

Heading east along a rail spur toward North Lombard Street, she noticed a stack of moldy concrete pipes next to the tracks, not far behind a sprawling food services company that faced the street. She spotted a rusted barrel at one end of the stack and thought it might make a good drop. It was overflowing with old rubbish and scrunched up against one of the pipes. It was accessible from the company's back parking lot but not visible from the street. When she checked it out, she discovered a hollow spot under the bottom rim and knew it would be a safe place to leave messages. She made a mental note of the barrel's exact location and went on.

She caught a bus near where Lombard branched off to North Columbia Blvd. and got to Hollywood an hour later in time for a free lunch at the senior center. There was no message from Tabor or James—but she left one for them.

Karla was back in North Portland by midafternoon and spent the rest of the day walking the area's main streets, commercial centers, and neighborhoods, noting landmarks, public buildings and businesses. That was knowledge that any homeless person needed to survive without a safe home to return to after a day out in the world. As she was learning about her new environment, she couldn't help but wonder where the crime families and gangs hung out. If she was going to fulfill her bargain with the FBI, she would have to find answers to that question.

She got back to the camp a little before dark and found most of the campers were congregating around the fire. A few were helping with a community pot of stew, to which quite a few people had contributed. Karla got thumbs up and mumbled thanks when she handed a bag of over-ripe vegetables she'd purchased from the sale rack at a nearby market to the young Hispanic woman who seemed to be in charge of cooking. When she took a seat on one of the stumps circling the fire pit, she saw that Baku wasn't anywhere to be seen. After a few minutes, a girl named Gretchen sat down next to her and lit a fat joint.

When Gretchen offered her a hit, Karla said, "No thanks, I'll pass for now." Gretchen nodded, let out a long-held breath, then passed the smoldering joint to a guy sitting on her other side.

"Have you seen Baku today?" Kala asked Gretchen a little later.

"He left this morning. Said he wouldn't be back until late."

"What's he up to?" Karla asked.

Gretchen gave Karla a blank stare, then said, "What's it to you? You a cop or something?"

"Hey—no big deal. I just got him a fifth of Jim Beam. My thanks for him getting me into this place. I just wanna give it to him, that's all."

Apparently satisfied with Karla's answer, Gretchen said, "He said he had a job today. Knowing him, he'll be in a mood to celebrate when he gets back. I'm sure he'll appreciate your gift."

"I'll wait up for him, then," Karla replied.

"Whatever," Gretchen said, then stood and walked off toward a little patch of woods where a latrine had been dug.

Around midnight, Karla was about to leave the fire pit where she'd been sitting alone and go to her tent. But as she started to get up, she heard scuffling along the trail from the railroad spur. A moment later Baku appeared at the edge of flickering light from the dying fire. Karla saw that he was unsteady on his feet. When he stopped abruptly, he swayed back and forth for a few seconds before dropping down onto one of the stumps, which barely stayed upright.

"Baku! Are you okay?" Karla asked, as she got to her feet and went over to where he sat hunched with his elbows resting on his knees, staring at the glowing coals and moaning quietly.

He raised his head and looked at the person standing in front of him. After a few seconds, he focused on her face, and asked, "Sue? Is that you?"

She smelled booze on his breath. Even in the low light she could see from his slack look and glazed eyes that he was *very* drunk.

"You've got to get to bed. Come on," she said in a firm voice. He didn't argue, so she helped him stand. Together they clumsily started toward his tent. She supported herself with her cane in one hand and half-dragged-half-pushed him with her other hand tightly gripping his heavily tattooed arm.

The next morning, Karla was on her second cup of coffee when she spotted Baku crawling out of his tent, blinking at the bright sunlight. She grabbed a cup off the makeshift table next to the fire pit and filled it from a pot sitting at the edge of the glowing coals. When she sat down across from where he sat on the ground in the shade of a big oak, she said, "Here, try this."

Baku reached out with a shaky hand and accepted the offering without comment and took a drink.

"You don't look so good," Karla said. "How do you feel?"

Before Baku could answer, he leaned to the side and threw up, coughing and gagging between bouts of violent retching.

"You must have really hung on a good one," Karla said, then got to her feet and headed back to the fire pit. A few seconds later, she returned with a plastic bottle full of water. "Drink this. Then you need to sleep it off," she said, thrusting the bottle in front of him. "You'll feel better later."

With some effort, Baku unscrewed the lid and downed half of its contents. After he drank the rest, Karla helped him up, guided him to his tent, and pulled the flap aside as he crawled in. "See you later," she said, knowing full well that he either didn't hear her or, if he did, didn't care.

After Baku fell asleep, and after another cup of coffee and a couple of day-old doughnuts, Karla headed toward the railroad spur with her pack and cane. When she got to the food services company parking lot, she made sure no one was around then went over to the barrel she'd told Tabor and James about. There was a folded-up square of paper and a burner cell phone sealed inside a small baggie in the hole. She glanced around and saw there were still no people in sight, then unfolded the paper and read it.

"This drop site is OK. We'll check every morning and night. Hide the phone here for an emergency. Destroy this note."

Karla crumpled up the note and put it in her pocket, then slipped the baggie-protected phone back into the space under the barrel. *So, the game is on,* she thought, as she walked toward Lombard and another day of checking out her new neighborhood.

When Baku woke and peered out of the tent's entrance, the sun was approaching the horizon, at least the horizon as defined by the top ridge of the western hills behind downtown Portland. Its golden reflection shimmered on the rippling surface of the Willamette River, only twenty yards from the edge of the camp and flowing north toward the Columbia. The first thing that came to his mind was the wad of cash he'd been paid the night before and was now safe in his pocket. "Gotta add it to my stash," he mumbled.

Ignoring his throbbing headache, he reached into his pocket for his money. "What the hell? Where is it?" he said to himself, as if he were under interrogation. Then it came back to him with clarity greater than expected for someone who'd been as drunk as he'd been the night before. The $600 from Zakim; meeting up with two other scouts at the *Bottom's Up* strip club on 82nd Avenue; unending rounds of drinks; stories and laughing; a young girl. Then what? *Those bastards must have stolen my money. Or was it her?* he wondered to himself.

With the panic of someone who realizes how much they'd screwed up, he frantically searched his other pockets, then looked around the cluttered tent. As he was tossing his dirty clothes from one spot to another, the flap opened, and a voice asked, "Hey, Baku, you awake yet? It's time for dinner."

"They stole my money!" he cried, before he fully realized what he was saying.

He looked up to see Karla staring at him. "Baku. Take it easy. Who stole your money? What money?" Then she noticed a cell phone half-hidden by the edge of his sleeping bag.

He saw where she was looking and quickly pushed the phone out of sight.

Karla didn't mention what she'd seen. Instead, she said, "Come on. Let's get you something to eat, then I'll help you find your money."

An hour later, Karla and Baku were sitting in a red-vinyl upholstered booth in Ted's Tavern on Lombard, the last of their soggy, ketchup-covered French fries too cold to eat. "Two more beers," Karla told the waitress as she cleared away their plates.

"You gotta pay for this. I don't have any money," Baku said, when the beers were set in front of them.

"No problem," Karla replied. Then, after a long silence, "What happened last night? Who do you think ripped you off?"

Baku took a drink of his beer. After he set the glass back on the table, he said, "I'm not sure. But it was either the two guys I was drinking with, or the little hooker I ended up with later—just before I left that place. It's kinda hazy. I was pretty much out of it by then."

"How much are we talking about?" Kala asked, trying to sound concerned rather than as if she were digging for information.

Baku took another pull on his beer. "A lot. I got paid for a job."

"Did they get all of it?"

"A hundred went on a tab when we got to the club. Each of us chipped in that much for food and drinks, and for the cover charge, too."

"What did that leave you?" Karla asked, once again trying to get a handle on the amount.

"After a hundred for the whore, I should have had $400. That sweet little girl must'a took it out of my jacket pocket when I was in the toilet."

'How'd you get back to the camp?"

"Zakim gave me a ride. He saw me walking up 82nd when he drove by."

"Zakim? Who's he?"

Baku stared at Kala for a few seconds, as if deciding what to say, then said, "Nobody special. Just someone I know."

"Lucky for you he came along at the right time. It would have been a long walk."

"Yeah, it would'a been."

Karla took a sip of her beer, then said, "You wanna go to the club and see what we can find out? I'll go with you."

"Wouldn't do no good. Those two guys won't be there. And trying to chase down the hooker could be dangerous. Pimps don't take kindly to that kind of thing."

"Couldn't you complain to the club—tell them what happened?" Karla asked, still trying to get closer to Baku's mysterious money source.

"That's the dumbest thing I ever heard. The club got their $300, that's all they care about. The last thing they'd want is someone poking their noses into what they don't control. Don't even think about going there."

Karla nodded acceptance of what he said, then asked, "How about Zakim? Can he tell you how to find those two guys? What did you call em before? Scouts?"

Baku swallowed the last of his beer and slammed the glass onto the table. "Forget about that name. Don't ever bring it up again. And stay out of my business. "Then he slid off the bench and hurried toward the front door, leaving Karla more determined than ever to find out what he was up to and who Zakim was. She ripped a page from a little notebook, scribbled a short message, left a twenty for the tab, and headed to the drop site.

Undercover Agent

Episode Four

The morning after Karla left a message at the rusty barrel drop site, Captain Tabor and agent James were sitting across from each other in an out-of-the-way North Portland café. Tabor glanced at the note lying on the table between them. "Does that name Zakim ring a bell? Or Baku?"

"Zakim does. Baku doesn't," James said, after he sat his coffee cup down and moved his egg yolk-smeared plate aside.

"Zakim Olahyinka," James said. "A big guy, Nigerian. Got legal residency as a kid through Temporary Protected Status—religious persecution . . . or whatever. He came to Portland from LA five years ago, apparently to open new territory for a Nigerian trafficking gang. We watched him for a while but couldn't get anything on him. Had to pull surveillance at the beginning of this year. Word on the street is, among other things, he runs prostitutes here and in Seattle—including underage ones. If he does, he's doing it under our radar. As for the strip club Karla mentioned in that note, it's a known hooker hangout, but we've never gotten solid proof of actual buys. Those 82nd Avenue bartenders and pimps must have sixth sense. They spot our undercover vice guys every time they go near it."

"Yeah. Our vice squad knows that place," Tabor said. "But they've never nailed anybody there either. Karla says this guy Baku called himself a *scout* and she suspects Zakim paid him for a job. What do you think that's about?"

At that moment, their waitress approached with a coffee pot in one hand and a check in the other. "Refills?" She laid

217

the check on the table and then filled the cups the two men pushed closer to her.

"Thanks," James said, smiling at the waitress. Picking up the check, he looked at Tabor and said, "I'll get this. The FBI's got a bigger budget than Portland Police Bureau does."

Ignoring James's remark, Tabor asked again, "Any ideas about what Baku might be doing for Zakim?"

"Could be lots of things."

"Like what?"

"I don't know," James said. "Maybe collecting payoffs, running dope, selling dope, checking up on his girls—guys like Zakim are into all kinds of things. Sometimes they use runners like this Baku dude for odd jobs, stuff they don't want to waste time doing themselves or give to regular gang members. It's like pick-up work, once-in-a-while jobs."

Tabor took a swig of coffee, then asked, "What should we tell Karla?"

"I'd tell her to go slow, to keep an eye on Baku, but not so close he gets suspicious. Under no circumstances should she try to get close to Zakim. He's a nasty bastard. If he suspected something wasn't on the up-and-up, he wouldn't hesitate to deal with her in the worst way."

"Right. I'll leave a message for her this morning."

A few days later, at one of her best panhandling spots, Karla called it a day in the middle of the afternoon after an elegantly dressed, elderly woman put a twenty-dollar-bill into the paper cup sitting next to Karla's neatly printed cardboard sign. On her way back to the camp, she checked the drop site but waited until she was in her tent to read Tabor's note. She understood the warning about Zakim, although she'd had no intention to visit him anyway—at least not until she knew more about who he was and Baku's relationship to him. But she still bristled at the thought of Tabor, or anyone for that matter, telling her what to do—or how. This was her gig. She would play it as she saw fit. Maybe that's why she didn't check the drop site every day. As far as Baku was concerned, she believed she was the best judge of how to manage him.

With that thought in mind, she checked to see if Baku was in his tent. When she found that he wasn't there, she went to the fire pit. He wasn't there, either. But Gretchen was, talking with Rosa.

"Any idea where Baku is?" Karla asked the two women.

"You still acting like you're his mother?" Gretchen snapped.

"He hasn't been around all day," Rosa said in a friendlier manner.

"Thanks," Karla said, ignoring Gretchen's comment, then walked off toward the railroad spur leading to Lombard. She stopped at the edge of the woods and surveyed the open space extending all the way to the food services company. There was no sign of Baku or anyone else approaching. She went back to the camp and took the path to the river's edge. Again, no sign of Baku. Confident that he was nowhere near, she beelined back to his shelter, avoiding the fire pit and taking care no one saw her.

Outside Baku's tent, she once more made sure there was no one around, then unzipped the flaps and ducked in. She quickly found the phone she'd seen earlier, put it in her pocket, and left, leaving everything else as she had found it.

Back in her own tent, Karla checked Baku's calls, able to do so only because of Tabor's instructions on how to use the mobile phone hidden under the drop site barrel. There were several recent calls, incoming and outgoing, all for the same number, which was one of the three in his contact list. It was the one identified with the letter Z; the other two were F and J. She wrote all of them down on a scrap of paper, including Baku's number. She put the phone back in her pocket, hid the paper with the numbers under her bedding, grabbed the unopened bottle of Jim Beam, and went back outside.

On her way to Baku's tent to return the phone, Karla heard scrunching footfall sounds behind her on the littered path. She spun around to see who it was. It was Gretchen, her spiky, orange hair glimmering like a strobe light in the bright sunshine streaming through the treetops.

"What are you doing in this part of the camp?" Gretchen barked in a voice louder than necessary as she came close enough to Karla to be threatening.

Karla planted her feet further apart, slowly raised the hand holding the bottle of whisky, and said, "I'm gonna leave this for Baku. You gotta problem with that?"

Gretchen glanced at the cane Karla had lifted off the ground a couple of inches, took a step back, and said, "All right. Go ahead. I'm watching the camp today, just doing my job, that's all." Without further comment, she turned and headed back toward the fire pit, leaving Karla to continue her task unobserved.

Karla woke from a nap as the sun was setting and joined some of the other squatters who were already at the fire pit for the community supper—fish stew from a salmon one of the Vietnamese guys caught off Kelley Point. An hour later, and halfway through the meal, Baku appeared out of nowhere, approached the circle, and yelled, "Hey, I'm back."

"Welcome home, Bro," someone said.

"Where you been?" someone else asked.

"Working," Baku said, then set a Fred Myer plastic shopping bag on the ground and took out two jugs of red wine. "This is on me."

Between Rosa's stew, Gretchen's dope, and Baku's wine, the meal turned into a party celebrating another profitable job that allowed Baku to not only provide booze, but also contribute generously to the camp's food fund.

People started drifting back to their shelters around eleven o'clock, happy, high, and tired. By midnight, Baku and Karla were the only ones left, sitting next to each other in front of the smoldering embers of Rosa's cooking fire.

"I'm glad you had a couple of good days and made some money," Karla said. "And I'm happy to see you back here alive. I was worried, especially since you didn't say anything about leaving."

"Don't worry about me. I can take care of myself. What I do is none of your business anyway."

"I'm not being nosey. It's just that after you were ripped off at that strip club I worry. I worry about the company you're keeping, too."

"What are you talking about? You're not my mother. Keep outta my life."

"Okay, okay. Relax. No problem." After a prolonged silence, during which neither one of them made a move to leave, Karla said, "I could use some cash. Is there anything I could for your buddy, Zakim?"

"Zakim? How do you know about him?" Baku responded with alarm in his voice.

"You mentioned his name at the bar the other night, before you disappeared. I figure he's your employer. I'd like to get some work from him if I can."

"You just a dumb, crazy-ass old woman. You don't even know who he is, or what he does. There ain't nothin' you could do for him. Best you stay away from Zakim . . . and what I do for him ain't none of your business. How many times do I gotta tell you to stay outta my life?"

"Hey . . . Baku . . . I'm sorry. I didn't mean to get into something I shouldn't have. How bout we forget the whole thing? Let's sample the present I got for you. It's by the entrance to your tent. Go get it and bring it back here for a nightcap. Go on."

"What present?" Baku asked, puzzled by Karla's sudden change of direction.

"Just something to express my thanks for you getting me into this camp. Go on, get it. I'm dying to see how good it is."

Baku returned a few minutes later, holding the black-label Jim Beam out to Karla. "Here—open it."

"This is supposed to be pretty good stuff. And I know you like good whisky. It's hundred proof, twelve years old. Cost me three days panhandling. But worth every penny for what you did for me . . .. Thank you, Baku. You're a good friend, I'll never forget that."

An hour later, with half of the whisky gone, most of it drunk by Baku, Karla was ready to restart her interrogation. But when she started to ask him about his work for Zakim,

Baku leaned forward, intending to pick up the bottle sitting on the ground next to the stump he was on, and fell forward. He landed hard in the dirt.

"You okay?" Karla asked as she knelt next to him.

Baku didn't reply as she helped him sit up. He was seriously drunk. After she managed to get him into a sitting position with his back against the stump and his legs stretched out in front of him, he said, "Gimme that bottle."

"You've had enough. Drink this," Karla said, and handed him the half-full cup of water she'd been drinking from along with her sips of whisky.

Baku slapped the cup away and said, "Gimme that bottle," slurring his words and stretching toward the Jim Beam just beyond his reach.

Karla hesitated a moment, then picked up the bottle, but held it in her lap. Baku stared at it for a second, then stuck out his hand, as if about to receive a gift. Looking directly into his heavily lidded eyes, she said, "Tell me about Zakim. What do you do for him?"

"Wha . . . what?" Baku stammered, with a look of confusion spreading across his face.

"I need money, Baku," Karla said with a level of firmness he couldn't ignore, even in his near-stupor state. "I gotta have an operation and need to pay a big part of the cost. No way I can raise enough by begging on corners or with the shop-lifting gang of street kids I run. I wanna work for Zakim, like you do."

Baku lunged for the bottle, but Karla pulled it back and gently deflected his hand. "Gimme that," he blurted out again.

"Tell me about Zakim," Karla replied, then moved the bottle a little closer to Baku's outstretched hand.

Baku's eyes darted around the area, as if checking to see if there was anyone else nearby. "What do you mean running shoplifting kids?" he asked.

"How'd you think I get money to spend on high-end booze like this? It ain't from panhandling. She held the bottle in front of his face, then pulled it back down to her lap. "Tell me about Zakim!"

Karla's jarring demand, and learning about her claimed gang of thieves, was enough to break through Baku's resistance. "He's my boss."

"What do you do for him?"

"Jobs."

"Come on, Baku. You can trust me." Karla handed him the bottle and he took a mouthful. He started to take another, but Karla grabbed it away, then asked, "What kind of jobs?"

He looked into her eyes for a second, then mumbled, "I find girls for him."

"Oh my god," Karla said as she rose to her feet and moved a few paces away. She suddenly turned and said, "Are you telling me that you find young girls who Zakim kidnaps?" The look on her face expressed the horror she felt at what Baku had told her. "How could you do something like that? "What happens to the girls?"

"I don't know—ain't none of my business. They're homeless kids, nobody cares about 'em."

"Don't you realize what that does to them? That their lives are destroyed?"

"Don't know nothin' 'bout that. Ain't none of my business. Anyway, he sells most of 'em to somebody else." His eyes were losing focus.

"How much does he pay you?" she asked, stepping closer and speaking louder.

"I get a hundred each," he managed to say, looking up at her.

"Is that what you were doing in Seattle?"

"Yeah. I found eleven. There's more homeless kids up there than here." Baku leaned forward and stared at the empty bottle lying in the dirt. "I gotta sleep," he said after a moment, then tried to stand. Karla grabbed his arm when he started to fall to one side.

"Come on. I'll help you to your tent," she said as she led him away from the fire pit.

After Karla got Baku through the flaps and on top of his sleeping bag, she felt around in the dark until she located his phone. She slipped it into her pocket and silently went back

223

outside, already thinking about what she would say to Zakim when she called him the following morning.

Undercover Agent

Episode Five

The night's unrelenting rain left the homeless encampment's fire pit soggy and its ground mired in mud, but it didn't deter the two dozen-plus squatters from starting their day like any other. A guy named Ricardo managed to get a fire going and Rosa made a pot of coffee. Some of the campers headed out to look for day work, to panhandle, or to go to one of the shelters where they could get a free breakfast. Others gathered around the fire and warmed or cooked whatever they'd scrounged the day before or found in the camp's common larder.

Groggy from a sleepless night, Karla sat with the others, drinking coffee and eating one of the over-ripe oranges a neighborhood market had donated earlier in the week. She noticed that Baku wasn't anywhere to be seen and assumed he must still be asleep. She figured he would sleep late because of his heavy drinking the night before. She needed to sneak his phone back into his tent before he woke, but not until after she called Zakim. The likelihood of Zakim taking a call was good if it came from Baku's phone. But it was still early, so she wanted to wait a while before she tried. She'd hidden the phone in her tent, not wanting to risk its discovery from the sound of an incoming call when she was at the firepit.

It wasn't only the rain that had kept Karla awake most of the night—it was also thinking about what she would say to Zakim. Learning from Baku about Zakim's trafficking in homeless girls made her even more determined to help take Zakim down. Forcing grown women into the sex trade was

225

bad enough, but it was another thing altogether to be stealing young kids off the streets and ruining their lives. She had to do something. Something more than just telling Tabor and James. What could they do without proof? Nothing! As she saw it, her job was to get that proof. After all, she was being paid as an undercover agent. It was time to start earning her wages.

While Karla was drinking her coffee and thinking about the call to Zakim, Captain Tabor was sitting in his unmarked car on the far side of the food services company parking lot talking to Agent James on his phone.

"No message this morning. I'll check again tonight," Tabor said in response to James's question.

"Think she'd do something stupid?" James asked.

"Like what?"

"Like lean on Baku too much. Or try to get close to Zakim. That's what."

"She seems to be doing okay with Baku. As far as Zakim goes, I don't think she'd take that risk."

"Oh yeah?" James said. "You wouldn't have expected her to attack a mafia hit man with nothing but a cane, either."

"That was different. She didn't have a choice. He was gonna kill her."

"I hope you're right," James replied. "Let me know when you get another message."

After the phone went dead, Tabor sat for a few minutes, wondering why James was so concerned about such an unlikely event as Karla hooking up with Zakim. Shrugging, he pulled out of the lot and headed back to precinct headquarters.

Meanwhile, in a windowless room at the rear of the J & L Transport truck depot in a rundown neighborhood on the southeast edge of Portland, Zakim Olahyinka was frowning at his phone. He'd punched in Baku's number, but there was no answer. "Where's that little son-of-a-bitch at? He ain't answering." He ended the call and looked at the man sitting across the table from him, Jack Severs, his guy in charge of getting the girls to where they were needed. "After you put

Jamal and Frank to work, go see what's up with Baku. We gotta have two more girls tonight to make up for the two from Seattle who got sick. They ain't doin' so good."

"The truck's gotta leave at midnight to make the noon transfer in Redding tomorrow," Jack replied.

"I know that," Zakim said angrily. "That's why I want all three of them scouts out there today. Stay on top of this, Jack. I don't want this order messed up. There's a lot riding on it."

As soon as Jack left, Zakim dialed another number. "We might have a problem with tonight's delivery," he stated without apology. He listened for a few moments, then said, "Yeah, I'll let you know," then ended the call.

As Karla was crawling into her tent she was surprised when Baku's phone started buzzing and quickly retrieved it from under her sleeping bag. The number on the screen was the same one she'd seen when she checked his calls the day before—Zakim's. "Damn," she mumbled. "Now what?" She didn't answer the call and put the phone in her jacket pocket.

"Don't do anything stupid," she said to herself as she headed toward the drop site. "I better talk to Tabor." But before she got to the edge of the woods, she decided to check on Baku first, to see if he was still asleep. She back-tracked to his tent, noting there was no one around to see her. Carefully moving the flaps aside and peeping inside, she saw he was still sleeping. *I've got time to figure this out,* she thought. *I'll slip the phone back in his tent, then leave a message at the drop site for Tabor. He'll help me decide what to do about Zakim.*

She took the phone out of her pocket and pulled the flaps further apart. But when she started to put the phone inside, it buzzed again. Without thinking, she jumped up, still holding the phone, and moved far enough away to not wake Baku. She looked at the number displayed in the window—Zakim again. Against her better judgement, she answered it, as if she'd been both compelled and waiting for this opportunity.

"Yes?" she said in a flat voice.

"Who is this?" a deep voice said after a slight delay.

"Hello, Zakim," Karla answered.

"Who are you?" Where's Baku?"

"Baku's okay. Right now, he's asleep. I'm a friend of his. My name's Sue.

"What the hell's goin' on? What are you doin' with his phone?"

Then an idea that had been bouncing around in her subconscious mind suddenly surfaced. "I've got something to offer you that will help your business. But . . . it'll cost you."

From the ensuing silence, Karla sensed the confusion Zakim must have been feeling. An unknown woman on the other end of one of his scout's phone was making an offer that made no sense. Someone who apparently knew what he was into. "Whoever you are, bitch, you're as good as dead if you ain't on the up and up."

"Meet me at Ted's Tavern on Lombard at noon, then you can judge for yourself." She cut off the call, went over to Baku's tent and yelled, "Hey, Sleeping Beauty. Time to rise and shine." Before Baku fully woke, she tossed the phone in without him noticing, then rose to her feet and walked off toward the fire pit. Her cane kicked up wet debris as she went. "There's still some coffee left," she yelled over her shoulder. "You better hurry. It won't last forever."

At a quarter to twelve, Karla was sitting alone in one of the booths across the room from half a dozen patrons scattered along the bar. A Grateful Dead song drowned out what little conversation there was, and a strong odor of stale beer permeated the thick air. A little after noon, when Karla was on her second cup of coffee, two men she'd not seen before entered. They stood near the door peering around the room. The tall, lanky one—black like ebony, bald, and with a jagged scar down one cheek—halted his search when he saw Karla. After she nodded, he motioned his companion, a burly, bearded white guy, to stay by the door. He looked around the room once more, then walked over to her table and slid onto the seat across from her.

His eyes, the color of dark night, bored into hers. "This better be good . . . Sue," he said coolly. There was an unmistakable undercurrent of threat in his calmness. "It would be a shame if you had to take a ride with my friend over there. He hates women. Something about what his mother did to him. Something he never got over."

Assuming it was him, she said, "Zakim, you don't have to threaten me. You'll like what I have to say." Her eyes fixed on his, unwavering, unblinking. She kept her trembling hands under the table.

Zakim held her gaze for a few seconds, glanced down at his over-sized hands folded on the table in front of him, then sat back against the vinyl upholstery. After a brief silence he leaned forward again, placed his hands palms down on the scarred surface, looked her in the eyes and said, "All right, Sue. What you got to say that's so important?"

"The FBI's out to get you and wants me to help them do it. They're paying me to go undercover, get close to your operation, to learn about your business.

Zakim's eyes widened, but he held her gaze. After a few seconds, he said, "You got a reason I shouldn't kill you?"

"I want to work for *you*," Karla said without hesitation. "They're forcing me to do this because of my record. And they're paying me, but it's next to nothing. For ten times what they're giving me, I'll be your eyes and ears—half a million over two years—twenty thousand a month into a Swiss account."

"You're either totally crazy or absolutely desperate for money to come to me with this bullshit. But I got to admit, you got guts." He turned toward the man still near the door and signaled him over to the booth. When he arrived, Zakim said, "Benny, take this dumb bitch for a ride and make it one way."

"Wait!" Karla said. "I go missing, they'll be on you like snakes on a rat. Hear me out."

Zakim motioned his thug to back away, then said. "You got two minutes."

"I can let you know their plans, what they know about you, if they're gonna make a move on you. I'll protect you by keeping you informed."

"How do I know you won't play both sides? That you wouldn't turn me in the first chance you get?"

"I figure you got a long reach. If I double crossed you, I'd be dead before I knew it. Like I said, I need money. Living on the streets doesn't provide opportunities to build much of a nest egg."

Zakim sent Benny back to the front door and waved the bartender to the table. "You got anything to eat here?" he asked.

"Burgers and fries."

"You want something?" he asked Karla.

"That sounds good," she said.

"Make it two. And two IPAs," he told the bartender, then turned back to Karla. "I'll kill your ass if you screw up my business. And if I can't, someone else will. If you do hook up with me, there'll be no way out. Once you're in, you're in to stay. You good with that?"

"No! I'm not good with that. The FBI's giving me a two-year deal. If I play their game, I'll get my record cleared and 50 K. I'll give you the same time. Then take the half million and disappear—Mexico or Costa Rica. Someplace warm and far away. That's all I want."

Before Zakim could answer, the bartender sat the beers on the table without saying anything, then went back to the bar.

Zakim took a long pull, then said, "Are those FBI guys watching you? Do they know you're here right now?"

"No. I'm sure they aren't following me. I've been checking. We communicate by messages at a drop site."

"Where's that?"

"Near the camp where I'm staying. The one Baku's at.

"You got a phone?"

"No."

Zakim took another drink, then asked, "How you gonna let me know if something's goin' down? What they're up to?"

Karla was silent for a while, then said, "I don't want a phone. They leave a trail. I'll go through Baku. Or else I'll use his phone. You'll have to tell him to let me."

The burgers arrived and the two of them ate in silence, as if they were digesting the possible consequences of their conversation as much as they were the overcooked meat and greasy fries.

After Zakim pushed aside his half-eaten burger and wiped his mouth, he said, "All right. I'm gonna give you a month to prove your value. If you show you're worth it, we'll go ahead with the deal. If not, you'll be taking that ride with Benny."

Karla shook her head and said, "That's not enough time. I need more to get their confidence. To learn about how they operate and what they got planned. At least three months."

"Two," Zakim replied with finality. Then, without saying anything else, he threw some bills on the table, slid out of the booth, and left through the front door. Benny, close behind his boss, glanced briefly at Karla as the door swung shut, returning the room to its cheerless gloom.

Undercover Agent

Episode Six

Karla was still sitting in the booth at Ted's Tavern, thinking about the arrangement Zakim dictated to her before he'd left a few minutes earlier. She had two months to prove her value as his spy on the FBI. Meanwhile, a few miles away, Special Agent in Charge, Hanna Marx, entered an FBI headquarters conference room with a frown on her face and a growl in her voice. "What's the status with the Hammer woman?"

Agent James stood and faced his boss. "She's moved to a camp where one of Zakim's men lives—a guy named Baku." "She appears to be gaining his confidence. We've set up a drop site and Tabor's keeping in touch with her. Now all we can do is wait and see what she learns."

Remaining by the door, making no move to take a seat, Marx said, "I'm getting questions from headquarters about the wisdom of using a homeless woman as an informant. Especially one with a background like hers. The cost may be a problem, too. I need something to show, soon. Do what you can to hurry things along."

"That could be dangerous," James said, uncomfortable with the direction Marx was taking.

"This isn't the Girl Scouts she's joined. See what she can do." Marx turned and left as abruptly as she'd entered, leaving James to contemplate the risks of stirring the pot too vigorously.

232

When Tabor checked the drop site a few days later there was no message from Karla, the third time in that many days. Looking around to make sure he hadn't been noticed by anyone, he returned to his car. Slumped low in his seat, he called James.

"What's up?" James asked.

"No message again. Maybe she's in trouble."

"Maybe. Whaddya think we should do?"

"The only thing we can do. Wait and see what happens. I'm sure as hell not gonna march into the camp and look for her . . . hold on . . . a woman's heading toward the barrel . . . it's her. I'll call you back."

Tabor eased out of his car and glanced around to make sure no one else was in sight. He walked across the parking lot, then along the rail track and caught up with Karla.

"We gotta talk," Tabor said as he came up behind her.

Karla spun around, her cane raised and ready to strike. "Captain!" She said. "What are you doing here? We can't be seen together," she added, glancing toward the woods where the camp was set up.

"There's no one around. Come on. My car's over there," Tabor said, nodding toward the parking lot.

Ten minutes later, they were sitting in Tabor's unmarked car on a quiet side street a mile away.

"It's been a week since we've heard from you. We were concerned," Tabor said.

"I'm doin' fine. Don't worry."

"All right. Any progress on getting a line on Zakim?"

"I'll let you know when I do."

"What about Baku? You any closer to him?"

"I'm workin' on it," Karla said, her irritation at Tabor's questions evident in the sharpness of her reply.

Sensing her growing discomfort, Tabor said, "Look, Karla. James is feeling pressure from Marx to show progress. The higher ups don't like the fact that the FBI's paying out this much money, either. You gotta give us something—something to keep the wolves away."

Karla took her hand off the door handle she was about to use to leave and turned to face Tabor. After a pause, she said, "I wasn't gonna tell you this yet, but I met Zakim a couple of days ago."

"What?" Tabor blurted out, "Whaddya mean you weren't gonna tell me? Are you nuts? What the hell's goin' on with you?"

"Take it easy. It's under control. I told him I run a gang of punks—shoplifting, a little burglary, stuff like that. That I know how to handle street kids. How I could help him. That I wanted to work for him. A line of bullshit, that's all."

"Oh. Is that all? How'd you get to him, anyway?"

"Through Baku. I used his phone."

"Jesus, Karla. You're in way over your head. You're playing with fire, and you're gonna get burned if you don't cut and run."

"I can handle it. Like I said, don't worry."

Tabor sat staring through the windscreen for a while, then said, "What'd he say . . . when you offered to work for him?"

"He'll give me a try. Two months to prove myself."

"How the hell you gonna do that?"

"I'll go with Baku the next time he has to collect street kids. I'll see what happens. I'll come up with something."

Tabor shook his head and said, "That won't do it. He's got guys like Baku to find and snatch homeless girls. You'll have to do more that. You're setting yourself up for a bad fall."

Karla was silent for a while, then, avoiding his gaze and looking out the front window, she said, "I also told him I was working with the Feds and that I could let him know about their operations. I'll have to give him something."

Tabor was stunned by what she said. "What? Are you insane?" he yelled and slammed his fists against the steering wheel. "God damn it, Karla. This guy's a ruthless, sadistic killer. He'll crush you like a bug if you don't give him some juicy FBI secrets. What were you thinking?"

Turning back to face Tabor, she said, "I was thinking I gotta do whatever it takes to get inside his organization—

that's what I was thinking. You know, like what Marx is paying me to do. I was also thinking we would be able to come up with something that would satisfy him but not compromise what you guys are doing. At least, not all that much."

"That's a tall order. You should have worked this out with us before your leapt into a hot frying pan."

"Yeah? Well I didn't, did I? Didn't have that luxury. But now it's done, so you better get a grip and start thinking about a plan. Right now, I'm going back to the camp, find Baku, and convince him to take me along on his next raid."

Dumbfounded by Karla's revelation, Tabor couldn't think of anything to say as he watched her climb out of the car and head toward the river. Her cane clacked loudly as she disappeared into the deep shade of the tree-lined sidewalk.

Karla found Baku by the Willamette River where a path from the camp ended in a small, grassy clearing. She sat down next to him without saying anything.

"What's up?" he asked, continuing to stare at the water. After a long silence, he said, "Zakim called. Said you're working for us now. That I should show you what we do. That you gonna help with the girls." After another long pause, he said, "What the fuck you up to?"

"Money, Baku. That's what I'm up to. Money to live by. Same as you."

"You think you can just push your way into my gang and do your share?"

"With your help, yeah, I think I can. And will."

"What I do is serious. Sometimes things get nasty. Don't always go easy. Sometimes me and my bros gotta get rough with them bitches. You up for that?"

"I nearly killed a man, didn't I? Have you? And my time in prison wasn't a tea party. I wouldn't still be alive after living most of my life on the streets if I hadn't been able to kick ass when I needed to. Don't underestimate what I'd do if I had to."

Baku looked at her for a moment, then said, "All right. I hope you're what you say you are cause we got a job to do, tomorrow."

"What kind of job?" Karla asked, wondering to herself if she really would be up to helping Baku and his pals kidnap innocent girls who would be forced into sexual slavery.

"The kind I always do. Snatching girls off the street. A delivery's set for Friday night. We got three days to round up at least a dozen, more than that if we can."

"Here in Portland?"

"Wherever we find them. From Vancouver to Salem. As fast as homeless and runaway kids are coming here, won't be no problem. It's finding the best ones that's hard—right age, healthy, decent looking, alone or in pairs."

"What age?" Karla asked, afraid of what the answer might be.

"Young, but not too young. The people Zakim supplies wants 'em between twelve and eighteen. Older than that, they mostly come from Europe and Africa. That ain't our business. Ours is kids."

"What do we do when we find them?" Karla asked, feeling sickened by the thought of what she was getting into.

"First, we spot ones who'd be good to take. Gotta remember where they are. That night, me, Frank, and Jamal, and now you, will make a drive-by snatch with the van. We gag and tie 'em up. After we collect as many as we can, we take 'em to a house, or some other building, where they're kept till either one of Zakim's guys takes 'em or they get picked up by somebody else. When they're put in a shipping container or truck, our part's done. We collect our money and say good night."

Karla fought to keep her voice under control. "Where will we take them?"

"We'll find out tomorrow night. It's different every time. Zakim don't take no chances."

"What's our plan for tomorrow?"

"You and me'll scope out the inner east side and any Max stops we can fit in. Frank and Jamal will hunt camps and other neighborhoods around the city. Tomorrow night we'll make the snatches. Then the next two days, same thing, different locations. You better get a good night sleep cause there won't be much chance for it the next couple days." Baku got to his feet and started toward the camp. "Dinner time. You comin'?"

A little after 3 a.m. that night, a lone woman with a cane made her way carefully across a weed-filled, dirt lot toward a rusty barrel. Once there, she knelt next to it and placed a Ziploc baggie in a hollowed-out space underneath. She stood, looked around, then returned to the wooded area harboring one of many makeshift camps sheltering Portland's homeless.

"She must have left this note late last night. It wasn't there when I checked yesterday around seven," Captain Tabor said to Agent James, who sat across the table from him.

"What's it say?" James asked after he put down his coffee.

Tabor looked around to make sure no one was within hearing distance, then read the note out loud. "Baku, two others, and me will kidnap some girls tomorrow night, and the next two nights as well. They'll be taken away Friday night. Don't know where they will be held. Maybe I can find out tomorrow and let you know. You have to rescue these girls without suspicion put on me."

"Jesus, Tabor. You said she wouldn't do anything crazy," James said. "You were sure as hell wrong about that. This is definitely crazy. How can we rescue a bunch of girls when we don't know where they'll be, how many there are, or who we'll be up against? And if that weren't bad enough, it can't look like we got a heads-up from Karla. This woman's out of control. If you don't . . ."

"Hold on! Okay. You're right. It's a tough situation. But we gotta deal with it."

At that moment, the waitress came to their table and refilled their cups, then asked, "Have you decided what you want?'

After she took their orders and left, James said, "Okay. There's a couple possibilities we could consider."

The two men sat talking and drinking coffee for the rest of the morning, ignoring the waitress's gentle hints to vacate their spot as the lunch crowd started filling up the place.

Tuesday morning dawned to a cloudless sky and gentle breeze. The familiar fragrance of the Willamette spiced the morning air that brought life to the camp. The smell of Rosa's fresh brew gave it a perfect edge.

"You ready?" Baku said at the entrance to Karla's tent, just loud enough to be heard.

"Be right out," Karla answered. "I'll meet you at the fire pit. I need coffee."

An hour later, the two mismatched Zakim foot soldiers were on a MAX train heading toward Southeast Portland. They were going to comb the inner industrial area for likely targets. The permissive attitude of Portland's civic leaders toward the homeless, coupled with a scarcity of affordable housing and increases in broken families, opened the flood gates to an influx of people of all ages seeking better opportunities, or perhaps just a safe place to sleep. Included in this seemingly unending influx were lots of young girls and women—plenty of targets for Baku and his gang.

Forty minutes, two transfers, and a short walk landed Baku and Karla in a maze of narrow streets, littered sidewalks, an assortment of bridges and highway ramps, dimly lit underpasses, and a confusion of abandoned and newly constructed buildings. Some of the people living on the streets in this area were in camps. Some were in pairs or small groups, some alone. Living conditions of the homeless ranged from camps like the one in North Portland where Baku and Karla were staying, to jerry-rigged structures of tarps, cardboard and scrap wood erected on sidewalks, empty lots, and along the sides of major roads. Some were nothing more than a sleeping bag or an odd assortment of worn and dirty blankets thrown down wherever there was a dry, empty space.

Walking every street, block by block, Baku spotted a dozen women or young girls who met his criteria for grabbing that night. Karla made a note about each one: what they looked like, their location, other people nearby, any information that could be used to make a clean snatch and safe getaway. When they returned to the Lloyd Center transfer point, they spent another hour traipsing around that area and identified several more candidates. They got back on the Max Yellow Line and to the camp in time for Rosa's stew and the opportunity to share with their fellow campers the gallon of red wine they'd bought along the way.

Karla had just nodded off when Baku shook her shoulder and whispered in her ear, "It's time. We gotta go." She opened her eyes to see him standing near the glowing embers of Rosa's fire while slipping on his backpack.

She grabbed her shoulder bag and cane, then said, "I'm ready."

Baku looked around, then in a low voice said, "Jamal and Frank's in the van. They're parked on Lombard. Come on."

Karla followed Baku as they quietly went past darkened tents and silent sleepers toward she knew not what, excited and scared at the same time.

Undercover Agent

Episode Seven

In the pitch dark of night, two mismatched figures hurried quietly along a dirt path paralleling an abandoned rail track that served a booming wartime manufacturing site decades earlier. The taller one, a wiry black man in his mid-twenties, was earnestly giving instructions to his companion, a white woman in her thirties who was struggling to keep up with his fast pace. Years of relying on her battered oak cane allowed her to keep her limp at a minimum and match the man's stride, although it took considerable effort.

"You'll stay in the van and cuff 'em when me and Frank take 'em in. Tape their mouth and eyes, then their legs. We'll hold 'em down for you, but you gotta do it fast. Can you do that?

"Don't worry, I'll do it. But why so fast?" Karla asked, suspecting she already knew the answer.

"Less chance of being spotted—and identified."

They walked on in silence

"There's the van," Baku said a minute later, pointing to a dark form half-hidden under a sprawling oak tree at the far side of an expansive parking lot belonging to the food services company.

One of the two men standing beside a late-model, windowless, dirty green Ford van greeted Baku in a low voice as he and Karla approached. "You're late."

Baku glanced at his phone. "Cool it, Frank. Five minutes ain't gonna kill us." He nodded at Karla. "This is Sue."

Pointing at a big black guy, he said, "That's Jamal." He turned to a white guy. "That's Frank."

Jamal said, "How's a crippled woman gonna do what's gotta be done?"

"Couple months ago, she beat a man half to death with that stick she's got there. She'll be all right," Baku said, unable to suppress a tinge of pride in his voice, or perhaps just unaware of it.

"She better be all right. If she ain't, that little stick ain't gonna do her no good," Jamal said, giving his head a flip so his long dreads swung around.

Knowing she needed to diffuse the situation, Karla took a step toward Jamal and stuck out her hand. "Glad to meet you, Jamal. Baku's said good things about you."

Jamal glanced at Baku, then reluctantly stepped forward and shook her hand, careful not to crush it with his powerful grip.

Frank watched in silence as Karla deftly brought Jamal to heel, then spat out, "Cut the shit, lady. We gotta get this show on the road." He slid the side door open and said, "You and me'll be in there. Baku's up front with Jamal, who's driving. When they spot a target and pull over, I'll jump out and help Baku grab her. When we get her in, you gotta be ready to do your part. There's plastic cuffs and duct tape in that box." He pointed at a wooden crate secured to the back of the passenger seat. "All right. Everybody ready?"

A moment later they were on their way.

Frank and Karla sat on the bare metal floor cater-corner from each other, legs stretched out in front of them. Although the interior was dimly lit, Karla was able to get a closer look at her partner. He appeared to be in his forties, had close-cropped blondish hair and was clean-shaven. Although a little shorter than she was, he was muscular like a weightlifter, and was heavily tattooed, including numbers and symbols at various places on his neck. He had the cruel eyes and cold look of a hardened criminal without limits to what he might do. In contrast to Jamal, whom she saw as a big teddy bear trying to be tough, this man frightened her. And Karla was not easily frightened.

Up front, in the passenger seat, Baku scrolled through entries in his phone from the day before while Jamal drove east on Lombard, taking care to stay under the speed limit. "Take MLK to the Lloyd District," Baku said. There's two that looked good on Eighth, just north of Clackamas Street."

Twenty minutes later, Jamal turned north on Eighth, pulled over to the curb, and doused the lights. "It's that blue-tarp shelter up there," Baku said, looking at a lone camp site in the dim shadows of a large tree halfway up the block. "Stay here. I'll check it out." He eased the door open and stepped onto the sidewalk.

"Get ready," Frank told Karla. "There'll be two of 'em if it happens."

Karla got two FlexiCuffs and a roll of tape from the crate and laid them next to her. Frank noticed her hands were shaking. "You gonna be able to do this?" he barked more as a challenge than a question.

"I'll do it," was all she said, holding his gaze until he looked away.

Then, a little less aggressively, he said, "Put pieces of tape on that." He nodded at a metal rod spanning two struts on the bare sidewall, "For their eyes and mouth."

She quickly did what he told her—four six-inch lengths of grey duct tape were then ready to be grabbed.

"Tear off the piece for their wrists after you wrap their ankles. Jamal will help hold 'em while you do it. You gotta be fast."

Karla nodded. "Yeah, I know."

A moment later, Baku eased open the door. "They're inside their tent, and there's nobody else around." He glanced up and down the street, then climbed back into his seat. He pulled the door shut but didn't let it latch. "Let's do it. Get your masks on."

Frank pulled on a black ski mask, then silently slid the side door open and got ready to jump out. Karla found a mask in the crate and put it on.

Jamal eased the van slowly up the street, lights off and keeping engine noise as low as possible.

When Jamal stopped next to the shelter, Baku and Frank rushed to the makeshift tent and ripped away the tarps. At the same time, Jamal shifted to park, stepped between the front bucket seats, and knelt next to Karla. "Get ready," he said, then glanced at the tape pieces hanging next to her. She took a piece and held it by its two ends. Her hands were no longer shaking.

The two girls woke to being jerked upright by someone yanking them by their hair and clamping strong hands over their mouths before they had a chance to cry out or speak a single word. Before they understood what was happening, they were being held down on a cold, metal floor. Tape was being stretched across their mouths, then their eyes. Attempts to scream and struggle were useless. They couldn't move their legs, then felt tight binding looping around their ankles. Someone roughly turned them face down and their hands were tightly taped together behind them. It hurt, and all they could do was whimper and roll their heads side to side, but it did no good. They were helpless, had no idea why this was happening and were overcome with fear.

In less than a minute, Jamal was back at the wheel, the doors were closed, and the van was moving ahead, not too fast, not attracting attention as it turned left on Broadway and headed to the next target on Baku's list.

It was a little after five a.m. when Baku told Jamal to head out to Fairview, a Portland suburb ten miles east along the Columbia River. Half an hour later, they arrived at a wooded, two-acre lot at the end of a dirt road off Sandy Boulevard. Jamal pulled up next to a double-wide, trashed-out mobile home and cut the engine. Baku got out and opened the side door of the van. "Let's get 'em inside."

As Baku was drifting off to sleep in his tent in the predawn hours, his phone buzzed. It was Zakim. "How'd it go?"

"Good. There's eight of 'em in the trailer."

"We need at least twenty. More if you can find 'em."

"Yeah. I know. We're going out again tonight—gonna get the ones Frank and Jamal spotted yesterday. Me and Sue gonna scout up some this afternoon, too."

"How'd she do?" Zakim asked.

"She did good. She'll be able to replace Max. Having four makes everything go better."

"All right. Guess I'll keep her around a little longer. But watch her close. There's something funny about her."

"Don't worry, I will."

An hour after she got back to her tent, Karla felt it would be safe to sneak out to the drop site while it was still dark. On her way out of the camp, she stopped by Baku's tent to make sure he was asleep. Light snoring from inside told her he was. Ten minutes later she slipped a plastic baggie with a note in it under the barrel, then hurried back to the camp. She was in serious need of sleep, knowing another long day awaited her.

"What's it say?" Agent James asked Tabor, who sat across the table in the restaurant holding the note from Karla he'd retrieved from the barrel drop site that morning.

> *Eight girls abducted tonight and kept in a trailer near the Columbia. I think it's east of town. But I don't know where. Will get more girls in the next two days. They'll be taken away at night the day after tomorrow. Do something.*

"We gotta get a fix on that trailer," James said.

"How we gonna do that? We don't even know what vehicle they're in, so we can't follow them."

James thought for a moment, then said, "We'll give her a location device to hide in the vehicle they're using. We'd know where they are every minute. I'll get one and meet you at the parking lot in an hour. You can leave it for her at the

244

barrel." James got up and hurried out the door, leaving the tab for Tabor, who this time didn't mind at all.

At twelve noon, Baku, Karla, Frank, and Jamal were sitting at a corner table in the Burrito King on Lombard waiting for their orders to come up. "Me and Sue gonna check out Northeast," Baku said to the others. "You two see what you can find along Route 30 toward Scappoose. Check along the river. We'll meet tonight at the same place. At midnight."

"What about the girls at the trailer?" Karla asked.

"Whaddya mean?" Frank replied. "They'll be there until they're gone. Whaddya expect, maid service?"

Karla turned to face Frank and said, "I expect humane treatment of those girls, that's what I expect. Water, blankets, loosening their cuffs. You got a problem with that?

Frank was caught off guard by Karla's sudden eruption, but quickly recovered and said, "We ain't running a girl's finishing school. They ain't gonna die in a couple a days. They'll be gone Friday night. So, get off your high horse and leave it alone. It's none of your damn business, anyway."

Karla knew this was a critical point in her relationship with this little band of lowlifes. Without a moment's hesitation, she plunged ahead. "Call Zakim. I wanna talk to him. Now!"

Baku was taken aback by her sudden demand. "What the hell you talking about? This ain't none of your concern. I ain't calling him just because you say so."

"Do it!" she said, slapping her hand down on the table.

Unable to tolerate anymore of Karla's outrageous behavior, Frank drew back his arm and uncoiled a swing at her face. But before he connected, Jamal, in a lightning-fast move, grabbed his wrist and twisted it backwards almost to the breaking point.

Frank suppressed a scream and groaned, "Okay. Let go."

Karla nodded at Jamal, who released his grip but didn't take his eyes off Frank. Ignoring Frank, she turned to Baku and said, "Call him!"

The intensity of her command, Frank's sudden blowup, and Jamal's quick action to protect her, shocked all of them. After a prolonged silence, Baku reluctantly said, "All right, but don't expect him to be happy about it."

"What?" Zakim answered when Baku called. "This better be important."

"Sue said she gotta to talk to you," Baku said and handed his phone to Karla without waiting to hear what Zakim would say.

"What's going on? What you want?" Zakim said angrily after Karla said hello.

"We gotta take better care of those girls," Karla said, charging ahead and ignoring Zakim's questions. "Leaving them tied and taped is torture, and it decreases their value. We'll get more for them if they're in better shape.

Surprised at Karla's boldness, but unable to ignore her reference to money, he held back the threat he had intended to make. Instead, after a slight pause, he said, "What are you saying?"

"Send someone out there to look after them. Keep 'em in decent shape. Locked up, or chained up, so they can't escape, but out of pain. They gotta have water and food, and access to a bathroom. They gotta be clean and look healthy so a buyer will see that they're getting something of value."

"Are you wanting that job? Is that what's this all about?" Karla detected suspicion in his questions.

"No! I don't wanna be a babysitter. The crew needs four people. I wanna keep doing what we did last night."

"I'll think about it," Zakim said, then cut off the call.

Karla handed the phone back to Baku, turned to Jamal and said, "Why don't you see if our food's ready. They don't bring it to the table. Gotta pick it up over there." She nodded at the counter where the cooks put the burritos when they're done. As Jamal was making his way to the food counter, Karla reached over and laid her hand on Frank's arm. "Every thing's gonna be okay, Frank. Just trust me." Their eyes met briefly before Frank yanked his arm away and mumbled, "We'll see."

"Yes, we will," she said, then turned to Baku with a grin and added, "Won't we."

Baku said nothing, just sat there shaking his head, wondering what this cunning woman was up to.

Undercover Agent

Episode Eight

After the second day of scouting targets, their abductions that night went as smoothly as it had gone the night before. The procedure was simple and when properly executed was unfailingly successful. The three critical elements were: targeting an appropriate victim, absence of witnesses, and speed. Baku and his team, Jamal, Frank, and now Karla, performed like a precision machine—it was impossible to resist its efficiency. The two-day flurry of activity resulted in the capture of seventeen girls or young women. They were chained to each other and crammed into an ancient mobile home on an abandoned, sprawling woodlot in a small, rural community northeast of Portland. After one more day of abductions, the captives would be sold to a human trafficking ring and disappear without a trace. This was the business Zakim Olahyinka, Baku's boss, was in, the supply of female chattel. Along with his other criminal activities, it was helping make him wealthy, far beyond anything he could have imagined as an orphan Nigerian immigrant in Los Angeles thirty years earlier.

But Zakim's despicable pursuits had not gone unnoticed, especially by the human trafficking team in the Portland regional FBI office. Although this group, under the leadership of Agent Darrel James, had been tracking Zakim for several years, they hadn't been able to obtain rock-solid evidence of his nefarious dealings that would stand up in a court of law— he was just too careful. But with Karla Hammer inserted into

Zakim's gang as an undercover agent, maybe, just maybe, they might obtain proof that would end this cruel enterprise. Now, with James's career on the line, everything he'd been working on over the past ten years suddenly depended on an unproven, untrained wild card—a middle-aged, homeless woman with a criminal record. What she would do in the next few days would determine the fate of this investigation, the careers of himself as well as that of Captain Tom Tabor of the Portland Police Bureau, and possibly that of Hanna Marx, Agent in Charge of the Portland FBI office. In view of these complexities, it's not hard to understand how important the response to Karla's command would be when sitting at a corner table in the Burrito King on Lombard with Baku and the other two gang members, she said, "Frank. Get me some of the green salsa."

Conversation suddenly froze, and all eyes focused on Karla. At first Frank didn't move and just stared at the woman he'd intended to hit a few minutes before but had been stopped by Jamal. A look of confusion flooded his face. When Karla didn't avert her gaze from him, Frank turned to Baku, then Jamal—neither said anything. This was between Karla and Frank.

"Well?" Karla said with considerable firmness, still staring at him.

Frank mumbled something inaudible under his breath, stood up and went to the counter and asked for more salsa. "The green kind," he said.

"Thank you, Frank," Karla said, when he placed the plastic container of salsa on the table in front of her.

"Eat up," Baku said softly after Frank sat down. "We got another big day ahead of us. And night, too."

Smiling, Karla glanced at Baku, then said, "I just love this color," as she spread the salsa over her burrito, knowing full-well that from that point forward, it was she who actually controlled this little crew of wanna-be gangsters.

Later that same day, after the camp was quiet and Karla knew that Baku was catching some much-needed shuteye before they embarked on the last night of abductions, she snuck away to the drop site. She retrieved the note and a plastic baggie Tabor or James had left for her. Back in her tent, she read the message with the help of a penlight.

> *Hide this magnetic locator chip*
> *in the vehicle where it won't be*
> *seen. We'll rescue girls at*
> *trailer. Tell Zakim you heard a*
> *rumor about an FBI raid.*
> *Maintain Zakim's trust at all*
> *costs. Destroy the chip after the*
> *raid.*

Around three a.m. that night, Jamal pulled the van alongside the dilapidated mobile home at the end of a barely recognizable dirt path and cut the engine. "All right, let's unload 'em," Baku said, as he opened the passenger side door and started to get out.

Karla reached over the seatback and grabbed his shoulder. "Get Zakim on the phone. I gotta talk to him."

"Come on, Sue. I can't call him every time you wanna tell him something. I'll give him a report later, like I always do. After everything's done, and when these bitches are got rid of."

"Call him. It's important," she repeated, and tightened her grip.

"Call him," Jamal said. "Do what she says."

Baku was startled by Jamal's demand and could tell he meant it. Even though he didn't want to, he clicked on Zakim's name.

"What?" Zakim answered.

Baku handed the phone to Karla. "We might have a problem. I got a message today to stay away from Baku's gang tonight. Don't know what it means, but I don't like it. The feds might be planning something. How would they know what we're doing?"

"You tell me. You talk to anyone about what you been doing?" Zakim demanded.

"That's a stupid question. Of course not. But I don't know about my friends here. Can we trust them? Is there anyone at your end that might be a mole?"

"You're the only one I know who talks to the FBI. Why didn't you tell me about this earlier today? Maybe *you* the one settin' us up. If you are, you're gonna be one sorry lady."

"We worked hard today getting these girls. I didn't have a chance to call you. You and me got a deal. I'm not gonna screw that up. So just take this warning for what it is. Don't let anything mess up this transfer. We got nine more tonight. That gives us a total of twenty-six. That's gonna be some good money—at least fifteen thousand each. Which, by the way, my team's gonna want a bigger piece of."

"*Your* team? What the hell you talking about? Baku's your boss. And the money ain't none of your business."

"Sorry, Zakim, I couldn't hear that. This phone battery's going dead." She ended the call, handed the phone back to Baku and said, "Let's get to work."

"What's going on?" Jack, Zakim's lieutenant, asked when Zakim slammed his phone on the table.

"I don't know. Sue told me she thinks the feds might be on to us. Could be nothing, but we can't take any chances, Gotta get those girls outta there soon as we can. Call Zorn and tell him to hurry up."

"I talked to him a few minutes ago," Jack said. "The truck's on I-5 this side of Salem. They'll get to Fairview in an hour or so. I'll take Larry and Tiger and meet him at the trailer, make sure everything goes okay, and collect the money."

"Pay off Baku's guys. If Sue gives you a hard time about how much she's getting, sell her with the other ones—half price. Zorn should snap her up if she's that cheap. On second thought, If he don't want her, get rid of her. Bury the body where it won't be found. I've had it with that pushy bitch."

"No problem. I'll keep you posted."

251

As Frank was taking the last girl from the van to the trailer, and Baku, Karla, and Jamal were inside preparing the girls for the transfer, the rumble of a heavy vehicle approaching along the dirt road caught his attention. "Come on," he said to the terrified young girl he'd pulled out of the rear of the van, her eyes and mouth taped, and her hands and feet tightly bound. He had to half-carry-half-drag her through the dirt toward the trailer door. When he got to the entrance, he yelled, "The truck's here."

"They're early," Baku said.

"Not all of these girls are ready," Karla yelled, her ski mask muffling her voice.

"Don't worry," Baku said. "Sometimes the buyer's early. They'll wait. Just hurry up. Jamal! Get them chains off those ones over there," Baku said, pointing at a group of girls cringing in the hall leading to a back bedroom. "Tape their eyes and chain 'em in threes."

The truck pulled alongside the van, but the noise of the engine didn't stop. Suddenly the trailer door flew open with a loud crash and two masked, camo-clothed men brandishing automatic weapons burst into the body-strewn room.

"Outside!" the one in front screamed in a strong foreign accent, motioning toward Frank and Jamal, who were close by tending to some of the girls. 'You too!" he said to Baku, then turned to Karla, "and you. Out!"

Once outside, Baku and his companions were confronted by two men in ski masks pointing guns at them. "On the ground," one of them ordered, also with an accent. The other quickly cuffed Baku and his gang with plastic restraints, bound their ankles, then checked them for guns. "They're clean," he said in a language Baku and the others recognized as Russian.

The four men then hastily took the whimpering and terrified captives, some led, some carried, some dragged, from the trailer to the truck and loaded them into its enclosed cargo box. Ten minutes later, the truck was gone.

Lying on the ground outside the trailer, hands and legs bound, Baku and his companions knew they had to tell Zakim what happened as soon as possible. Frank rolled and scooted his body to a position where Jamal could work his hand into Frank's pocket and withdraw a switchblade. After Jamal cut Frank's plastic restraints, he freed the others. But as Baku was getting his phone out, they heard and saw an SUV emerge from the woods and speed into the clearing where the trailer was sitting. When it came to a halt, Jack jumped out and ran to where they stood.

"We gotta get these girls outta here. The feds might be coming."

"It's too late," Baku yelled. "The Russians took them."

"Whaddya mean?" Jack screamed, as two more of Zakim's gang members got out of the SUV and joined him. Baku described what had just happened, emphasizing how certain he and the others were that the hijackers spoke Russian.

"I gotta call the boss," Jack blurted out. But before he could punch in the number, they all spun around to where another SUV was speeding into the clearing, followed closely by two more.

"What the hell is this? Jack cried out. Who are these guys?"

The lead SUV slid to a stop and four Kevlar-clad men jumped out and rushed forward, aiming automatic rifles at the seven Zakim gang members huddled in front of the trailer.

"On the ground," one of the men yelled. "Now!"

Seconds later the two other SUVs pulled up. Suddenly there were eight more armed men approaching the trailer.

Two of the men made a quick frisk of the gang, finding and taking away pistols from Jack and his two buddies.

"Check inside. Find the hostages," another of the men said.

"There ain't no hostages here," Baku hollered." Who are you?"

The man who had ordered the trailer search went to where Baku lay on the ground. He pulled a small black leather wallet from his pocket and flipped it open to display a bronze-colored badge. "FBI," he said. "You're under arrest for kidnapping."

Before Baku could respond, a man came out of the trailer and said, "There's no one here."

"Looks like you're in the wrong place, mister," Jack said.

Ignoring Jack, the FBI man said, "Check the woods. They gotta be here someplace."

A few minutes later, one of the FBI leader's men rushed up and said, "No sign of any hostages, Sir."

"Where are they?" the leader asked Jack.

"I don't know what you talkin' about."

"What are you and these people doing here?" the FBI man asked aggressively, looking around at the Zakim gang.

"We're having a book club meeting. Is there a law against book clubs?" Jack answered.

The FBI agent fought hard to control his rage, but realizing he had no evidence to act on, he turned to his men and yelled, "Let's go. There's nothing here."

As soon as the FBI team was gone, Jack called Zakim. "The Russians ripped us off. They took the girls. Must have been the Ratsov gang."

"What? The girls are gone? I'll kill that bastard Ratsov if he did this."

"About a half hour ago," Jack said. "Then a bunch of FBI storm troopers showed up looking for the girls. They left a few minutes ago."

"Damn! What the hell's going on? How'd Ratsov *and* the feds know about tonight. We got a leaky faucet we gotta fix. And fix it fast."

"Want me to question Baku's gang?"

"Yeah, later. First, we gotta get those girls back." Zakim said, panic evident in his voice. "You got a description of what they were driving?"

Jack got a description of the truck from Frank and Jamal and told Zakim.

"That fits hundreds of trucks, no way we'd be able to locate it. Bring Baku and the others back here. Then we'll figure out what to do."

Meanwhile, miles away in Northeast Portland, the twenty-six traumatized female abduction victims were being admitted into the emergency trauma ward at Emanuel Hospital under the supervision of FBI Agent Darrel James. So far, his cursory questioning hadn't yielded information that would be helpful in proving who was responsible for their capture. After the attending physicians told him to leave, he called his boss, Hannah Marx. "We know who hijacked these girls from the information provided by Hammer, but from what the girls tell me, they were kept in the dark—never saw anything. They have no idea who grabbed them, or where they were taken, except that it was three men and a woman. They could tell that from their voices."

"All right. Go home and let the doctors get on with their work. I want a detailed report on this operation tomorrow morning. And I want the Hammer woman here, too. By the way, well done."

Undercover Agent

Episode Nine

As soon as Karla and the rest of Baku's gang got into the van to go to Zakim's headquarters, she took the location chip from where she'd hidden it and slipped it in into her pocket. In the rush to leave, no one noticed. Then, as Jamal was climbing into the driver's seat, she yelled, "Wait! I left my pack in the trailer. Gimme a minute."

When she got out of the van, she threw the chip as far away as she could, went into the trailer to get her pack, then hurried back to the van. "Let's go," she said as she pulled the rear door shut.

Jamal hit the gas and followed Jack away from the trailer in a cloud of dust.

Thirty minutes later, Jamal pulled into a bay in Zakim's warehouse in Southeast Portland and cut the engine. The van's rear door flew open and Jack, holding a pistol at his side, said, "Everybody, inside."

"Why the gun?" Frank asked as he climbed out the back.

Jack waved the pistol in Frank's direction. "Just go."

While Jack herded Baku's gang into a back office in the warehouse, in another part of town, FBI Agent James was on the phone with Captain Tabor.

"It's four in the morning. What's goin' on?" Tabor, roused from a deep sleep, asked irritably.

"We got the girls They're at Emanuel Hospital. But Karla, and the rest of Baku's guys are at Zakim's headquarters in Southeast.

Tabor tried hard to clear his head. "That's great, at least about the girls. But. what do you want me to do about Karla?"

"Shouldn't we get her out of there? Zakim's gonna figure that she set up the bust of his shipment. He'll kill her . . . or worse."

It took a few seconds for Tabor to respond. "Darrel . . . calm down. Take a breath. Put yourself in Karla's shoes. She's no dummy, right? She's done okay so far, right? Let's think this through."

"But . . ."

"Darrel! Stop!" Tabor glanced at his wife, who was stirring awake, then threw the covers off his side of the bed and sat up. "Meet me at the Starbucks at 102nd and Stark in thirty minutes. We'll figure out what to do."

Zakim was on the phone when Jack came into his office and took a chair in front of his boss's massive desk. "Don't worry," Zakim said into his mobile more confidently than he should have. "We'll get those bitches back. Looks like it was Russians that got 'em." Then, after a pause, "I don't know. Maybe they followed Baku, my guy who was snatching the girls." Another pause. "No way. Baku's loyal. Ain't no way he'd do that. He's one of us. Maybe it was one of his gang that tipped off the Ruskies. I'm gonna get on that now—I'll call to you later." Zakim ended the call and told Jack to bring in Jamal."

"Sit down," Zakim said when Jack led Jamal to Zakim's desk. "Jack, leave us alone. I'll call if I need you."

"Zakim watched Jamal take the only other chair in the room, directly in front of his desk. "Who told the Russians about tonight?"

"I don't know nothin 'bout that. Don't think it was none of us. We just doin' our job. Getting' it done."

"How'd they know about the transfer? About the girls?"

"No idea."

"What about Karla? Think she might be a mole for the cops—or the Russians?"

"I don't think so. She's a hard-ass, but a good one. She keeps us focused. Even got Frank under control. She's okay."

Zakim was silent for a moment, then said, "Is she trying to take over from Baku?"

"No way. She supports him. She helps him keep on track, that's all. Like a mother—or something. She made it easier on those girls, too."

"All right. Tell her to come in."

A minute later, Karla was sitting in the chair across from Zakim.

"What happened tonight?" Zakim said accusingly.

"That's what I was gonna ask you—*boss*. How all our work got blown away in a Russian shit-storm. Three nights of precision snatches pissed away in less than ten minutes. You think we spent three nights doing this for the fun of it?"

"Knock it off, bitch. Remember who you're working for. Show some respect."

Karla sprung from the chair, leaned forward and planted her fists on top of the desk. "Don't ever call me that again. I'm not your bitch! Or anybody else's. And I want to know what's going on around here. Because it doesn't seem like you know. If you did, you'd be finding out how those Russian bastards knew what we were doing. And it's not because any of Baku's team ratted us out. We're in this to make money, and we sure as hell wouldn't do that by cozying up to the Russian mafia.

Zakim was shocked by Karla's sudden eruption and at first wasn't sure how to react. But he quickly regained his composure. "Sit down. *Somebody* has to be talking to the Russians, if it was them, or the Feds, if they were involved. If it ain't you or another one of Baku's crew, then who?"

Karla let her expression of rage relax and sat down. "If you're sure it wasn't someone close to you, then maybe there is no mole. Maybe somebody got a fix on us and has been following us all this time. Or maybe they put a tracker on one of our vehicles. There's all kinds of hi-tech gadgets they could use to track what we're doing. Could be the Russians followed us, watching us collect the girls, and waited to grab them before the buyer showed up. We shouldn't automatically assume someone inside this organization is an informer. There's too many other possibilities"

Zakim didn't say anything for a while. Finally, he said, "It's the Russians. They been wantin' to get into this game for a long time, but we've kept them out 'cause we're better at it. We control the market, from Mexico to Seattle. Twenty girls a month, that's our average. It's not our main source of income, but it's enough to make a difference. I ain't gonna lose it to those bastards."

"Whaddya mean it's not our main source of money? What else is there?"

"Nothin' that concerns you. Your job is to help Baku and help him supply the girls."

"I'm getting bored with girl-snatching. Anybody with half a brain can do that. I can do more. Let me help with these other things, whatever they are.

Again, Zakim fell into silence, as if he were analyzing Karla's words. Then, "I'll think about it. Now get the hell out and tell Baku to get in here."

While Zakim was interrogating members of his gang, Agent James and Captain Tabor sat at a corner table in the Starbucks, as far as possible from the only other customer. "Fill me in on what went down tonight," Tabor said. And I'm still pissed that my guys weren't in on it."

"Like I told you before, Chief Marx wanted this to be an FBI action. You know, politics."

"I get it. So, what happened?"

"Our guys pretended to be Russian. They had a location from the chip Karla planted in their van, so it was no problem finding them. We timed the raid so it was before Zakim's buyer got there. We knew about the pickup time from phone calls we monitored."

"Sounds like it was a success. Congratulations."

"Thanks. But Karla should get the credit for it. She made it happen."

"Right. So, the question is, what danger is she in now?" Tabor asked.

"The more I think about what she's been able to do so far, the more I think she'll bullshit her way past any suspicion that she was responsible for a tipoff resulting in the fake Russian mafia guys stealing their girls. At least I hope so. She's penetrated this far into Zakim's world, why wouldn't she be able to keep going?"

"She's pretty good at this, isn't she." Tabor swallowed the rest of his coffee. "All right, let's see what happens over the next couple of days. But if we don't hear from her by the day after tomorrow, we're going in after her. Okay?"

"Okay. I'll set it up with Marx."

It was around noon when Karla woke. When she opened her eyes, she instantly remembered she was back in her tent in the North Portland homeless camp and felt a wave of relief come over her. As her head cleared, she remembered Jamal bringing her and Baku back to the camp early that morning after hours of grueling interrogation by Zakim about the loss of the girls the night before and about how the FBI showed up a few minutes later. She remembered how after a while she'd shut Zakim and his relentless droning out of her mind, but whatever they told him must have been enough to convince him that Baku's gang was in the clear. Then she recalled her conversation with Zakim about his gang's other activities. How she had tried to wheedle herself into whatever else he was into but was kept out by his refusal to talk about it. She'd planted the seed, though, and now all she could do was to wait to see what sprouted. But there was one thing she was certain of—she wasn't going to let that sowing go untended until it yielded results."

Karla found Rosa at the fire pit and managed to get a couple of sandwiches and some coffee from her, promising to replenish the common larder with new supplies later that day. Then she went to Baku's tent where she found him still asleep. "Wake up! We got stuff to talk about."

A few minutes later, Baku crawled out and joined Karla in the shade of a nearby Douglas fir.

'Here's a sandwich . . . compliments of Rosa."

Baku took the sandwich and the coffee without saying anything.

Karla didn't waste time getting to the point. "What else is Zakim into besides selling girls?"

"What are you talking about? If he was, how would I know, anyway?"

"You've been with him long enough to know a lot. Tell me."

"Why you wanna know that? It ain't none of your business. There's some things it's better not knowing about."

"Baku. You trust me, don't you?"

"Yeah, I guess so."

"Okay. I'll be honest with you. Zakim needs my help. Last night he told me that some of his other deals were in danger of going bad. And that he saw how I helped you get more focused on collecting the girls, and how Jamal and Frank were doing a better job, not causing you so many headaches. He told me how pleased he was with how you're running your operation now."

"He said that?"

"Yes, he did. He also told me to talk to you about how I could help him with his other problems."

"Why didn't he tell *me* that?" Karla sensed the skepticism in his question.

"He was going to but was interrupted by a phone call. Must have been from someone he reports to, because he seemed kinda scared. He told me to leave so he could talk in private."

Baku hesitated a moment, then said, "Maybe it was from a guy in LA named Olatunji."

"Oh yeah. Zakim's mentioned him to me once. Said he was the big boss."

"That's right," Baku said. "He's in charge of everything."

Everything? What's that mean?"

"All the stuff the gang's into."

"Besides girls? What else?"

"We're not supposed to talk about it," Baku said defensively, as if he knew Karla wouldn't let up until she got answers.

"It's okay. He was gonna tell you to fill me in on our other activities before he got that call from Olatunji."

"He was?"

"Yeah. He was. I wouldn't lie to you. You should know that by now. I'm your partner, and partners trust each other."

Baku took a swig of the coffee, then finished the sandwich. "You sure he wants me to tell you all what we're doing?"

"Sure as sure can be," Karla said as she moved closer to Baku then pressed the RECORD button on the recorder in her coat pocket."

Late that night, in a conference room at the FBI center in Northeast Portland, Agent James and Captain Tabor huddled over a tape player. "This is a goldmine," Tabor said after the tape ended. Forty-seven minutes that could bust up Zakim's gang and put him and his buddies in jail for a long time."

"Maybe," James said. "We need solid proof. Without it, it'd just be the recorded word on a low-level errand boy against Zakim and a team of hot-shot defense lawyers. And the recording was made without the guy's knowledge. Anyway, we knew about some of this stuff. Although not the gun smuggling—that's helpful. But we need more than this."

Tabor set the player to rewind then refilled their cups with the last of the coffee. "If you knew about the drug dealing and murder for hire activities, and all the rest, why haven't you arrested him?"

"Because we don't have solid proof. We've got plenty of suspicion, some circumstantial evidence, but nothing that would satisfy a judge."

"So, this tape is of no value?"

"I wouldn't say that. It points us in another direction—the guns. If Karla could find out where Zakim warehouses them, and we find them in his possession, we'd have him on a major Federal charge."

"That would put her at considerable risk."

James didn't say anything in response to Tabor's observation.

Tabor stood and slipped on his jacket. "I don't like it. Nosing around other things Zakim's doing could get her killed."

James stood and prepared to leave with Tabor. "That's what we're paying her for, isn't it?"

Undercover Agent

Episode Ten

Karla found Rosa at the firepit adding wild mushrooms to a soup pot resting on a bed of glowing coals. Karla set two sacks of vegetables on the ground. "Here's some stuff for the larder from vendors at the farmers' market."

Rosa glanced at the bags. "Thanks. I'll use them for a stew tomorrow. Maybe someone'll bring in some meat."

"I'll see what I can do. I'm gonna be on the streets in the morning."

"Beef, if you can manage it. Oh, yeah. Baku was looking for you a while ago."

"Is he still around?"

"He said he was goin' to the river. I don't think he's come back."

Karla found Baku sitting in his regular spot on a steep bank overlooking the slow-flowing Willamette. "Rosa said you were looking for me. What's up?"

"Zakim wants to see you."

"How am I supposed to get there? It's on the other side of town."

"Jamal's parked on Lombard—at that strip mall where the laundromat is."

"I'll go after Rosa's soup's ready. I gotta eat something."

"He said as soon as you can get there."

"Did he say why?"

"He don't tell me nothin'. Not like he does you."

"Are you coming with me?"

"He didn't tell me to, so I guess not."

Twenty minutes later, Karla approached Jamal's van. Two men got out, Jamal on the driver's side, Zakim's bodyguard, Benny, on the passenger side. She didn't like seeing Benny and knew it wasn't a good sign. Before she could get away by ducking behind the adult video shop next to the laundromat, Benny yelled, "Don't make me chase you. Get over here."

"Karla limped to where Benny stood waiting. "Must be important if Zakim sent you to fetch a cripple lady like me when Jamal could have done it on his own."

Benny ignored her comment and opened the side door. "Get in."

Karla tossed in her walking stick and scrambled after it. She noticed that the inside handle had been removed, same for the rear door.

Since there were no back seats, she sat on the floor with her back against the driver-side wall. After they were under way, she scooted close to Jamal's seat. "Jamal. What's going on?"

Benny spun around. "Shut up. Get back there," nodding toward the back of the space.

Jamal glanced at her in the rear view mirror and their eyes locked for a second, but he said nothing.

A few moments after the van pulled into the backlot and up to the loading dock behind Zakim's warehouse, the side door flew open and Benny said, "Get out," then moved back from the door. After Karla got out, Benny grabbed at her arm. Karla jerked away and stepped back a pace. Benny raised his hand to hit her, but Jamal jumped in front of him. "No need for that. She won't be no trouble."

Benny started to say something but didn't when he saw the steel in Jamal's eyes, a look he'd not seen before. He also saw how Jamal stood with one foot forward, his shoulders turned at a slight angle, and his hands held in loose fists at chest-level. He was as tall as Jamal, but thirty pounds lighter and twenty years older. "Back off, Brother. No problem." He turned to Karla. "I'm gonna take you to Zakim."

Karla followed Benny up to the dock, her walking stick clanging on the metal steps. They went through an entrance next to a closed overhead cargo door and down a long hall, past two closed doors, then stopped before one painted red. Benny knocked four times. A second later a buzzer went off. He turned the handle and pushed the door open to reveal an office with a large desk, some filing cabinets, and a single chair in front of the desk. Zakim sat behind it like a king on his throne.

Following Benny's command, Karla sat in the chair. After Benny left the room, in a stone-cold voice Zakim said, "I know it was you who set us up. What else have you told them?"

If Karla was scared, she didn't show it. "It wasn't me. I'm on your side, remember?"

"Cut the crap. One way or the other, you're gonna tell me everything. Make it easy on yourself."

Karla knew from his controlled calm and unwavering gaze that he was convinced he was right and would be unrelenting in learning the truth. "Why do you think it was me?"

"Gretchen's been keeping track of what you been up to. She saw you put something under that barrel where you leave messages—the night of the delivery. Before she could get it, a man did. She followed him to his car. She said it looked like an unmarked cop car. That's why I *know* it was you."

"I left a message there, like I always do. If I didn't, they'd suspect something was wrong. But I didn't tell them about the girls being transferred that night."

"Bullshit. Jack found a locator chip in the weeds near the trailer today. You must've tossed it away when you went in to get whatever you left behind."

"I didn't—"

Zakim didn't let her finish. "Benny!" he yelled, then buzzed the door. When Benny came in, Zakim said, "Take this bitch outta here and get the truth out of her."

Before Karla could say anything, Benny grabbed her by the hair and jerked her out of the chair. "Let's go. You don't wanna be late for our appointment." She clutched her walking stick as he marched her through the doorway into the hall. When Benny opened the last of several more doors and shoved her into the room, he was surprised to see Jamal. "Wadda *you* doin' in here?"

Jamal took a step toward Benny. "Let her go. She's coming with me."

Benny pushed Karla aside and took a six-inch switchblade from his pocket and clicked it open. "You stupid son of a bitch. Get the hell out of here. This ain't none of your business."

Jamal ignored the knife and moved to where Karla stood near the door. "I'm leaving all right . . . and so is she."

Holding the knife in front of him, Benny stepped toward Jamal. Anticipating what was coming, Jamal threw a punch at Benny. Benny ducked, blocked Jamal's next swing, then plunged the knife into Jamal's belly. He sliced the blade sideways a couple of times before pulling it out. Jamal grunted and staggered backwards, then dropped to the floor. When Benny turned toward Karla, he doubled over when Karla, holding her walking stick like a shovel, rammed it into his groin. Excruciating pain shot through his body like an electric shock, and just as paralyzing. Before he could recover, she smashed the cane on top of his head. Then, holding it like a baseball bat, with every ounce of strength she could muster, she delivered a cracking blow to the side of his skull, landing it above his ear and opening a long, deep gash. He collapsed onto his side and stayed down, not moving, or breathing.

She checked Jamal's pulse, gently closed his eyes, then snatched his phone from his coat pocket. Wanting to get away from the bodies, she stepped into the hall and pulled the door shut behind her. She knew she had to call Tabor, but without Zakim hearing. She opened one of the other doors and entered a long room. The first thing she saw was a bench with half a dozen automatic rifles on it. Looking around, she saw wooden crates stacked along a wall. Then she noticed a bunch of pistols on another bench, and more wooden crates underneath. She knew at once this was what the feds needed to take down Zakim—solid evidence of gun trafficking.

Agent James was waiting for his burger and shake at Burgerville when his phone buzzed. He answered at once when he saw Tabor's number in the caller ID window.

"Karla's in trouble. She's at Zakim's. We gotta go in."

"Slow down. What's going on?"

"She just called. One of Zakim's guys was gonna rough her up, but another guy got himself killed when he tried to intervene. Then Karla killed the one who killed him—with her cane. She hit him like she did the mafia guy. Then she found a room full of guns. Zakim doesn't know any of this. She thinks he's still in his office.

"How many others are there?"

"She hasn't seen anybody else, but she didn't know for sure."

"I'll call in a SWAT team. I'll meet you there as soon as I can . . . down the block . . . at that welding shop. I'm on my way. Cancel that order," he yelled at the cashier as he ran out the door.

After Karla ended the call to Tabor, she looked around the room she was in and noticed another door in the far corner. Hoping it might lead to a way out of the building and escape without having to pass Zakim's office, she opened it cautiously and peered into the dark interior. She found a wall switch and turned on the overhead light. She was stunned by what she saw—bundles of cash stacked on shelves lining two of the walls. There were packets of twenties, fifties, and hundreds, banded in packs she estimated to contain at least fifty bills, maybe more. There was no other door and no windows.

She hesitated a second, then grabbed a duffel bag off a nearby table and started stuffing bricks of bills into it. She noticed that $10,000 was written on the band around the ones with hundreds. She knew she wouldn't be able to take all of it but was determined to get as much as she could. When the bag was full, mostly with hundreds, but also some fifties and twenties, she returned to the gun room and cracked open the door enough to peek into the hall. There was no one there, and no sounds. With her cane in one hand and the heavy bag in the other, she headed toward the door to the loading dock. She struggled with the weight and concentrated on being as quiet as possible.

When she got to where Zakim's office was, the door was ajar. She stopped, afraid of being seen as she passed by. She heard him talking, but with short pauses, obviously on the phone. He sounded excited.

"How many are there?" A few seconds later, apparently on a different call she heard Zakim say, "Jack! Seymore just told me a bunch of feds are by the welding shop. Yeah, like they're waiting for something—or somebody. I think we're gonna get raided. We gotta get outta here. Yeah! Now! Pack up as much money as you can. Get Benny, kill the woman. I'll meet you two out back in a couple of minutes."

Karla heard noises from Zakim's office, like a laptop being slammed shut, and then papers, or files, being thrown into a bag or case of some kind. Then a chair scraping the floor and footsteps approaching the door. She looked around and saw another door a few feet behind her. She stepped back, set the satchel down, opened the door, grabbed the money, and got into the room just as Zakim came out of his. She didn't have time to close the door all the way, but in his haste Zakim didn't notice.

Karla saw at once that she was in a small bathroom, and that she still had her cane and the duffle bag. She heard Zakim's footsteps receding down the hall toward the loading dock. A moment later, she heard another set of footsteps racing along the hall, possibly toward the room with the money. *Must be Jack*, she thought. But at that point, she didn't care, she just wanted to get away—before Agent James and his guys and Captain Tabor got there. Let them pick up the pieces—the guns, the money stacked on those shelves, whatever was stashed in the other rooms. Let them catch Zakim, and Jack, sort out the two bodies, Benny and Jamal, they'd deal with all of it without her. She just wanted to get away—with her bag of money, money she'd earned—fair and square.

She looked around the room and immediately saw it—a window covered by a draw-down shade. She discovered that it looked out on a narrow, fenced-in side yard containing scattered debris and trash barrels. When she unlatched and tried to open the window, it gave enough to get her cane under it and pry it up high enough to crawl out. She punched her cane through the screen, tossed out the bag and walking stick, then squeezed through head-first, plopping onto the wet ground without hurting herself. There was no one in sight, although she heard heavy boot steps and men barking orders from around the far corner. She heard Zakim yell something, then a barrage of gunshots, more orders being barked, then silence.

The fence was too high to climb, especially with the heavy bag. If she was going to get away with the money, she would have to get past the loading dock. She edged along the building wall, listening for the sounds of men—it was still quiet. *They must be inside*, she thought, and peeked around the corner. There was no one there, just several SUVs, two police cars, and the SWAT team minibus. She didn't see anyone near the vehicles or the gate. This was her chance—she stepped around the corner and headed toward the street.

"Stop! Put down the bag and the stick. Get on the ground."

She glanced to where the voice came from and saw a man on the loading dock pointing an automatic rifle at her. Yellow letters across his Kevlar vest said *FBI*.

"On the ground," he yelled again.

Karla dropped the bag and started to kneel down, but suddenly froze in place when Captain Tabor came out of the door and saw what was happening.

"She's one of ours," Tabor yelled at the FBI guy.

The FBI guy gave Tabor a long look, then lowered his gun and said, "Who is she?"

"She's FBI, undercover. I gotta get her outta here so she won't be identified."

The SWAT guy stared at Tabor for a moment, then lowered his rifle and said, "All right."

Tabor scrambled down the steps and told Karla to come with him. She picked up the bag and followed him past two bloody bodies lying near Jack's SUV. When she glanced at them, she saw it was Zakim and Jack.

A few seconds later they were at Tabor's car. "What's in the bag?" he asked after she put it on the back seat.

"Personal stuff." She got into the front seat and didn't say anything else until Tabor pulled out of the lot, made a couple of turns, and headed toward the freeway.

"Personal stuff? Like what?" he asked.

"You know—clothes . . . and other stuff. Nothing you'd be interested in."

"You sure?"

Karla looked at him, and he glanced at her, their eyes making direct contact. "Sure as sure can be," she said, then, suppressing a smile, turned away. "Where are we going?"

"FBI headquarters. Marx wants to debrief you, get your statement."

"Now? Can't she do it later? Like tomorrow?"

"What's wrong with now? You got something you gotta do?"

Before Karla could answer, Tabor's phone buzzed. "Yeah?" he answered. He glanced at Karla while listening to whomever it was that called. Then, "I'm with her now. On our way to see Marx for a debriefing. We'll be there in about half an hour." He ended the call, then said, "That was James. He's gonna be at Zakim's warehouse for a while. They found lot's of stuff to occupy them. Bodies, money, guns, dope, computers, and files. A real treasure."

Karla was quiet for a while, then said, "Before we see Marx, I need to stop by a bank in Hollywood. The one across the street from the furniture store."

"Why?" Tabor asked.

"I want to leave this stuff with a friend who works there. I don't want to take it to the camp. Stuff gets stolen there sometimes."

Tabor shook his head, then said, "A bank won't take that much . . . *personal stuff* . . . they have to report anything over $10,000 to the government. Would you want that?"

Karla didn't say anything for a while, then, "Okay. Then I need a storage locker."

"Are you sure you want to do this? What about me? You're putting me in a tough position."

Without hesitation, Karla said, "Yes, I'm sure. I earned it. It won't be missed, anyway. As far as you being in a tough position, you don't have any idea what's in that bag. And I'm not gonna tell you, either. As far as you know, it's clothing I had at Zakim's for when I had to change into something more fitting to the occasion."

"Karla—"

"I told you . . . I'm sure. Sure as sure can be. So, drop it."

Tabor drove on in silence for a while, maneuvering through the building afternoon traffic. Finally, he glanced at Karla and said, "All right. I don't like it, but we'll do it your way. There's a self-storage place on Northeast Halsey, not that much out of our way."

"Thanks."

They continued on, neither of them saying anything. Fifteen minutes later, Tabor pulled into a fenced-in parking lot of a self-storage complex and Karla went into the business office alone. She took the duffel bag with her.

Twenty minutes later they were back on their way to FBI headquarters. Karla was the first to break their uncomfortable silence. "You wanna get something to eat after this thing with Marx is done?'

"Thanks for asking, but I need to get home. Tonight's my wife's book club and I gotta baby sit."

"You have a baby?"

"Two teen-age daughters. I guess I'm old fashioned, but I don't like leaving them alone."

"No problem. I wouldn't mind getting back to the camp, anyway. Rosie's cooking's as good as most restaurants. I want to see about Baku, too. See if he's been arrested. You can drop me off at that wine shop near the Max station in Hollywood. I'm gonna treat my fellow campers to some high-end wine for a change. I've always wondered what the good stuff tastes like."

Tabor gave Karla a sly look and said, "Well. from now on you'll be able to drink all the expensive wine you want with that stash of so-called personal stuff. I suppose you'll be leaving the street life too, right?"

Karla didn't answer for a while, just stared out the passenger window at the congestion of cars and trucks and at the neighborhoods they were then passing by. Finally, she said, "It depends on what Chief Marx has to say."

"What Marx has to say? What do you mean?"

"Maybe she'll want me to stay on. After all, you can't deny I helped bring down a crook you hotshots weren't able to get by yourselves. There's gotta be more crooks out there she'd like to bring down, don't you think? If I'm gonna be an undercover agent whose supposed to be a discarded, harmless homeless woman lost in the shadows, then I'd better be living that life, right?"

"You mean you'd stay on with the FBI? You'd risk your life again? Those bastards nearly killed you. Next time you might not be so lucky."

"I don't need luck when you've got my back. You were in my corner this time, you'd be there again, wouldn't you?"

"Karla! You're talking crazy. You're not trained for this kind of work. This thing with Zakim was a fluke. Next time could be a lot worse—like getting killed."

"That *is* a good point, Tabor. Maybe I can convince Marx to get me some training. It would be nice to know how to defend myself with something besides my trusty walking stick. Although you'll have to admit, I haven't done too bad with that as my only weapon, have I?"

"Karla! God damn it. I'm serious. This is a crazy idea."

"I'm serious, too. And it's not a crazy idea. I did something worthwhile for the first time in my life, and I'm proud of what I did. And another thing. I like living the way I do. Few responsibilities to weigh me down, friends who accept me as I am, a cozy tent and a warm sleeping bag. So, get off your high horse and let me be who I am. Who I wanna go on being. Okay?"

Tabor started to say something, but realized they'd arrived at the FBI complex security booth.

"Tabor and Hammer to see Marx," he said to the guard.

"She's expecting you, Captain Tabor. You can park over there," the guard said, pointing toward a visitors' spot near the main entrance.

Five minutes later they were ushered into Marx's office rather than into the conference room they'd been in during previous visits.

Marx stood and walked around her desk to meet Karla and Tabor. "Miss Hammer. It's nice to see you again. We have a lot to talk about. Hello, Captain Tabor."

"I was thinking the same thing," Karla said as she shook Marx's outstretched hand.

Marx pointed at the couch. "Make yourselves comfortable. Would you like anything to drink?"

Tabor started to say something, but Karla jumped in. "I don't have much time right now. Let's just get down to business."

Marx arched her eyebrows, obviously taken aback by Karla's abruptness. "I suppose you're referring to the twenty-five thousand dollar payment we owe you."

"That's part of it."

"Part of it? What's the other part?"

"Job training. That's the part we need to talk about."

The End

Jack and Storm

Episode One

Small town, Northwestern United States; 2079 AD

Jack was tired after a long day at his job as a security
guard. He'd logged four hours of overtime because his regular
partner was out for three weeks with a broken leg. Still, with
two demanding youngsters, the extra pay was a godsend, so he
would just bear the exhaustion and rake in the benefits. It was
dusk when he finally got checked out by his supervisor and
headed home, loping along Central Avenue at a brisk pace. He
wanted to get home in time to give Storm, his mate of four
years, relief from the little mutts, play rough and tumble with
them, and maybe take them for a romp in the park before
dinner and sleep time.

He hadn't gone more than a few blocks when he heard a
siren approaching from behind. Then he noticed a surge of red
and yellow flames low in the sky and caught the unmistakable
odor of smoke. It was up ahead in the next block. He was
trained in rescue work, so without hesitation he broke into a
fast run and reached the conflagration a few moments later. A
group of panicked and distraught people was gathered on the
sidewalk across the street from a three-decker apartment
building engulfed in a blazing inferno.

"My baby! She's still in there!" one of the women
screamed. Her cries didn't drown out mumblings of derision
directed at him by a few of the folks standing there, and he
noticed unfriendly looks by others. But used to such

discrimination, and realizing how dire the situation was, Jack ignored them, dashed across the street, bounded up four cement steps, and rushed through the open door.

The heat he crashed into inside the burning building was like a brick wall, but he kept going, hurling toward the sounds of a baby crying somewhere down a hall filled with smoke but not yet with flames. He held his breath and ran as fast as he could, his eyes chafing from the searing heat, trusting his hearing to lead him to the baby. He crashed through the half-open door into the baby's room where the temperature was less intense and was relatively smoke-free. He snatched up the infant, thankfully wrapped tightly in a blanket, careful not to injure her with his powerful jaws. Glancing around the room, he saw a window open just wide enough for him to fit through. When he jumped out, he landed on top of a garbage bin, managed to keep his balance, dropped to the ground, and ran with the child to where its mother waited desperately with open arms and tears flowing down her cheeks.

The baby was unharmed, and Jack was joyfully proclaimed a hero. He was applauded by almost everyone there and graciously accepted their praise. He answered questions by the Fire Department Chief and posed for photos to document his heroic rescue. But as the interrogations wound down, and he prepared to leave, a gaggle of TV news reporters and cameramen showed up. He reluctantly gave in to their insistent demands for interviews, although what he really wanted was to get home to Storm and their two rambunctious but lovable youngsters.

Back at work the next morning, Jack again encountered a blitz of attention. Much of it was praise for his bravery, but some, from those who resented him because he was different, ranged from rude indifference to outright threats. In fact, because of possible physical harm to Jack from a few of his more aggressively prejudiced coworkers, his supervisor took him off his regular shift and assigned him to an abandoned government facility where he was the only guard on duty. But even with Jack posted to that remote location, the town's mayor managed to track him down and summon him to city hall for an official recognition and congratulations ceremony the following day. With all this attention, Jack worried that it might interfere with his career and just wanted to get on with his quiet life as it had been before he'd saved the baby. But between an unrelenting tsunami of social media, extensive TV and newspaper coverage, and the mayor's heavily publicized event, that naïve wish turned out to be impossible. As a result, his life was changed in a way he never could have imagined.

The next day, Jack and Storm arrived at city hall a few minutes before the mayor was scheduled to meet them at the main entrance. The mayor's deputy had planned a grand entrance with the mayor personally escorting Jack and Storm into the rotunda lobby where TV cameras would be stationed for a live broadcast of the award ceremony. Most of the people involved in this event, other than Jack himself, understood the ceremony was intended to make the mayor look good in this election year as he cast aside discriminatory barriers to beings like Jack and his mate and magnanimously acknowledged Jack's heroism.

Unfortunately, the regular security guard at the entrance to city hall had been in an accident on his way to work that morning and a temporary replacement had been hurriedly recruited from a neighboring town. He must have led a hermit's life, because he didn't recognize who Jack was when Jack and Storm approached the main entrance. He rudely told them they'd have to use the delivery entrance around back. That's how such creatures were always treated, and there were no exceptions. Not wanting to cause trouble, Jack started to walk away, intending to go around back where he and Storm would be allowed admittance.

"Jack!" Storm shouted, "where are you going? We were told to meet the mayor at the front entrance. That's what we're going do, no matter what this hick says." The guard took a few steps back when he saw the fierce look Storm gave him.

"Come on, Storm. It's' not worth arguing about. You know how they feel about our kind. We've gotta play by *their* rules to get by in *their* world."

But Storm, with irrepressible outrage distorting her striking facial features, bumped Jack aside, moved forward to a spot directly in front of the confused guard, and snarled, "What's wrong with you? Don't you know who he is? He's Jack Lupus, that's who. And I'm his mate, Storm Lupus. We were invited by the mayor." Her angry protest was loud enough to attract the attention of those inside the building. Before the replacement security officer could manage a response to Storm's verbal attack, the mayor's aide was suddenly standing next to him. He nudged the guard aside and led Jack and Storm through the entryway, apologizing profusely for the embarrassing mishap and promising that the security guard would be dealt with appropriately.

"He was just doing his job, He didn't know who I was," Jack remarked. But the deputy either didn't hear what Jack said, or if he did, didn't care.

Jack and a somewhat calmed Storm followed the deputy past the security checkpoint, through a short entry hall, and into an ornate lobby. They were greeted by a rousing reception—a ring of chairs was filled with clapping and cheering citizens and city workers who'd been coerced to attend another of the mayor's frequent public functions. TV cameras hovered behind the circle of chairs. A podium stood on a low dais with microphones on it. Standing at the podium with outstretched arms and a tooth-flashing smile that could dim the intensity of the sun, was the mayor himself, the honorable Silas J. King, now in his fifth term and in the middle of a bitter battle for his sixth.

His opponent, Miss Geraldine Hope, the libertarian city council president, was running on the usual tried-and-true anti-corruption plank, but also advocated an "equality for GMAs" theme—proposing to repeal discrimination laws against Genetically Modified Animals.

Among all the minority populations King had to put up with, he despised the wolf family most of all. In his view of the world, and in agreement with most of his fervent supporters, they were no more than freaks foisted on society by Satan-ruled East Coast devil-worshiping scientists simply because they wanted to test their ability to challenge the power of the one and only true God. Freaks he had to accommodate because of federal laws that superseded laws passed by the city council of his own town. So, to placate liberals whose votes he still needed to retain the power of his office, he had to play the part—show compassion, demonstrate acceptance, and acknowledge their rights. So here he was, forced by political expediency to bestow the honor of "Hero" upon this humanized wolf bastard for simply doing what he'd been programmed and trained to do, and in so doing, cheating the city out of an award he should not be entitled to.

The mayor's hypocrisy didn't fool Storm—she had a keen ability to read human body language and emotions. She'd always been less inclined than Jack to willingly accept restriction imposed on their species by the ruling majority. It was obvious to her that they'd been relegated by the town's power-brokers to a rung even lower than other minorities. But she also understood Jack's acceptance of their situation—play along to get along. And, like Jack, she also understood the futility of defying age-old prejudices by people toward anyone outside their own group. But she didn't like it and was more prone than Jack to express her hostility, even at times to a point of insurrection. It was in this state of mind that she stood calmly next to Jack listening to the mayor recount Jack's actions the previous night, claim credit for his own tenure's success at creating community harmony, and promise further progress in his next term. Then, with a major surprise that turned their world upside down—not only was Jack awarded a key to the city and a huge wreath of red and yellow roses, but also a cash award of two-hundred-thousand dollars, anonymously donated by a wealthy citizen. With that astounding announcement, and a brief thank you statement by Jack, the ceremony ended with crisp one-hundred-dollar bills and the gold-plated key being stuffed into the pack strapped to Jack's back. After Storm instructed the mayor's aide to send the flowers to the rescued baby's family, and in a state of near-disbelief at their good fortune, she and Jack made their exit from the rotunda past a line of applauding citizens.

Jack and Storm hadn't even made it half-way along the hall toward the front entrance when the mayor leaned close to his aide and whispered, "That two-hundred-grand would be helpful to my campaign."

When the mayor's attention was directed toward a reporter requesting a quote about the ceremony, the aide nodded at a burly man standing at the edge of the crowd as if he were awaiting instructions. The man quickly turned and followed Jack and Storm out of the building.

Jack and Storm

Episode Two

When Jack and Storm left city hall, they headed toward the bridge over the river and to their assigned living area on the other side. "We'll stop at the bank on the way home and deposit this cash," Jack said as they broke into a fast lope.

Five minutes later, Jack slowed his pace and said, "I don't like the look of those men standing at the bridge ramp. Something's not right."

Storm slowed to match Jack's pace. "Yeah. I noticed them, as well. Five of them . . . like they're waiting for something."

"Like us, maybe?"

"Probably. Us and those dollars in your pack."

Jack and Storm stopped in the deep shade of a huge cedar tree. They were still a hundred yards from the bridge. Jack looked around, then said, "We've got to get to the other side, deposit this money, then get home to the pups. But that's the only bridge within twenty miles. Our other choice is to swim, but this pack is heavy, and I wouldn't want to get the money wet. Besides, the river is filthy and polluted with chemicals and sewage waste."

"Then there *is* no other choice," Storm said. "Let's just go on like we normally would. If they make a move to stop us, we'll break into a fast run, out maneuver them, and get across the bridge. They probably wouldn't chase us into our part of town. Anyway, we could outrun them if they tried."

Jack was quiet for a moment, looked around again, then said, "All right. That's what we'll do."

When he said that, Storm sensed that something had abruptly changed. It was in the resonance of his voice. She glanced at him and saw it in his appearance as well. His ears were pitched forward, his eyes were wider, and his mouth was open just enough to reveal rows of flashing white teeth. His neck hackles were raised, and his tail was straight out. His body was slightly lower to the ground than usual. "Let's get this over with," he growled with an intonation she'd not heard before.

"Jack?" Are you okay? All of a sudden you're different."

"I'm not different, Storm. It's just another part of me, a part until now I've been able to keep under tight control. I'm not gonna let those goons get this money. It's our way out of this back-water town. I've had it with being branded a second-class citizen because some genetics company wanted to see how hybrids like us would turn out. We're nothing more than experiments turned loose in society. We just happened to have been consigned to a particularly miserable place. This reward is a chance to go somewhere we'd be welcome. Maybe even be with others like us. If we let those thugs, if that is what they are, take this chance from us, we'll regret it the rest of our lives. So, if I seem to be different from what I was a few minutes ago, it's more likely the *real* me is surfacing. I have a feeling we'll find out soon. Are you with me?"

Storm shifted her stance, then said, "I hope they don't try to stop us. But if they do, you're right, we can't let them take the reward money. We'll have to do whatever it takes to get past them. Yes, I'm with you."

A hundred yards in front of the two partially humanized wolves, Stan Grift stood at the bridge ramp with his arms hanging at his sides. He clutched a heavy oak billy club in his right hand. Four other men were lined up behind him, each holding a club of some sort, each with hatred in his eyes but fear in his guts. They'd seen pictures of wolf-human hybrids before, had heard rumors of their ferociousness when riled, and had seen photos of Jack in the local newspaper, but their guts twisted into even tighter knots as they watched Jack and Storm advancing as if they were unafraid, unconcerned about the supposedly fierce foes they faced. And when the men saw how big Jack was, they realized he was far larger than they'd expected.

"Hold the line," Stan said without taking his eyes off the approaching couple. "Think about the grand we'll each get when we deliver that backpack. Follow my lead, stay where you are until I say otherwise. Remember, even though they talk like us, they're still just freak dogs, that's all. Nothin' we humans can't handle."

Jack and Storm came to a halt five yards short of the ramp. Jack took a single step forward. "We need to cross," he said in a strong voice. "Move aside."

Grift matched Jack's advance, then said, "You can pass after you pay the toll."

Jack held the man's eyes and said, "There's no toll on this bridge. Never has been. Move aside," he repeated.

"Well, there's a toll now. That pack on your back will do."

Jack took a step forward. Storm moved up to his side and growled softly. As if answering her back, Jack growled more loudly, then said," Toll or no toll, we're crossing this bridge. We're not paying you anything, so get out of our way." His voice was more like a snarl than his usual humanized wolf intonation.

"It's not that easy, Dogboy. Have your bitch undo the pack and drop it on the ground. Then you can be on your way."

Understanding that the man was not going to let them pass without getting the pack, Jack slowly edged forward, his eyes darting back and forth between Grift and the men lined up behind him.

Seeing the wolf approach as if preparing to dart past him, Grift raised the club over his head ready to slam it down on Jack if he came closer. That movement was all it took to spark Jack into action. He bolted forward, then quickly twisted to the left as the club flew downward past his head. But unexpectedly, Grift swiftly followed the swing of the club with a powerful kick with his steel-tipped boot to Jack's shoulder. The power of the blow and intense pain caught Jack off guard and allowed Grift to land another clout onto his back. Jack staggered but managed to avoid the next swing. But then, as Grift raised his club for another try, Storm vaulted high over Jack and locked her powerful jaws around Grift's wrist, instantly crushing bone and drawing blood. Grift desperately tried to shake off Storm's vice-like grip and screamed for his men to attack. While Grift was occupied with Storm's frenzied assault, Jack turned to intercept the man rushing to where Storm was then mauling Grift's shoulder, and with a single arching leap, sank his teeth into the man's throat and shook him like a ragdoll. When blood gurgled out of the man's mouth and open wounds, Jack flung him aside and spun to meet the next attacker. This one was quicker on his feet. With a vicious kick, he deflected Jack's attempt to grasp his club-wielding arm. But before Jack recovered from the kick, Storm, having abandoned the badly disabled Grift, already had the man on the ground and was tearing flesh from his thigh as he screamed in agonizing pain. The two remaining thugs, seeing what the two wolves had done to their companions, took off running toward the town center.

With two of the assailants seriously wounded, a third dead, and the other two run off, Jack and Storm were able to catch their breath and consider what had just happened. Storm was visibly shaken, staring at the man moaning on the ground with his bloody leg in shreds. Then she looked at Grift clutching his mangled shoulder desperately trying to stem fountains of blood spurting in all directions. "Jack, what have we done?"

Jack nudged the one whose throat he'd ripped open. There was no response. He glanced toward the town. "Humans would call it self-defense if they'd done what we just did. But for us, it'll be *murder* if how they've treated us in the past is any indication."

Storm, following Jack's gaze, said, "You're right. But what's scary is how easy it was. And how it felt . . . I don't know . . . natural? What's happened to us?"

"I'm not sure. But I'd do it again if I had to. And yes, it *was* easy. And it did feel good, like that's who, or what, I am—a wolf. But right now, we've got to get out of here. Those two men will spread the word as soon as they get into town and all hell will break loose. Between the police and gun-toting vigilantes, the manhunt will be relentless. Let's go."

Wolves have been clocked at forty-miles-per-hour, and Jack and Storm beat that by a fraction on their way to their den and the two young wolf pups awaiting their return. Storm insisted on the pups quickly eating as much as they could, as she and Jack did themselves. Then, with nothing other than the pack full of cash on Jacks back, they left what had been their home for the past three years and the section of the town designated for them and them only. They headed north into an expanse of dense woods flanking the western side of the Rocky Mountains and extending almost a hundred miles to the Canadian border. They intended to get as far away as possible from the town, the men who would come after them, and the country that had created them and thrown them into an alien society that wanted nothing more than to destroy them.

Jack felt safer when they reached the forest where its dense canopy concealed them from surveillance drones that would have been launched by then. A bigger threat now was a robot sniffer dog that could follow their scent trail. Jack had seen them during his training and knew how effective they were. They'd have to find a body of water large enough to wash away their traces, even if it meant getting the money wet—it would eventually dry out. They traveled at a quick pace for the rest of the day—resting only when the pups were too exhausted to continue—then into the night, closer and closer to the border. The astounding endurance of wolves for running served them well and they kept well-ahead of any pursuing trackers.

Finally, in the dark of night, Storm caught the odor of lake water off to the west and they headed in that direction. Moonlight filtering through the treetops allowed safe passage through the forest's dense undergrowth. Soon they came across a small creek that led them to what they were looking for, a large lake that filled a long valley leading northward, into Canada.

When they halted for a brief rest before entering the lake, Jack suddenly perked up his ears and turned toward the woods they'd come out of. "Hear that sound? It could be a robot crashing through the woods."

Storm stood silent, listening." "No . . . wait . . . yes, I hear it now . . . it's far away but seems to be coming this way."

"Storm, you and the pups swim to the upper end of this lake. I'll stay here and take care of the robot. If I don't, it'll circle the lake until it picks up our trail again. I'll find you as soon as I can."

"Jack! You can't destroy that thing. Aren't they indestructible?

"I'll have to trick it by giving it a false lead. That'll give us enough time to cross the border before other trackers find us. You'd better get going." Jack watched as his family entered the water and headed toward the middle of the lake, noticing how close Storm stayed to the pups, who were already good swimmers, just not as fast as their mother.

Jack and Storm

Episode Three

When Storm and the pups were halfway across the lake, Jack waded in and swam parallel to the shore for almost a mile to the mouth of a wide river. He got out of the water, rolled in the dry sand to leave a strong scent, then ran along the riverbank into the woods for a mile or so. At that point he swam across the river, got out on the other side, and continued into the woods. When he'd gone what he thought would be far enough, he carefully doubled back on his tracks all the way to the river. Once there, he rode the rushing current back to the lake, then swam to where he figured Storm and the pups would be waiting.

After reuniting at the upper end of the lake, Jack and his family continued their run north. Their hunger was satisfied by half a dozen mice and a rabbit Storm had caught after she and the pups had reached the rendezvous point.

Meanwhile, the robot dog that had been tracking them had traced Jack's scent along the small creek that led to the lake. When the robot lost the scent at the lake's edge, it did what it was programed to do in cases like this. It traveled along the shore until it picked up the scent again at the spot where Jack got out of the lake where the river entered into it. The robot followed Jack's scent along the riverbank to where it ended again. Eventually, after exploring an increasingly wider area, the robot picked up the trail on the opposite bank and followed it deeper into the woods. Confusion set in when the trail suddenly ended again where Jack had stopped and doubled back. As Jack predicted, the hapless robot spent the rest of the day fruitlessly circling at greater and greater distances from where the scent disappeared until its battery died. With its signaling devices deactivated and its computer shut down, it was transformed into nothing more than an incredibly expensive hi-tech gadget lost in the woods, destined to slowly turn into a pile of rusty metal unless its operators found it.

Two days later, Jack and Storm and the pups were snaking their way down the forested western slopes of the Canadian Rockies, skirting few-and-far-between human settlements and isolated cabins they either heard or saw from a distance. Realizing they would not be able to survive indefinitely in a wilderness for which they were ill-prepared, Jack and Storm had gradually concluded they should try to locate other genetically modified wolves like themselves: to discover how those GMAs were surviving, whether it was by joining human communities like Jack and Storm had been inserted into in the States, or as isolated communities of creatures like themselves. He'd heard rumors that other humanized GMAs had fled the prejudice and discrimination of the U.S. for what was supposedly a more tolerant Canada, but so far, they'd not encountered any.

But Jack and Storm's uncertainty about their future was about to change because unbeknownst to them, they'd been followed for the last few hours by a pack of eight Grey Wolves. The situation came to a head as evening twilight set in when that pack suddenly emerged from the surrounding underbrush in a treeless clearing with their teeth bared and hackles raised. They silently encircled Jack's family and blocked their way forward. Adhering to the ancient and deeply embedded ways of the wolf, the pack had no choice but to confront the interlopers who'd violated their territory.

Jack halted and Storm beckoned the pups close to her side as she moved next to him. When Storm started to say something in human-speak, Jack growled softly, and she remained silent. Jack looked at the pack surrounding his family. Some of them crouched low to the ground, some sat on their haunches, others stood unmoving, but they were all intently focused on Jack and Storm's every move. A second later, the emboldened leader of the pack, solid black and larger than the others, stepped stiff-legged toward Jack and halted five yards in front of him. Jack saw a long scar on one side of his face and a ragged, torn ear, obvious signs of the wolf's experience as a fighter.

Jack and the black wolf glared at each other, neither daring to make a first move. Jack was a head taller and probably fifty pounds heavier than the pack leader, which may have been why the leader seemed hesitant to attack. Suddenly, one of the other wolves, who was close to where Storm stood with the two pups, dashed forward and grabbed one of the pups by the scruff of its neck and turned to scurry off. But before he got more than a few feet, Storm hurtled toward him, sank her razor-sharp fangs into his flank and ripped it open to the bone. The wounded wolf yelped, dropped the panicked pup, and scrambled away from Storm as fast as it could. At the same instant, Jack spun away from the leader and leapt to where Storm had been standing before she attacked the wolf to rescue her pup.

Jack glared at the other wolves, as if daring them to make a move. But when Jack had spun away to protect the other pup, the alpha male edged forward. Sensing that movement, Jack whirled back around to meet the black wolf when it suddenly hurled itself at Jack, obviously intending to attack from behind. Jack instantly shifted sideways, pivoted hard counterclockwise, and slammed the full force of his massive body into the shoulder of the attacker, knocking him off balance and preventing his flashing teeth from ripping into him. Before Jack could follow with a counter-attack, Storm leapt over him and landed with her jaws clamped around the pack leader's throat, who'd stumbled over a fallen limb when Jack knocked him aside. Storm pinned him to the ground and the vanquished wolf yowled to signal his capitulation to her dominance as she mercilessly tightened her stranglehold.

With both pups in tow, Jack moved to where Storm held the black wolf down and motioned her to release him. After the defeated leader struggled to his feet, with blood dripping from his lacerated neck, Jack stepped closer, looked down at him, and growled menacingly. The humiliated and cowering wolf looked around at the pack. When none of them came to his aid, many of them avoiding his pleading eyes, he whined pitifully and skulked into the woods. His tail was between his legs and his ears were laid back, and without further resistance, he yielded his position as pack leader to the new alpha male.

Storm went to where the other wolves had been attentively watching Jack and the defeated leader and went from wolf to wolf, halting before each one. In every case, including confronting the largest and oldest female, the pack members crouched down to acknowledge her as the pack's new alpha female. A moment later, several of the wolves went over to the pups and nuzzled and licked them with great affection, assuring them of their acceptance into the pack.

When Storm rejoined Jack, he started to say something in human speak but caught himself before the words came out. He looked at Storm, then surveyed his pack. Instead of barking or growling, he did something he'd heard of, but had never done himself—he pointed his nose toward the evening sky and howled. The sound he made was scratchy and wavering, not at all like a proper wolf howl. But then, on the second attempt, he howled with more confidence. The howl was not only powerful but had a tone that was pure and eerily haunting, as if he were voicing an ancient memory buried deep in his ancestral past, an expression of his true self, the central core of the alpha wolf he now was. His third howl was in concert with Storm's, whose higher pitch was a pleasant contrast to Jack's lower one. Then, in an exultant harmony of howls, all the other members of the pack joined in joyous celebration of their new leaders. Even the two pups, already at ease in their expanded family, did the best they could.

From that moment on, there was never a human word uttered by Jack and Storm within hearing range of the pack. However, for many years to come, remnants of their former life emerged in the form of lingering tales about a pair of huge wolves who were able to keep their pack of gray wolves safe from human predators by means that would require deep understanding of the ways of man. How to outwit humans, even the most determined hunters intent on eradicating a species with which they were unwilling to share a world they were convinced they and they alone had the right to dominate. The truth of those stories, nor the fate of two hundred thousand dollars rumored to have been carried off from a small town in Oregon years earlier by a giant wolf, was never known one way or the other. Except, that is, when a pair of old wolves told their descendants stories about living among humans in a far-away land, and always in a secret language spoken only in the confines of their own den.

The End

www.ingramcontent.com/pod-product-compliance
Lightning Source LLC
Chambersburg PA
CBHW031101260626
47172CB00001B/166